2

-

2

A Pig of
Cold Poison

Also by Pat McIntosh

A Pig of
Cold Poison

Pat McIntosh

Constable • London

Constable & Robinson Ltd
3 The Lanchesters
162 Fulham Palace Road
London W6 9ER
www.constablerobinson.com

First published in the UK by Constable,
an imprint of Constable & Robinson, 2010

First US edition published by SohoConstable,
an imprint of Soho Press, 2010

Soho Press, Inc.
853 Broadway
New York, NY 10003
www.sohopress.com

A copy of the British Library Cataloguing in Publication
Data is available from the British Library

UK ISBN: 978-1-84901-012-2

US ISBN: 978-1-56947-650-5
US Library of Congress number: 2010004127

Printed and bound in the EU

1 3 5 7 9 10 8 6 4 2

Mixed Sources
Product group from well-managed
forests and other controlled sources
www.fsc.org Cert no. SA-COC-1565
© 1996 Forest Stewardship Council
FSC

For Ellissa,
who has blue eyes but a much nicer disposition

Chapter One

Although he was watching closely when the mummer was poisoned, it took Gil Cunningham several days and three more poisonings to work out how it was done.

There were many more people in the hall of his sister's house than he had anticipated. The weather had been mild for late October, and not all the guests were in their winter-weight finery, so that the wide, light chamber and its two huge window bays each as big as another small room seemed to be crammed with furred wool set next to rustling taffeta-lined brocades, with a top-dressing of black silk hoods and jewelled hats. Gil, checking on the threshold with his wife on his arm, cast a glance round and muttered to Alys:

'Sweet St Giles, she's asked half the High Street. She'd never have noticed if I'd stayed at home.'

'We have a good company,' observed Alys's father, the French master-mason, at Gil's other side. Alys, ignoring them both, handed her plaid to the journeyman who had let them in, paused to ask after the man's family, and went forward across the buzzing room to embrace her sister-in-law Kate, who sat enthroned beside the cradle, her crutches propped against the arm of the great chair and her gigantic waiting-woman on guard beside her.

Kate and her husband, Gil's good friend Maister Augie Morison, had launched on the process of entertaining most of the burgh council of Glasgow and their families, in

1

small batches, with the twofold purpose of showing off their newly extended house and their baby son to Morison's fellow merchants. As the child's godparents, Gil and Alys were naturally expected to be present at this first occasion, but Gil had obeyed his sister's stringent invitation with some reluctance. He had a report to compile for his master the Archbishop of Glasgow, and two legal documents to compose before the week was out. Either would have been a preferable occupation for the afternoon, if he could not borrow a horse and ride out into the autumn sunshine. Instead here he was, in his good blue brocade, required to make civil conversation about nothing in a group of people he did not know well.

'There is Francis Renfrew the apothecary,' stated Maistre Pierre. 'And Maister Hamilton. I suppose they would start with their neighbours, indeed. They had to suffer the worst while the building went on.'

'Aye, Gil,' said their host, appearing beside them. 'And yourself, Pierre. I'm right glad to see you.'

'How is Edward?' asked Gil, nodding towards the cradle. Morison's face broke into his lambent smile.

'Oh, he's well enough,' he said, with unconvincing modesty. 'I think he's going to be a reader. He listened to every word on a page o *Floris and Blanchflour* last night.'

'Do you tell me?' said Maistre Pierre, suitably impressed. 'At ten weeks of age?'

Gil preserved his countenance and gestured at the company.

'Who have you got here today?' he asked. 'Looks like a town meeting.'

'Not so many,' pronounced Maistre Pierre. 'There is Dod Wilkie the litster, who is Hamilton's friend, and is that also Wat Forrest from the Drygate? It is to be hoped nobody falls ill today in the burgh, if both of the established apothecaries have closed up shop to admire wee Edward.'

'It's worse than that,' confided Morison in amusement. 'We're to have the Play of Galossian acted later for the company, seeing it's the season, and it seems young

2

Bothwell, that has the potyngar's booth at the Tolbooth, is one o the band I've asked in to play it. There won't be a potyngar of any sort at liberty in the town. Bide there till I get you a glass, maisters, and then we'll go talk to Adam and Dod yonder.'

He slipped away past three seated women. Gil identified Mistress Hamilton in ill-judged light blue velvet, Nancy Sproull the wife of Wilkie the dyer, and the hugely pregnant Meg Mathieson, second wife of Maister Renfrew the burgh's senior apothecary. Meg shifted uncomfortably on her seat as his eye fell on her, but none of the three looked up from their intent dissection of someone else's reputation, and Maistre Pierre said:

'Galossian? Does he mean that tale of champions and death and healing?'

Gil nodded, still surveying the room.

'I have never understood why such things should be seasonal.'

'It always has been,' Gil answered absently. 'Any time from All Hallows Eve –'

'That is today,' observed his father-in-law.

'– to New Year. I suppose it celebrates the death of the old year and the coming of the new one. Out in Lanarkshire every parish has its own version, and the young men go about playing it in houses and farmyards and get rewarded with ale.'

'Better, surely, to play out tales from Holy Writ,' said Maistre Pierre in faint disapproval, accepting a brimming glass from Morison. 'Your health, maister.'

Following his friend between the clustered backstools, Gil listened to the snatches of conversation. The chamber was not in fact as crowded as it had seemed at first sight, although all the guests had brought their ladies; unless one counted the baby and his nursemaid, and Morison's small daughters and their stout black-browed nurse who were handing little cakes and sweetmeats, there were no more than two dozen people present, and most of the men had retired into one of the big new windows in a comfortable,

3

argumentative group. In the further window, three women seemed to be discussing herbs for the complexion, two black cloth veils leaning together with one head of soft brown waves.

'You want to choose him a young lassie, she'll be by far more biddable.' That was Francis Renfrew, striking in tawny velvet braided with crimson silk, his wide-brimmed bonnet close to Wat Forrest's neat black felt.

'That depends on the lassie, Frankie,' observed Maister Forrest. 'An older one will be the more grateful to get a husband.'

Whose marriage were they hatching? Gil wondered. Could Wat be turning his mind to his brother's future? Adam had been a year ahead of Gil at the grammar school. He must be nearing thirty, it was full time he brought a wife and her dowry to the business in the Drygate, but by all accounts *biddable* was not a word to apply to Renfrew's younger daughter.

An even less biddable lassie paused in front of him, holding her wooden platter up level with her chin so that he could reach it.

'There's two cakes each,' she warned him, 'and you get one of the marchpane cherries. But there's plenty quince zozinzes.'

'I'll take a quince lozenge, then,' Gil said, 'and leave some cakes for other people. Thank you, Ysonde.'

His sister's younger stepdaughter gave him another penetrating grey stare.

'Some folk's taking more than two cakes,' she said. 'If you don't take one now you might not get any. Wynliane and me made them,' she expanded. 'Nan helped.'

'I see.' Gil took a cake obediently. 'Has Mistress Alys had hers yet?'

'Yes, and she said it was good.' Ysonde waited. Realizing his duty, Gil took a cautious bite of the greyish morsel, and nodded with emphatic pleasure. 'You can get another one if you like. But I'm not giving any more to him.' She glowered at someone beyond Gil. 'He laughed when I said how many, and then he took a great big handful.'

'That was ill mannered,' Gil agreed, swallowing the final crumbs. The little cake was perfectly edible; Nan Thomson, who was now shepherding the older girl out to the kitchen with an empty tray, must have had more to do with it than Ysonde would admit.

'You didn't bring your baby,' she observed.

'No, we didn't,' he agreed. And he isn't our baby, he thought, and it's beginning to matter. 'John's only two, so he couldn't take the sweetmeats round like you and Wynliane. He'd eat them all.'

'So he would,' she agreed solemnly. 'I'm not eating these ones. We kept ours back in the kitchen. Now you have to go and talk to people, Mammy Kate said.'

'Is that right?' Gil looked around him. 'Who will I talk to?'

'I don't care.' Ysonde tossed her head. 'They're all growed up and boring.'

She turned away and marched past Wat Forrest just as he said rather firmly, 'Frankie, you ken fine my brother has another in mind. I see no purpose in arguing the matter.'

'If he goes that road, you'll rue it, Wat,' responded Maister Renfrew, 'and so will he.' He rose and stalked off into the window bay, the set of his tawny velvet shoulders suggesting annoyance and indignation. Was that a threat? Gil wondered, and turned away, not wishing to catch Wat Forrest's eye at such a moment.

As usual at events like this, the men and women were conversing separately. Alys, easy to find in her apricot-coloured taffeta, had settled beside her sister-in-law and was bending over the cradle with a sour-faced young woman in a huge Flemish hood whose black silk cap must surely be wired to make it stand up like that. The three women nearby were still intent on someone else's reputation, but Agnes Hamilton, wife of Andrew Hamilton the

5

master-carpenter, looked up briefly and smiled at Gil from among her chins.

In the nearer window the men had broken into smaller clumps. Renfrew had joined Maistre Pierre, who was already deep in conversation with Wat Forrest's brother Adam and a small sturdy man in bright green broadcloth faced with sunshine yellow, Wilkie the dyer, who had probably not produced those difficult shades in his own workshop. Morison had moved on to speak to his neighbour Andrew Hamilton, and nearest to Gil two younger men he knew slightly were discussing apothecary business while the target of Ysonde's displeasure, seated sideways on a backstool, swung one leg and stared at the painted beams above him, humming tunelessly.

Gil looked closer at this man. He had taken him at first for a stranger, but he was startled to find he recognized him. It was Nicol Renfrew, eldest son of the apothecary, who had been in the same year as Gil at the grammar school and who had been a strange, scrawny, twitching boy with restless hands and feet and a tendency to blurt out whatever remarks came into his mind, generally trimmed with foul language, which had got him beaten on a twice-daily basis despite his undoubted ability in Latin and geometry. Here he was, filled out, even slightly plump, calm and sleepy-eyed, smiling up at the painted vines. Hooking a stool closer with his foot, Gil sat down next him.

'Aye, Nicol,' he said. 'I heard you were back in Glasgow.'

'Gil Cunningham,' said the other man after a moment, and produced a high-pitched chuckle. 'So what you doing here? Did you ever see such a parcel of stuffed sarks, and the auld man the worst of them? I'd never ha come, but he insisted.'

Perhaps the man was less changed than he had thought. Gil ignored this remark, and went on, 'Where is it you've been? The Low Countries? Did I hear it was Middelburgh?'

'So they said,' agreed Nicol vaguely, and waved a hand. 'Could a been anywhere. They spoke Latin,' he added. 'And the Saracen tongue.'

'What are you doing now you're back?' This was harder work than it should be. 'Do you work with your father?'

Nicol shrugged one shoulder, and swung the foot again. 'He's no need of me. He's got Jimmy Syme and my dear little brother, he's not needing another to fetch and carry. So Agnes and Grace does that, when they're not fetching for my new mammy.'

High Street gossip swirled in Gil's head. Syme was Nicol's brother-in-law, four or five years younger than him, wedded to the elder daughter perhaps two years since and now standing over yonder conversing stiffly with the same dear little brother, and Agnes was the younger girl. Whatever the older was called, it was not . . .

'Grace?' he queried.

'My blessed wife.'

'Your wife? Good wishes on the marriage. When was that?'

'Last Yule, or thereabout.' Nicol's heavy-lidded gaze lifted above Gil's head, and his vague expression warmed. 'Speak of the devil.'

The woman moved forward from behind Gil as he rose to greet her. He had a swift impression of height and slenderness, a modest gown of dark silk brocade and foreign cut, then light grey eyes met his and he found himself read, assessed, evaluated, in the time it took her to curtsy and smile at him. She must be nearly his height, and fully as intelligent as Alys.

'Introduce me, Nicol,' she prompted, an odd lilt to her voice.

'Grace,' said Nicol offhandedly. 'Gil Cunningham. We were at the grammar school,' he enlarged.

'Grace Gordon,' she supplied resignedly, and leaned forward to kiss Gil in greeting. 'I'm aye glad to meet a friend from Nicol's boyhood.'

7

'The surname explains the accent,' Gil said, seating her and reaching for another stool.

'Aye, I'm a Buchan lass,' she agreed, 'though I met Nicol in Middelburgh.' A movement by the door to the kitchen stair caught her eye; she turned to look at the girl just crossing the chamber, and apologized. 'I wonder what Agnes has been up to now?'

'She likely stepped out to ease hersel,' said her husband. 'Leave the lass alone, why can't you? She's seventeen.'

'That's exactly why I can't leave her alone,' she said patiently, 'and neither Meg nor Eleanor is fit to have an eye to her the now.' Ah, that was the older daughter's name, thought Gil, pleased to get that called back to mind. 'Och, she's brought Meg the lavender cushion, that's all. She must have run round to the house. Forgive me, Maister Cunningham, I should leave family business at home. Aye, Nicol and I met in Middelburgh.'

'You'll find it damp here,' Gil offered, as a harmless gambit.

'I do, but at least I don't miss the east wind.'

'What's to talk o but the weather?' said Nicol irritably. 'East wind, west wind, damp or cold, so? Even my faither canny sort that, whatever else he can order.'

'Then tell me about this play we're to see,' said his wife. 'Who might Galossian be? We've no tales o him in the nor'east, though we've plays enow. Is it comical, or are we like to weep at it, Maister Cunningham?'

'Both, I suspect, depending on the acting,' he offered, and she laughed, a sound as attractive as he had thought it might be. 'It's an old tale of battle and the hero's death, with a doctor who comes in to cure him.'

'And who plays the doctor? I hope it's someone well qualified!'

'I've no notion,' Gil admitted. 'Augie said it's the company that young Bothwell from the Tolbooth runs with, so maybe he'll take that part.'

'Bothwell,' said Nicol, and produced that high-pitched

chuckle. 'Tammas Bowster's company, wi Bothwell playing the doctor?'

'So Augie said.'

'Tammas Bowster, and Nanty Bothwell from the Tolbooth. *Galyngale ne lycorys Is not so swete as her love is.* Does my faither ken yet, Grace, d'you think?'

'I've no notion,' she said quietly. Gil glanced from her to Maister Renfrew the elder, who was now deep in discussion with Maister Wilkie, opened his mouth to ask what the exchange meant, and found himself forestalled as Ysonde popped up in front of him.

'Mammy Kate wants you,' she said abruptly. 'But you're no to make Baby Floris cry.'

She disappeared back into the crowd as swiftly as she had appeared, leaving him wondering if he had heard right. Nicol had just quoted *Floris and Blanchflour*, and then . . .

'Oh, you heard right,' said Kate when he reached her. Alys, still hanging over the sleeping infant, looked up, her eyes full of laughter. 'Never mind that now, Gil, have you heard yet what Augie's done? It's young Bothwell's company he's asked to play Galossian for us. I thought Renfrew would have an apoplexy when I told him myself just now.'

'So Augie told me,' Gil said. 'Is it a difficulty, Kate?'

'You could say that, Maister Gil,' pronounced her waiting-woman Babb from behind the great chair.

'It is,' Kate said anxiously, looking about her. 'Where is Agnes Renfrew?'

'Yonder with Nell Wilkie,' said Alys, pointing into the window without raising her hand from the carved rim of the cradle. Glancing that way, Gil identified the two unmarried girls, the bare heads tilted together so that gold curls and oak-brown waves mingled. Wat Forrest's wife was with them, and seemed to find their conversation amusing. 'And, Kate,' Alys went on, 'is the armourer's lad not in the same company?'

'Aye, Mistress Alys, he is,' agreed Babb. 'He plays the hero, they tell me. And the glover's in it and all, playing Judas that does all the speaking.'

'Dan Gibson and Tammas Bowster,' said Kate, and sat back. Finding Mistress Hamilton looking at her across the chamber she smiled brightly, and said, so only Gil and Alys could hear, 'Trust Augie, he never knows – Gil, we must just make the best of it, and hope the lassie behaves, but will you be on the alert for any trouble? And I don't like the look of Meg Mathieson, either. I never expected her to be here.'

'Best of what?' Gil asked. 'I don't think I know any more than Augie.'

'The apothecary and the armourer lad's both been courting her all year,' said Babb with relish. 'But she canny decide which she favours.'

'And her father favours neither,' Alys completed.

'So that's what Nicol meant.'

Ysonde materialized beside them, peered possessively into the cradle, and said, 'You leave our baby alone. That's Mammy Kate's baby. Mammy,' she went on, before any of the adults could react, 'there's men in the kitchen talking to Ursel, and one of them's got his face all black, and one of them's wearing a bed-sheet. Is that for the play?'

'A bed-sheet?' said Kate in surprise. 'Over his clothes?'

'No.' Ysonde reflected briefly on this. 'On his head.'

The journeyman who had admitted them earlier appeared at the kitchen door and crossed the chamber to his master, who heard what he had to say and clapped his hands for silence.

'The players are here, neighbours,' he announced. 'If we make oursels ready, they'll be up any time to entertain us.'

Two sorts of bustle began at his words, the women shifting chairs and arranging themselves with Babb's help, the men drifting reluctantly into the main chamber from the window space. Morison's household clattered in from the kitchen and retired to a corner, the grizzled steward Andy glaring sternly at the younger maidservants, who had a tendency to giggle. Gil watched all in some amusement, having found himself a place against the wall.

'Och, it's only the old play,' said one of the two girls Alys had pointed out. 'What's so wonderful?'

'Guard your tongue, Nell,' said the dyer's wife briskly, and thrust a backstool at her daughter. 'Here, set that for Meg, next Lady Kate, and come and get another.'

So that was Nell Wilkie, with the soft brown hair, a comely young woman but nowhere near as striking as her friend. Agnes was a plump little soul, with a head of gold curls, a pretty face, huge blue eyes, and a kissable mouth. A wise father would have had her married off before now, which probably meant that Maister Renfrew was not wise where his younger daughter was concerned. The cut and quality of her blue silk gown suggested the same.

'There is Maister Renfrew's new wife,' commented Maistre Pierre in his ear. 'Meg Mathieson. I am surprised she has come out. Do you suppose it is twins?'

'No way to tell,' said Gil, watching Agnes seat her burgeoning stepmother, place an assortment of cushions at her back and hand her a fan of swan's feathers. 'Could be a consort of four voices, by the size of her.'

His father-in-law guffawed, then straightened his face hastily as Maister Renfrew passed them, towing his younger son by the sleeve of his green brocade gown.

'You'll stand by your sister,' he was saying, 'and oversee her behaviour, and no argument from you.'

'She's none of my –' began the young man, a handsome youth if he had not been at the spotty stage, and swallowed as his father turned to glare at him. 'Aye, sir.'

Neither Agnes nor her stepmother seemed pleased to see their menfolk; Agnes greeted her brother with a sniff and a flounce of her blue silk skirts and the stepmother, not many years older, eyed her husband warily as if uncertain of his mood. He smiled kindly at her, which seemed to alarm her more, patted her shoulder and turned away to join Gil and Maistre Pierre, tucking himself in beside the mason's wide furred gown.

11

'I'll just stand ower here,' he said softly, 'where Meg canny see me. She's the sizey a house, you'd think she was carrying a football team, and it makes her carnaptious.'

It took perhaps a quarter-hour of stir and argument to get the company seated in a half-circle round the door which led to the kitchen stair. Mistress Hamilton was in a draught, Nancy Sproull the dyer's wife could not see past Eleanor Renfrew's headdress and Andrew Hamilton the younger, all of thirteen and very grown-up in dark brown broadcloth, had to be separated from a glass of Dutch spirits his parents had not seen him acquire. Gil dealt with that for Kate without alerting either parent, the other problems were solved, the two little girls settled at Kate's feet, Nicol Renfrew was persuaded to move his backstool beside his wife's, and the audience was declared ready.

Morison nodded to his steward, who signalled in turn to a journeyman standing ready by the door, and the man slipped out to the kitchen. A distant set of ill-tuned small-pipes struck up a discordant noise; feet sounded on the stairs, there were three loud knocks on the door, and it was flung wide.

'Haud away rocks, haud away reels!' began a stentorian voice, and Judas entered.

Gil knew two or three versions of the play, but had not seen this company perform before. The other actors filed in behind the piper, whose small-pipes were eventually silenced, and bowing to their audience launched into the traditional song about Hallowe'en while their Bessie wielded a broom inexpertly round the legs of stools and backstools. They carried garlands of coloured paper and withies; their costumes were the usual mix of old clothes and ingenuity, discarded gowns turned to the lining, card mitres for Judas and St Mungo painted and stuck with gold braid, the Bessie character with plaits of horsehair dangling from her vast linen headdress, a bedspread train pinned to her ample waist. The two champions wore real, rather battered armour, though their swords were of wood, and one had his face blacked with soot. Gil had seen both combatants in the armourer's workshop. Which of them was Agnes's fancy? he wondered.

Judas was declaiming his next speech now, announcing the coming fight. His acting style was striking, ornamented with huge dramatic gestures which bore no relation to the words he was using, so far as those could be understood; the accent used by Lanarkshire folk on a stage had always puzzled Gil.

The young apothecary from the Tolbooth was indeed playing the doctor in an imposing tall hat of black paper. He was a stocky fellow, buttoned into a too-long gown tucked up over a shabby belt of scarlet leather, a vast scrip hanging at his side. He had glanced once at Agnes Renfrew, conspicuous in her blue silk, then stood silent against the wall while all were introduced.

'If you don't believe the word I say,' Judas ended, with sudden clarity, 'call for Alexander of Macedon, and he'll show the way! Alexander! Alexander! Alexander!'

'I know Alexander,' announced Ysonde. 'Our Da's got a poetry book about him.'

Her sister shushed her, but Judas bowed to her, and declared, 'Aye, bonnie young lady, and here he comes the now!'

The black-faced champion came forward into the acting space, saluted the company with his sword, mumbled Alexander's speech about how he had conquered the world except for Scotland, and summoned Galossian as the champion of all Scotland to come forth and fight him. As the champion's name was called the requisite three times, Gil found Maistre Pierre's elbow in his ribs, drawing his attention to Maister Renfrew on the mason's other side.

One glance, and Gil shared his father-in-law's concern. The apothecary's face was engorged with apparent rage, a vein throbbing wildly in his temple under the silk bonnet whose crimson matched his brow and cheeks, his bulging eyes fixed on Agnes, who in turn was gazing adoringly at the young man in the buttoned gown. Gil was just in time to see her brother nudge her, and then pinch her arm viciously. A commotion of her skirts suggested she had kicked him in return.

'Frankie, you should sit down,' suggested Maistre Pierre quietly, putting his hand on the apothecary's arm. Renfrew started at the touch, and looked round, gasping for breath. On the other side of the room Augie Morison had noticed and was watching anxiously.

'Will I find you a seat?' Gil asked, while Galossian detailed his defence of Scotland. The man could speak well, but the tale seemed to involve more giants and other heroes than other versions. Renfrew shook his head, but reeled as he did so, and Gil nodded to Morison, slipped quietly past the apothecary and fetched one of the green leather backstools from the nearer window space. Once persuaded to sit down, Renfrew shut his eyes for a moment, then reached for his purse, opened it clumsily and fumbled within for a small flask of painted pottery, which he unstopped and tipped to his mouth. Whatever it contained, its effect was rapid; the man's breathing settled, his colour began to improve. The people nearest had turned to look, but the players were reaching the exchange of insults between the two champions, and their distraction was brief. Morison, watching carefully, relaxed and sat back.

'I'm well,' said Renfrew irritably, waving his free hand at them. 'Leave me be, I'm well.'

'I stay with him,' said Maistre Pierre quietly. Gil nodded, and returned to his place; across the intervening landscape of black silk French or Flemish hoods his sister caught his eye, but he shook his head. Beyond her Alys smiled at him, and turned her attention to the play, where to the children's delight the champion of Scotland, describing his armour, had just reached the immortal line:

'My arse is made of rumpel-bone! I'll slay you in the field!'

St Mungo handed his garland to the Bessie and stepped forward, straightening his mitre. 'Here are two warriors going to fight,' he intoned, 'who never fought before. Galossian bids you cheer him on, or he'll be slain in all his gore. A-a-amen.'

The champions bowed formally to one another and to Kate as the lady of the house. Then, apparently taking his opponent by surprise, Galossian swung on his heel, bowed and performed a crashing salute of sword on buckler, his eyes fixed on Agnes Renfrew. Agnes went scarlet; several of the older ladies nodded with sentimental approval, but Maister Renfrew's colour rose again and by the wall the young apothecary in his buttoned gown looked grim.

'Lay on, lay on!' ordered Alexander rather desperately. 'I'll rug you down in inches in less than half an hour!'

'He said that before,' observed Ysonde.

Galossian turned, took up an obviously rehearsed position, and the fight began. Gil, watching critically, felt it had been carefully practised, and amounted to a display. It was certainly very impressive, with much shouting, stamping, and crashing of the wooden swords on the leather-covered bucklers, and ranged right across the chamber and back again. The players cheered both warriors impartially, and when St Mungo encouraged them again the audience joined in. The two little girls squeaked and shrieked with excitement, young Andrew Hamilton forgot his sulks and jumped up and down, and at length, with a mighty blow which only just missed his helm, Alexander was struck down. He fell his length, and Galossian raised his sword in response to the audience's cheers, then fell on top of his enemy.

'Why's he dead?' Ysonde asked. 'He winned!'

Nicol Renfrew produced that high-pitched laugh. St Mungo stepped forward again, and declared the champion slain, while the Bessie attempted to sweep both corpses off the stage.

'A doctor!' exclaimed Judas. 'A doctor for Poor Jack!' The entire company called for a doctor, in a deep mutter which made Kate's older stepdaughter scramble on to her knee, shivering. 'Ten merks for a doctor!' said Judas.

The mutter changed to a a strange, hissing, grumbling, *Here-he-is-here-he-is-here-he-is*, at which Gil felt the back of his neck crawl, and Wynliane whimpered and buried her head in Kate's sleeve. The young apothecary stepped away from the wall, and marched forward importantly, elbows akimbo.

'Here comes I, a doctor, as good a doctor as Scotland ever bred.'

Kate was coaxing the little girls to look up and watch the funny man. The dialogue continued, much hindered by the Bessie, with the old, old jokes localized for Glasgow (*Where have you travelled? Three times round the Indies and the Dow Hill, and twice across Glasgow Brig*) and the long recital of what this doctor claimed to cure (*The itch, the stitch, the maligrumphs, the lep, the pip, the blaen, the merls, the nerels, the blaes, the spaes and the burning pintle.*) The women laughed at that, the men ignored the joke, Judas and the doctor bargained at length over his fee while the two slain champions lay getting their breath back, and finally the doctor opened his scrip, announcing loudly:

'I've a wee bottle here that hangs by my side, will raise a man that's been seven year in the grave.'

He held up a little flask of painted pottery, very like the one Maister Renfrew had taken from his own purse, paused for a fraction of a moment, and pointed to it with the other hand.

'Seven year?' repeated Judas. 'What's in it?'

'Twelve herbs for the twelve apostles,' began the doctor, 'and three for the Blessed Trinity –'

Gil looked round the room. Most of the audience was engrossed, laughing at the by-play between Judas and the Bessie, who had clearly worked together before. Grace Gordon sat by her husband, elegant and modest, hands folded in her lap, watching the doctor intently, critically. Agnes Renfrew was also gazing at the doctor, her father and brother were both glowering at her again, Andrew Hamilton the elder had fallen asleep, Nancy Sproull was looking thoughtfully at Renfrew's wife.

16

'Two drops to Jack's toes and one drop to Jack's nose,' pronounced the doctor. He drew the stopper with a flourish, frowned at the little flask, and bent to apply the treatment. Judas and the Bessie stepped silently backwards while, beside the tight-lipped Maister Renfrew, Maistre Pierre wondered audibly why the hero had changed his name. 'Rise up, Jack, and sing us a song!'

'I canny,' protested the recumbent Jack.

'Why no?'

'I've a hole in my back would hold a sheep's heid!'

'We'll ha to repeat the treatment.' The doctor bent with another flourish. 'Three drops to your beak and two to your bum. Rise up, Jack.'

Jack scrambled up, grinning under his helm, rubbed at his mouth and then raised both arms in a champion's salute when the audience applauded. Alexander got to his feet, St Mungo came forward again, and the actors all launched into the final part of the play, a mix of traditional songs about Hallowe'en and improvised compliments to the company present. While they sang Jack rubbed occasionally at his mouth, and cast languishing glances at Agnes Renfrew, who studiously ignored him while her father glared at her and the piper went round with a green brocade purse decked with ribbons, shaking it hopefully at the audience.

'What, have we to pay for them to finish?' demanded Nicol Renfrew, and laughed again. His wife patted his arm, and drew up her dark silk skirts to find the purse hanging between gown and kirtle; around her the other women were doing the same, and the men were reluctantly fishing at belts or in sleeves. By the time the piper reached Gil his purse was well filled and jingling. Gil added his contribution and a word of praise, and the man grinned and moved on.

The actors were still working through the Hallowe'en songs. Alexander had caught his breath, and was singing lustily, but Jack was breathing hard. *What for fighting and blood he bled, Greysteil was never so hard be-sted*, Gil thought.

It occurred to him that the player was becoming redder in the face rather than recovering a normal colour. The doctor, next in line, threw the champion an anxious look, spoke to him under cover of the singing. Jack shook his head, and then reeled, staggered, caught at Judas's sleeve and went down on his knees, dragging the other man's reversed gown off his shoulders as he fell.

'Rise up, Jack!' hissed Judas, hitching up his gown. One or two people laughed doubtfully, but Jack went on down, sprawling on the polished wooden planks of the floor. Judas bent to lift him, but could not get him to his feet; the other players sang on with determination as the fallen man was dragged aside. Gil, getting a closer view of the red face and rapid breathing, came to a swift conclusion. Whatever ailed him, the man was badly stricken. The children should not see this.

He looked across the chamber to find the servants, and caught the eye of the nurse Nan. Jack's feet shuddered in the beginnings of a convulsion, Judas exclaimed in alarm, and before anyone else moved Gil picked his way through the audience, lifted Ysonde from her post at Kate's feet, grasped Wynliane's wrist and drew her after him. Nan met him at the door to the upper stairs as the exclamations began.

'Let me go!' said Ysonde, trying to squirm free. 'Want to see the end!'

'It's ended,' said Gil. 'There's no more play. Go with Nan, poppets.'

Nan, her black brows startling in a face pinched with sudden alarm, nodded thanks to him and gathered the indignant children to her.

'Come, we'll go up and make the baby's bath ready,' she prompted. 'Maister Gil's right, the play's ended.'

Gil stood at the door until they vanished up the stairs, then turned to look at the scene in the hall. His sister was staring at him, her hands clenched on the rim of the cradle, Alys had risen in her place, all the apothecaries in the room had converged on the fallen mummer, and the rest of the audience was still gaping, trying to work out what had happened. His eye fell on Grace Gordon, sitting tense and pale beside her husband, gaze fixed on the man's quivering feet.

'Gil!' said Kate sharply. 'What's happened to the man?'

'Is it poison, do you think?' said Maistre Pierre beside him.

'I fear so. Assuming he hasn't taken an apoplexy,' Gil qualified, 'or dropped with the plague.'

'Plague?' repeated the woman nearest him in sudden alarm. Eleanor Renfrew, he noted, annoyed with himself for using the word aloud. 'Is it – is that –?'

'No, no,' said Maistre Pierre soothingly, 'your father will tell us in a moment, mistress. I am sure there is nothing for us to worry about.'

'Get the armour off him,' recommended Maister Wilkie from his post near the window. 'It's likely stopping him breathing.'

'What's best to do for him, maisters? Should we carry him to a bed?' asked Morison, on the margin of the group kneeling round the mummer. They ignored this; they were consulting in tones of slightly forced civility, while Judas and the other players stared at them and Anthony Bothwell, still clutching the bright pottery flask, said incredulously:

'What's come to him? His breath was short – is it the armour right enough?'

'The heart is very slow,' pronounced James Syme, one hand at the pulse in the mummer's throat, 'and there is a great excess of choler, judging by the colour of his skin.'

'The breathing is getting more rapid,' observed Wat Forrest gravely, 'and shallower.' His brother nodded, practised fingers on the stricken man's wrist.

'He's been eating almonds, you can smell them,' contributed Robert Renfrew. 'That's warm and moist. It's led to a sudden imbalance, maybe –'

19

'It's waur than that, Robert. I suspect –' said Robert's father heavily. The five of them exchanged solemn looks, and the others nodded.

'Aye, Frankie,' agreed Wat Forrest. 'I'm agreed.'

'Agreed on what?' demanded Morison. 'What can we do for the poor fellow?'

They looked up, and Maister Renfrew got to his feet.

'A priest,' he said. 'We should carry him to bed and bleed him, and I'll send Robert for the needful to make a cataplasm to his feet, but a priest is the most urgent matter.' He looked about the high light chamber, over the shocked faces. 'Well, Agnes,' he said brutally, 'so much for making your own choice, lassie, for here's the one of your sweethearts has slain the other.'

Someone screamed.

'What?' said Bothwell in horror. 'I never – I didny – and it was only a couple drops touched his mouth, he never even swallowed – it must ha been something he ate –'

'Cold pyson,' said Renfrew, 'and powerful at that, if a few drops can kill a man, and we all saw you minister it, my lad.' He stepped forward, and snatched the painted pottery flask from the other man's hand, and held it up. 'What could be in this, to slay him in the space of a few Aves?'

'No!' Bothwell protested, and turned to look at Agnes Renfrew, who had risen to her feet and was staring white-faced and horrified at her father. 'No, it wasny –'

'Small use to deny it,' declared Renfrew, 'and by Christ I'll see you hang for it, man, for I'm master of our mystery in this burgh and I'll not have the profession brought into disrepute in this way. Seize and hold him, Wat, Adam, and I'll thank you to send for the Serjeant, Augie.'

'No!' said Bothwell again. The Forrest brothers grasped his shoulders, and he looked from one to the other of them, appalled, but did not struggle. 'No, I never!'

The stricken mummer's feet drummed on the floor in another convulsion, and his breath rattled. Augie stared at him in distress, crossed himself, then turned to find his men with quick instructions. As two of the journeymen vanished down the kitchen stair Gil stepped forward to intervene.

'I'm none so certain it's Bothwell's doing,' he observed. 'Why would anyone choose to minister pyson to the man like this, in front of as many witnesses?'

'Why would I pyson any man, let alone Dan Gibson?' demanded Bothwell, staring round at a ring of hostile faces. 'He's a good fellow, we've aye been – save for us both – and she, she, she favours me so far's –'

'Aye, and little use in that,' said Renfrew with satisfaction, 'for I'd other plans for the lass long afore this. Here, Robert, here's the key to the workroom, you ken what to fetch.'

'Are you saying,' said Dod Wilkie, suddenly catching up with matters, 'the man's deid, Frankie?'

'Deid?' shrieked someone across the chamber.

'As good as,' said Wat Forrest.

Kate pulled herself out of her chair, took her crutches from Babb, and thumped forward, saying firmly, 'Bear him into the next chamber, poor man, and lay him on the bed. You his friends can stay with him or go down to the kitchen as you think best, and Ursel will bring you some aquavit, which I've no doubt you could do with. Jamesie, Eck,' two of the journeymen started and came forward, 'fetch a rope and take over fro Maister Forrest. And for the rest of us, neighbours . . .' She looked about her, gathering up attention despite the rival attractions in the chamber, and smiled crookedly. 'I'd planned a few diversions for Hallowe'en, ducking for apples and the like, but it hardly seems right now. When the Serjeant gets here he'll likely want to get our witness to what happened –'

'I never saw,' said someone hastily, 'for I was talking to Barbara here.'

'I did,' said another voice, 'I saw him shake the bottle to stir up the pyson –'

'No, I –' began Bothwell.

Somebody uttered a heartfelt groan.

21

'So we'll need to wait here,' continued Kate, as the limp form of the champion was borne out of the room by two of the other mummers. The apothecaries followed in a solemn group. 'Andy, would you and Ursel have them bring up more wine and another bite to eat.'

'We'll no all can stay here,' pronounced Nancy Sproull from her post beside Renfrew's wife. 'We need to get Meg home to her own chamber, or she'll be here longer than you care for, Lady Kate.'

'Never say it, Nancy!' said Renfrew, turning back from the door.

'Oh, I'll say it, Frankie, whether you choose or no.' She laid a portentous hand on Mistress Mathieson's belly, and nodded as the younger woman gasped and the great dome heaved under her touch. 'Her time's on her.'

'So she was right about her dates, then,' said Renfrew.

'*Ah, mon Dieu!*' said Maistre Pierre.

There was an appalled pause, into which Mistress Mathieson delivered another shuddering groan. Then Nicol Renfrew said, with his high-pitched laugh:

'No doubt of the brat being yours, Faither, when it picks sic a moment to arrive.'

Chapter Two

By the time the Serjeant arrived the gathering had split into several parts.

At Mistress Sproull's announcement the remaining men among the guests had taken themselves hurriedly into one of the window bays again, their backs to the goings-on. Gil would have joined them, but for a feeling that the flustered Augie needed his support. Kate, however, went into immediate action.

'I'll see to this, sir,' she announced, one hand on Morison's arm. 'You make certain Maister Renfrew and his colleagues have all they need. Here's Gil can help you, and Alys, I'd be right glad of your –'

Alys looked round and nodded from where she was already conferring with Mistress Sproull.

'There is still time to get her home,' she said, 'since it is only next door, but also we should send to tell her mother and the midwife.'

'Aye, you're right, lassie,' agreed Babb, stroking Mistress Mathieson's perspiring forehead with one large gentle hand, 'we've time, but we'd best no stand about, just the same.'

Leaving Maister Renfrew issuing curt instructions to Kate and to the women of his own household, Gil followed Morison as ordered, and found himself recalling the way his mother had addressed his father as *my lord* in company, formal and respectful and at times extracting the same expression of deep but wary relief as he had just seen on Morison's face.

In the hall-chamber, the sick man had been laid on the great bed, the plaids and mantles which had been laid there bundled on to a stool, the embroidered counterpane hastily drawn back and mounded at his feet. The remaining mummers were huddled by the wall while the Forrest brothers and James Syme conferred in low tones at the bedside. Morison hurried to join the apothecaries, saying anxiously, 'How does the poor laddie? Is he – is he still –?'

'He's still alive,' said Syme, 'but I fear we must prepare for the worst. Is the priest sent for, Augie?'

The other champion sobbed aloud at this, scrubbing at his eyes with the cuff of his doublet and smearing soot on the back of his hand. Judas patted him clumsily on the shoulder. Gil crossed the room to join the men and offer sympathy, got them to sit down on the padded bench which matched the hangings of the bed, and drew a back-stool to one end of it so he could see their faces. Robert Renfrew hurried in as he seated himself, carrying a heavy leather case and a silver basin and followed at a more measured pace by his father.

'Tell me about this,' Gil said encouragingly to the mummers, trying to ignore the bustle. 'That's not the way the play should go. What was meant to happen?'

They all stared at him, and then the Judas pulled himself together and said wearily, 'Well, the champion should rise up and all be – all be well again, maister. That's what the play's about, see.'

Gil nodded agreement. 'Was anything else different, before Danny fell?'

They looked at one another uneasily, and Judas, who seemed to be the spokesman, said, 'No. No that you'd call different, considering.'

'Considering what?' Gil summoned patience.

'I'll no believe it,' said the St Mungo. He pushed his mitre back to scratch his head. 'Nanty's a good fellow, he'd no do sic a thing.'

'Here's the priest,' said the piper quietly, as a stir at the chamber door signalled the entry of Father Francis Govan from the Franciscan house across the way. One of the maidservants entered with a jug of hot water, staring round-eyed, and lingered until pushed out by Wat Forrest. His brother was using mortar and pestle to bruise some powerful-smelling herbs.

'Nanty and Danny had words,' said Judas reluctantly. 'Down in the kitchen yonder, afore we come up to play the play.'

'And what was that about?' Gil asked. Again they looked at one another uneasily.

'About the lassie Renfrew?' said the Bessie. He had removed his headdress, which lay at his feet like a mound of washing; closer inspection showed that Ysonde was right, and the main component was a bed-sheet, nine or ten square yards of heavy linen. The fellow's neck muscles must be strong, Gil thought, to carry that on his head. 'See, Nanty was out in the yard getting a word wi her when we should ha been all in the kitchen setting out the moves.'

'And Danny took exception to that?' Gil prompted.

'He gaed out to the yard,' said the piper, 'called him in, demanded what they'd had to say at sic a moment.'

'And Nanty said it was nothing, and nane o his mind,' supplied Bessie. 'A bit of a ding-dong they had, though it was just a shouting match, they never flung fists.'

'We got them calmed down,' said St Mungo, 'and we sorted out all the moves, and sat down wi a stoup of ale to wait.'

'And then,' took up Judas, 'if Nanty wasny getting another word wi the lass on the stair, just afore we came up. I spoke sharp to him, but the limmer gied me a bit snash herself, and slipped away back to the company. And as well, too,' he added darkly. '*I've saved your play*, she says. Did you ever hear? She'd ha felt the rough side of my hand if she'd waited, whoever her faither might be.'

When Gil stepped out into the hall, he found Kate just despatching Babb and two reluctant journeymen with the groaning, white-faced Mistress Mathieson established in a great chair, to carry her next door to her own house, escorted by her stepdaughters who appeared to be engaged in a savage whispered quarrel. Several people looked round as he emerged, but he shook his head.

'No change,' he said. 'Is the Serjeant not here yet?'

'William must have gone further afield to find him,' Kate speculated. 'The man's never about when you need him.'

'And Our Lady send that Eleanor doesny miscarry and all, what wi the excitement,' commented Grace Gordon as she gathered up the last of the fans and cushions. 'You'll remember this gathering your life long, Kate.'

'I wish I thought I could forget it,' said Kate wryly.

The two women exchanged kisses, and Grace left, with an anxious look at her husband, who waved his fingers at her but did not move. Alys came to tuck her hand in Gil's, whether giving or seeking reassurance he was uncertain though he was glad of her touch. Kate braced herself visibly and looked round the hall at her remaining guests. Mistress Hamilton and the quiet young wife of Wat Forrest, who had hardly spoken in Gil's hearing all afternoon, had begun discussing childbirth with Nancy Sproull. Nancy's daughter Nell had retired to a corner and seemed to be struggling with tears. The men were still under siege in the window bay, Andrew Hamilton and Dod Wilkie discussing some matter of burgh council business with Maistre Pierre, Nicol Renfrew sitting humming tunelessly and swinging one foot again, and young Andrew Hamilton staring alternately at the door to the hall-chamber and at the despairing figure of Nanty Bothwell at the far end of the room where he sat bound to a backstool and guarded by two journeymen in watchful pose.

'I wonder how long we –' Kate began, one hand at her breast.

'There is little we can do but wait till the Serjeant comes,' Alys observed, 'and pray for that poor man. Gil, do you think it can have been an accident?'

26

'I don't believe Nanty Bothwell intended to poison Dan Gibson,' he said cautiously.

She gave him an intent look, and nodded. Kate, easing at the bodice of her dark red gown, said, 'Of course it was an accident. I've dealt with the man, when I wanted straightforward simples rather than a compound wi honey at five times the price, and he's intelligent and civil, and so is his sister. As you said, Gil, he's not such a fool as to poison the fellow afore all these witnesses. I'm right sorry we've had to take and tie him. I had Jamesie fetch him a bite to eat and drink, poor man.'

'There's a sister, is there?'

'Her name is Christian Bothwell,' said Alys. 'She is often at the booth, but I think she does a lot of the stillroom work. I think her a good woman.'

'Where is Serjeant Anderson?' wondered Kate distractedly, still plucking at her gown.

'Kate, are you laced too tight?' Gil asked. She looked down, colouring, and snatched the hand away.

'Edward,' she said. 'He needs to be fed.' She looked about the chamber as if expecting to see the baby hidden in a corner.

'Mysie has taken him above stairs,' Alys said. 'I'll fetch her down. Where will she bring him?'

'Not here,' said Kate, with a helpless glance at the men still ostentatiously talking matters of state. Nicol Renfrew gave her a happy smile and another tiny wave of his fingers.

'Augie's closet,' Gil suggested.

He had just returned to the hall with a list of instructions for Morison, leaving Kate and Alys to settle down with the baby, his nurse Mysie, and a jug of ale, when a portentous knocking at the house door announced the Serjeant. Admitted by Andy Paterson the steward, the burgh lawkeeper proceeded into the hall, a big man in an expansive blue woollen gown with the burgh badge embroidered on the breast. He was followed by one of his constables bearing a coil of rope and a pair of rusty manacles.

'Guid e'en to ye, maisters. Aye, Maister Cunningham,' he said, looking about him. 'So what's this about murder being done? Strange how I'm aye finding you next to a murder.'

'Daniel Gibson,' said Gil, ignoring this, 'fell down deathly sick at the end of the mummers' play.'

'Is the rest of the company well?' asked the Serjeant sharply.

'So far as I knew,' Gil answered, impressed despite himself. The man did not usually ask such pertinent questions.

'A terrible thing! We all saw him pysont,' Mistress Hamilton announced with relish. 'Poor man,' she added.

'Gibson was playing Galossian,' Gil supplied, 'and it seems as if he could have been poisoned by the drops the doctor uses to cure him. Maister Renfrew and his partners, and the Forrest brothers, are working on him now.'

'He's a deid man, then,' said the Serjeant, 'for nobody could survive that much curing.' He laughed at his joke, and looked about him. 'Where is he, then? I'll need to see him, deid or no, and where's Nanty Bothwell? Ah, you've got him ready for me.'

The door to the hall-chamber opened, and Morison emerged, his velvet hat in his hand.

'Serjeant,' he said. 'I thought I heard your voice. Thank you for coming so prompt. It's a matter of violent death, right enough.'

'Death?' said Nancy Sproull sharply. 'Is the poor fellow dead, then?'

In the window Maistre Pierre turned to look at them, and pulled his hat off. The other men did the same, one after another, and Nanty Bothwell, between his two sentinels, bent his head and muttered a prayer.

'He died just now.' Morison crossed himself, and most of his hearers did likewise. 'Father Francis was wi him.'

'God send him rest,' said Andrew Hamilton. His son was silent and round-eyed.

28

'Aye, well,' said Serjeant Anderson, 'that's clear enough, I'd say. Pysont by the man that's his rival in love, so I hear, and all these folk witnesses to it, is that right?'

Nanty Bothwell looked up with a despairing 'No!' but most of those present nodded, and there was a general chorus of agreement. Nancy Sproull said:

'Aye, as Agnes said, we all saw him give poor Daniel the drops that slew him.'

'I'm none so certain,' said Gil. 'Bothwell seemed as dismayed as any of us at the man's taking ill.'

'It was hardly anyone else in the chamber ministered the pyson,' objected Maister Wilkie. He clapped his green bonnet back on his bald patch and came forward into the room. 'There was none of us anywhere near the man – aye, nowhere near either of them, till the moment Dan Gibson fell down.'

'That's truth,' agreed Maister Hamilton.

His stout wife nodded, her chins wobbling, and young Andrew said clearly, 'They were all there in the midst of the room, see, and the rest of us round the outside.'

His mother looked at him fondly, but Nicol Renfrew said, with that irritating giggle, 'It was the wrong flask he had.' Everyone turned to stare at him, and he put his head back and looked owlishly from face to face. 'You could see that,' he added, and giggled again.

'How could you tell?' Gil asked carefully, trying to recall the moment when the flask had appeared from the doctor's great scrip.

Nicol waved a hand, grinning. 'It just was.'

A reply Ysonde might have made, Gil thought.

'This gets us nowhere,' declared the Serjeant. 'See here, Maister Cunningham, you're paid of my lord Archbishop to look into murders, so it's only natural you should want to look further. But I'm paid wi the council to keep this burgh safe, and what I'll do to that end is arrest the man that pysont Daniel Gibson, that you've got held there waiting for me, and there's the sum of it. Where is the poor fellow, sir?'

'Yonder, in the hall-chamber,' said Morison, with a help-less glance at Gil, while Wilkie and Maister Hamilton made approving noises and the scrawny constable looked resigned.

'But if there's some doubt about the flask –' Gil began, swallowing anger.

'Ach, nonsense,' said Maister Hamilton roundly. 'We've only this daftheid's word on that, and he's the one that tellt our Andrew Dumbarton Rock was on fire.'

Nicol flourished one hand and bowed, still grinning, and young Andrew went scarlet and glowered at his father. The Serjeant, ignoring the exchange, summoned his constable and proceeded grandly towards the door Morison had indicated. Gil, following him, paused as he found Maistre Pierre at his elbow.

'The man is safe meantime, if he is in the Tolbooth,' the mason observed in French. 'But I agree, it is not at all a certainty.'

'I'm not happy,' Gil admitted, 'but there is too little to go on. Better to let him take the fellow up, I suppose, while I ask questions further afield.'

In the hall-chamber the apothecaries were packing up their equipment, a set of wicked little knives, the basin in which the cataplasm had been mixed, the packets of strong-smelling herbs which went neatly back into the leather case. Robert Renfrew, holding a bowl of blood, stood aside for the Serjeant to enter and his father looked up from his herbs and said:

'Aye, Serjeant. It's murder right enough. Have you arrested the fellow?'

'In good time,' returned Serjeant Anderson, sailing towards the bed. 'Poor Danny. A good lad, so I believe.' He removed his hat briefly, and replaced it, then nodded at the mummers still seated in a row where Gil had left them, four of them numb and silent, the other young champion now sobbing into his hands. 'Aye, fellows,' he went on. 'A bad business, a bad business. It just goes to show what fol-lowing your heart can do to a young man.'

Maister Renfrew closed down his case and fastened the strap. Its lid was ornamented with the same sign as hung over his door, the sun rising out of a mortar.

'He's brought the craft into disrepute,' he said grimly, 'and I'll see him hang for it.'

Gil turned away from the doorway and moved across the hall, towards the seated prisoner, but before he had taken two steps there was a hammering at the house door, an urgent voice shouting, 'Let me in! Let me in! Is Nanty there?'

The two journeymen guarding the prisoner looked at one another blankly; Morison emerged from the hall-chamber, Andy Paterson the steward could be heard clumping up the kitchen stairs, but Gil himself was nearest. When he opened the door the woman on the other side of it almost fell in out of the twilight, still saying, 'Is Nanty here? Let me see him! What's ado?'

'Christian!' exclaimed the prisoner.

She straightened up, looking round for him, and hurried to his side. 'Our Lady save us all, Nanty, what's amiss here? They tellt me – they tellt me – it's never true, is it? A man dead, and by your hand?'

Bothwell looked up at her, his face working.

'Danny's dead,' he said. 'It wasny by my hand, Christian, I swear it, but he's dead none the less.'

She stood over him, some of her fears allayed, and set a hand on his shoulder. She was a stocky woman, older than her brother, dressed in a decent gown of woad-blue worsted, the ends of her linen kerchief knotted behind her head, her apron stained with the different colours of an apothecary's stock-in-trade. She had come out without a plaid.

'You don't need to swear it for me, my laddie,' she said, with fond untruth. 'I'd never ha believed it, whoever tellt me it. But what's ado then? Why are you bound like this?' She turned, looking round the chamber, and her eye fastened on Gil. 'Is it you that's in charge, sir? Why is my brother being held?'

31

'There's a man deid, Christian,' said Wat Forrest's quiet wife. Barbara Hislop, that was it, Gil thought.

'He pysont Danny Gibson,' said Maister Wilkie bluntly, 'no matter what he swears on, for we all saw it happen.'

'But how?' she said, staring at him. 'You all saw? How would that happen, in front of a room full of people, and none of them raise a hand to stop it?'

'All sudden, it was,' said Mistress Hamilton. 'We'd none of us a suspicion, till he fell down in a fit.'

'It must ha been something in the flask, Chrissie,' said Bothwell, swallowing hard, 'but whatever it was I never put it there.'

'Aye, and what flask?' she demanded. 'I've got your flask here.' She put a hand under her apron and drew out a small pewter flask, which she shook. 'You left it below the counter, I'd just found it when Girzie Murray from the Fishergate cam in by the booth and said you were taken up for murder.'

Well, well, thought Gil. So Nicol Renfrew was right.

'It was this flask, mistress.' James Syme stepped past Morison where he still stood open-mouthed in the door of the hall-chamber, and held up the painted pottery object which had emerged from the doctor's great scrip at the vital moment.

'That looks like one of –' she began, and bit off the words.

'We all had some of that shipment,' said Adam Forrest from behind Syme. 'You ken that, Christian.'

Morison pulled himself together and came forward, saying, 'Maisters, I think the Serjeant wants to ask us what happened, and then we're free to go, and I'm right sorry to have had to keep you here so long.'

'No trouble,' said Andrew Hamilton the elder in cheerful tones, 'I'd stay longer than this in company wi your clarry wine, Augie.'

'So can you untie my brother, sir?' demanded Christian Bothwell.

32

'No, no, we'll no untie him the now,' announced the Serjeant, emerging in his turn from the hall-chamber. 'He's safe where he is till Tammas and me's ready to take him away.'

'Away? Are you arresting him? But he never – I'll not –'

'He's guilty, woman, and no use to protest,' said Wilkie.

'If it wasn't the right flask,' said Gil, nodding at the little pewter one which Christian still held, 'where did you get the other one? The one you used?'

'Why, I –' began Bothwell, and stopped, staring in horror at the bright glaze of the flask in Syme's hand. Sweat broke out across his brow, and he closed his mouth, swallowed, and said, 'I – I forget.'

'No point in questioning him here,' said the Serjeant. 'I'll get all the answers I need out of him, down at the Tolbooth. Now, maisters, mistresses, I've heard from the man's fellows, and from the potyngars that treated him, I'll take your account of what passed, if it's convenient, and then I'll get away out your road.'

'What's in the right flask?' Gil asked.

'This and that to make a smoke when it's opened.' Christian drew the stopper and waved her hand, and a cloud of sinister bluish vapour trailed after the open flask.

'There's no harm in it,' said her brother wearily, 'but it looks good.'

'And in the other?' Gil looked from Syme to his colleagues. 'What would you say killed Danny Gibson? Can you prove what's in the flask in any way?'

'What, taste it ourselves?' said Robert Renfrew. He had found a discarded tray of sweetmeats. 'I think no!' he said, and popped a marchpane cherry into his mouth.

His father frowned at him, and said heavily, 'That's a task for one of us, I'd say, it being apothecary business. There's ways to prove pysons, though something that acts so swift and in small quantity – aye, well, the craft will tell.'

'The craft will tell,' agreed Syme, 'though it takes great learning to prove a poison.'

'I'll take that on, Frankie,' offered Wat Forrest. Syme looked annoyed. 'You've trouble enough in your household the night, without extra work.'

'Aye, I should be away,' admitted Maister Renfrew reluctantly, 'and see how the lass is doing. They'd ha sent word if the bairn had come home, I suppose. But I'd as soon see Bothwell took up for murder afore I go.'

'No, no, just you get away, maister,' said the Serjeant, with slightly forced civility, 'and let me speak wi these worthies. Then we can all get home to our supper. Maister Cunningham, if you want to run about testing pysons, I'll no stop ye, and if Maister Forrest wants to take the nasty stuff away wi him I'll be just as glad no to have the care o sic a thing myself, but I'll ha Nanty Bothwell safe in the cells at the Tolbooth in any case, so he'll no slay any more folk.'

'We'll never dare entertain again,' said Kate. She spoke lightly, but her eyes were shadowed.

'No, no,' said Maistre Pierre comfortingly, a wedge of pie halfway to his mouth. 'Once the poor fellow is buried you can be sure it will all be forgotten.'

'Aye, but the quest,' said Morison. 'The whole town will be there to hear. There was a crowd at the gates the now, when I saw the Serjeant off the premises.'

Alys patted Kate's arm. 'Better to wait, as my father says, till the poor man is buried,' she said, 'but after that, you must hold a gathering for a great many people, and hold your head up and wear all your jewels. And Augie must wear the King's chain.'

'And invite the Provost,' said Gil, 'and our uncle.'

'And your neighbours,' added Alys. 'You are right, Kate, Grace Gordon is well worth the knowing. When did you say they came home, she and Nicol?'

'In May, was it? Poor soul, she'd have had her own bairn by now, but she miscarried within days of reaching Glasgow, and kept her chamber a month or more after it.

34

She's well now, I'd say, but –' Kate glanced at Alys, and stopped in mid-sentence.

The last of the other guests had eventually left, still exclaiming about the afternoon's entertainment, but Kate had begged the mason's party to wait on and eat a bite of supper in private with them, saying, 'I've no idea what's left in the house, it could be thin fare, but we could both do with your company.'

In fact it was a substantial meal before them, the more so since Kate picked at her plate of cold raised pie and refused the mould of rice and almonds which Ursel had sent up with apologies.

Morison cast her an anxious glance now, served Alys with a wedge of onion flan, and said, 'I'm less than convinced it was murder under our roof, anyway. Young Bothwell seemed as stricken as any of us by the man's death. Can you do aught about it, Gil? After all, you – you got me –'

Kate shivered. He dropped his serving-knife to put a comforting hand over hers.

'I feel very sorry for that poor woman, his sister,' said Alys. She and Kate had been in time to witness the removal of the prisoner, with Christian's angry attempts to interfere restrained by Nancy Sproull and a more sympathetic Barbara Hislop.

'I'm not convinced it was murder by Nanty Bothwell,' said Gil. 'I'll report to my lord and get his instruction, but I agree, Augie, I should be asking questions already, before folk forget what they saw.'

'And what did we see?' asked Maistre Pierre rhetorically. 'The only opportunity to poison the man while the players were there in the hall,' he gestured with his third slice of pie at the door of the small chamber where they sat, 'was when the doctor put the drops to raise him up.' He grimaced at the irony implied. 'But was there some other way it could be ministered?'

'The sword?' said Morison.

'Was wooden,' said Gil, 'and they never struck flesh. It was a very clever display,' he added, 'they were well practised.'

'The armour?' suggested Alys. 'Something they ate or drank in the kitchen?'

'Christ preserve us,' said Morison, 'I never thought o that. Kate, should we –?'

'I'll ask Ursel,' said Kate with more resolution. 'She was to give them ale, she'd likely serve it from the barrel or from a common jug, but she might ha noticed something.'

'The man was rubbing at his mouth,' Gil recalled, 'just before he collapsed. Did the drops go on his mouth, Alys? I think you saw better than I did.'

'The second time,' she agreed. 'The first time he only touched the man with the lip of the flask, but the second time when he said, *Three drops to your beak*, I saw them fall.'

'If that was the moment,' said Maistre Pierre, 'it worked with astonishing speed.'

'He fell down within a quarter-hour,' said Alys.

'Less,' said Gil. 'The length of a *Te Deum*, maybe.'

'I can't bear this. Let's talk of something else,' said Kate. 'Tell me how John does.'

Nothing loath to discuss his foster-son, Maistre Pierre launched into an account of how the boy had escaped into the garden that morning, and had been found seated on the stone bench beside the wolfhound Socrates, singing to a blackbird.

'He has a sweet little voice,' said Alys, 'and very true.'

'Well, his father is a harper,' Kate pointed out, 'and his mother could sing, by what you tell me.'

Morison had turned his head, listening to a disturbance elsewhere in the house. He pushed his chair back, but before he could rise the chamber door was opened.

'Maister?' said Andy Paterson. 'My leddy? Here's Adam Forrest out in the hall, wanting a word wi Maister Gil, and I've two o the mummers in the kitchen on the same errand. What'll I do wi them all?'

'Give the mummers some ale and bid them wait,' said Kate decisively, 'and ask Maister Forrest if he'd care to step in here and join us, and bring him a glass and trencher.'

Adam Forrest, much embarrassed, refused food but was persuaded to some more of Morison's claret.

'My good-sister Barbara keeps a good kitchen,' he said, 'we'd our supper already, though none of us was that hungry, what wi one thing and another.'

'Nor are we,' agreed Morison, in flagrant disregard of Maistre Pierre's laden plate. 'It's a bad business, Adam.'

'Aye, a bad business,' agreed Adam, 'and I'm right sorry to ha troubled you at your meal, Lady Kate, but –' He slid a sideways look at Gil. 'I just. It's a bit.' He ran a finger round the rim of his wineglass. 'I just –'

'Go on,' said Gil encouragingly.

'Well. Will you be looking further into the business, Gil?'

'He will,' said Kate and Alys, speaking together.

Gil suppressed irritation and said, 'I'll report to my lord, but I think he will want me to investigate, aye.'

Adam sat back and nodded in obvious relief.

'You don't think Maister Bothwell guilty?' Alys said.

'I'd never ha taken him for a pysoner,' said Adam simply. 'It's what we all deal in, certainly, the most of an apothecary's trade is in things that will kill in some quantity or another, but we're sworn to use our skills to support life, no to end it, and Nanty's a good craftsman, I'd never ha thought he'd bring the craft into disrepute this way, no matter Frankie Renfrew's opinion.'

'Do we know yet what was in the flask?' asked Maistre Pierre. 'Your brother was to prove it, I think.'

'He was just setting to that when I came out,' admitted Adam. 'We were both of us right puzzled by it. It's a kind of a whitish liquid, like almond milk, though I couldny say if it smells like almond milk too, for we never got too close to it, seeing what it's done to Danny Gibson.'

'And what was that?' said Gil. 'What signs did you observe before he died?'

'Gil, must we hear this again? You saw him too,' objected Morison, taking Kate's hand.

'I'm no apothecary,' Gil said quietly. 'I'd as soon hear what the trained man saw.'

'Well, we all saw him,' said Forrest with confidence. 'Nanty said he never swallowed, it was only a couple of drops touched his mouth. But with that minimissimal dose, he went short of breath even after he'd had time to recover from the battle, there was a great excess of choler which made his face red and caused him dizziness so that he fell down.' He closed his eyes to recall the scene better, and Kate bit her lip and turned her face away. 'His breathing was fast and shallow, with a great strain on the heart, leading to seizures,' he recited, as if he was composing a report, 'which eventually slew him.' He crossed himself. 'We did what we could, the five o us, but it's my belief there would never ha been any saving him, no matter what remedies we tried.'

'It sounds like no ailment I ever heard of,' said Alys. 'It could only be poison, I am certain.'

'And I,' said her father, 'and the rest of Glasgow I suppose, but what poison? And if it did not get into the flask at young Bothwell's hand, then whose?'

'The flask,' said Gil. 'I thought Mistress Christian recognized the flask. The one that was used instead of Bothwell's own. That bright pottery is distinctive.'

'Well, no, it isny,' said Adam awkwardly. 'We've all three got some, all three o the businesses. We use them for the luxury goods. It was a barrel we had from Middelburgh, of painted ware out of Araby or somewhere. Frankie ordered it up last spring, and took the most of the batch, but Nanty had five or six, and me and my brother took a dozen.'

'In proportion as you trade in the burgh,' said Maistre Pierre, wiping his platter with a piece of bread. 'You have your custom well apportioned between you. Maister Renfrew trades in luxuries, in cosmetics and expensive fine goods, you and your brother have the middle part of the market and young Bothwell serves the poorer sort that can yet pay for *materia medica*. All works out well, I should say.'

'I'd say so,' agreed Adam, 'though I've noticed Frankie – well, enough of that.'

'So whose was that flask?' Alys asked. 'One of Maister Bothwell's, or another?'

'We'd need to count them all afore I could tell you that,' Adam admitted. 'They're each a bit different, but hardly enough to tell one on its own like that. I don't see it could be one of ours, but I can check,' he added.

'Would the other mummers know where the flask came from?' asked Morison.

Kate glanced quickly at him, and said, 'You could speak to them in the kitchen, Gil, rather than bring them up where their fellow died. Maybe Maister Forrest would have some questions for them and all.'

Gil led Adam Forrest obediently down to the kitchen, reflecting that his sister had probably heard enough of the day's troubles. In the big, busy room the mummers were easily picked out, two grey-faced men surrounded by most of Morison's household, who were plying them with sympathy mixed with questions about what the Serjeant had asked them and what he would do next. Without their disguises it took Gil a little while to identify them. Then he recognized a gesture, the angle of a head, and realized that they were the two mitred characters, Judas and St Mungo, probably the senior men in the group.

'Tammas Bowster and Willie Anderson,' said Adam behind him. 'Willie's kin to the Serjeant, but I ken no ill of Tammas. He's a glover in the Thenewgate.'

Andy Paterson looked round at this, saw them standing at the foot of the stair from the hall, and called for silence, into which Gil said politely, 'May I come into the kitchen? My sister sent us down. I think these fellows wanted a word wi me.'

'Aye, that we did,' said the man who had played Judas, getting to his feet. 'A word in private, maybe, maister?'

'Take a light into the scullery,' suggested Ursel the cook, a spare elderly woman in a clean apron. 'And mind your good gown on the crocks, Maister Gil, they're no all scoured yet.'

Perched uncomfortably on the wooden rack where the pots were dried, Gil watched the two mummers brace themselves for speech. They were both quite tall, St Mungo bearing a strong resemblance to his kinsman Serjeant Anderson, the glover leaner and younger with a confident manner which suggested he was his own master. The rushlight Adam had carried through from the kitchen showed them exchanging awkward glances.

'It's like this, maister,' said the glover after a moment. 'We'd a word among ourselves, the –' he checked, pulled a face and went on – 'the five o us that's left. Davie Bowen's no making much sense, poor lad, he's that stricken by his fellow being deid all in a moment like that, but the rest of us are agreed, and we put our heads thegither, and we, and we –'

'And we put our hands in our purses and all,' offered Willie Anderson.

'Quiet, Willie, let me tell it. And the thing of it is, maister, by what we've heard, you see into secret murders like what's happened here for Robert Blacader, and we thought, maybe you'd consider seeing into this one for us? For it's certain it was murder, Danny was fit and well afore the play began, and it wasny ever Nanty that done it, and we've –' Bowster dug in the breast of his leather doublet and drew out a pouch. 'We've gathered a fee to you, the day's takings and a wee bit from each of us and all. Only maybe,' he admitted, with a deprecating look, 'it'll no be enough, wi you being a man of law and all.'

Taken aback, Gil stared at the two, trying to think what he should say.

'It might no take that much doing, for a learned man like yoursel, maister,' said Willie Anderson ingratiatingly. 'There might be enough there in wir purse.'

40

'You said you'd be taking it on anyway,' said Adam Forrest from the shadows. 'Did you no?'

'I said I'd report to my lord Archbishop,' Gil corrected. 'It's for him to decide whether he wants me to go into the matter.'

'Is that right?' said Bowster in dismay. 'Blacader's decision?' The two mummers looked at one another uncertainly. Anderson recovered first.

'If he was to decide against you,' he suggested, 'maybe you could just look into it a wee bittie anyway? Maybe as far as wir purse would take you?'

Gil shook his head, more in disbelief than anything else, but Adam said, 'No harm in that, surely, Gil?'

'If I'm to report to Robert Blacader, I need more to tell him,' said Gil. 'Why are all Anthony Bothwell's friends so certain he's innocent, for a start? And I need to know more about the play, and all the players. This is no place for –'

'Gil?' The scullery door creaked open, and Alys stepped in, holding up her apricot silk skirts with one hand. 'Gil, here is Mistress Bothwell wanting a word.'

'Maister Cunningham?' The woman's voice was high with anxiety. 'Maister, will you act for my Nanty? He's there in the Tolbooth, John Anderson's got him in chains, he's as innocent as a babe of any poisoning. Will you act for him, and clear his name?'

Chapter Three

Gil was having difficulty keeping his face straight.

He knew it was inappropriate. One man had died and another was facing torture, trial and possibly hanging. Bothwell's friends were deeply anxious for him, his sister was almost frantic. But never before had what felt like half of Glasgow come separately and asked him to take on a case. He feared he was not concealing his amusement well; Alys had looked at him quite severely before she left for home. The remaining supplicants, meanwhile, were gazing hopefully at him by the light of the hall candles, where they had all adjourned after Mistress Bothwell's outburst.

'The evening's wearing on,' he had said when they came up the stairs. 'Adam, if I call by the shop tomorrow, I can find out how your brother has proved the flask, and get a longer word wi you.'

'Aye, fair enough,' agreed Adam, 'but I'll wait and see Mistress Bothwell to her door, I think.'

'No need,' Alys had said quickly. 'Mistress Bothwell will lie at our house tonight.' Her eyes met Gil's. 'They have one servant, who sleeps out,' she added. He nodded, with some reluctance. In her present state it was hardly right to let the woman go home alone, and though he would have preferred not to offer protection himself he would certainly lose an argument with Alys about the appearance of partiality.

'I'm right grateful,' admitted Mistress Bothwell, pleating up the hem of her apron between small hard hands. 'I'd

42

not – I canny fancy sleeping in an empty house, after sic a day.'

'Better Maister Forrest walks us home now,' said Alys, at which Adam made sounds of assent, 'and my father may stay and help you talk to the mummers.' She looked about her. 'Take this light into the window there and I will send him to you.'

So now, seated on one of Morison's good tapestry back-stools, he poured the men more ale, handed a beaker to his father-in-law, and said, 'Why are you so certain it was none of Bothwell's doing?'

They looked at one another and shook their heads.

'Ye just canny think o Nanty doing sic a thing,' said Anderson. 'He's aye that sweet-tempered, never a man to hold a grudge or, or –'

'He's been good friends wi Danny Gibson,' said Bowster. 'Until these last two-three month when they both took a notion to the lassie Renfrew, they were scarce out of one another's company in leisure time, for all I heard.'

'Went drinking thegither, went out to the butts on a Sunday,' agreed Anderson.

'Did their being rivals for the little Agnes make a difference?' asked Maistre Pierre. The two shook their heads again.

'They wereny spending as much time thegither,' offered Bowster, 'but they were friends enough when we met for the play. The lassie's well watched, ye ken, she'd have a word for them if her faither's back was turned, but it's no as if either lad got that close to her.'

'And yet they quarrelled in the kitchen here,' Gil said. 'Was that over Agnes?'

'Aye, well,' said Bowster uncomfortably. 'It was just shouting. A cause Nanty had a word wi the lassie. Seems they'd pledged no to get the advantage o one another.'

'Tell me about Danny Gibson,' said Gil. 'He's one of the armourer's journeymen?'

'Aye, he's – he worked for William Goudie,' said Bowster.

'The armourer, ye ken,' said Anderson. Gil, who had dealt with the burgh armourer for years, merely nodded. 'Him and Davie Bowen both, which is how their fight was that good, seeing they had leisure to practise it any chance their maister would let them.'

'It was good,' agreed Gil, with the thought that anything to be salvaged from the afternoon might be a comfort to Gibson's friends. 'I don't know when I last saw a display as accomplished.'

'Has Maistre Goudie been told?' asked Maistre Pierre.

'Aye, I've tellt him,' Bowster said, sighing, 'I've tellt the two houses where we were engaged to play the play the morn, I've let Archie Muir know that leads the other company in case he wants to take on the engagements in our place. I think I've tellt the most of Glasgow, maister, and it's no been easy.'

Gil took the hint, and poured some more ale.

'Has either man enemies?' he asked. 'Bothwell or Gibson, I mean. Have they quarrelled with anyone else lately?'

The two mummers looked at one another again, and Anderson shrugged his shoulders.

'No that I ever heard,' he said.

'Nor me,' agreed Bowster, and raised his beaker.

'No rivals at anything else, no insults, nothing like that?'

'Nothing like that, that I ever heard,' Bowster said, emerging from the beaker. 'A'body that I tellt just now that the lad was dead was right cut up about it, and all, and couldny believe it was Nanty's doing.'

'Now, the flask,' Gil said, accepting this. 'When did you see it was the wrong one?'

'When Nanty drew it out of his scrip, I wondered,' said Bowster, frowning. 'See, he holds it up and points to it,' he held up his beaker and imitated the gesture, 'and tells how there's all the herbs in it, and I saw then it was the bonnie paintit one. He'd said he'd not use one when I asked him afore, a cause they're too expensive if it got dropped, and I thought, well, he's changed his mind.'

44

'I thought that and all,' agreed Anderson.

'But then when he opened it, there was no smoke like there should ha been,' Bowster went on, 'so it never made any sense when Sanders and me backed away. That's our Bessie,' he explained, when Maistre Pierre looked puzzled. 'Sanders Armstrong, that's whitesmith off the Fishergate. But that's the first I kenned of it being the wrong flask.'

'Bothwell never mentioned it earlier?' asked Maistre Pierre.

'No that I heard,' said Bowster. He looked at Anderson, who shook his head blankly. 'It might be he mentioned it to one of the other lads, I could ask them if you like, but it was a bit – down in the kitchen yonder, where we was supposed to robe up, and black Davie Bowen's face, and that, it was going like a fair what wi the company above stairs and folk running up and down to fetch wine and cakes and the like, and that wee lassie getting underfoot –' He grinned wryly. 'Asked poor Davie whether he was the Deil or St Maurice, she did. He didny ken what to say, the poor fellow. So as for hearing what any one of the lads said to another, it was a matter of who I was standing next to, that's who I heard speaking, and I never heard a word of the wrong flask.'

'No that I ever heard him mention,' said Christian Bothwell. 'No enemies, none to wish us ill in Glasgow at least.'

'And outside it?' Gil asked.

They were sitting by the fading hearth in the hall of the mason's big sprawling house further up the High Street. When Gil and his father-in-law finally returned home they had found Mistress Bothwell here in colloquy with Alys and Catherine, the aged French lady who had been Alys's duenna before their marriage. At Gil's entry the wolf-hound sprawled next to the ashes leapt up and hurried to greet him, tail swinging, and he had to acknowledge the animal's welcome before he could speak. By the time he had persuaded his dog to lie down again, Alys had also come forward to greet him with rather more dignity and say softly in French:

'I have let her tell me nothing, Gil, all is still for you to ask.'

He acknowledged this with a quick smile, and touched her hand. She returned the smile and slipped past him to see about something in the kitchen, and he went towards the hearth, taking the opportunity to study the guest while Maistre Pierre was expressing sympathy for her troubles. She was still dressed as she had been when she first hammered at Morison's door in the twilight, though she had discarded the stained apron and released the long ends of her kerchief to hang down at her shoulders, in the custom of an older woman whose day's manual labour was done. Her face was broad and plain, though her features were well proportioned; she looked strained and anxious in the candlelight, but her smile had a sweetness about it as she bade goodnight to the dignified Catherine.

'Outside Glasgow,' she said now. 'Well, there are those we hold enemies, but they might not hold us enemies, having got the better of us.' She noted his startled look, and folded her hands in her lap. 'We're no Glasgow folk by birth. Nanty and me were raised in Lanark,' she said carefully, 'and trained by our faither, that was apothecary in the town. But when he died there were those that claimed the shop and the workshop and all that was in it as payment for his debts, and we left Lanark and came here instead.'

'That was two years or so since, I think,' said Maistre Pierre. She glanced at him and nodded.

'Had your father's creditors any connections in Glasgow?' Gil asked.

'No that I'm aware.'

'And your brother has built up his business,' observed Maistre Pierre, 'supplying the low end of the market, trading in pence rather than merks and turning over a tidy sum. Or so Maister Forrest tells me.'

'That's kind of him,' she said obscurely. 'Aye, we serve the Gallowgate and the lower town, wi packets of plain herbs and a few standard cures that sell well, and private consultations, discretion assured.'

'No quarrels arising from that?' Gil persevered. 'A failed treatment, someone who doubts your discretion? What do the other two apothecary houses think of your work?'

She looked blankly at him, then said, 'I see what you're asking me. No, I've no mind of anyone that holds a grudge at us. Not all treatments succeed, you'll understand, but the most of our custom recognizes that. Our discretion's never failed that I mind, and as for the other houses, Wat and Adam are good friends, and Frankie's aye treated us wi civility. We're no looking at the same trade, after all. It might be a different tale if we were after his fine goods custom.'

'What was in the flask your brother should have carried?' Gil asked.

'This and that, to raise a bit of smoke when it's opened,' she said, as she had before. 'It's harmless, so long as you didny drink it or the like, and makes a good effect. Nanty devised it himself.'

'And it was the right stuff in the flask,' he persisted.

'You saw me open it, maister. It was the right stuff – at least, it smoked the right way.'

'How did he come to leave it behind?'

She shook her head. 'Likely he took it out of his scrip to fill it, while he was at the booth, and forgot to put it back afore he went out to the play. Better ask him yoursel, maister, if that Serjeant will let you anywhere near him. He wouldny let me in the cell to speak wi him, just took the food and the blanket I brought and sent me away from the door.' She suddenly turned her head away, but her eyes glittered with tears in the candlelight.

Careful questioning built up an image of decent people, a fond sister, an easygoing and hardworking brother, a close friendship with the dead Danny Gibson.

47

'Until the two of them took a notion to that silly wee lassie of Renfrew's,' Mistress Bothwell said wearily.

'Is she so silly?' Alys asked, crossing the hall from the kitchen stair. She had tied back the sleeves of her silk gown, and was carrying a wooden tray with several beakers and two steaming jugs. The dog Socrates thumped his tail in greeting, and Gil rose to draw a stool to the hearth to serve as a table.

'If she thinks her faither would ever let her wed wi my Nanty,' Mistress Bothwell answered, 'she's more than silly, she's daft. He'll give her a new gown if she asks it, or a feast for her birthday which was how she and Nanty met, but he's got her marriage sorted, I'll wager, and Frankie Renfrew takes interference from nobody, the more so since Andrew Slack dee'd and left him senior man in the craft within the burgh.' She accepted a beaker from Alys, sniffed, tasted, and threw her an approving look. Alys smiled in response, and poured from the other jug for Gil and her father.

'I would have thought your brother a good prospect,' observed Maistre Pierre. 'A man with his own business, another apothecary, a good age for her –'

'Nanty's wife will have to work hard,' Mistress Bothwell countered, 'to earn her keep and her bairns' when they come. It's our own business, but we're still building it up, maister.'

'It was clear enough this afternoon Maister Renfrew does not approve,' said Alys. 'And you, Mistress Bothwell. Would you see it as a good match?'

'No.' She took a sip of her steaming beaker. Gil raised his eyebrows, and she said with more hesitation, 'I'd be wary of any connection wi Frankie Renfrew. A man wi his own opinion on everything's bad enough, one that canny let others alone wi their own ideas is more than I can take. He'd be present in the booth or the workshop daily directing what should be done or sold or ordered up. It's enough trouble now to get him to put our wants on the docket for Middelburgh without altering them to what he thinks best, we'd never get the simples we needed if he had a share in the business.'

Gil was unsurprised, soon after they had retired, to hear Maistre Pierre's distinctive loud knock at the outer door of their apartment. He padded across the further chamber in his stocking feet to admit his father-in-law, who said without preamble, 'It must be some enemy of the young man, whatever the sister says.'

'Or of both of them,' said Alys, at the door of their bedchamber. 'Or perhaps someone who dislikes Agnes Renfrew, or apothecaries in general.'

'Hmm.' Her father considered this, seating himself at Gil's gesture in his usual chair by the cooling brazier. 'I suppose.'

'Or it could have been an accident after all,' said Alys. She began to unpin her velvet headdress, and turned away into the other room to finish the task before the looking-glass.

'All the man's friends are agreed that it's out of character,' Gil concurred, lighting another candle from the one he held. 'And it does seem a clumsy way to go about it, to poison your rival in front of half the High Street. What puzzles me is this business of it being the wrong flask.'

'We must find where that one came from,' said Maistre Pierre. 'And how it was exchanged for the right one, and by whom.'

'And whether Bothwell knew it was that flask when he opened his scrip. Did either of you think he seemed surprised to find it?'

'He might have been,' said Alys from the bedchamber. 'I wonder if he paused just a little when he touched it in his scrip.'

'I was watching Frankie Renfrew,' admitted the mason. 'But I thought Bothwell as amazed as the rest of us when his friend fell, which suggests he did not know it to be lethal.'

Rustling sounds suggested Alys was unlacing the apricot silk with its wide sleeves. Gil, who would normally have helped her in this task, put aside the thought of the solid, slender warmth of her ribcage between his hands, and said resolutely, 'I must speak to Wat Forrest tomorrow, to find out what he has discovered. And to young Bothwell himself.'

'If the Serjeant will let you,' said Maistre Pierre gloomily. 'He has decided the man is guilty, as has Frankie, I suppose.'

'I'll go to the Provost if he won't,' said Gil. 'But Alys, you could find out for me, if you will, if all the flasks Bothwell took from the joint order are accounted for, or if that could be one of them.'

'Yes,' she answered thoughtfully. Silk rustled again. 'We must check those. But we need to account for the ones that went out to customers with some preparation in them, as well. It could be one of those.'

'She is right,' said her father. 'And there is another thing I wonder at about young Bothwell. If the father's substance all went to pay his debts, where did these two get the money to set up in business in Glasgow?'

Alys emerged from the inner chamber, fastening a bed-gown about her, and came to sit down with her comb.

'Their mother's portion?' she hazarded. 'It needn't be much, if the season was right. They needn't even have a physic garden. So much of an apothecary's stock-in-trade is there for gathering in the countryside at the right time of year. Enough coin to lay in some ginger and liquorice, and a good eye for growing things, and perhaps a few crocks and mortars and paper for packaging, and you have the start of your trade.'

Maistre Pierre shook his head. 'It puzzles me. Why Glasgow? Why not Edinburgh or Linlithgow, or another nearer town to Lanark?'

'That's a good point,' said Gil. 'It may not be relevant, but who knows what is relevant at this stage?'

Alys turned to smile at him, her face half obscured by the sheet of honey-coloured hair which gleamed gently in the candlelight.

'I'll see what I can learn,' she said again. 'And Gil – I know you would rather not have her here, but she would have been alone in the house tonight if she went home.'

'Aye, very true,' said Maistre Pierre. 'It was a wise decision, *ma mie.*'

Gil made no answer. After a moment she continued, 'Gil, has anyone else prayed for the poor man?'

'Father Francis was there,' he pointed out.

'No, I mean for Nanty Bothwell. Whatever happens, he has lost a friend, and he probably gave him the poison that killed him. He needs our prayers.'

'I have a Mass said for him tomorrow,' said Maistre Pierre. 'And we can remember him in our devotions tonight. I have no doubt Catherine has already done so.'

She was silent for a few strokes of her comb, then said, 'If it is not poison in the painted flask – well, no point in speculating on that yet, I suppose. The man fell so soon after the drops touched him it seems most likely to have been that. If we are right, we need to establish what it was, and how it got in the flask, and what it was doing there.'

'Who was it intended for, and who put it there,' Gil added.

'We said that before,'said Maistre Pierre. 'If the young man forgot or mislaid the right flask, he must have replaced it at some time. But why with one full of poison?'

'It could simply have been someone's store of the poison,' said Alys slowly, 'and lifted by accident. The stuff already in the flask, I mean, and the flask simply taken as a substitute.'

'That's possible,' said Gil cautiously. 'But would a practised apothecary use what was in the flask without knowing what it was?'

'There was no label on it, was there?' asked the mason.

'None when I saw it,' said Gil.

Alys combed reflectively at her hair for a little while, then said, 'What of the other people who were there? How did they look when the man fell? Father, you remarked on Maister Renfrew's fit of rage, but that happened long before the flask appeared.'

'Shock? Surprise? I didn't see their faces,' Gil said.

'Shock and surprise,' agreed Maistre Pierre. 'Amazement. One or two thought it still part of the play, I suppose. Then you moved, Gil, and several watched you. I could not think what you were at myself.'

'It seemed most important to get the children out of the chamber first.'

'Yes, indeed. Kate mentioned that while she was nursing Edward,' said Alys. 'She was grateful, Gil. Wynliane still has nightmares, and seeing a man die in such a way would certainly set her off.' He grunted, slightly embarrassed. 'I looked at my father first, and Maister Renfrew beside him. He seemed amazed. Then you moved, and then when I looked again all the apothecaries had rushed forward, except for that one, is it Nicol Renfrew? Who stayed in his seat and laughed. Such a strange man.'

'He always was strange,' Gil said. He described Nicol as he recalled him from their schooldays, and she listened carefully, but said:

'And the women were all shocked, I think. Poor Nell Wilkie was very distressed, I found her weeping in a corner later, but of course she could not leave until her parents did. She kept saying, *It's horrible, it's just horrible.* I wondered if she had a liking for either man herself. And what with Meg beginning in labour like that as well, both her stepdaughters were overset. It's fortunate Grace is a woman of sense, for if I'd to rely on Eleanor Renfrew –' She bit the sentence off, and applied her comb again.

Her father stirred, and broke his long silence with, 'Well, well, we were all shaken. Violent death in the midst of rejoicing – I hope it is not an ill omen for young Edward, or for the house. Now what must we do tomorrow? Who must we speak with? The brothers Forrest, I suppose, Maister Renfrew, Mistress Bothwell.'

'I can do that,' said Alys, 'if you speak to Maister Renfrew, Father. See if you can find out about the other flasks. We can hardly trouble the rest of the household while Meg . . .'

'I'll talk to the Forrests and to the accused man,' said Gil into the pause, 'and see where that leads me, but I'd best get a word with the Provost first of all.'

'Do that,' said his father-in-law. 'And now I suppose you have better things to think of than talking of murder. I go to my bed. Goodnight, my children.' He got to his feet, and they bent their heads for his blessing. At the door he halted, and clapped Gil on the shoulder, nodding.

'Something else to think about,' he said cryptically, with a flick of the eyes towards Alys as she retreated to their bedchamber. 'A good thing, I think.'

'It's a puzzle,' said Wat Forrest, looking sourly at the painted flask. 'It's pyson right enough, and strong pyson at that as Frankie said, for it slew a couple sparrows and a seamew that fancied the bread and all, much the same way as poor Danny.'

'The same way,' Gil repeated.

'Well, allowing it was smaller creatures,' said Adam.

'Aye,' agreed his brother. 'It acted much quicker, wi no seizures, they just fell over and twitched a time or two, even the seamew, that's a lusty bird.'

I haue brought a remedy with me that is the grettest poyson that euer ye herd speke of,' Gil said thoughtfully.

'You have?' said Wat quickly. 'Ha! You're at your quoting from books again. Find me a book wi this in it, then, for as to what it is, Gil, I've no more notion than when I started.'

'Have you decided what it isn't?'

'Oh, we've started a list,' said Adam.

They were in the Forrest brothers' workroom, a powerful-smelling place lined with shelves. A wall of pottery jars, each carefully labelled in the neat script taught at the grammar school, faced an array of mysterious pieces of glassware and metal tubes. There was a scrubbed and much-stained bench in the middle of the room, and a small charcoal burner gave off a welcome heat but was not, Gil suspected, there to warm the occupants although the day outside was bright and cold, the wind biting. At the other side of the chamber, by the window which gave on to the shop, Wat's quiet wife Barbara Hislop, niece of the late Andrew Slack, was working at something in a lead mortar between trips into the shop itself to deal with a customer. It was amazing how much of the Upper Town needed rice or nutmegs or digestive lozenges this morning.

'There's a few substances you can set aside immediate,' Wat said helpfully, 'that never take the form of a liquid, or else demand heat to liquefy them. Then there's the colour, which is like watered milk, that lets you leave aside those that are said to be green or yellow or the like, and the smell, for I'd think there's no smell from the flask, though to tell truth I haveny got that close to it. No strong smell, we'll say. And we'll do without proving it by taste, for I've a wife and a bairn to think of.' The wife looked round at this; they exchanged a glance, and she smiled slightly and addressed the mortar again.

'So we're no much forrard,' said Adam.

'We know now it's poison in this flask, the one that was in Bothwell's scrip,' said Gil. 'If we knew what it was, it might tell us who put it there, but there could be other ways to find that.' He nodded at the bright thing sitting innocently on the workbench. 'Knowing where the flask itself came from would help.'

'Well, from Araby,' said Wat.

'We had a dozen, as I tellt you,' said Adam. 'There's seven still on the shelf yonder,' he pointed at the furthest rack, 'and we need to go through the book and check, but

I think the other five's accounted for, gone out holding one preparation or another for the gentry trade.'

'That's assuming they're still in the houses they went to,' Gil observed. 'If you let me have a list, I'll see to tracking them down.'

There was a pause, in which the brothers looked at one another.

'I could see to that,' said Barbara Hislop in her soft voice. 'I delivered the most of them, after all. I could call by each one and ask if it's still there.'

'Aye, that's the way,' said Wat in relief. Gil, recognizing that confidentiality was a requirement in other professions than his own, nodded with some reluctance.

'Maybe you'd do more than ask, mistress,' he suggested. 'If you could try to set eyes on each one, and make a note of it, that would be better. I wouldn't need to see your note unless you learn aught the Provost has to hear,' he added, 'but I'd as soon know it was writ down somewhere just what you learned.'

Wat frowned at this, but grunted agreement. His wife looked at him, then into the mortar; pushing it to one side she covered it with a cloth and said, 'I'll go out the now, while folk are still in their houses. How was Christian the day, sir?' she added shyly. 'Adam said she was to lie at your house. That was kind in you.'

'She's worried for her brother,' Gil said. 'She went down the town early, to see to the booth and get a loaf to send in for him to break his fast.' He glanced at the window. 'I'd best be away to the Tolbooth and speak to the man myself.'

'Tell him he has our prayers,' she said, and both the brothers agreed with emphasis.

'Spoke to the Provost,' repeated Serjeant Anderson.

'You can send a man up to the Castle to check, if you like,' said Gil pleasantly.

'No, no, I'll tak your word for it, maister.' The Serjeant reached for his keys, rose in offended dignity from his great chair and turned towards the stair which descended from the far side of his cluttered chamber. 'Come and get speech wi our pysoner, then. I've no put him to the question yet, I was waiting on instruction from the Provost myself and he'll likely want him up at the Castle. Forbye my lord Montgomery hasny returned the pilliwinks he borrowed off me the last time he was in Glasgow.'

Suppressing the thought of what thumbscrews would do to a man used to such fine work as rolling pills and measuring tiny quantities of their ingredients, Gil followed the Serjeant down to the row of three small cells where miscreants were held until justice came their way.

'We've no that much room,' admitted the Serjeant, 'seeing the Watch lifted a couple of lads on the Gallowgate last night, suspicion of pickery, and the ale-conners had a bit trouble yesterday and all, so we've a hantle of alewives, causing of mob and riot . . .' He paused as a volley of shrill invective struck them from the alewives' cell. 'But just the same I put him in on his own, seeing it's no right to ask other folk, even ill-doers, to share a cell wi a pysoner.' He was unlocking the furthest cell as he spoke, and now unbarred the door and opened it cautiously, peering in. 'Right, Anthony Bothwell, here's a man of law to question you why you did it.'

Bothwell was on his feet when Gil stepped into the cell, a blanket round his shoulders, the end of a loaf in one hand. He ducked his head in a bow, stammering, 'Maister Cunningham! This is right kind of you –'

'Wait till he's questioned you afore you call him kind,' said the Serjeant. 'Just kick the door and shout a bit when you want to leave, maister, I'll hear you in time.'

As lock and bar clunked into place Gil looked round and sat down cautiously on the stone slab which served as a bed.

'Your sister's loaf reached you,' he observed.

Bothwell looked down at the crust. 'Aye. How is she? She's aye – she's –'

'She's out at the booth here,' Gil said. 'She's feared it might be attacked if she left it unattended.'

'Aye. I thought o that too, in the night,' said Bothwell. He took two paces across the cell and two back, and turned to Gil, spreading his hands, the crust shedding crumbs on the filthy floor. 'What am I to do, maister? I never pysont Danny, whatever the Serjeant says, but he'll not hear me. I lay all night thinking, what of my sister? She'll never wed now, we'll never get a tocher thegither for her, who'll go to an apothecary that's been accusit of pysoning a man?'

'You'd be surprised what folk can forget,' said Gil. 'Your sister's asked me to look into this business. She'll not believe you guilty, and nor do the Forrests, nor the other players.'

'My thanks for that, maister,' said Bothwell.

'So sit down, man, and tell me where the flask came from.'

'The flask?' The other man stared at him. 'Was it – was it the flask right enough?'

Gil detailed Wat Forrest's observations. Bothwell heard him out in silence, and suddenly sat down on the bench and covered his mouth with the back of his free hand.

'I'd been sure,' he said after a moment, 'sure as anything, it was something he'd eaten afore the play. So it was pyson, and it was me gave it to him, and neither of us ever thinking –' He broke off, and rubbed at his eyes. 'Poor Danny. God ha mercy on him. And on me.'

'Amen,' said Gil. 'So where did the flask come from? Is it one of your own?'

'No, it –' Bothwell stopped, staring at Gil in the dull light. After a moment he looked away, and said slowly, 'Aye, I suppose it is.'

'You must know.'

'Aye, it is. It's one of mine. One of ours.'

'So what was in it and when did it get there?' The other man shook his head, staring at the ground. Gil looked at him in some puzzlement. 'You must know,' he said again. 'Why were you carrying that one rather than the other?'

There was another pause. Then Bothwell drew a deep breath, exhaled hard and said, 'Maister, you've just tellt me I killed my nearest friend. I'm no thinking that well. Can I get a bit of time to get my head clear?'

'I've aye found,' said Gil deliberately, 'that the sooner I ask the questions, the better the answers I get.'

'No in this case,' said Bothwell.

'Well, let's talk about something else. Have you enemies in Glasgow? Anyone that dislikes you enough to get you accused of murder?'

'Me?' said Bothwell in blank amazement. 'No! No that I – no.' He shook his head.

'Why Glasgow anyway? Why did you settle here after you left Lanark?'

Bothwell grimaced. 'Our grandam was a Glasgow woman. We'd kind memories of her.'

'And the move was a good one?'

'Oh, aye. Till now. Wat and Adam have been good to us, and Frankie's aye free wi advice and encouragement.' He shot Gil a wry look. 'Seeing we're hardly after the same custom.'

The same remark as his sister had made.

'Tell me about Danny Gibson,' said Gil. 'What kind of a fellow was he?'

'A good friend.' A painful half-smile. 'We seen eye to eye on so many things, it was no wonder we both –' He stopped, and there was another pause.

'Both went after the same girl,' Gil supplied.

'Aye.'

'Which of you did she favour?' Another shake of the head. 'Neither of you? Do you tell me a young lass like Agnes Renfrew contrived to be even-handed between you?' Surely not that empty-headed little creature – Alys could have managed it, he thought, but Alys is by far wiser.

'Look, we can just leave Agnes out of this,' said Nanty

58

Bothwell. 'She's got nothing to do wi it, I tell you. I never slew Danny out of jealousy or for any other reason, it was a foul mischance, and no point in asking questions.'

'What did you and Danny have words about in the kitchen before the play?'

'We never did,' said Bothwell, looking up indignantly.

'I've heard different. You had speech with Agnes Renfrew out in the yard, and then hot words with Danny in the kitchen.'

'Oh.' Bothwell looked down again. 'That. Aye, well, I saw Agnes in the yard and stepped out – just to pass the time of day,' he said fluently, 'no that she was able for much conversation for she'd to run home on some errand for her stepmother, seeing it's just next door. And then, well, Danny was angry at me for getting a chance at speaking wi her when he hadny. We'd an agreement. We'd pledged,' he said, with a sideways glance at Gil. Tears sprang to his eyes, and he suddenly put his hand over his mouth again. 'Ah, the poor fellow,' he said behind it.

'And then you spoke to her again on the stairs. What did she have to say then?'

'Nothing. She was on the stair, I met her there. By happenstance.'

'Are you sure it was happenstance? You'd a lot to say to each other, for a chance encounter.'

'Why are you questioning me? You know the whole tale, that's clear,' said Bothwell. 'I tellt you to leave Agnes out of this, forbye.'

'No, for I don't know what she meant by saying she'd saved the play.' There was no answer. 'What had she to do with the play?'

'Nothing,' said Bothwell firmly. 'Ask her. Ask her faither. Do you think Frankie Bothwell would ever let his lassie near a company of mummers?'

'Right,' said Gil, rising. He kicked the door and shouted loudly for the Serjeant. 'I'll do just that, man, for if you'll not help me to the truth I'll get there another way.'

* * *

59

Below the painted sign depicting a marble mortar and pestle a crowd was gathered about the door of the Bothwells' booth. Its demeanour seemed to be peaceful, but Gil hastened his stride along the side of the Tolbooth, past the other small booths and stalls with their array of enticing wares spread out in the chilly sunshine.

'No need to hurry,' said the capper from his doorway, knitting-wires unheeded in his hand. 'They'll be there a while yet.' Gil checked to look at the man, who went on, 'I canny interest you in a good new bonnet, maister? No, I thought not. Trade's been as quiet the day so far, they're all along by Christian's door trying to hear what's to do wi her brother.'

'I'd like to know the same,' said Gil, rather grimly. The capper threw him a jaded look and ducked back into his booth, taking up his thread of wool again.

Christian Bothwell was behind the counter in the booth, dispensing packets of herbs and folded papers of pills, a snippet of news or thanks for a word of sympathy along with each. To his surprise Gil recognized his wife beside her, neat this morning in her everyday blue gown and plain black silk hood, taking the money and counting the change as if she had done it all her life. He managed to catch her eye over the heads of the crowd, and she smiled at him, spoke quietly to Mistress Bothwell, but made no effort to leave. With some trouble he elbowed his way to the front, and the two women finished the transaction they were occupied with and turned to him.

'So did you get a word wi Nanty, sir?' asked Mistress Bothwell.

'I did. He's not saying much.'

'Pennyworth of treacle, lass, and I've my own pig here,' said a stout woman, elbowing him aside and thumping a pottery jar down on the counter. 'That's a terrible thing about your brother, and all.'

'Is it the shock, maybe?' Mistress Bothwell said to Gil, smiling automatically at the woman and passing the pottery pig to Alys.

'I'd say not.' Gil looked round at the crowd, nodded to an acquaintance, and resisted the attempts of another woman with a basket of strong cheese to push past him to the counter. 'I need to get a word wi you, mistress. There's a few things you could tell me.'

Alys was already lifting the money-box away into the booth, and Mistress Bothwell reached for the ropes that held the counter in place.

'Get round to the door and I'll let you in,' she said. 'Forgive me, neighbours, I need a word wi this man of law, you'll agree Nanty needs all the help he can get the now. I'll open the shutters again in half an hour,' she promised. 'Your pig'll likely take that time to fill, the treacle runs that slow this weather, Maggie.'

There were some groans, and a few disgruntled comments, but the woman with the cheese seemed to speak for most when she said, 'Aye, Christian, take all the advice you can get. Is that no the man that got Maister Morison let off when he found a heid in a barrel?'

Inside the booth, with the shutter closed and the door latched again, it was nearly dark. Alys materialized at his side in the shadows, tucked her hand in his, and said, 'Will he not answer your questions?'

'He'll tell me nothing about the item he had,' Gil said quietly, well aware that they were far from private. 'Nor how it came to be in his scrip instead of the other. Can you shed any light, mistress?'

'No,' said Mistress Bothwell from across the little space. 'I found the pewter one in here when I lifted the counter to close up, the way I said, long after he'd left to gather wi his friends. The wee filler was there wi it, I thought like as not he'd been mixing a fresh batch of the smoking potion and filling it into the flask and maybe been interrupted by a customer and put the whole thing under the counter out the way.'

'That sounds reasonable,' Gil agreed. 'But the other. Where did he get that, and when did it come by its fill of poison? Is it one of your own?'

'One of ours? It might be.' By her voice she was thinking carefully. 'Frankie Renfrew would have us take a half-dozen out of a shipment he had from Araby, and I've no recollection we've used any of them. We don't trade wi the luxury end of the market, maister. They should all still be in their straw wrappings in the basket where I stowed them.'

'And where would that be?' he asked.

She laughed abruptly. 'A good question.'

'They are not here, are they?' said Alys. 'Could they be in your house?'

'Aye, very like. I'll tak a look if it's important, maister.'

'I think it is important,' said Gil patiently. 'We need to find out where it came from and how it came to be in his scrip with poison in it, and if your brother won't tell us we have to find out another way.'

'But why won't he say? That's madness, if it's sic an important matter. It wasn't just us that had some,' she said, still thinking it out. 'Frankie ordered six dozen, I think he said, and five of them was broken or chipped past using for the business. We took a half-dozen, Wat and Adam had a dozen, so Frankie must ha had near fifty. Even Frankie Renfrew isn't going to trade fifty flasks like that in a year.'

'But why would either the Forrests or Maister Renfrew wish to do you such an ill turn?' Alys asked.

'It might not be Frankie himsel.'

'Mistress Hislop is to check that all theirs are accounted for,' Gil said.

'Barbara's a good lass. You'll can trust what she says.'

But can I? Gil wondered. Beside him, Alys said:

'Might my husband go by your house just now and ask your servant to look for the basket? Would it be easy for her to find?'

'No,' Mistress Bothwell said bluntly. 'I stowed it out of her way. She's a capable woman, but she's right clumsy. I'll not have her crashing about in my workroom. I tell you what, maister, if you would wait while I go home the now, seeing you're in a hurry, I could fetch out the basket and bring Leezie back wi me to gie me a hand here while I'm about it.'

'I could come with you,' said Alys hopefully. 'Gil can guard the booth on his own, I am sure.'

'If you're doing that,' said Gil, 'leave me a light of some sort.'

Chapter Four

Maister Goudie's shop along the Thenewgate was also beset by a number of lads and men old enough to know better, who were hanging about the door in the hope of setting eyes on the surviving journeyman. When Gil stepped into the shop an older man looked up from his work on a ball-ended dagger, perhaps thinking that here was a genuine customer. Through the window behind him the two apprentices were visible in the yard behind the shop, at their endless task of rottenstoning the plate mail. There was no sign of Davie Bowen, but Goudie appeared from the drawing-shop to one side, ducking past the leather curtain, slate and pencil in hand and spectacles on nose.

'And how can we help you, Maister Cunningham?' he asked. 'A new dagger, is it, or a helm? Or I've a bonnie back-and-wame would just about suit you, all of new plate and just a wee bit chasing on the breast –'

'I'm not buying today,' Gil said regretfully. 'Maybe at the quarter-day. I just stepped by to condole with you after yesterday.'

Goudie crossed himself, and in the tail of his eye Gil saw the other man do the same.

'That's a kindness, sir. Aye. A shock that was, I can tell you. When they brought Davie home, weeping his heart out, the poor lad, and tellt me – aye, aye, a shock like no other.' He paused, and peered hard at Gil. 'Did Tammas Bowster tell me you were present when it happened, maister? I wonder, would you come up and let me know what came about, and maybe the mistress and all? Billy, you'll mind the shop a while, man? I'd be right grateful, Maister Cunningham. Davie's made very little sense, I'm sure we can all understand that, but I'd thought better o Tammas than the fool's tale he gave me.'

'I'd be glad to,' Gil said. And thank you, St Giles, he thought. What a piece of good fortune.

He found himself bustled through the drawing-shop, past rows of hanging parchment measuring-strips and wooden patterns, past a well-thumbed book of designs on the wide bench, and up the stairs to the living quarters. Here a lean, motherly woman in striped homespun exclaimed at Goudie's introduction, and pressed him to sit down by the brazier and accept oatcakes and a cup of buttered ale while he explained all to them. He went over the tale of Danny Gibson's death, and they heard him out with more exclamations and sighs.

'So Tammas had the right of it,' said Goudie. 'I couldny credit it myself, that he just fell down and died. And at Nanty's hand, forbye. Is that no dreadful, mistress?'

His wife nodded, wiping at her eyes with the tail of her headdress.

'The poor lad,' she said. 'But it wasny Davie's fault, that's clear enough. I'm grateful for you telling us that, maister.'

'I wish I'd never let them practise in my yard,' said Goudie glumly.

'How is Davie?' Gil asked.

'Laid down on his bed wi a draught,' said Mistress Goudie. 'I'm no one to coddle the lads, you'll ken, maister, but he's in no state to work. He said he never slept. Poor laddie, he sat here at the fire weeping and telling me he wanted to dee hissel, I think he's feart it was something he'd done that caused Danny's death.'

'He's aye been soft, that lad. Billy's fit to work the day, why not Davie?'

'William Goudie, you shed a tear or two yoursel last night,' challenged his lady.

'Tell me about Danny,' Gil requested. 'What kind of a lad was he? Was he well liked? Had he any enemies?'

'Not that I ken,' said Mistress Goudie firmly. 'He was a bonnie lad, not out of the ordinar in any way, civil enough round the house and in the work place,' Goudie nodded agreement to this, 'got on well wi his fellows. Behaved hissel as well as a lad that age will do, went to Mass wi the rest of us. A bit fussy to feed, he would never touch anything wi nuts in, couldny stand nuts. It made fast days a wee bit difficult, but no more than that.'

'Did he make jokes, play tricks, anything that might have annoyed someone?'

'No that I ever heard,' she said doubtfully. 'He was – he was aye sic a kind laddie,' she finished, and sighed and dabbed at her eyes again.

'What did he do for his leisure?'

'Went drinking,' supplied Goudie, 'went out to the butts on a Sunday, played at the football on a holiday. Much like his fellows, as Mistress Goudie says.'

'Did he belong to any league or band?' Gil asked. 'Any of the altar companies, or a football side, anything of the sort?'

'No that he ever mentioned,' said Mistress Goudie, thinking. 'He supported St Eloi's altar along at St Mary's, like all the hammermen, but I never heard him speak of any other league he had to do wi. And the lads do talk, the three of them,' she bit her lip, 'times they'd forget I was present, as if I was their mother.' The end of her headdress came into use again, and she turned her face away.

'Did he have anything of any value?' Gil asked. 'I'm still trying to find a reason why he would be killed.'

'But surely they're saying it was Nanty Bothwell's doing?' questioned the armourer.

'I'm casting all round about,' Gil said. 'I'll look at all the possibilities. Did the lad have anything worth stealing, mistress?'

'No that I ever saw.' She looked across the chamber. 'I packed his gear all up into his scrip, for his faither to

66

collect when he – aye. So it's there, maister, if you wish a look at it. He hadny that much.'

This was true. Two spare shirts, one badly worn, two pairs of hose, two doublets and a leather jerkin; comb and shaving gear, a woodcut of St Eloi brandishing the newly shod leg of the horse which stood docilely beside him on the remaining three. Drawers and other linen, a pair of shoes, a pair of boots, made a separate bundle. On one of the doublets was pinned a pewter badge of St Mirren.

'Did he have a bow?' Gil asked.

'I arm my laddies myself,' said Maister Goudie. 'So I keep a half-dozen bows for their use. He'd his choice of any one of them, and the same for blade and buckler, to take out to the butts.'

Gil shook his head. 'There's nothing here to kill for, that I can see,' he said.

'Bothwell must ha done it,' said Goudie. 'But it's a strange way to go about getting rid of your rival, to use poison on him wi half the burgh looking on.'

'I can't make sense of that,' Gil said. 'Were they rivals right enough? Did Danny ever talk to you about it, mistress?'

'Oh, they were rivals,' agreed Mistress Goudie. 'At least so far as they both had a notion to the lass, and she had a notion to the both of them. I saw her a time or two at the market, wi a maidservant at her heels,' she divulged, with a rueful smile. 'She'd stop by the potyngar booth at the Tolbooth, and pass the time of the morning, and then she'd be along here not a quarter hour later and keeking in at our shop door, though what business a young lass would have in an armourer's shop – well, it did no harm, or so I thought, though it's led the lass into grief after all. But the two lads was friendly enough about it, and as good friends as ever when the lass wasny about.'

'Perhaps she was even-handed then,' Gil said. 'Bothwell told me she was. He said they had an agreement, too – he and Danny Gibson, I mean.'

'Young fools,' said Goudie, without heat. 'Danny naught but a journeyman, Nanty Bothwell still to make his way in his trade – her father thinks by far too well of himself to wed her to either, and so I told them both a time or two.'

'Aye, you did that, Goudie,' agreed his wife, 'but did you expect them to listen?' She sighed again. 'Och, poor laddies. The both of them. What a business.'

'Where did he go drinking?' Gil asked as he rose to leave.

'Now that I can say,' pronounced Mistress Goudie. 'He and Billy would argue over the best alehouse, and Danny aye swore by Maggie Bell's house, just across Glasgow Brig.'

Tammas Bowster the glover was seated at the window of his shop, stitching intently at the many scraps of fine leather which went into a glove. Gil recalled the white kid-skin he had bought in Perth in the summer. Perhaps this man could make it into something suitable for Alys, he thought.

When he stepped into the shop Bowster raised his head with a sour look, but his expression lightened as he saw Gil and he got to his feet, saying hopefully, 'Is there any word, maister?'

'The Serjeant hadny heard from the Castle when I was there,' Gil said. 'I came by to see if you'd recalled anything new that might help me.'

'You'll take it on, maister? You'll see into how poor Danny came to be pysont?'

'I seem to be doing that,' Gil admitted. The glover set aside his work and put a stool nearer the brazier.

'Hae a seat, maister, and I'll answer your questions. I've not recalled anything,' he admitted, 'but if you prompt me who knows what might come to mind. Was that you at Goudie's door the now? What's the word o Davie Bowen?'

'Overcome by grief. Mistress Goudie was quite anxious about him.'

Bowster nodded. 'He's aye a soft laddie, a gentle soul. I think his daddy put him to the armourer in the hope it would harden him. And yet he's that good with a sword and buckler.'

The two were hardly exclusive, thought Gil.

'Tell me about yesterday,' he said. 'Where did your company gather? Here, or at Goudie's?'

'Aye, at Goudie's. Nanty was a bit after the tryst, last to arrive, he said he'd had a run of custom and his sister not back yet from the house. Then when we were all assembled, and certain we'd our guises all complete, we went up to Morison's Yard in a body wi the piper playing.'

'Your piper,' said Gil. 'Who is he?'

'Geordie Barton, dwells in the Fishergate. No a bad piper, kens more tunes than some of them, but he can put away the ale like it was the last brewing in the country.'

'And Nanty never said he had the wrong flask?'

'I've been thinking about that,' said Bowster. 'He never said aught about it at all, and you ken, I think that would be a cause Davie and Danny were getting right anxious about the play. It was Davie's first time afore other folk, you'll understand, and he was a wee thing on edge. Nanty likely said nothing about changing anything for fear of –'

'Of course.' That made sense, though it cast no light on when the change had occurred. 'So from Goudie's you all walked up to Morison's house, and went to the kitchen door.'

'It's a fine large kitchen. And the auld wife there – Ursel, is that her name? – was right friendly, though she was rare taigled with the company above in the hall, and sending up food. She gave us ale and gingerbread, and let us disguise oursels in her scullery, and then we waited in her kitchen till they were ready for us in the hall.'

'And when did the two of them quarrel? Nanty and Danny Gibson?'

Bowster thought about this.

'A'most as soon as we stepped out into the kitchen,' he said at length. 'I was last out, for I was helping Bessie wi his headdress, and they were going at it by then. I think by what they were saying, Danny had come into the kitchen and saw Nanty out in the yard getting a word wi the lass, and then she went off somewhere, so Danny never got his turn to speak wi her.'

'But Nanty didn't leave the kitchen again till you came up the stair?'

'I'd not say that,' said Bowster cautiously. 'He slipped away up the stair himsel afore long, and I found him getting another word wi the lass in private. At which I tellt him, if him and Danny quarrelled again, what would it do to the play, and the lass says that about *I've saved your play*, and goes away up to the hall.'

'And you've still no notion what she meant by that?'

'Never a one.' Bowster lifted the strips of leather on his bench and turned them in careful fingers. 'Unless maybe Nanty was for leaving us and she's persuaded him to stay, but that makes no sense, he was enjoying his part.'

'He says they met on the stair by chance,' Gil observed. Bowster shook his head sceptically. 'Did the lass come through the kitchen, or had she come down the stair from the hall?'

'I never noticed. But there was that much coming and going, and some of the men were in and out at the door, the fellows of that household I mean, she could easy ha come in that way and me never see her, for I was taken up wi seeing that the champions never took too much of the ale-jug when it came round.' He pulled a face. 'I once saw an Alexander hurt bad, for that the Jack was drunk when they fought, and missed his swing.'

'I never thought of there being so much to see over, in taking charge of the play,' Gil said. 'The ale was in a common jug, was it?'

'Oh, aye, which she, Ursel I mean, filled from the household barrel in the corner of the kitchen,' the glover assured him. 'We all had a pull at it, to wet our thrapples for the singing, and a bit of her gingerbread off the tray. It hadny any gilt on,' he added reflectively, 'but it was right good gingerbread.'

'Ursel makes good gingerbread,' Gil agreed. He sat thinking for a space, while Bowster fidgeted with the strips of leather. 'So the first you knew of it being the wrong flask,' he said at length, 'was when it appeared out of Nanty Bothwell's scrip, in front of everyone.'

'Aye, like I told you,' agreed Bowster.

Gil got to his feet. 'That's a help,' he said, with partial truth. 'I'm getting things clearer in my mind, though I still don't see how it happened. I'll have more questions afore I'm done, I've no doubt.'

Bowster rose likewise.

'If I can answer them,' he said, and then, casually, 'Is there any word from the Renfrew household? Is Mistress Mathieson –?'

'Still groaning,' said Kate. 'Poor lass, she's having a hard time of it, they're saying. I've sent Babb twice today, with my snakestone and then a cup of one of Mother's remedies. The house is full of her gossips, settled in for a long wait.'

They were seated where the sun streamed in at one of the great bay windows, while in the other the two little girls played some complicated game involving their dolls, a wooden horse and a handful of the red and yellow leaves which were now blowing about the yard. Kate checked that they were engrossed, adjusted the screen by the cradle to keep the light out of her baby's face, and picked up her sewing again.

'Tammas Bowster asked me if there was word,' Gil said.

'I've no doubt he did. Grace told me Meg's father chose our neighbour for her, over the glover,' Kate said circumspectly, 'as being better able to provide for her. There's no doubt that's true, but I'd say she'd have preferred the other.'

That explains that, thought Gil, watching her hands as she stitched, and suddenly thought of young Mistress Mathieson's expression as she looked at her husband. Kate was developing their mother's tendency to be right about things.

'I've spoken to Andy,' she went on, 'and to Ursel. The mummers had ale, out of one jug, and gingerbread from a common tray, while they were in the kitchen. There was all sorts coming and going, so it's possible someone spoke to the – the man that died, and gave him something else to eat or drink, but nobody saw any such thing, though they all agreed he'd had a shouting match with young Bothwell. I think Gibson was mostly talking to the Judas after that.'

'Kate, that's excellent,' he said. 'It bears out what the mummers themselves have said. I've another question for you to ask your household now.' She looked up, eyebrows raised. 'I think Agnes Renfrew slipped out to fetch something for her stepmother. Which door did she use?'

'The hall door,' said Kate firmly. 'At least – I saw her leave that way, Jamesie let her out. There he is in the yard, Gil, you could ask him if he let her back in. Is it important?'

'It's something that puzzles me.'

Out in the yard, Jamesie was quite willing to leave his task of stacking tin-glazed pottery dishes on the rack opposite the gates, but when Gil explained his question he scratched his head in thought.

'I'd say I never let her back in,' he pronounced after a moment. 'I mind letting her out to go back to her own house, for that her mammy needed some special cushion, as if our cushions wasny good enough for her, and she laid her plaid over her shoulders when she left. That's how I mind it, I'd to fetch the plaid from the bed in the good chamber where we'd laid them all, and I'd to try twice to get the right one, but she'd ha need of it. That bonnie blue gown she'd on wouldny keep the wind off her.'

'But she never came back by the hall door,' Gil prompted.

'No, I'd say she didny. You could ask Andy,' the man suggested. 'Maybe he let her in after I'd gone from the door. Which I did once all the guests was arrived.'

A little searching located Andy, assisting his master in the counting-house in sorting through the bills for the coming quarter-day. Both men listened to his question, but shook their heads.

'I mind seeing the lass as she returned,' admitted Augie, 'but I only caught sight of her in the midst of the hall, with the cushion in her arms. Kate did offer Mistress Mathieson her own herb cushion, but it seems she wanted this one.'

'I never noticed,' said Andy. 'Here's that docket from the *Sankt Nikolaas*, maister, wi the clarry wine on it. If Jamesie didny let her in, Maister Gil, she never came in by the hall door, for I'd have heard her rattling at the pin. You could ask if Ursel noticed her in the kitchen, or one of the lassies. They were quite taken wi all the fine clothes,' he added, inspired, 'maybe they'd ha taken note if she cam in that way.'

'A good thought,' Gil said. He returned to report this to Kate, and found Ysonde hanging over the cradle, cooing to its sleeping occupant. As he sat down she said in honeyed tones:

'Wee Baby Floris, all s'eepy. You're no to wake him,' she added to Gil, and whisked off to the other window and the game with her sister.

Gil raised his eyebrows at Kate, who said solemnly, face straight, eyes dancing, 'That's what Ysonde calls him, because she and Wynliane are in a book, but Edward isn't.'

'Oh, aye, and Augie said he'd read *Floris and Blanchflour* to him,' Gil recalled. 'I hope his life has less adventure in it than Floris's.'

'So do I, indeed. Did Jamesie have anything useful to say?'

Gil recounted his information and Andy's suggestion, at which she made a note in her tablets to speak to the two maidservants.

'Is it a matter of the time she returned?' she asked.

'Something like that.'

'I wish we'd never thought of entertaining,' she said, sighing. 'Bad enough Meg going off into labour that way, but this other – ah, well. What's done's done.'

'When did Augie ask the mummers in?'

'Two days afore. Tuesday, I suppose,' she said in some surprise, 'it's still only Friday today. He told me about it on Wednesday, there was no time to do anything, other than warn Meg –'

'So the household knew?'

'The women did,' Kate said. 'I don't think they told our neighbour himself. They may not have wanted to. He's a hard man to cross, in chamber, hall and counting-house, it seems, and considering how he looked when I did tell him, I'd have kept quiet if I was in Meg's shoes too.'

Gil thought about the events here in the hall. 'Kate, when it happened – did you get a sight of any of the other faces? Did any of them seem . . .' He paused, groping for words.

'Was anyone affected out of the ordinary?' she supplied. He nodded. Of his four surviving sisters Kate was his favourite, and the closest to him in temperament and thought. Of course she knew what he meant. 'I never noticed,' she went on. 'I wasny well placed to see the faces. Maybe Babb or Andy would be more help.' She paused, needle in the air. 'I'd think one or other of the women, Nancy or Barbara or Agnes Hamilton, might call by this afternoon before they go in to wait on Meg. I'll ask them and all – circumspectly.'

'I too have little to report,' said Maistre Pierre, spreading potted herring liberally on his wedge of bread. Further down the long board young John McIan, perched on his nurse's knee, shouted something unintelligible and waved a crust. Nancy hushed him, but the mason grinned at his foster-son, waved back, and continued, 'Maister Renfrew was willing enough to talk to me, but all he would say was that the young man is guilty, and must hang for it.'

'Is there any word of Meg?' Alys asked.

Her father shook his head, swallowed a mouthful and said, 'No, it seems she still labours, poor woman. I did not stay long, the household is manifestly in turmoil, full of strange women, and only the two young men are in the shop. I got word with Frankie by enquiring how he did after yesterday.'

'The two young men,' Gil repeated, handing the last bite of his bread and herring to the dog sitting politely at his elbow. 'Robert and Nicol, do you mean?'

'Robert and young Syme, the son-in-law. I had forgotten about Nicol.'

'Did you ask about the flasks?' Alys prompted.

'I did. He would not entertain the thought that it could be one of his.'

'But it must be,' said Alys. 'Kittock tells me a lad came from the Forrests' shop to say all theirs are accounted for, and the six that the Bothwells took were still in their packing, safe in Christian's stillroom, with the docket of receipt as well.' She looked at Gil across the table. 'We spent a good time exploring the room. She was very willing to tell me about all her stores, and we must have opened every container in the house. There was nothing that answers to Adam Forrest's description of what is in the flask.'

'Nor in the booth,' said Gil. 'Like you, I looked in every pig and flagon in the place. None of them held poison – at least, not that variety,' he qualified. 'Unless it's very thoroughly hidden, or there is no more than went in the flask, it isn't in the booth.'

'Nor in the house,' she agreed.

'I hope you have both washed your hands before you ate,' said Maistre Pierre.

Beside him Catherine, who had been masticating potted herring on white bread with the crusts removed, set down her beaker and said in her elegant toothless French, 'It is very remarkable that so many of the young man's friends have asked you to prove him innocent.'

'Half of Glasgow,' Gil agreed.

'Except,' she went on, nodding in acknowledgement of this, 'the Renfrew girl. And yet he had spoken to her just before the play, I understand.'

'I wondered about that too,' said Alys. 'Perhaps she can't get away to speak to Gil. They must all be at sixes and sevens just now.'

'The household of Maistre Renfrew is a large one, and I think not all its members are willing to be ruled by their master. Nevertheless,' she raised one liver-spotted hand to prevent Maistre Pierre interrupting, 'I do not see why that should lead them to poisoning and murder.'

'My thoughts exactly, madame,' Gil said, smiling at her. He had held the old lady in respect already, but since his marriage he had come to admire her perception and tact. As for how she acquired her information, it was clear that though she spoke no Scots she understood it well. Now she bent her head in reply to his comment, and said to Alys:

'You should call on the household, *ma mie*, to pay the duty of a neighbour.'

'So I thought,' agreed Alys.

John, squirming down from Nancy's lap, pattered up the length of the table, ignoring attempts by other members of the household to distract him, paused to insert his soggy crust into Socrates' willing mouth, and halted beside his foster-father's tree-like knee.

'Up!' he commanded. Maistre Pierre hauled the boy on to his lap, pulling the child's long tunic down over the little fat legs in their woollen stockings.

'That daughter,' he said disapprovingly, 'the younger one, is particularly unruly. You would never have behaved like that, Alys.'

Her quick smile flickered. 'It was never necessary,' she said with composure. 'Gil, what will you do this afternoon? Who do you need to speak to?'

'Most of Glasgow,' he said. 'John, would you like a piece of apple? I'll have to speak to Renfrew myself, I suppose, and the men of the household. I can hardly disturb the women just now. I called on Maister Hamilton and Maister Wilkie before I spoke to Kate, but neither of them had much more to offer, and of course their wives were from home.'

'Morple,' ordered John, extending a hand, fingers wriggling. Gil handed him another slice of the apple, and Socrates' nose quivered in indignation.

'He must say *If you please*,' Alys prompted.

'Pease,' said John obligingly, and beamed, displaying some well-chewed fragments. He was a handsome child, with a strong look of his father the harper, and seemed to be intelligent as well as musical. Gil, who was his legal guardian, was beginning to think in terms of the universities of Europe, and set aside each quarter as much as he could of the income the boy had from his dead mother's property towards that end.

'Ed ockies,' announced John, holding up one foot so that his red stocking showed.

'Red stockings,' Gil agreed. 'Mammy Alys knitted them.'

He caught sight of Alys's expression as she watched the child, but before he could say anything Catherine announced, 'Then we must all go about our various tasks. You may tell Mistress Mathieson I have prayed for her, and also for her infant, *ma mie*.'

'Well, if it's one o mine,' said Maister Renfrew sharply, 'he must ha stole it. I've no wish to go through my books to prove it, for such a one as him, and I see no point in adding the charge of theft to a charge of murder forbye, but that's the beginning and end of it, Maister Cunningham.'

'Do you think?' said Gil mildly.

'Aye. Or else the sister's lying.'

77

'My wife said she saw the six still in their straw,' said Gil, 'and the docket itemizing six flasks of Araby ware in your own writing, lying beside them. That seems clear enough to me.'

'Aye.' Renfrew tapped irritably on his tall desk. In his workaday clothes of brown wool he was a less flamboyant sight than yesterday, but the two grouse feathers pinned in his felt hat by a brooch with a huge chunk of amber suited well with his bearing. Elbows out, shoulders squared, neck stretched, he had met Gil's question about the painted flasks with lively indignation. 'So he must ha stole it, whether from my shop or from one of my customers.'

'The curious thing is, he says it's one of his,' said Gil.

'The man's a pysoner. Small wonder if he's a leear as well.'

'You've made good use of the shipment, I think. They're bonnie things. I saw you had one about you, yourself.'

'Aye,' said Renfrew. 'There's two sizes, see, though I kept all the bigger ones for my own business, and the wee one holds a good quantity for the kind of draught that's taen in a minimissimal dose. I've gave out a few in the last year.'

'Have you any thoughts about what the poison itself might be?'

Renfrew blinked slightly at the change of subject, and his high colour lessened as he applied his mind to this question. He stared distantly at the shelves of his work-room for a space, while Gil looked round him. This business, as the other apothecaries had made clear, was aimed at the higher end of the market, with an emphasis on such luxury goods as cosmetics and perfumes, dyestuffs and sealing-wax and the more expensive foodstuffs. The outer room, which was the shop, was lined with sacks of raisins and rice, almonds and figs, pigs of honey and treacle, glass jars of lavender water. The workroom was laid out differently from Wat Forrest's, but held a similar assortment of alarming equipment. Some of the jars on the crowded shelves were marked with a black cross, some had parchment or paper covers with writing on them. The nearest mortar held a quantity of large pale seeds which Renfrew had been pounding at when Gil came in; the box beside it was labelled with a flourish *Nux pines*. Do pines have nuts on them? he wondered. Not in Scotland, for certain.

His attention was recalled as Renfrew shook his head portentously.

'I don't deal in pyson as such,' the older man admitted, 'save maybe for killing rats, so it's no a matter where I've great practical experience, but I've read as wide in the subject as any man in Glasgow. It's not arsenical salts, that's for certain, nor any of those that acts first on the belly, which cuts out a great number. It worked *instanter*, which lets us set aside all the slower ones, you'll appreciate.' Gil nodded at this, but Renfrew went on without looking at him, 'I'd say it might be one of those that can be got by infusion or maybe distillation from plants, seeing it was in that cloudy liquid form, but I'd need time wi my books to get any closer. Has Wat never come back to you wi an answer?'

'Not yet,' Gil said. 'If that's the case, it's something a good apothecary could brew up for himself, is it, rather than something that has to be imported from the Low Countries?'

'If that's the case,' said Renfrew, 'aye.'

'Is Anthony Bothwell a good enough apothecary to do that kind of thing?'

'I suppose he might be,' admitted Renfrew with reluctance.

'What about his sister?'

'Oh, never. Women are all very well for carrying out the wee tasks,' he elucidated, 'concocting sweetmeats, compounding an ointment or reducing an infusion, all my lassies can deal wi sic matters, though times they overdo it,' he added bitingly. 'But the great tasks are men's work. Women hasny the application, you see, on account of their natures are more cold and moist than ours, it means you canny rely on them.'

'I see,' said Gil, comparing this assertion with what he knew of the women in his life. It did not seem to match. 'So you think this must be something Bothwell himself distilled.'

'It could be,' said Renfrew, 'and that's as close as I'll say. We'll ken more when Wat has done proving it.'

'If Bothwell's that good an apothecary,' said Gil casually, 'why did you not like the match for Agnes?'

Renfrew's colour rose again.

'That's no concern of yours!' he exclaimed. 'I'll wed my lassies where I choose!'

'Just the same I'd ha thought,' Gil persevered, trying to keep the same casual tone, 'that since you've wedded Eleanor to one apothecary you might ha chosen another for Agnes.'

'I can do far better than that for her,' said Renfrew angrily. 'She's a bonnie wee thing, and she'll have a good tocher, and once I let it be known –'

'So why not Bothwell?' Gil asked. 'He's a hard worker, he's built up the business from nothing in a couple of years.' He and his sister, he qualified in his mind, and I hope she'll forgive me for ignoring her contribution. 'I'd have thought he'd seem like a good husband for any girl, until this happened yesterday.'

'Aye, well, it's as well I'd no thought of consenting to either of her choices,' said Renfrew triumphantly, 'or she'd be betrothed to either a pysoner or a corp by now.'

Rounding the corner of the Tolbooth, Gil encountered Eleanor Renfrew, a maidservant behind her. She was a plain young woman, with the same big blue eyes as her sister in a sour face both pinched and puffy with pregnancy. She was warmly clad against the sharp wind, the hood of her heavy cloak drawn over her everyday linen headdress and a plaid over all concealing her size. She did not seem to have been to market, since she had no basket or packages with her, and the servant was yawning.

'Good day, mistress,' he said, raising his hat. She curt-sied, and would have moved on, but he said, 'I was by your father's house just now. There's still no word of your good-mother.'

'Likely no,' she said. 'It's no going well.'

'Might I have a word, mistress?' he asked. 'We could get a seat in St Mary's Kirk –'

'Our Lady love you, no!' she said. 'I've spent all morn-ing there on my knees asking aid for Meg, my back's like toothache, and I'm about out of my head wi boredom. I was just on my way home, for I can tell my beads there as well as in St Mary's, so you might as well come along.'

Wondering what use such grudging prayers would be, he turned to accompany her, and was surprised to be led into a wynd just above the Tolbooth.

'I thought you'd have stayed under your father's roof,' he said. 'There's certainly room in that house.'

'Syme wished to have his own place.' She raised the latch on the door of a small narrow house, and stepped inside. 'Buttered ale, Maidie, and then we might as well get on wi the supper. Hae a seat, maister.'

She looked about her with evident pleasure, shedding cloak and plaid to hang behind the door. The chamber was sparsely furnished, but the few pieces were good, and there were embroidered hangings at the windows to keep the draughts out. A door at the back led into the kitchen, where Maidie was now rattling crocks, and a stair in the corner suggested at least one upper chamber. Syme must be doing well out of the business to cover the rent here, Gil thought, surrendering his own plaid.

'What was it you wished to say?' she asked, sitting down by the brazier and poking at it with a piece of kindling.

'Yesterday, at my sister's house,' he said. 'Would you tell me what you saw?'

'What I saw?' she repeated, startled. 'A bad business, that. I hope Lady Kate's none the worse of it today. As for what I saw, maister, why, the same as a'body else. Nanty

Bothwell gave Danny Gibson something that slew him, with all the guests looking on.'

'That's true,' Gil agreed. 'Did you know the flask he had?'

She shrugged. 'They're all over Glasgow. One of a batch my father had from Middelburgh and sold on to the other potyngars.'

'No way to tell whose it was?'

She laughed sourly. 'Ask at my brother Nicol, why don't you. He'll likely have a name for it.' Gil raised his eyebrows. 'Daftheid that he is, he has names for everything about him. He's no so bad as he was, when he was a boy you had to call his platter Barnabas and his eating-knife Maister Lute or he would eat nothing. It would surprise me not at all if he had a name for the very flask and told you where it had been afore Nanty Bothwell showed it to the company.'

'Now I think of it,' Gil said slowly, 'when we were at school he had names for both inkhorn and penknife. And yesterday he was very sure it was the wrong flask.'

'I think we'd all jaloused that by the time he spoke.'

'Have you had a word with your sister since then? How has she taken it?'

'Ill, I'd say,' she turned to accept the steaming jug from the maidservant, 'but I've never spoken wi her. She slammed away into her own chamber as soon as we got Meg up the stairs, and then I was packed off out the house.' He nodded; it would be bad luck, he knew, for a woman carrying a child to be under the same roof as another in labour.

'Did she seem badly affected?'

'She was gey quiet, which is no like her. I'd have said she'd had a shock,' agreed Mistress Renfrew, 'but then so had the rest of us. It'll not suit her, to have one of her admirers hanged for poisoning the other,' she added.

'Has she favoured either of them over the other?' Gil asked carefully, leaning forward to take a beaker from her. The buttered ale was not as hot as he would have liked, but well spiced.

'I'd not have said so. But I've not spoken to her of them more than once or twice. I'm not round the house as much now I've my own place to see to,' she looked round her again with satisfaction, 'and she's not like to confide in me anyway.' She saw Gil's raised eyebrows. 'We don't get on, maister. There's none of us gets on, save for Meg, poor girl.'

Gil, whose siblings had squabbled and then made up on a daily basis throughout his childhood, concealed his thoughts on this.

'So you'd not know which she would have preferred,' he prompted.

'Neither of them, like I said. No point in preferring either one anyway, she likes keeping them hanging round her heels, but she kens fine the old man will have a match for her soon.'

Does she? Gil wondered. And does she accept the idea?

'Who will he choose?' he asked.

'You don't think he'd tell us? I'll say this for Syme, he listens to what I have to say. My faither never minded me in his life, and for all Agnes can get anything she wants out of him – did you see that gown she had on yesterday? – she'll not dare cross him either.'

He drank some of the buttered ale, and changed the subject. 'Do you think it was a deliberate poisoning?'

'How would I –' She stopped. 'No,' she said at length, 'I'd say not. Nanty Bothwell's a decent man, and he's got sense enough to see that would never work. What good to get rid of your rival if you're clapped in the Tolbooth in chains?'

'Or by anyone else?'

'Not likely, surely? Danny Gibson was a decent fellow too by all I've heard. Agnes wouldny harm her two lap-dogs, and none of the rest of us . . .' Her voice trailed off; she thought for a brief space, then looked at him with what seemed to be genuine reluctance. 'The only thing I can think – Robert's one for malicious tricks. He sent Meg a pair of gloves at her birthday, all in secret so the old man took it they were from,' she bit her lip, 'from someone she knew. He blued her ee, she'd to keep the house for a week till it faded. Then Robert boasted of it to Syme, and denied it when Syme told the old man, which led to – But I don't see how he could ha done this. It must ha been a mischance of some sort.'

'If it was a mischance, where might the poison have come from?'

She shook her head. 'I've never a notion. Do they ken what it is yet?'

'One of the plant infusions, we think.'

'Our Lady save us, that's little help.' She pulled a face. 'What's more, sir, any of us, any woman in Glasgow that's got a stillroom, could make up such a thing if we knew what to infuse. There's some skill in the work, but more in knowing what to put to it, and to get something that acted so quick I'd say you'd need to look for someone well up in the craft.'

'You're better up in the craft yourself than your father gave me to think,' he said deliberately.

She snorted. 'Him! He'll not admit the women in the house do the most of the work. It's Grace makes half the face-creams and that, as well as his drops for his heart, and me that makes the other half, and Agnes and me that makes the sweetmeats. Syme's a good worker, and knows the trade,' she added approvingly, 'which he should, having been my faither's journeyman, but all our Robert ever does is stand about looking useless and eat the sweetmeats.'

'And your brother Nicol?'

'What use a daftheid like him? If I'd my way I'd send him away again, wi his moonstruck ideas, and keep Grace wi us for the sake of the business.'

'What ideas are those?'

'Och.' She paused to think, looking at her empty beaker. 'He'd give the old man willowbark tea for his heart, and such nonsense. All stuff he's got from some foreigner he met in Middelburgh. As for what he thinks about the

84

circulation of the blood, you'd need to hear it.' She set the beaker back on the tray beside the jug. 'Was there anything else you wanted to ask, sir, for I'll need to get on wi the supper.'

'How do you think it happened?'

She looked blank for a moment. 'You saw how it happened as well. Oh, d'you mean how it got into the flask? I've never a notion, like I said already. There's aye potions and pysons lying about an apothecary's shop, maister, but my faither has us all trained well, we'd label sic a thing.'

'What, a label reading "poison"?'

'Little use that for the servants,' she observed. 'No, it's a big black cross, well inked in, stuck or tied or drawn on the cover-paper. So if it was something from our house, it ought to ha been labelled.'

'And has your family any enemies?' he asked, digesting this.

'Enemies? No more than most of the burgess houses of Glasgow, sir. Success breeds envy. No, this was apothecary work, maister, and the apothecaries mostly gets on well enough.' She rose. 'Now, the kale willny chop itself, and Maidie's got enough to do. Where did I leave your plaid?'

Chapter Five

'It seems very silly,' said Alys, avoiding two men with a barrel slung on a pole between them, 'to take you away from the house just to accompany me a few doors down the street.'

'Never you fret, mem,' said Jennet happily, looking about her. 'The work'll get done anyway, we were about finished in the kitchen, and it's not right you should go about on your own now you're a wedded lady. Is that no that Mall Hamilton that used to work for Lady Kate's man?'

'Very likely,' said Alys, pausing before the apothecary's door. 'She dwells just off the High Street, I recall. Do you want to come in with me, Jennet, or would you sooner have an hour's liberty?'

'Och, I'll come in and get a word wi them in the kitchen here, and then I'll be handy for when you take your leave.'

Alys nodded, and pushed open the door. A string of little bells slung on the inside jingled cheerfully as she stepped into the shop. It was a light place, with a big window to the street rather ostentatiously closed by glass both above and below. Behind the counter, to one side of the door, James Syme was weighing rice into folded papers, surrounded by boxes and bags which all stood open to assist the birth upstairs. Jennet had followed her in and stood inspecting the merchandise critically while she enquired after the Renfrew women.

'My good-mother's groaning still,' said Syme, shaking his head sadly. He was a handsome man rather younger than Gil, with waving golden hair and a pink skin, but had a way of speaking as if he was imparting a valuable secret, even if he discussed the weather, which Alys always found irritating. 'I fear it's not going well, that's a full day and a night since she was taken wi't and the bairn not come home yet.'

'Poor woman,' said Alys with a surge of sympathy. She had never attended a birth, even with Mère Isabelle in Paris, but all she had ever heard – 'If there's anything I can do?'

'We're doing all we can think of,' said Syme, slightly offended. 'If you think you know anything new, you're welcome to suggest it. Maybe you'd like a word wi some of them?' He glanced at the linen-swathed jug she carried, then turned away to open the door into the house. A ragged, pain-filled scream reached them, and Syme grimaced. 'You'll can find your way by ear, I've no doubt.'

Alys knew the house slightly, and knew that most of the ground floor was given over to the shop and various store-rooms and workrooms. Leaving Jennet to make her own way out to the kitchen, she went quietly up to the floor above, sparing a thought for the difficulty of getting Meg up the stairs yesterday. Stepping into the hall from the stair she checked, startled to find the two youngest members of the household locked in a furious, whispered argument, so intent on their hostility they did not notice her.

'– nothing to do wi me, and none of your business either, Robert Renfrew!' hissed Agnes. 'So just keep your nose out where it doesny belong, and leave me alone!'

'You've got rid of one of your two lapdogs,' retorted Robert, 'you'll no get rid of me so easy, you sleekit wee jade!'

'I never! It was nothing to do wi –'

'Where'd he get that flask, then? They're saying it's no one of his own –'

Another of those screams issued from the door at the far end of the hall, and Agnes flinched. Robert looked up.

'What's she girning for?' he said contemptuously. 'You'd think she was deein, the noise she makes.'

'She's screaming because it hurts,' said Agnes fiercely. 'Get away to a keeking-glass and burst your plooks if you canny be helpful, and keep out of my business, you kale-wirm!'

Robert turned, aiming a skilful kick at his sister's shins as he did, and caught sight of Alys in the door from the stair.

'Oh, Mistress Cunningham,' he said, and bowed politely. 'Come to wait for news? My good-mother's in yonder, as you can tell.'

Alys acknowledged this and moved forward, saying only, 'How are you, Agnes? That was a bad day yesterday.'

'It was,' agreed Agnes, tears springing to her eyes. 'It was – I canny believe it yet.'

'Strange, that, seeing you planned it,' said her brother.

'I never! It was nothing to do wi me!' Agnes sprang forward like a whirlwind, there was a ringing slap and she was gone, her feet sounding on the stairs to the floor above, leaving her brother staring and nursing his reddening cheek. The spots Agnes had mentioned stood out white against the rising colour. Alys curtsied and turned away hastily.

At the further end of the hall there was a pair of chambers one beyond the other. The outer one was bustling with women heating water over the fire, warming linen, passing an ale-cup round from a small barrel decorated with ribbons and a green garland. A close-stool behind a screen made its presence known. Mistress Hamilton was nearest the door, already flushed with the heat and the strong ale, specially brewed for the event. She greeted Alys with pleasure.

'Have you come to wait for news, lassie?' she asked. 'It's not going well.' She dropped her voice. 'Her mammy's in a right state of worry for her, and Mally Bowen's been sent for.'

'I'd have thought she'd be here from the start,' said Alys.

'It was Eppie Campbell they'd engaged,' explained Mistress Hamilton, 'for that she's a friend of Meg's. But Eppie wished Mally sent for a couple hours since. They're saying the bairn's maybe the wrong way round, poor lassie. Here comes Marion Baillie, that's her minnie, the now.'

Mistress Baillie emerged from the inner room, followed by another of those screams, at which the woman stopped, biting her lips, and put a hand out to steady herself on the court-cupboard she was passing. Alys flinched in sympathy and moved forward, nodding to Nancy Sproull and then to Grace Gordon, and curtsied to the older woman.

'I'm Alys Mason,' she explained, 'from a few doors up. I brought this.' She held out the little jug she carried. 'It's hot water with honey and aquavit and a sprig of thyme.'

'She drinks any more, she'll driddle the bairn out,' remarked Nancy Sproull. 'Grace was just giving her something and all.'

'It might put some strength into her,' Alys said. 'How is she?'

'That's a good receipt.' Mally Bowen materialized beside them. 'She's right weary since I turned the babe. I'll try her wi some of that the now.' She took the jug and retreated to the inner room. Mistress Baillie shook her head, and wiped her eyes with the back of her hand.

'That's kind, lass,' she said. 'Oh, my poor lassie. It's no – it's never –'

'It's hard for you to watch,' said Alys, putting a hand on her arm. 'Can I do anything?'

'I don't know what's to do for her. She's – we've got her lying down for now, she's that weary, and it's no dropping as it should, even though they turned the bairn – we'll have her back in the chair shortly, but –' The incoherent speech broke off, and Mistress Baillie drew a deep breath and looked at her intently. 'Did you say you were Alys Mason?' Alys nodded. 'Were you no at that gathering yesterday?' She nodded again, and the other woman looked about them at the bustling room, then put a hand

89

on Alys's shoulder. 'Come out here if you will, lass, till I get a word.'

Out in the hall Robert Renfrew was still standing about, but left ostentatiously when he saw them. Ignoring him, Mistress Baillie towed Alys to one of the window spaces and said with quiet urgency, 'Were you present at these mummers? Can you tell me what happened? Grace told me a bit, but she'll never say aught that reflects on Renfrew and I can make no sense of Eleanor's version, and that Agnes has barely left her chamber since they came back here. And Agnes Hamilton's a good soul, but –'

'Yes, I was there – is it worrying her?' But surely, thought Alys, the – the pressures of bringing a baby to birth should overcome all else. Maybe not.

'I think that's what's eating at her,' agreed Mistress Baillie, and rubbed at her eyes again. 'She canny give her whole mind to the task, she canny let go and let the bairn come. She's fighting everything we do.' She was a plump, attractive woman, not much past forty and still with most of her teeth, but her face was haggard with worry and lack of sleep, and her mouth worked as Alys looked at her. 'Tell me what happened, lassie, will you?'

Obediently, Alys recounted the tale of the afternoon, of the substitute flask and how the first any of them had realized that something was wrong was when the champion fell the second time. The other woman listened closely, and shook her head.

'I see it,' she said. 'My lassie was feart it was –' She stopped and looked at Alys. 'She never did a thing wrong,' she said fiercely. Alys nodded. 'But she favoured Tammas Bowster, and her faither would take Renfrew for her, no matter that he's older than I am, and her heart's no been in the match.'

'That is hard,' said Alys. 'But surely now she has the baby –?' At least she has the baby, said a little voice in her mind. My father liked my choice, but I have no baby yet.

'Aye, and it's Renfrew's bairn, no doubt of that, whatever he said to her when she was first howding. But

90

Tammas was there yesterday, I take it, with the other mummers?'

'He was,' agreed Alys.

'I think my Meg's feart it was Renfrew tried to pyson Tammas Bowster and slew this Gibson by mischance.'

Alys stared at her, aware that her mouth was dropping open. Recovering it, she said, 'No, indeed, it could not have been, for nobody told Maister Renfrew about the mummers until he arrived at the house. He was not best pleased, my good-sister said, but there was little he could do about it by then.'

'Was it not the flask Renfrew aye carries on him that pysont the man?' asked Mistress Baillie doubtfully.

'No,' said Alys firmly, 'for my husband saw him drink from that himself, while the mummers were acting the play. It was another flask.'

'Would you tell her?' Mistress Baillie seized Alys's hands in a painful grip. 'Lassie, would you tell her that? It might – she might let go if she hears it, she can stop fretting and think of the bairn instead.'

'Yes, if you think it proper for me to be in the same chamber,' Alys said diffidently. 'I'm not – I've no –'

'Oh, never mind that! Anything that will help my lassie,' said Mistress Baillie. She set off towards the door, then checked as another ragged scream tore at their ears. 'Oh, my poor Meg!' she exclaimed, tears starting to her eyes. 'Oh, how can I bear it?'

'She's more to bear than you have, Marion,' said Maister Renfrew, coming into the hall from the stair. 'How is she? Is she making any progress?'

'None,' said Mistress Baillie bluntly. 'We've tried all the receipts you sent up, all the charms, all the prayers. She's bound up in the birthing-girdle from St Thenew's, she's got a knife under her pillow, the jasper-stone, Lady Kate's snakestone, that strange thing Caterin Campbell sent round, she calls it Our Lady's sea-nut – none of them's done her any good. If you'd unlocked your workroom when I first asked you this would never ha come about.'

'Superstitious nonsense – and that room stays locked now, the way things vanish. It's coming to it, when I've to lock my workroom against my own household.'

'And if you'd listened to me about her dates,' persisted Mistress Baillie, unheeding, 'she wouldny have been at Morison's yesterday getting frightened into this state.'

Her tone was biting; a lesser man would have quailed, but Maister Renfrew merely said, 'Well, it's the lot of women. Can Grace do nothing?'

'Grace gave her some of Nicol's drops, but it's no done much good,' said Mistress Baillie. Behind Renfrew a maid-servant entered the hall and padded past them. 'It takes one who's been through it to support a lass, especially her first time.'

'Here, Isa,' said Renfrew, ignoring this. 'What are you about here, woman? There's no word yet, there's no call for you to be up here! Away back to the kitchen.'

'I'm here to empty the close-stool,' said the woman, 'since it willny empty itsel, as any woman could work out.' She bobbed without respect, and went on into the crowded room.

Her master stared after her in exasperation, and Mistress Baillie said, 'Oh, get away to your prayers, man, for it's about all you can do for Meg now. You and your pine nuts!'

Renfrew bridled at this, but said sharply, 'We've got prayers being said for her at the Greyfriars, and Eleanor's along at St Mary's on her knees, seeing she can hardly come about the house till the bairn comes home, the way she is. So if you'll no have me in the chamber –'

'It's Mally Bowen won't have you in the chamber, you ken that as well as I do,' said Mistress Baillie. 'So you might as well get along to St Mary's yoursel, maister.'

She turned towards the door, then stood aside to let Grace Gordon emerge.

'Grace!' said Renfrew curtly. 'I've been seeking you.'

'I was away for another dose of the drops,' Grace said quietly.

'One dose is enough. She's no needing more. Come wi me the now.'

Alys, following Mistress Baillie, caught sight of Grace's expression. What was it? she wondered. Resignation, apprehension, fear? She slipped past the other girl and into the hot, busy room, where the ale-cup was going round again. Mistress Hamilton was embroidering an account of a cousin's recent delivery; Alys, who had heard parts of the tale before, moved on quickly, but Nancy Sproull caught her arm, peering up at her with those dark-fringed grey eyes not entirely focused.

'Alys,' she said solemnly. 'Alys, you're a sensible lassie and a good Christian soul and all.'

'I try to be.'

Mistress Sproull pulled her down to breathe ale at her. 'Would you do me a favour, lass? Would you call by our house and get a word wi our Nell?'

'With Nell?' Alys repeated in surprise.

Nell's mother nodded, still with that juridical solemnity. 'She's right grieved by yesterday's trouble,' she divulged in a hoarse whisper. 'She'll not stop weeping. See if you can talk some sense into her, lassie?'

'I'll try,' promised Alys, disengaging herself with some trouble.

In the birthing chamber it was slightly less hot, and quieter between Meg's bitter pangs. She was laid on her side on a truckle-bed, clad only in a sweat-damp shift, her hair loose and clinging to her swollen face. Bound round her, under her sagging breasts, was the birthing-girdle, a strip of parchment cut to the height of Our Lady and inscribed with grateful prayers, and charms of one kind or another were strapped to her arm or her bare thigh.

'Mammy, make it stop,' she moaned as Alys entered. 'I don't want a bairn, take it away!'

Mally Bowen, wife of Serjeant Anderson, the burgh layer-out and most experienced midwife, had both hands and one ear applied to her belly, and her mother was already bending over whispering to her. Mother and daughter turned to look at Alys with identical expressions of hope.

'Here, what's this?' said Mistress Bowen, straightening up. 'There's no room for you in here, my lass, you've none of your own –'

'She's got a word for Meg,' said Mistress Baillie, 'that willny wait, Mally.' The two exchanged a significant glance, and Mistress Bowen stepped away from the bed to join a younger woman by the shaded window. Both were wrapped in linen aprons, stained with blood and – and other fluids, thought Alys. She was astonished by how alarming she found it to be here. Is it because I have no role, no responsibility? she wondered. Or is it another reason?

'Alys?' said Meg weakly, reaching out a hand to her. She drew close, and knelt down in obedience to the hand. 'Is that right, what my mammy says? Did you see –?'

'My husband saw,' said Alys, trying to sound reassuring. 'He saw your man drink from his own flask, while we all watched the mummers. So it was never your man's flask that Nanty Bothwell had in his scrip. It was nothing to do with him what happened.' And if the logic of that is not rigorous, she thought, this girl would never see it at the best of times and right now she's incapable of thinking it out.

'O-oh!' Meg let her head fall back on the pillow, tears starting to her eyes. 'Oh, thanks be to Our Lady!' Her mother wiped at her brow with a damp cloth, making soothing noises. 'I should never ha doubted –'

She caught her breath, and clapped both hands to her belly.

'Oh, aye,' said Mistress Bowen, bustling forward from the window with her colleague. Alys stepped hastily back from the bed, and found herself elbowed against the wall. 'That's more like it, then.'

'It's no the same as it was,' said Meg weakly. 'It was – it was –'

'Aye, it's no the same.' Mistress Bowen turned back the folds of the linen garment which Alys now realized was not a shift but a man's shirt, and groped expertly between the massive, blue-veined thighs. 'That's a clever lass. No long now.' She paused as another of the spasms seized her patient, and as it eased she said over her shoulder, 'I think we'll have her in the chair now, Eppie.'

Alys, caught between the bed and the window, watched in alarm as the three women raised Meg and transferred her to the birthing-chair, where she lay limply, thighs spread, her head thrown back on her mother's breast, while the two midwives inspected her privities. This was not how one had ever imagined – it was not how the birth of the Virgin or of St Nicholas was shown – they could never depict a saint in such an extremity, she realized. The priests would never believe it. And Kate has done this, been through this, she thought, horrified, and yet she loves her baby.

Although Mistress Bowen had said it would not be long, it seemed to Alys that she stood trapped by the window for a hundred years while Meg laboured through the last stages of bringing her child to birth. She was aware of a stirring at the door to the outer chamber, of voices and exclamations as well as of Meg's increasing cries of pain, the encouraging words of the two midwives, the reassuring murmurs from Mistress Baillie, but her attention was entirely on Meg, on this dreadful process of bringing a child into the world. She seemed to be reduced to a single point of attention, without hands or feet or body, only a pair of eyes and a mind which tried but was unable to reject what it was seeing.

Finally – finally – Meg screamed in what seemed like a death-agony, the two women on their knees exclaimed together, there was a flurry of movement, a sudden thin high wail. The entire world and everything in it seemed to pause for a moment, and then all the women in the other chamber sighed at once. Meg exclaimed joyfully, her weakness forgotten:

95

'Oh, let me see! Let me see! Is it a boy or a lassie?'

'It's a bonnie wee lassie, and the image o her daddy,' said Eppie exultantly, and raised the baby up to its mother's reaching arms, the cord trailing. 'Gie her your titty, Mammy, till she kens you.' Over Meg's shoulder her eye fell on Alys, and her expression changed. 'Here, my lass, have you been here the whole time?'

Alys nodded dumbly. Mother and grandmother were already crooning over the scarlet, sticky, crumpled creature in Meg's arms, counting its toes and calling it *Wee Marion* and *Bonnie wee lass* while it nuzzled for Meg's dark nipple. Mistress Bowen, with a glance at her colleague, got stiffly to her feet and came round the end of the truckle-bed.

'I'll say this for Frankie Renfrew, he makes bonnie bairns. Come away, pet, it's a hard thing to witness your first time,' she said. 'You should never ha been here.' She put out a bloodstained, reeking hand to offer support, then withdrew it as Alys recoiled, shuddering. 'Aye, away out and get some of the groaning-ale, lassie, that should settle your wame.'

'Bide there,' said Grace Gordon, 'till I find you something to restore the spirits.'

'I never thought of it being so – so –' Alys subsided on to the bench Grace had indicated. 'Should you not – there is the father to be told –'

'I'll let Eppie do that,' said Grace, 'seeing it's the howdie's right. And the gossip-ale was going like a fair without my aid, and will go better still now the bairn's at the breast.'

She had found Alys adrift in the house on legs which did not seem to belong to her, and taking one look in her face had steered her to her own bedchamber. The room was full of kists, most of them ranged in the space under the bed, and, despite the array of expensive clothing of good wool and fine brocade which hung on pegs round the walls and behind the door, smelled not of moth-herbs

96

but, unaccountably, of apples. Now Grace opened a further door and vanished into a small light closet, where Alys could hear her moving things. Glass clinked, pottery tapped. After a moment she emerged with a cloth, which she used to dab at Alys's hands and wrists. The familiar, comforting scent of lavender water rose from it.

'D'you want to talk about it?' Grace asked. 'I take it you witnessed the birth?' Alys nodded wearily. 'Aye, there's good reason they shut us out. Did Mally turn the bairn, then?'

'I suppose. She said she did. Do you not wish to join the rest of –'

'No, I'm well enough here.' The cloth moved on to Alys's temples and brow. 'Just sit quiet. You're no howding yoursel?'

She shut her eyes, but managed to shake her head under the gentle attentions.

'How long since you were wedded?'

'Nearly a year.'

'Time enough.'

'And you?' Think about something else. Make conversation as one was always taught. Good manners are earthly salvation, as Mère Isabelle once said, though Catherine would not agree.

'The same. Nicol and I were wedded last Yule in Middelburgh, and came home here in May.' Her lips tightened briefly.

'And a – a sad homecoming for you, I think,' said Alys, pulling her thoughts together. 'You haven't – you aren't –?'

'No.'

Change the subject, thought Alys.

'How did Nicol think, to find his father wed again?'

Grace shook her head, smiling wryly. 'No best pleased, I think, the more so that the letter must ha gone astray and we'd never heard of the marriage, though he'd heard of ours. Nicol and Frankie don't get on, you'll ha jaloused, and that was just another coal on the fire. Mind you he's no quarrel wi Meg herself, poor creature.'

She put the cloth in Alys's hand and rose to fetch a pottery cup from the closet, stirring it as she crossed the chamber. 'Drink this, my dear. It should help a bittie. And never fear, you've had a fright the now but they aye say it's a different matter when it's your own.'

Alys shuddered at the thought. There, it was back in her mind again. She drank obediently from the cup, though her teeth rattled on the rim, and tried to concentrate on what was in it. Honey, and rose water, and – Not myrrh, but something resiny. What could it be?

'You know apothecary work?' she asked.

'I do. That was how Nicol and I met,' Grace admitted.

'That must have been a help when you came here. Another pair of hands is always an asset.' Particularly when they don't have to be paid, she thought.

'Aye, when they don't need a wage,' agreed Grace, echoing her thought. 'I've found a place here. I do the most of the stillroom work, now Eleanor has her own house to run. Frankie likes to carry a good line in stillroom wares, for them that's too lazy or busy or unskilled to make their own.'

'Lavender water,' said Alys. 'Quince lozenges.'

'Aye, those were my quince lozenges the bairnies were handing round yesterday, that I made from a barrel of quinces we got last month. A good shipment, the most of them were fit for use.' The other girl hesitated, and Alys recognized what was coming next. 'That was a terrible thing that happened. Your man acted well, getting the wee lassies out of the chamber afore they knew what was going on. He's a good man.'

'He's the best in the world,' she said firmly, and smiled a little with stiff lips at the thought of Gil.

Grace laughed, but it was sympathetic. 'My! But has he learned aught about how it happened? Was it Nanty Bothwell's doing indeed, or –'

'He's still trying to find out.' Conversation, conversation. 'I think Agnes has taken it badly, poor girl. To have one of your sweethearts accused of poisoning the other –'

'I've no notion how she's taken it,' said Grace. 'She's not left her chamber since we got Meg to bed, and she'll speak to nobody.'

'To nobody at all? I saw her earlier, arguing with her brother in the hall.'

'Did you so? We sent food up, but she's not eaten it, and the servant-lass that's been her bedfellow since Eleanor wedded says she never uttered a word. Even Nell Wilkie couldny get in to speak wi her. I suppose Frankie must ha been thinking about Meg, or he'd have dragged her out by now, but as it is she's been let alone. She must be coming round a bit.'

'She must surely be in great distress. Maister Renfrew seems certain it was deliberate poisoning, but everyone else who knows the young man thinks it was an accident.'

'I've little acquaintance wi him,' said Grace. 'Or his sister.'

'She seems a good woman, and very fond of her brother.'

'No guarantee he's innocent.'

'Agnes spoke to the one man yesterday, and not to the other, and it was the one she slighted that died. That was unfair.' Where are my manners? she thought in faint puzzlement, but it seemed as if she was floating high in the air, above such considerations.

'Did she so?' Grace turned her head to look at her. 'How did she manage that? Oh, when Meg would have her fetch her own herb-cushion, I suppose. *So privilie caught he the prettie wench.*'

'Yes, that was it, so the mummers told us. Would she not talk to her sister just now?'

'To Eleanor?' Grace laughed shortly. 'They don't speak unless they have to.' She met Alys's eye, and smiled rather bitterly. 'It's a warlike house, this one. What is it Holy Writ says? A house divided against itself?'

'How so? Is it some great quarrel among them? Their mother's will, or something?'

'Nothing so likely,' said Grace. 'They just don't get on. I never believed Nicol when he tried to tell me, no till we came here to Glasgow and I saw the truth of it myself.'

Alys contemplated this idea.

'I have no brothers or sisters,' she admitted, 'but Gil had seven, and I think he is good friends enough with those that live. He's very close to two of his sisters. Does Nicol –?'

'Nicol and Robert were at one another's throats within an hour of our entering the house. Agnes spent that whole day flyting at him, making fun of his every word – he's his own way of – he doesny aye . . .' She paused, seeking for words.

'I've noticed,' said Alys, and suddenly found herself choking back a laugh at the thought of Nicol's way of saying things.

'Eleanor was easy-osy at first, but now she's defied him to come near her, in case he afflicts her bairn. And since he'd come home without permission, Frankie wasny well pleased. There was a thundering argument over the supper, all about his inheritance, and who was or was not a partner in the business. In fact, it was only Meg that made us welcome,' Grace recalled.

'It must be strange to have a good-mother younger than yourself,' observed Alys, thinking of her own mother-in-law, elegant, powerful and terrifyingly perceptive. Meg Mathieson would never be any of those, but she was still Grace's mother-in-law. The idea was very funny. 'Do you get on wi her?'

'Oddly enough, we all do,' agreed Grace. 'She's a sweet-natured lassie, when –' A quick glance at Alys's face. 'When she's in her own self.'

'Grace?'

Nicol Renfrew was standing in the doorway, looking slightly puzzled to find Alys there. His wife rose and went to meet him, her hands out. He returned her kiss, saying, 'What's eating at the old man? And did you hear we've a new sister? Meg's finally dropped her bairn.'

100

Alys shut her eyes at the words, but had to open them again, because the image of Meg screaming in the birthing-chair was lurking behind her eyelids.

'I heard,' Grace said. 'Are you pleased?'

He shrugged. 'Well enough, I suppose. It doesny touch me. What's eating at Frankie? He was in a rare rage about apples down there, and about you never consulting him, and then ranting at Robert. Eppie Campbell had to tell him the news twice afore he heard her.'

'We've spoken of it,'Grace said. 'Never worry. I brought a second barrel of apples up here this morning, and filled all the boxes we had wi apple-cheese, and he's concerned it willny all sell afore it goes off.'

Nicol giggled in that strange way. Alys found herself laughing aloud in sympathy, and he cast her a glance, but said to his wife, 'Why would you do that, lass? Just to annoy him?'

'I don't annoy your father if I can help it, Nicol, you know it,' she said, with a sudden intensity. 'I wanted to work wi apples the day, nothing more than that. Are you well, my loon?'

'I'm well enough,' he said indifferently. 'That's Gil Cunningham's wife, is it no?' He nodded to Alys, and smiled slyly. 'I know what you've given her.'

'Only a speck,' said Grace.

'And why are the two of you in here talking, anyway? You should be at the gossip-ale getting drunk wi the rest of them. The hall's full of drunken women.' He giggled again.

Grace patted his cheek. 'That's your answer,' she said. 'We'd no wish to get drunk, Alys and me, so we're in here talking instead.'

Alys watched them. The cloud on which she appeared to be floating was descending slowly, and she was thinking more clearly. Apart from her own, the only marriage she had observed at close quarters was Kate's. Both were love matches; she thought this one was not, though it was evident the two were fond of one another, and she wondered what Grace had brought to the marriage. Perhaps her skill, if it was that great.

'You never talk to me,' said Nicol discontentedly. 'You talk to Frankie, and Meg, and all them. I wish you'd talk to me instead.'

'I'll aye talk to you, my loon,' said Grace, turning to look intently at his face. 'Sit down now and talk wi the two of us. Do you need some of your drops?'

'No, for I'm going out. I've a message to you from the old man. He bade me tell you,' he ticked them off on his fingers, 'the shop's about out of lavender water, he wants more brought down, and where was the small glass gourd, oh, and his drops is getting low. Here's Blue Benet.' He handed her another of those painted flasks, studied his hands, and giggled. 'Aye, that's the lot. Now I'm away out.'

'Will you be back for supper?'

'Aye, likely. I'm going to tell Tammas Bowster that Meg's brought home her bairn.'

He slouched out of the room, and Grace watched him go, tight-lipped. After a moment she sighed, and smiled, and said, 'He's a kind man, my Nicol, whatever else. Did you ken his mother?'

'No, for she died long before we came to Glasgow. Maybe Agnes Hamilton knew her,' Alys suggested. 'Is it you makes up Maister Renfrew's drops? I saw him taking some yesterday. And Nicol has some as well.' She heard herself giggling as Nicol had done. 'Drop, drop, drop, everyone has drops. Do you make his too? Does Robert have drops?' She closed her mouth firmly, alarmed by the words which were falling out of it. Dropping out of it. What is wrong with me? she wondered. Where are my manners flown to?

'No,' said Grace quietly. 'It's his father makes those up.' She came to sit down, gave Alys another of those sharp, assessing looks, and nodded. 'Aye, you'll do. Do you want to sleep a bit? Put your feet up on the bench.'

'No, I don't want to sleep.' It seemed like a very bad idea. There might be dreams waiting. 'I'd rather talk,' she said hopefully. 'Tell me how you met Nicol. Did you love him when you were wedded?' That's better, said the watchful voice in her head. You can ask any woman that kind of question.

'I favoured him,' said Grace, smiling slightly. 'He's well learned, and mostly civil, and the – the man that taught us both would have us wed.'

'Was that in Middelburgh? Will you go back there?'

Grace sighed. 'I'd like to. We'd friends there, and elsewhere in the Low Countries.'

'Then why not go?'

'Frankie won't hear of it. Now we're here, he says, we can stay and take a hand in the business. Which doesny please the rest of them.'

'Why not? I'd have thought they'd like the extra help.'

'Aye, but there's the extra outgoings.' The other girl sighed again. 'And the questions it raises about Nicol's place here.'

'Surely he is the eldest son?'

'Aye, and Frankie sent him into the Low Countries to learn his trade,' Grace said rather bitterly. 'But now he's learned it, Frankie won't hear what he says. All he does is cry him down a fool. I'd say he's decided Syme and wee brother Robert can be bent to his purpose better than Nicol ever could. So Nicol's to stay here and do nothing, while his father takes me for –' She bit that off.

'Why did you come back to Scotland?' Alys asked.

Grace gave her a rueful look. 'You're full of questions the day, aren't you no? Well, I suppose that's my doing, and you'll mind little enough of it the morn.'

'I like to know things,' said Alys happily. She had come down from her cloud now, but was feeling pleasantly relaxed, though some of her thoughts did not seem to be in her control. 'So why did you come back, if Nicol dislikes his father so much?'

'I'm not right sure,' said the other girl. She rose and went to the window, looking out of the glazed upper portion over the bleak garden and fiddling with the turn-button on the shutter below it. 'Time we gathered the last of the autumn simples,' she noted. 'I suppose Nicol was determined, and I'd a notion to see where he grew up. But all we've done in coming here is make Frankie the more resolved that Nicol's to have no part in the business, or the proceeds, and nothing like his share of the property in the old man's will.'

'He has his rights,' said Alys, 'but that's unkind. It's a father's duty to see his children established in the world.'

'Aye, well, he says he's already done more than Nicol deserves.' Grace left the window, and looked down at Alys, the grey eyes considering her carefully. 'I should start another batch of his drops. It takes a day or two while the virtues combine.'

'Maister Renfrew's drops? I saw him take them,' Alys said again. 'They worked right well, and quickly at that. Is it his heartbeat that troubles him, or the threat of an apoplexy?'

'Excess of choler, properly, together wi he's no a young man though he will behave as if he's twenty. I think I have all the simples here to put to them.'

'Then I should get away and leave you to your work.' Alys rose, finding her legs more certain than they had been. 'I'm right grateful for your help, Grace.'

'Och, never mention it,' said Grace. 'Are you fit to go home alone yet? Aye, I think you are. Had you a lassie wi you? I'll call her.'

'N-no,' said Alys, with sudden decision. 'Jennet's in the kitchen here. Send and tell her, if you would, I've stepped next door to see my good-sister, so she may go home in her own time. Kate will want to hear the news of –' She swallowed. It was all still there in her head, waiting to pounce. 'News of Meg.'

Chapter Six

It was probably fortunate, Gil thought later, that the Serjeant greeted his request to speak to the prisoner again with nothing more offensive than:

'Forgot what you'd asked him, have you? Aye, he's still where he was. But you'll ha to be quick, the Provost sent for him a bit back and I'll have him up to the Castle for questioning as soon as Tammas Sproull gets back from his dinner. And the quest on Danny Gibson's cried for the morn's morn,' he added, unlocking the door to the end cell.

'I won't keep him long,' said Gil, biting back a sharper answer. He stepped into the cell as Bothwell got to his feet, looking alarmed. 'I'll shout when I'm done.'

The Serjeant barred the door and went away, grumbling under his breath. Gil looked at the prisoner, who said, 'Is it – is it more questions? For I've said all I have to say, maister.'

'Have you?' said Gil. 'That's a pity.' He sat down cautiously on the bench, and looked up at Bothwell. 'You haveny told me all you have to tell, that's for certain, and I'm getting a bit displeased about running round Glasgow finding out things you could have told me yourself in the first place.' Bothwell eyed him warily. 'Do you want to hear what I've learned?'

'I'd sooner hear how my sister does,' the young man admitted.

'Well enough, but not best pleased wi you, for the same reason,' said Gil. 'Now, she found the pewter flask, the one

105

you should have had in your scrip, under the counter when she closed up the booth, and the filler alongside it. She thought likely you'd been filling it and been interrupted by a customer. Tammas Bowster says you came late to the tryst at Goudie's, saying there had been a rush of custom, which would fit wi that.' Bothwell looked steadily down at him, his face giving away nothing. 'Where did Agnes get the one you used in the play?'

'I told you, it was one of ours,' said Bothwell, startled into speech.

'Your sister says not. The six you had from Renfrew are still in their wrappings where she stowed them.'

'It was a spare one he . . .'

'He what?' prompted Gil as that statement halted in mid-air.

Bothwell bent his head and muttered, 'I forget.'

'Who gave you it, Nanty? It's important. Your life hangs by that flask, you understand me? As things stand, the assize will likely find you slew Danny Gibson and you'll be sent to Edinburgh for trial, and I wouldny give much for your chances there if you'll not defend yourself.'

Bothwell turned away from him, shaking his head. Gil stared exasperated at his back, and said, 'I'll tell you what I think happened. I think Agnes gave you that flask, and I think she got it from somewhere in her father's house. Had you agreed that beforehand? Is that why you left the pewter flask behind?'

'No!' said Bothwell, swinging round indignantly. 'No, we never – are you saying I'd plotted wi Agnes to slay Danny? She wouldny do sic a thing!'

'Then who did?' demanded Gil. 'Somebody poisoned Danny Gibson, and I need to find out how it happened, and if it was a mischance I'd like to know who keeps that kind of strong poison lying about Glasgow and why, so I can avoid him.'

'No me, maister!' said Bothwell. 'I've no a notion what it was. Has Wat never sent to let you know?'

'Not yet. Maister Renfrew thought it's most likely one of the plant infusions, but he said he'd need time wi his books to be certain of it.'

'A plant infusion.' Bothwell stared at the wall for a moment, much as Renfrew himself had done. 'Aye, there's a few things that – you'd not believe what can brew up into pyson, maister. Yew, bindweed, monkshood, there's half a hedgerow could kill and the other half cure.'

'I'm aware of that,' Gil said grimly. 'Now will you tell me the truth about that flask, or will you hang for Agnes Renfrew? *My deth ich love, my life ich hate, for a lady shene*, is that it?'

There was a taut silence, which lasted and lasted. Finally Gil sat back and crossed one leg over the other. 'Well, then, what will you tell me? How well do you know the lassie Renfrew? Have you had much converse wi her? What do you know of her family?'

'N-nothing,' admitted Bothwell. 'I've not – I've not been that concerned to speak of them wi her – we met when he gave a feast for her birthday, two month since. All the craft was invited, and one or two neighbours, and there was dancing. We – she stood up wi me for a couple of branles, and a country-dance, and we'd a good laugh thegither, and I, I, I was right taken wi her.'

'What did her father do about that?' Gil asked.

'Bid her dance wi young Andro Hamilton.' Bothwell pulled a face. 'She wasny well pleased, as you'd imagine. Thirteen, is he? He's no more, certainly, though he's a likely lad.'

'And when did Danny Gibson meet her?'

Bothwell looked aside. After a moment he said, 'He and I were chaffing at the booth a couple of days later, and Agnes passed by wi a basket, on her way to the baker's. Danny was as taken wi her as I was, and she –' He stopped, and rubbed his eyes with the back of his hand. 'She was aye even-handed,' he said. 'If she spoke wi one of us she'd speak wi the other.'

'She never had the chance to do that yesterday,' observed Gil. 'Where did she get the flask from?' There was no answer. 'Nanty, if you'll not help me to the truth, I canny help you, and what will your sister do without you?'

'Wed Adam Forrest?' said Bothwell.

'He'll not take her if you hang for a poisoner.'

There was another pause, and finally Bothwell burst out with, 'I canny tell you more than I have done, maister! Can you not see that?'

Descending the steps to the street, Gil spied his father-in-law approaching, conspicuous for his size even without the huge grey plaid round his shoulders. The mason, seeing him, altered his path to meet him, and clapped him on the back.

'Ah, Gilbert! And what success so far?' he asked.

Gil shook his head. 'I seem to be going round in circles,' he admitted. 'Where are you bound just now?'

'The new work. Well, it is hardly new,' qualified Maistre Pierre, 'but we have had to take that gable down almost to the foundations. I go to see how Wattie has progressed.'

'I'm told Danny Gibson drank in Maggie Bell's ale-house,' said Gil. 'I'll cross the river with you, and we can get a jug of ale once you've spoken to Wattie.'

The suburb of the Gorbals was the usual haphazard mixture of poorer cottages and tall stone houses, the habitation of those who were either too poor to live in the burgh or wealthy enough to ignore the burgess regulations about indwelling. In the midst of these was the leper hospital, the roof of its little chapel of St Ninian rearing above the walls. Maistre Pierre's new project was easy to pick out as they strolled down the steep slope of Bishop Rae's bridge; the client was extending an existing stone house, which was swathed in scaffolding, propped with sturdy oak beams, and open down one side like a toy house Gil had seen once in the Low Countries.

'I take it Maister Hutchison has moved elsewhere while you're working,' he said.

'He has.' Maistre Pierre grinned. 'He has moved his family in with his good-mother, so he is very anxious that I finish. I tell him, if he had waited until the spring, it would all have gone much faster. At least we get the founds dug for the new wing.'

Waiting for the mason to finish listening to his foreman's complaints, Gil gravitated to the smithy near to Maggie Bell's tavern, where the usual crowd of onlookers was watching the smith and his two assistants. There was something endlessly fascinating about the way the iron came out of the fire, cherry-red or yellow or even white, soft enough to change shape under the clanging hammers, growing darker and duller as it took its new form.

'Gil Cunningham,' said a voice over the fierce hiss of the cooling-water. He turned, and found Nicol Renfrew by his side, grinning aimlessly. 'I saw you at the Cross. What are you doing over this side the river?'

'Getting a drink at Maggie Bell's, when my good-father finishes speaking to his men.'

'I'll join you. You ken that's where Danny Gibson drank?'

'I do,' said Gil, looking curiously at the other man. 'Who told you that?'

Nicol shrugged again. 'Folk tells me a' sorts of things. I never remember who said the half of them. Maybe I saw him myself, or maybe it was Tammas Bowster, poor fellow.'

Maistre Pierre emerged from the building site, took in the situation, and waved at the tavern. Gil turned towards the wooden sign with its painting of St Mungo's bell, saying, 'You know Bowster? Do you know any more of the mummers?'

'I know Sanders Armstrong,' offered Nicol, 'that's their Bessie. And I know Geordie Barton that plays the pipes. But I don't know Willie Anderson, I don't like him.'

'Did you know they were going to be at Augie's house yesterday?' Gil asked curiously.

'I did.' Nicol giggled. 'Tammas tellt me. But I never tellt the old man. Did you see his face when he knew? I thought he'd have an apoplexy.'

Gil ducked in at the low door of the alehouse, and made for the corner where Maistre Pierre was already established with a large jug of ale and three beakers. Nicol wandered across the crowded room behind him, nodding to one or two people and bowing to Mistress Bell herself where she stood threateningly beside the barrel of ale.

'I like it here,' he said as he sat down.

'It makes a change,' said Gil.

'My faither never crosses the river,' countered Nicol. 'Do you ken my minnie has a wee lassie?'

'A lassie?' Gil repeated. 'Are both well?'

'Oh, aye, they're fine.'

'My congratulations to your father,' said Maistre Pierre heartily. 'He must be pleased?'

Nicol shrugged. 'Likely. I never asked him. Mally Bowen said it looks like him, they tell me, so at least he can stop casting that up at poor Meg.'

'Casting up what?' asked Gil.

'He reckons she played him false,' said Nicol as if it was obvious, 'the same as my mammy did. But now he kens he was wrong.'

'Here's good fortune to the bairn,' said Gil, recovering his countenance, and raised his beaker. They all drank, and he went on, 'Tell me something, Nicol. How did you know it was the wrong flask Nanty Bothwell had yesterday?'

Nicol shrugged. 'It just was,' he said again.

'Which one was it, then?' Nicol gave him a doubtful look. 'I've heard you can tell between them. It's the patterns, isn't it?' Gil prompted, aware of Maistre Pierre watching in puzzlement.

'They're all different,' Nicol said at last. 'Same as people. Nanty should ha had Billy Bucket, that stays in his scrip for the play. He's made of pewter and holds the smoking brew. But he never had him, he had one of the crock ones instead. Allan Leaf, it was.'

'And where does Allan Leaf usually stay?' Gil asked. 'Not in Nanty's scrip, I take it.'

'No, not at all,' agreed Nicol. 'He's often in my faither's purse, for he holds his drops that Grace makes up for him.'

'Where did you see him last, before Nanty had him?'

Another shrug. 'Might ha been in the workroom. There's three of them, you see, that do the same task, and when one's done he puts him to wait and gets another from the cabinet. I just gave Blue Benet to Grace to fill up for him.'

Was there a reason, Gil wondered, why these were all men's names? Was Nicol's world peopled entirely by male objects?

'That is very clear,' said Maistre Pierre, refilling their beakers, 'but if the flask you call Allan Leaf was in the workroom, which I am sure your father said was locked, how did it come to be in young Bothwell's scrip?'

'He did say that, didn't he?' said Nicol, and giggled. 'Perhaps he flew.'

'What are the drops for?' asked Maistre Pierre curiously.

'His heart, mostly,' said Nicol. 'Likely it's something the Saracen learned Grace in Middelburgh when we were there.'

'A Saracen?' said Maistre Pierre, his eyes lighting up. 'You have spoken with a Saracen medical man? Doctor or surgeon?'

'He trades in *materia medica*,' said Nicol with that sudden return to rationality which kept disconcerting Gil, 'and has knowledge you would never credit of what all his stock can do.'

'Who was the poison intended for, do you think?' Gil asked.

'Well, never for Danny, the poor devil.' Nicol looked round the tavern, nodding again to Mistress Bell at the tap. 'He drank in here, you ken, and there's not a soul in the room that you'd say was his enemy. A decent lad.'

'So it seems,' said Gil. 'I don't believe Nanty poisoned him for your sister's sake either, so what was it all about? I can make no sense of it. Who was the poison for?'

'Why, for my faither, a course,' said Nicol, opening his eyes wide. 'Who else?'

'For your –' Gil stared at him, then closed his mouth, swallowed and said, 'Then who put it there? Whose doing might it have been? Robert?'

Nicol shrugged again in that irritating way.

'Could ha been. Could ha been any of us,' he said, and giggled. 'Save maybe my minnie, poor lass, for though she'd likely have the will to do it she'd not have the skill.'

'You are seriously suggesting,' said Maistre Pierre, 'that one of your family has tried to poison your father?'

'I'm never serious,' said Nicol, and giggled again. 'Well, no very often. I hate him, Grace hates him, Agnes hates him, Robert hates him, Eleanor hates him, Meg –'

'Maister Syme?' Gil prompted.

'Jimmy? No, he's all right. There's none of us hates Jimmy, save maybe Eleanor since she has to live wi him.'

'But does he dislike your father?'

'No, why would he? He's wedded him to Eleanor and made him a partner. Jimmy's done well enough out of it all.'

'Why do you hate your father?' asked Maistre Pierre.

Nicol gave him a sideways look. 'He's no easy to love,' he said, 'save as Holy Writ instructs us. I'll respect him, I'm grateful when he insists on it, but I hate him as well.'

'Was he not pleased when you came home?' asked Maistre Pierre.

'No,' said Nicol. After a moment he half laughed. 'We came in just at suppertime, and met wi Meg, poor lass, and they sent for Eleanor and Jimmy, and we all sat down to supper. We'd barely set a knife to the meat when Frankie said, *You needny think you've any more claim on the business. I'll make Grace's bairn my heir afore you*, he said.'

'A pleasant homecoming,' said Maistre Pierre, pulling a face.

'Give him his due,' added Nicol after consideration, 'he was civil enough to Grace, made her welcome, said that about her bairn, mixed her a cup of hippocras wi his own hands after he'd made one to Meg.'

He reached for the jug and poured more ale into all three beakers.

'But you say she hates him,' said Maistre Pierre, puzzled. 'Why should she hate him? She scarcely knows him.'

'She's seen what he did to me,' said Nicol, as if it explained everything. Perhaps it did, Gil reflected, if Grace loved her husband.

'I have always thought Maister Renfrew a good member of the burgh council,' observed Maistre Pierre, 'and a respectable burgess. He is well regarded in the burgh chamber.'

'No guarantee of probity,' Gil commented.

Nicol grinned at that. '*A true saying,*' he said in Latin, *'and worthy of all men to be believed.* I saw your wife in our house, Gil Cunningham.'

'She was to call there with some remedy for Mistress Mathieson,' said Gil.

'I wouldny know about that. She was talking to Grace. She'll maybe learn more than she bargains for. Grace is a wise woman, and clever as well.'

'So is Alys,' said Gil.

'Aye, they were cracking away. But you'll need to have a care to your wee wife, Gil. She'd had a fright, I'd say.'

'What makes you think so?' said Maistre Pierre in concern.

Nicol shrugged. 'Just by what Grace had given her. And the look of her. She wasny looking bonny.'

'Did she say what was wrong?'

'I never spoke wi her. What will you do about Allan Leaf and Billy Bucket? Will you tell the Provost? Only, I wouldny like to say all that afore the assize.' He gave Gil a sideways, sheepish smile. 'They would laugh. Folk do, when I tell them the names of things.'

'I need to report to him,' Gil said. 'I'll try to keep Allan Leaf out of it.' And what was troubling Alys? he wondered apprehensively. Was it simply the fact of a near neighbour's successful delivery, something which had reduced her to envious tears already this autumn, or had she uncovered some fact she would not wish to tell him? Either was possible, and the second would be easier to deal with.

'But tell me,' said Maistre Pierre curiously, 'what would cause your father to believe your mother played him false? You are patently his son, you are all four like enough –'

'I hope not,' said Nicol, and giggled. 'I've no wish to look like Frankie Renfrew, I can tell you, for he's never been – well, enough for that. It's an auld tale, maister, and forgot long afore you came into Glasgow I suppose. My mammy was Sibella Bairdie, and she was widowed already when she wedded Frankie. I was born eight month after he bedded her, and he cast it up the rest of her life.'

'But you –' Maistre Pierre stopped, looked carefully at the other, and shook his head. 'If you do not wish to be told how you resemble him in the face, I will not say it, but consider only your hands. They are as like to Maistre Renfrew's as my daughter's are to mine.' He held his own big square paw out across the table. 'You see, hers are the same shape, though smaller and finer made, and her fingernails grow like mine, each one. Study hers when you have the chance, and then study your own against – against Maistre Renfrew's.'

'My hands.' Nicol studied his, palm and back. 'Well, well. Now Frankie's hands I'd accept gladly, for he's right defty, whatever his other faults.' He looked at his hands again, right and left, rubbing at the nails with his thumbs, and then earnestly at Maistre Pierre. 'You've given me a thing to think on, maister.'

'I never heard the tale either,' said Gil as they made their way back across the bridge. 'I suppose as a boy I'd have no interest in such matters, and likely Renfrew kept it quiet enough at the time.'

'Likely,' said Maistre Pierre. 'But to raise a lad in the thought that he was some other man's son, with evidence like that before him – my opinion of Renfrew is diminishing daily.'

'You've given Nicol something to think about, as he said.' They had left him with a fresh jug of ale at his elbow, considering his hands by Maggie Bell's rushlights as if he had never seen them before.

Maistre Pierre shrugged. 'Nevertheless, it can have nothing to do with Danny Gibson's death. What did Mistress Bell have to say?'

'Nothing new.' Gil paused to peer over the parapet at the river muttering past the stonework of the great pillars. 'She has a good memory. How long since we were there last? Eighteen month? Yes, it was May of last year, when we – just before you took on young John. She recalled my name, and asked after Nan Thomson's daughter, who I think is wedded to some Dumbarton tradesman by now, so I have every hope that she's right when she says Danny drank there regularly, never caused trouble and had no arguments with anyone. A likeable lad, she said, and would be sore missed.'

'Well,' said Maistre Pierre after a moment. 'It had to be checked.'

'It had to be checked. No, this that Nicol had to say about the flask is of more use. I think I have to stop procrastinating and beard his father in his workshop.'

'Hmm.' His companion leaned on the parapet beside him, considering the water below them. The Clyde was shallow here, running over sandbanks and around small islets, but occasional deeper pools showed dark brown in the yellowing late afternoon sunlight. Autumn-brown leaves from the trees further up the river bobbed on the current. After a moment Maistre Pierre said, 'It was an accident.'

'I'm sure of it.'

'Who do you suppose is the intended target?'

'The man himself, I'd have thought, as our friend said,' said Gil, suddenly conscious that people were trudging past them up the slope of the bridge. 'He's the likeliest target in the house, I'd have said. Unless . . .'

'Unless?'

'Unless he prepared the stuff himself to deal with either his son or his wife.'

'If they all dislike one another as much as the son suggests,' said Maistre Pierre with distaste, 'surely it could be intended by any one of the household for any other.'

'The sister – the elder daughter – gave me the same impression,' Gil said absently. 'And she also made it clear any of them would be able to prepare the stuff. It was from her I got the idea our friend yonder might have recognized the flask, and she was right in that.'

'Well.' Maistre Pierre straightened up. 'As you say. If the father is the target we must warn him, and if instead he is the poisoner, then by warning him we may save someone's life. Let us do it now.'

They walked on in silence down the northward slope of the bridge and into the town, through the bustle of the Fishergate and Thenewgate preparing for darkness, shopkeepers bringing in goods which had been laid out for sale, a baker crying the last of his wares before the day's end, an alewife overseeing the transfer of a large barrel from her brewhouse to the alehouse across the street. Two of the burgh's ale-conners lurched past them after a good day's work as they reached the Burgh Cross, and the Serjeant proceeded majestically down the Tolbooth stair. Gil hardly noticed them; he was considering the information he had, trying to construct a complete image from it. He felt there was still some vital piece missing, or perhaps more than one. It might help if he knew what the poison was; he wondered whether the Forrest brothers had learned anything useful.

'Do you know what ails Alys?' said Maistre Pierre suddenly.

'What ails – no,' said Gil, surfacing with difficulty. 'That is, yes, in general,' he amended, 'though I don't understand why it matters so much to her. Just now in particular it's likely Meg Renfrew's baby.'

'I suppose. But our friend yonder thought she had had a fright.'

'Yes,' said Gil. 'I am concerned. I'll go home as soon as we've spoken to Maister Renfrew.'

'I never thought you indifferent,' said Alys's father unconvincingly. 'But so few things frighten her, I am puzzled.'

'So am I,' said Gil. He looked about him, and realized that they were before Renfrew's door. 'Sweet St Giles, the gossip-ale is skailing.'

It was indeed. The pend which led to the house door was full of hilarious women, clinging to one another and shrieking at some joke which Gil felt it was as well he had not heard. Two of them were supporting Agnes Hamilton, no easy task at the best of times, and calling for her servants to be sent for. Someone else, her headdress slipped forward over her face, was sitting on the doorstep alternately demanding lights and singing raucously about a hurcheon.

'*Meet we your maidens all in array, with silver pins and virgin lay,*' Gil said, with irony. He took a pace backwards, and exchanged a glance with the mason; as one they turned and made for the shop doorway.

Inside, James Syme and young Robert Renfrew started nervously at the jingling of the bells on the door, then relaxed as they saw two men entering. Robert stepped forward with an automatic smile, saying, 'And how may I help you, sirs? We've apple-cheese the now, just new in. Were you wanting my faither?' he went on, the smile diminishing as he recognized them. 'Just he's a wee bit taigled just now. Was it to offer good wishes for the bairn, or –?'

'I can imagine he is,' said Gil, 'but I'd like a word just the same. We've learned a bit more about what happened yesterday, and I'd like his opinion of the matter.'

'He's in the house,' Syme informed them as Robert returned to his position at the counter and helped himself to some sweetmeat from under the counter. 'Maybe you'd have a seat till the passage is free?' He inclined his head towards the other door, through which more shrieking laughter reached them. 'It might be easier.'

'Much easier,' said Maistre Pierre.

'We'll wait,' agreed Gil.

'Robert, is there a seat for the gentry?'

'Yonder,' said Robert unhelpfully, pointing. Syme tightened his lips, but brought two stools forward and seated them politely.

'A bad business, yesterday,' he said. 'Has Wat found what the poison might be? He's never sent word here, if so.'

'I've heard nothing either,' Gil said. 'Is your sister Agnes still shut in her chamber, Robert?'

'Likely,' said Robert indifferently. He reached under the counter and brought out another sweetmeat, which he popped into his mouth. He did not offer to share the supply.

'The lassie was quite overset,' confided Syme unnecessarily. 'It's no wonder if she's shut herself away. She's young yet, and still inclined to be foolish, no like my wife.'

'Hah!' said Robert explosively, but did not elaborate. Gil eyed Syme speculatively, thinking that the man seemed to hold Eleanor in more regard than she did him.

'I'd a word with Mistress Eleanor earlier,' he said. 'She tells me she and Agnes and your good-sister do a lot of the stillroom work for the business.'

'That's true,' admitted Syme. 'That's very true. We've been able to expand the range, what's more, since our good-sister came home. She has a few strange receipts from some learned Saracen she met in the Low Countries. Her rose comfits sell well, they're not quite like any –'

He was interrupted. The cacophony beyond the house door had been reducing as the good ladies of the High

Street made their way out to go home, but suddenly a new, shrill, perfectly sober voice burst on their ears.

'Do you believe my daughter now, Frankie Renfrew?'

'Aye, I'll believe her.' That was certainly Maister Renfrew. 'The bairn's a Renfrew right enough. She's the image of Agnes and Robert when they were born.'

'Are you no to apologize, then?'

Syme rose, turning towards the door as if to cover it, stop the exchange somehow. Gil moved to look out of the green window at the wriggling shapes moving in the street.

'Apologize? What way would I apologize? It's your daughter should apologize to me, woman, forever leading me to think other.'

'Just because Sibella Bairdie played you false, man, doesny mean all women's to be tarred from the same pot. My Meg's an honest wife, and you'll treat her that way from now on, or I'll have your hide for cushions, maister potyngar. And just you mind that.'

'Oh, aye, I'll mind it.' The latch rattled, the door opened, Maister Renfrew stepped through into the shop, saying over his shoulder, 'And maybe you'll mind that this is my house, woman, and treat me wi civility.'

'Aye, when you're civil to my lassie!'

Renfrew shut the door on this retort, snarling, then caught sight of Gil and stiffened.

'Oh, you're back, are you?' he said. 'Were you wanting something?'

'We are come to wish good fortune to the bairn,' said Maistre Pierre hastily. 'Are both mother and babe well?'

'Oh, aye, well enough.' Renfrew pushed his felt hat forward, scratched the back of his head, and sighed deeply. 'I was a fool to marry again. I wish I hadny thought of it now.'

'Me too,' muttered Robert.

His father looked sharply at him, but Syme broke in, smiling, 'Admit it, Frankie, there's advantages to being a married man.'

119

'Might we have a word, Maister Renfrew?' said Gil.

'What about? If it's the poison Bothwell used, these two had as well hear it, it's of as much interest to them as to me.'

'Not entirely,' said Gil. 'In your workroom, maybe?'

Renfrew unlocked the workroom and led them in. Gil looked round again, admiring the long scrubbed bench below the window, light even this late in the day. There must be room for more than one person to work at a time.

'All the potyngary work happens here?' he said.

'Aye, it does. What's this about, maister? I've all to see to, and the bairn's godparents to choose.'

'Syme and his wife and your good-daughter,' said Maistre Pierre. 'There, it is simple. Frankie, we are concerned for you.' Renfrew frowned enquiringly at him. 'We think that the flask that held the poison was one of those which should hold some drops which you take –'

'What? Havers, man, it was one of Bothwell's own –'

'No, sir,' said Gil patiently, 'we are quite certain all Bothwell's are accounted for, and so are those Forrest had. We should check what you've given out already,' he added, with little hope, 'in case it was one of those, stolen from whoever you sold it to, but we are quite certain it was –'

'Rubbish!' exploded Renfrew. 'How would he get hold of it? I never heard such nonsense. My workroom's locked, the supply of flasks is still in the barrel there in the corner, all in their straw, and the spare ones Grace makes up for me are here –' He turned to the shelves beside him, and patted a small, expensive sample of the cabinetmaker's craft. 'In this cabinet.'

'How many flasks do you use?' Gil asked.

'I keep three for the drops. Grace fills the three at a time, and puts them by here for me, and when I empty one, as I did this morn, I pass it to her. Then when I get to the third one she makes up a fresh batch.'

Gil frowned, working this out. Something did not tally.

'You leave it all to your good-daughter?' asked Maistre Pierre curiously.

Renfrew shrugged. 'I can trust her well enough wi that. The receipt's clear, she's capable of following it right, and it makes her feel useful forbye. I maybe need to bid her strengthen it,' he added thoughtfully. 'I feel as if the humours are unbalanced again the day.'

'Much has happened in the day,' observed Maistre Pierre.

'I'd have thought she was useful for more than that,' said Gil. 'She seems both skilled and competent.'

'You'd be surprised,' said Renfrew, with a sudden bark of laughter. 'You'd be surprised. Aye, she's a useful lassie, particular at making apple-cheese. I canny interest you in a box? Anyway, maister, the spare flasks,' he picked open one of the many little doors in the cabinet, 'would be with Grace, lying empty and waiting to be filled, or else here for my use. So it canny have been one of mine that Bothwell had, and when I think of the help I've given that lad, the advice and the stores I've put in his way, it fair makes my blood boil that he should misuse the craft that way.'

The doors of the cabinet bore labels with writing on them. Gil bent and looked closely, but found the words much abbreviated. *Absint., Tanac., Alc. mol.,* he read. The open cavity was unlabelled and empty; there were stains on the light wood which smelled vaguely herbal, though the cabinet and the whole chamber smelled so strongly of spices and drugs it was hard to identify one odour. Maister Renfrew, appealed to, agreed that it was the same way as his drops smelled.

'The last two or three you finished,' said Gil, 'did you give them to Mistress Grace yourself?'

'Oh, likely. Or I'd gie them to Frankie or to Robert to pass on to her. So it gets to her, it's no great matter.'

'But none has been missed?'

'And the one in your purse now, Frankie?' asked Maistre Pierre across the denial.

'It's the right stuff,' Renfrew said irritably. 'I lifted it this morning and I've had two or three doses in the day. I ken my own receipt. What are you trying to show, Peter? Are you suspicioning Bothwell intended to leave it here for me?'

'Not Bothwell necessarily,' said Maistre Pierre, 'but we have wondered if it was intended for you.'

Renfrew stared at him, then laughed again.

'No,' he said. 'No, I'll not entertain it. That's a daft idea. Besides, there's nothing goes on in my workroom that I'm not in control of.' He closed the little door, and looked at them curiously. 'You're serious in this, aren't you, Peter?'

'We are,' said Gil. 'Is there anyone in the house capable of brewing up such a poison?'

Renfrew shrugged. 'Robert and James and me, we're all busy at sic things from time to time. Nicol likely could and all, daftheid though he is, I trained him well. So aye, any of us, maister. But as I said, there's naught occurs in my workroom but I'm in charge of it, whoever's handling the bellows. No, I canny see that it could ha been aimed at me. Whatever sort of an ill-doer he is, Bothwell would never ha had the chance to set it in here, and nobody under my roof could do sic a thing, for reason that I take care of all the potyngary stuffs that would pyson a man.'

'The workroom was locked yesterday, you say?' asked Maistre Pierre.

'It was. You saw me unlock it the now. It's aye locked when I'm out of the house or when the shop's empty.'

'Is there another key?' Gil asked.

'Aye, Jimmy has a key, being a partner in the business, but he keeps it close as I do.'

'And do you have any more idea what yesterday's poison might be?'

'None.' Renfrew opened the workroom door, a little too quickly for his son who was revealed within a yard or so of the other side. 'Robert, have you no work to occupy you?'

'Aye, Faither,' returned the young man, 'but it's all in the workroom where you were just now.'

'Get on with it, then, afore I take a stick across your back,' said his father sharply. 'Jimmy, I think Peter and his good-son are just leaving.'

'No,' said Gil apologetically. 'I need a word with your daughter Agnes.'

'Wi Agnes?' Renfrew stared at him. 'Why?'

'As you said yourself, sir,' Gil pointed out, 'one of her sweethearts has slain the other. I'd say Sir Thomas will want a word wi her and all, and it's plain she can help me. I've given her most of the day, since she's not left her chamber, but I must speak wi her now.'

'You've no need to speak to Agnes,' said Renfrew crisply. 'An empty-heidit lassie like her can add nothing to what the rest of us saw.'

'I'll fetch her,' offered Robert, still in the workroom doorway. Gil looked at the young man, and saw the smirk just vanishing from his face.

'I come with you,' said Maistre Pierre.

'I'd sooner speak to the lassie in her own chamber,' said Gil, 'with maybe one of the other women at her side.'

'She's nothing to hide from her faither,' pronounced her father in menacing tones.

'Then you'll not need to be present, sir,' suggested Gil.

Renfrew grunted sourly at that and turned to the house door. 'You'd best come up, then,' he said.

'I'll come and all,' said Robert. 'I want to hear what she has to say.'

With a faintly gleeful air he preceded them through into the house, up the newel stair into the hall, up a further flight.

'What is a hurcheon?' asked Maistre Pierre absently as they passed through a succession of ostentatious rooms, their wooden furnishings pale and new, and the hangings bright and fresh even in the dwindling daylight.

'*Hérisson*,' translated Gil. 'Hedgehog.'

Finally Robert kicked at a shut door and flung it open, saying, 'Agnes? Here's the Provost's men come to take you up for poisoning Danny Gibson.'

'Robert!' said Gil sharply, but it was drowned in Agnes's shriek of terror. She had been lying on the handsome tester-bed which occupied most of the chamber, and she sprang up and off the bed on the far side, all in one movement, white-faced, petticoats flying, stammering:

'No! No, I didny – I never –!'

'Robert, you're a fool!' said his father.

'Come, come, Agnes,' said Maistre Pierre reassuringly. 'You know enough not to pay attention to what your brother says, no?'

'I never –' repeated Agnes, and then the sense of these words penetrated. 'You mean it's not – he was –' She swallowed, and turned a savage face on her brother, showing little even teeth. 'Our Lady's nails, I'll pay you for that one, Robert, I swear it, if it's the last thing I ever do.'

'*There was joye to sen hem mete, With layking and with kissing swete.* Thank you, Robert,' said Gil, without sincerity. 'I'm sure your father can spare you now. Likely Maister Syme would like your help to close up the shop.'

'Aye, get away, Robert,' said Renfrew. 'That was a daft trick. And we'll ha none o your sarcasm, maister,' he added. Robert gave Gil an ugly look and slunk out, and Renfrew entered the chamber, saying to his daughter, 'Here's Maister Cunningham wants to ask you about yesterday, Agnes. Speak up and answer him the truth, lassie.'

His face cracked in a half-smile, and the girl relaxed slightly, and came round the end of the bed. Her cheeks were wet, as if she had been weeping, and Gil saw that she was still trembling from the fright her brother had given her.

'Shall we have some light, and then sit down?' he suggested.

Seated by the opened shutters, he studied Agnes again in the light of the yellow sunset. She did not look as if

124

she had slept; the blue eyes were dark-ringed, the gold curls uncombed, and she clasped and unclasped her hands, apparently unaware that she did so. Maistre Pierre was watching her with some sympathy.

'You know your good-mother has a wee lassie,' Renfrew said.

'I could hardly miss it,' said Agnes. Not so distressed as she seems, then, Gil registered.

'Where did you find the flask, Agnes?' he said abruptly. She reared back like a horse sharply reined in, and stared at him, mouth open, eyes very wide.

'Find it?' she said after a moment. 'Me?'

'You gave it to Nanty Bothwell on the stair,' Gil said. Renfrew looked from his daughter to Gil, open-mouthed in indignation.

'Why would I do that?' she countered boldly. Definitely not so distressed as she seems, thought Gil. 'What would I – does he say I gave him it?'

'Never mind what he says,' said Gil. 'I'm interested in what you say. Where did you find it?'

'What's this about?' demanded Renfrew. 'My lassie never had aught to do wi the flask. I told you all that below stairs the now!'

'I never had it,' she said resolutely, shaking her head. 'It was nothing to do with me.'

'I've heard a different tale,' said Gil. 'You saved the play, you claimed. Where did you find the flask?'

'Why would I have the flask?' she said. 'It's nothing to do wi me, is it, Daddy? You keep all those things in your care, locked in the workroom, we never get a sight of them, what would I be doing passing one to Nanty Bothwell?'

'That's what I'd like to know,' said Gil. 'Nanty forgot to lift the one he should have had with him, so he asked you to find him something that would do, when you slipped back here to fetch your good-mother a cushion.'

'Why are you accusing her like this?' demanded Renfrew. 'What's the proof you have?'

125

'I never did anything of the sort,' said Agnes, sounding alarmed. 'You canny show I did, either!'

'Aye, what proof?' demanded Renfrew again.

'She was seen talking to Nanty, out in the yard, when she left Morison's house,' said Gil. 'And seen afterwards, talking to him on the kitchen stair. That was when she said she'd saved the play. You brought Nanty that flask, Agnes, and it killed Danny Gibson. Was that your intention?'

She turned her face away from the light, putting one hand up to cover her eyes.

'Do you think I'll ever forget how he died?' she whispered. 'You canny torment me like this, maister. Daddy, stop him! I never –'

'That's nothing to say to the matter!' said Renfrew angrily. 'It's all hearsay! How could she get the flask, let alone whatever was in it, when the key to the workroom was in my purse all the time?'

'Did you know what you'd lifted?' Gil asked. 'Did you know it was poison? Did you plan to have one lad kill the other and be hanged for it?'

'No, I never. Where would I get something like that?' she asked, without looking round. 'Tell me that, maister! My faither keeps control over all that moves in this house, and certainly over all that's to do wi the craft. How would I find sic a flask, let alone poison to put in it to–' Her face crumpled, and she covered it with her hands again. 'Oh, the poor laddie!'

'Danny died. Nanty will hang,' said Gil deliberately, 'unless we can show it was a mistake, that he'd no knowledge of what was in the flask. One of your sweethearts has died, but you could save the other one by telling me the truth, Agnes.'

'That's more than enough!' exploded Renfrew.

He got to his feet and patted his daughter's shoulder, and she turned to bury her face in the waist of his woollen gown, wailing, 'Send them away, Daddy!'

'Aye, never fret, my lammie. That's all you get, Maister Cunningham. I'll not hear any more of this nonsense, and

I'll answer no more questions myself. Away and tell the Provost it was Nanty Bothwell done it.'

'How long will you stay in your chamber, Agnes?' asked Maistre Pierre suddenly. 'You are needed out in the house. Your good-mother is abed, there is the house to run –'

'I'll see to what needs decided under my own roof, Peter Mason,' said Renfrew angrily. 'There now, my pet, they're just away.'

'If you change your mind, Agnes,' said Gil, 'you can send word to my wife.'

Chapter Seven

'I'm no that keen on your story,' said Sir Thomas Stewart, Provost and Sheriff of Glasgow. He pushed aside his notes on Danny Gibson's death, and blew his nose resonantly into a large linen handkerchief. 'Confound this rheum, a man canny think straight wi his head full of ill humours. Tell me it all again, till I see how it will sit wi the assize.'

He huddled into his huge furred gown, tucking his hands up the sleeves. Gil obediently began again at the beginning, and recounted what he had learned so far. Sir Thomas listened attentively, blowing his nose from time to time, and shaking his head.

'I'm still no convinced,' he said at last, 'and what's more I think the assize will never understand it. You're saying you think this lassie fetched a flask from her father's house, that turned out to hold poison, and it was all an accident. But the lassie denies it, so does her father, and you've given me no reason why Frankie Renfrew should have strong poison lying about his place and not recognize it.'

'I've been unable to speak to the lassie alone,' Gil corrected, 'and her father won't hear of what I say, and laughed at my suspicions.'

'I'm no surprised,' said Sir Thomas. 'He keeps a tight hand on his household, does Frankie, he'd never accept sic a notion, and no more do I. Is that the best you can do, Gilbert?'

'Bear in mind, sir, I've yet to hear from my lord Archbishop, I'm acting on my own account for now, so I can hardly insist on speaking to Agnes against her father's wishes. I've no notion whether she'd tell a different tale if I did. I'd hoped my wife might get a word with her, but she's –' He broke off, unwilling to expand further on that. 'She hasn't succeeded yet,' he finished. 'There's been no word from Stirling, I take it?'

'No, no, I think there hasny. Walter clerk would ha brought it to me if there had.' Sir Thomas hooted gloomily into the handkerchief again and wiped his eyes with his embroidered shirt cuffs. 'Confound this rheum. No, Gilbert, I'm no willing to give you a direct order to question the lassie. It seems to me there's little enough to connect her with the matter, other than that it's one of her two admirers that's slain the other. I'll put young Bothwell to the question in the morning, and see what light he'll cast on the matter, but –'

'She was heard speaking to him,' Gil pointed out.

The Provost shook his head again. 'So was the lad who died heard speaking to him, you tell me,' he said, 'and those two had high words. That's a better argument for why he's dead, though how Bothwell came by the poison so quick after the quarrel – did anyone think to search him or his scrip?'

'No, I didn't,' admitted Gil in some embarrassment. 'When I learned the flask he should have carried was left in the booth, I thought no further of it. That was unwise.'

'Aye, well, maybe John Anderson searched it, though whether he'd write down all he found is another matter.' Sir Thomas rubbed thoughtfully at his reddened nose. 'No. Now, this flask that has the poison in it. We've got Bothwell and Frankie Renfrew both claiming it's Bothwell's, your wife's witness that it isny because all the ones he had are still in the packing and the docket wi them, and that daft Nicol Renfrew saying it's one of his father's that should have drops in it. If that's right, and Nicol knows the flask, how come Frankie doesny? No, no, Gilbert,' he added as Gil opened his mouth to interrupt, 'I heard you the first time, but it's how it will look to the assize that matters. Quiet, now, and let me think.'

Gil sat hopefully, watching the older man. Sir Thomas must be in his forties, a small neat balding individual, usually dressed with quiet, rich good taste. Today, packaged in several layers of different furred garments, he resembled a disaster in a skinner's workshop. He was tapping on the desk before him now, considering the quest on Danny Gibson.

'Aye,' he said finally, drawing the papers toward him. 'I'll tell you what, Gilbert. I'll direct the assize to the cause of death, and order them not to consider who's guilty here. They'll no like it,' he admitted, 'for they aye relish getting someone took up for slaying or murder, but they'll have to live wi the disappointment for once. Then if you're right, and my lord agrees, we can follow it up, and if you're wrong, well, we've got young Bothwell locked up anyway, though I've a notion John Anderson would like rid of him. It's no very convenient having a lodger in the Tolbooth.' He blew his nose again. 'Confound this rheum. I'm away to my supper and my bed, and hope I feel more like the thing the morn's morn. My lady's got some remedy or other for me to take, but to be honest I'd as soon a good dram of usquebae.'

'Very well, sir,' said Gil, concealing his reaction. 'When will you question Bothwell?'

'Oh, that's for the morn and all,' said Sir Thomas, rising and clutching his furs about him. 'I'll not risk standing about there in the tower just now, all in the damp and cold. Bid you goodnight, laddie, and I'll see you in my court.'

Gil left the Castle in some annoyance, but by the time he reached the Wyndhead he was more resigned to the situation. It seemed as if he had spent the entire day asking questions to no effect, and now Sir Thomas had put a stop to any further action this evening, except perhaps to find out what Wat Forrest had learned. However it was late in the day, darkness had fallen and the denizens of the upper town were making their way home for supper, and the evening was sufficiently cold that after speaking to Wat it was attractive to think of doing the same, and then of sitting by the fire, discussing what they had learned so far with Pierre and Alys.

Yes, with Alys. And what was wrong there? he wondered, with a rush of anxiety.

When they left the Renfrew house Maistre Pierre had set off to speak to his men at the other site by the cathedral, and Gil had gone straight home, to discover that though nobody in the main house knew she was there, his wife was in their dark lodging, curled up in the bed in her kirtle, dry-eyed and silent in a tight little ball. Socrates, who was not allowed on the bed, had been wedged in firmly at her side with his chin on her shoulder, and had made it politely clear to his master that he felt his mistress needed him. Alarmed and puzzled, Gil had lit candles, spoken to Alys, stroked her hair, tried to find out what was troubling her, but she would not speak except to tell him to go away. Obeying might not have been wise, he was aware, but he did not know what else to do.

He paused at the top of the Drygate, standing under the torch on the corner of someone's house, to consider matters. In the last couple of months she had been quite unwell when her courses began, but a brief reckoning of the calendar had already told him that that was probably not the answer, and the dog's response suggested something different. Nicol's remark that she had had a fright might be nearer it. Where had she been this afternoon? She was going to call at the Renfrews' house, and Jennet had said something about Kate. Neither of those should have been alarming, the social events round a birth were women's work after all and Kate would hardly – unless she and Kate had discovered something she disliked.

He thought about that. Alys was inclined to make friends with the people involved in a case, and he was sure it did not help her to be impartial. Look at how she brought Christian Bothwell home, he reflected. If she had learned something this afternoon which reflected badly on

131

Christian, or on Agnes Renfrew, would she have retreated from it in this way? No, probably not, he decided. Her ability to face unpalatable facts was one of the things he valued about her. So how unpalatable must something have been to reduce her to the state in which he had found her earlier? Perhaps Kate can tell me, he thought, I can go there after I speak to Wat. He set off down the Drygate, pulling his plaid up against the wind.

The Forrest brothers were closing up the shop, Wat fastening the shutters while Adam swept the debris of the day's trading out into the street. They both looked up when he halted beside the door.

'Gil,' said Adam hopefully. 'Have you learned anything?'

'Nothing,' said Gil. 'Whatever I ask, it leads me no further. I'm more certain than ever it was an accident, but I canny prove it, and Nanty willny speak.' He looked from one man to the other in the light spilling from their doorway. 'Have you learned aught about the poison?'

'No really,' said Wat. He shook the shutters to check they were secure, and gestured to Gil to enter. 'Come and I'll show you what I've done so far.'

'You'd hear Meg Renfrew had a wee lassie,' said Adam, following them in. 'The image of Frankie, so the howdies said.'

'I did.'

Gil waited while the brothers stowed the last oddments about the shop, closed the box with the money and lifted the candles. Leading the way into the workshop, Wat said, 'He'll be after me within the week to betroth the bairn to our Hughie, I'll wager.' He set the box down within his sight and nodded at the pottery flask where it sat bright and innocent on the bench in the candlelight. 'Now, this. We've tried this, we've tried that, we've tested it for colour and for how quickly it boils, for how it mixes with oil and milk and butter.'

'Butter?' repeated Gil, startled.

132

'There's some poisons can be combined with goose-grease or butter, to smear on the skin or work into a glove or the like,' said Wat. He caught sight of Gil's expression, and grinned. 'If you're wishful to poison someone, man, there's a way to it, whatever care your victim takes.'

'So I see,' said Gil. 'And does this stuff work that way?'

'No need,' said Adam. 'It slew Danny just from touching his skin, we think. The best we can do is that it's some plant infusion or distillation.'

'But there's this.' Wat drew on a scorched and stained glove and reached for a small dish. 'We emptied it out into a glass, to get a better look at the colour, and when we poured it back, there was this left as residue. You'd be surprised what gets past the searce.' He carried the dish to the light, and poked with a spill at one of the objects which lay on it. 'You see?'

'I see it.' Gil moved his head this way and that to get a better look at the fragments. 'What would you say it is? It looks to me like scraps of nutmeat. A broken almond, or the like.'

'I'd say the same,' agreed Wat happily, 'and Adam's agreed. It's about the hardness of nutmeat, and by daylight it's white, like cream rather than like milk.'

'Almonds. Who mentioned almonds?' Gil recalled. 'When the lad fell, someone – aye, it was Robert Renfrew – said he'd been eating almonds, for you could smell them on him.'

'I mind that,' agreed Adam. 'You could smell them, the boy was right for once.' Gil glanced at him, and he grimaced. 'He's not a natural apothecary, young Robert, for all Frankie says.'

'I never heard that you could brew a poison out of almonds,' said Gil doubtfully.

'Nor I,' agreed Wat. 'Nor there's nothing in the books we have. Mind, if you put the right things to it, you can brew poison wi anything, but this hasny the look of something that's been brewed from a complex receipt. The more you put to a compound, the muddier it gets.'

133

'Not if it's distilled out,' Adam reminded his brother.

'Frankie was working with some sort of nuts this morning,' Gil recalled. 'The label said *Nux pines*. Could that be it?'

'Pine nuts?' Wat guffawed. 'Frankie? I wonder who those were for?' He grinned at his brother, and added to Gil, 'They're reputed excellent for –' he gestured expressively – 'propping up what willny stand. They're no poisonous, save you take too many, and you'd need to eat a sackful at a sitting for that.'

'I've heard they eat them in Italy and places like that,' said Adam. 'Gil, have you learned anything at all yet?'

'A little.' Gil leaned against the bench and summarized what he knew or suspected so far, while the two men listened with lengthening faces. When he finished, Wat shook his head.

'I've aye kent it was a quarrelsome house,' he admitted, 'but I never thought it was that bad. I'm more than ever glad I turned Frankie down yesterday. I'd say your choice is a better one, Adam.'

Gil, keeping his face blank, asked, 'Would you have said any of the household had the skill to produce this?'

'Frankie himself,' said Wat, 'for he's good at his trade. Jimmy, a course, and likely young Robert would know how though whether he'd achieve it I couldny say. How much Frankie's taught his daughters I've no notion. But it's hard to assess another's craft without seeing them at work.'

The Morison household was preparing to sit down to supper. The great board had been set up in the hall, the two young maidservants were shaking out the linen cloths to go over it, and the little girls and their nurse were waiting to set out the spoons and wooden trenchers. As Gil followed Andy Paterson across the chamber, the older child, Wynliane, intercepted him, looking up earnestly at

134

his face. Her eyes were blue, darker than Agnes Renfrew's. He paused, and smiled at her.

'Good evening, Maister Gil,' she said in her soft voice, and bobbed a child's curtsy. 'Will you stay for supper?'

'He better not,' said Ysonde from her nurse's side. 'Isn't enough pastries.'

'Ysonde,' chided Nan. 'That's no a polite lassie.'

'Well, there isn't,' asserted Ysonde.

Gil went on to find Kate, his mood lightened slightly as it always was by contact with Ysonde. His sister was inspecting some linen with Babb in the next chamber, supported on her crutches and holding up one end of a long cloth opposite a candle.

'It looks well enough by this light,' she said to Babb. 'Set it aside and we'll have another look by daylight. Will you stay to supper, Gil?'

'Ysonde says there aren't enough pastries,' he reported. Kate rolled her eyes. 'I'm expected at home. I only called by to ask if you had seen Alys this afternoon.'

'I did,' she agreed, accepting two corners of the cloth from Babb and waiting while the big woman lifted the folded end of the cloth. 'I gave her a message for you.'

'Was she well?'

'Well enough. Sit down a moment,' she said, glancing at him, and helped Babb put the final folds in the cloth. 'There, put it on the plate-cupboard, Babb, and we can search for stains by daylight. Ask Ursel if the supper will wait a quarter-hour, would you?'

'She'll likely no be pleased,' Babb warned, 'she's wanting to go next door to hear about the mistress's groaning-time.'

'Offer her my apology,' Gil said guiltily, sitting down on a chair against the wall. 'I didn't mean to hold back your meal, Kate.'

Kate, reared as strictly as he had been in the principle that one did not upset the kitchen, merely nodded, and turned to clump over to sit beside him, propping her crutches across her knee.

'I spoke to my lassies,' she said as Babb left the room. 'They noticed Agnes come in by the kitchen door, right enough, and they were both certain that she looked at young Bothwell as she came in, not at the lad who died.'

'And yet she had spoken to Bothwell earlier, so it should have been Danny's turn. It's proof of nothing, but it is suggestive. Did she speak to anyone?'

'No, they said she went straight to the stair.'

'Thanks for this, Kate. I've another question for your kitchen.' She raised her eyebrows. 'Ask Ursel, if you would, if anything she served the mummers had almonds in it.'

'Almonds? Like marchpane, or the like?'

'Anything of that sort,' he agreed.

'I'll ask her.' She looked at him sideways. 'Now why are you asking me if Alys was well? I'd my doubts about her myself, Gil. She seemed right shaken. She ate all the cakes on the tray, which is not like her, she usually takes one or two for manners, no more. She – it seems she witnessed the birth next door, and by what I hear Meg's time was none of the easiest. I had to ask her direct before she'd admit it. I think she's had a bad fright.'

'Oh.' He swallowed, dismayed. 'What – I mean, how – how alarming would that be?'

Kate gave him another sideways look, amusement in her face.

'I'd not have wanted Augie present,' she said.

He digested this, and after a moment braced himself, saying, 'Thanks, Kate. That must be it. I'd best be up the road and see what I can do.'

'She may not want your help,' Kate observed. He looked sharply at her. 'Gil, how do you get a bairn in the first place? It might take another woman to comfort her.' He stared, working out her meaning in growing embarrassment, and she bit her lip. 'I'd come back with you, but there's the men's supper here –'

'No.' He rose. 'See to your own household, Kit-cat. I need to sort this myself, whether she'll let me or not.'

She looked up at him rather anxiously.

'Bid her come down here the morn's morn,' she suggested. 'I'd take it as a favour – the – the quest on Danny Gibson's called for nine of the clock. I could do wi the company.'

He nodded. 'Thanks, Kate,' he said, and gripped her shoulder briefly.

'Ursel's saying,' announced Babb in the doorway, 'that the supper'll spoil if she keeps it back any longer, so if Maister Gil's no staying he'd best be off out the road, my leddy.'

'You see where Ysonde gets her manners,' said Kate resignedly. 'Goodnight, Gil.'

To his astonishment, and initial relief, Alys was in the hall of her father's house, overseeing the same tasks as had been in hand at Morison's Yard. Socrates was lying on the hearth watching her carefully, though he scrambled up when Gil entered and came to explain his earlier dereliction of manners, tail wagging, ears deprecatingly flattened. There was no sign of Christian Bothwell; she must have decided to stay in her own house this night.

'Am I late?' he asked, acknowledging his dog's apology.

'No,' said Alys lightly, with a tense note in her voice which he recognized. 'We waited supper. I thought you were working.'

'I was.' He turned to wash his hands in the pewter bowl set by the door, peering into the sparkles of candlelight on the water as if they might tell him how to handle this. 'I called by Morison's Yard,' he added, lifting the linen towel. 'Kate asked me to bid you down there tomorrow, while the quest is held. I'd assume the men will all go up to the Castle.'

'Likely.' She finished setting out the spoons, added the small salt from the plate-cupboard, inspected the table, and nodded. 'Bid them serve as soon as they like, Kittock. I'll call the maister.'

Over supper she maintained the same light manner, discussing something Socrates had done during the day, to the dog's evident embarrassment, and reporting what Nancy had said about John. Gil and her father, after an exchange of glances, supported her in this; Catherine silently absorbed stockfish-and-almond mould, and further down the table the mason's men exchanged the day's gossip with the maidservants. Gil caught two different versions of what Meg Renfrew's mother had said to her son-in-law, and some speculation about why Danny Gibson had been poisoned.

'Shall we have music?' said Maistre Pierre as the board was lifted. 'It's a good time since you played the monocords for us, *ma mie.*'

'No,' said Alys unequivocally. 'We have the case to consider.' She brought the jug of wine over to the hearth and arranged herself on the settle, tense and upright. Socrates lay down heavily on her feet. 'We need to compare what we know.'

Slightly to Gil's surprise, Catherine joined them. The old woman would usually have retired to her own small chamber after supper, where he was aware she regularly spent some hours at prayer before sleep. Tonight she sat quietly in their midst, beads in hand, lips moving, eyes downcast under the black linen folds of her veil, although midway through Maistre Pierre's account of their interview with Nicol Renfrew Gil realized that her attention was not on her beads but on Alys.

'Can he really tell one flask from another?' said Alys at the end of her father's recital.

'He seemed quite certain he could,' said Gil. 'We could test it. It must be part of the way his mind works.' He ventured to put his arm along the back of the settle, behind Alys. She glanced up at him, with a tiny grimace which might have been a smile, then frowned at her hands. The dog looked up at them both, beat his tail twice on the boards and lowered his nose on to his paws again. 'He thinks he last saw that flask, Allan Leaf he called it, in the workroom waiting to go up to Grace to be filled with Frankie's drops.'

'But the workroom was locked,' Alys said. 'Agnes must have found it somewhere else.'

'He was also certain the poison was for his father,' observed Maistre Pierre, 'although Frankie himself found the idea ridiculous.'

'One would, I suppose,' said Alys thoughtfully. 'What if I told you such a thing?'

'I should laugh in your face,' he agreed, 'but then I think I am a good master.'

'Probably Maister Renfrew does too. If it was not for him,' said Alys, 'if it was intended for Danny Gibson, then how could it have happened? Could Nanty Bothwell be lying? Could he have done it alone?'

'I'd say not,' said Gil. 'There's too much circumstance against it. He would have had to lay hold of a flask, not one of his own, and he had to have it ready before the mummers came to Morison's Yard. And why go to so much trouble, why not use his own flask?'

'If he used his own flask it would be known to be his doing,' said Maistre Pierre.

'He could hardly avoid that, in the face of half Glasgow.'

'But he claims it is his flask in any case,' said Alys. 'No, that doesn't seem logical. Then could he be in conspiracy with Agnes?'

'I'd believe it of her,' said Gil, 'but not of him. He's quite clear-headed enough to see that he must be found guilty, as things stand.'

'And if it was some other,' said Alys slowly, 'Robert for instance, conspiring with Agnes or not –'

'Or Renfrew himself,' Gil offered. 'If he keeps such close control over his workroom as he claims, it's hard to see how any other could make the stuff in his house.'

'Yes, but whoever it was, they could not know in advance that the flask would be needed. No, that doesn't hold up. Which leaves us with Agnes alone,' she finished, pulling a face, 'acting on the spur of the moment. Father says you spoke to her,' she said to Gil.

'She denied all,' said Gil, and Maistre Pierre nodded agreement. 'I thought she was more angry than distressed, though she put up a good imitation of it.'

'I think she is genuinely distressed at the death of her sweetheart,' said Maistre Pierre. 'She is also frightened. No doubt if she did provide Bothwell with the flask, she has seen that she must be suspected.'

'Angry?' said Alys. 'But with whom? As if she had not expected what happened? She might blame Bothwell for her situation – after all if he had not forgotten the flask and asked her help, she would not be involved.'

'Assuming he did ask her help,' said Gil. 'They both deny all this.'

'The safest road for both of them,' said Maistre Pierre.

'But when Renfrew announced that the boy had been poisoned,' said Gil, the scene in his sister's hall coming vividly to mind, 'he asked Bothwell what was in the flask.'

'And Bothwell,' said Alys, clapping her hands together, 'turned to look at Agnes!' Socrates sat up expectantly.

'Exactly,' said Gil. 'They gave no signal, but he clearly associated the flask with her.'

'So where have we got to?' asked Maistre Pierre. Catherine raised her head and looked at him, then went back to her beads. The dog lay down again with a resigned sigh.

'It looks as if Agnes gave Nanty the flask,' said Alys, 'but neither of them knew it held poison.'

'So if that is the case, who is guilty in Gibson's death?'

'I'd need to ask my uncle,' said Gil. 'I suspect the two of them must share some guilt, but if it was an accident, not murder, there would be a fine, kinbut, payable to Gibson's father or kin, with the guilty parties all in their linen at Glasgow Cross for penitence, rather than hanging.'

'Perhaps if we told Agnes that, we might persuade her to confess,' said Alys.

'I cannot see that young woman in her shift at Glasgow Cross,' observed the mason.

'Meanwhile, where did the poison come from, and why was it sitting about where Agnes could find it? I'd like to search the house, but Sir Thomas isn't convinced, and without a direct order from the Provost Frankie would never countenance it.'

'*Ah, mon Dieu*, what a thought,' said Maistre Pierre.

'Eleanor Renfrew,' Gil recalled suddenly, 'tells me they label poisons with a black cross. Agnes would have recognized that, I'd have thought. It must have had no mark.'

'Simple carelessness?' asked Maistre Pierre disapprovingly. 'To keep a pig full of poison standing about the place unlabelled? If that is the case, we do no more business with them, Alys, I think.'

'But where did it come from?' Gil repeated. 'Nobody we spoke to has recognized what it is.'

'Or at least has admitted to recognizing it,' Alys put in.

He nodded at that. 'You're right. Whoever brewed the stuff, he would hardly admit to knowing it now. The Forrest brothers are probably safe,' he added, 'they seem to be testing the flask quite thoroughly. They found scraps of what looks like nutmeat at the bottom of it, as if it had got through the bolting-cloth.'

'Nutmeat?' said Alys. 'Do you mean they think it was brewed from nuts? I wonder what that might be? I never heard of a poison like that.'

'Nor had Wat.' Gil grinned, and retailed the conversation about the pine nuts. Maistre Pierre guffawed much as Wat had done, but Alys listened seriously.

'He is right, they are not poisonous except in vast quantities,' she agreed. 'But I had not heard of that virtue in them. I must check my *Hortus Sanitatis*. I wonder – Meg's mother, Mistress Baillie, said something about pine nuts when she was abusing Maister Renfrew. Could they have been for his own use?'

'Myself, I have no wish to ask him that either,' said Maistre Pierre.

'No, but,' said Alys slowly, 'his wife was –' She caught her breath. Catherine looked up but did not speak, and after a moment Alys went on, 'Meg was in childbed, what was he doing preparing something of that sort?'

'To be ready for later?' Gil suggested. 'Maybe he wants a son from her. Or perhaps he has a mistress, or planned to –' he glanced at Catherine, but she had bent her head to her beads again. – 'visit Long Mina's, or some such place.'

'The man has a new young wife,' Maistre Pierre said. 'How many women does he need, in effect?'

'And does it mean he is planning to poison someone?' asked Alys.

Gil sighed. 'I think, from what Eleanor tells me, any of the Renfrew household is at least capable of making up whatever it is. Poison is a woman's weapon, or so I've read, but in this case it seems to me the men must be included as well, even Frankie.'

'Robert would be my favourite,' said Maistre Pierre darkly.

'Let us consider them,' said Alys. 'Who might wish to poison someone, who might be a likely target.' Socrates opened one eye as she bent to draw her tablets from the purse which hung under her skirts, then closed it again when she sat back slightly and took the stylus out of its slot in the carved cover. 'Maister Renfrew himself. Not a pleasant man, I think.'

'He might wish to rid himself of Nicol out of dislike,' said Gil slowly, 'or of the wife if he thought she was cheating him, but surely not any of the others of the household? He seems to favour Robert, he has wedded Eleanor off, Agnes is his pet.'

'The good-mother?' suggested Maistre Pierre. 'Mistress Baillie, I mean.'

Alys nodded, and made a note.

'Nicol himself,' she said. 'He hates his father, he dislikes his brother and sisters. Is he unbalanced enough to poison them from dislike alone? Or is there some benefit we can't see?'

'*Cui bono*? I suppose he could fear that Robert would take his place in the business,' said Gil slowly, 'but Nicol has changed since we were boys. It might be something he's taking now has settled his mind, but he's by far calmer than he used to be, almost out of the world at times. Just the same, I think his state is still what Aristotle called *akrasia*, or in Latin *impotens sui*, not master of himself.'

'Behaving inconsistently,' said Alys, 'not in accordance with any discernible principles. Yes, I see. That would fit. So is he capable of killing, do you think?'

'For something he cared about, maybe, and I wouldn't think he would care enough about the business to kill for it. He'd rather go back to the Low Countries, I think.'

'Grace asked him if he needed some of his drops,' said Alys, and unaccountably blushed darkly in the candle-light. 'Perhaps that's what has changed him.' She made a note. 'And Robert?'

'Robert dislikes everyone,' said Gil. 'His father, Agnes, probably Syme, certainly Nicol, possibly his stepmother. But he's not someone I could imagine leaving a flask of poison about unlabelled by accident.'

'So that if he left it,' said Alys, 'it was where his intended victim would pick it up. It becomes more and more important to know where Agnes got it from.'

'Nicol said that everyone likes Syme,' said Maistre Pierre reflectively, 'but it does not mean that Syme likes everyone.'

'I'd say he'd no good opinion of young Robert,' agreed Gil. 'And I suppose it would be to his benefit to be rid of Renfrew, though the method might be bad for trade.'

'And the women,' said Alys, writing busily. 'I think we can dismiss Meg as poisoner, though not as victim. She has no training, and –'

'She must know stillroom work,' Gil observed. 'If she learned that a given receipt would brew up poison, she would be as able to follow it as you would. And Frankie said much the same of Grace Gordon,' he recalled.

143

'I suppose you're right.' She made more notes on her list. 'Does Grace have enough reason to poison anyone, so far as one ever does? She loves Nicol, I think, though it was not a love-match, and surely she hardly knows his family. But Meg's marriage is certainly not a happy one,' she added. 'She might wish to be rid of Maister Renfrew. I know I would, if I was wedded to him.'

'Would you use poison, in such a case?' Gil asked, half serious. She looked up at him, shook her head, and went on writing. 'We can probably leave Eleanor out of it, in that she lives elsewhere now, but Agnes is fully capable of making and using such a thing.'

'But if it was hers,' said Maistre Pierre, 'she would not have given it to Bothwell, unless she intended the result.'

'I think we must include Eleanor,' said Alys. 'She is probably about the house daily.' She bit the end of her stylus, and studied her list. Gil looked over her shoulder, and said:

'It gets us nowhere, you know. It looks as if everyone in the household would cheerfully dispose of any of the others.'

'We need to find out where in the house Agnes got the flask from,' said Alys. 'It's a pity her father insisted on being present when you spoke to her.'

'I don't know how we do that. Likely she won't confess to you either, now we've had that tale from her. I have no direction yet from the Archbishop, so I can't question her more pressingly,' said Gil. 'And you know, whoever brewed the stuff itself has committed no crime so far, unless it was Agnes after all. There's no law about making up poisons, only about using them on fellow Christians.'

'There is the moral crime,' said Alys. 'The burden of guilt in having provided the means of Danny Gibson's death.' She shook her head wearily, and closed up her tablets. 'It must be wrong to do this. It's one thing to draw up such a list as a – an exercise for the mind, it's another entirely to use it to speculate on which of our neighbours

144

might be planning to poison another. These are Christian souls, and –'

'If it offers a means to prevent a Christian soul from committing murder,' said Catherine unexpectedly, 'your list has done that person a great service, *ma mie*.'

'As always, madame, you are right,' said Maistre Pierre. 'And now, I suppose, having decided that we cannot decide, we had as well go and sleep on it. Will you go to the quest on Danny Gibson, Gilbert?'

'I think I must,' said Gil, watching Alys brace herself. For what? he wondered. For privacy with him? For what he might ask her? 'Sir Thomas may change his mind and decide to call my evidence.'

Crossing the dark drawing-loft, the light from their candle making leaping shadows of wonderful curves and angles from the wooden patterns which hung from the ceiling beams, he reached out to take her hand. She did not withdraw it, but let it lie quietly in his, and when he drew her to a halt she stood beside him, her shoulders tautly braced. The dog sat down and leaned against her knee, looking up at her face.

'What is it, Alys?' he asked her. 'Something is wrong. Can I help? Can I put it right?' She shook her head. 'Is it something I've done?'

'No,' she said. 'No, Gil, it isn't you.'

'Is it something about Christian Bothwell? Or about Agnes?'

'No! No, it's nothing like that.'

'Wouldn't it help to talk about it, then?'

'No.'

'Have you tried prayer?'

'Yes.'

'What about a distraction? Would that help?' He let go of her hand to reach up and caress the line of her jaw within the drape of her black linen hood, and she reared back to snatch at his wrist and freeze, staring at him, her eyes round and dark with distress in the candlelight. Socrates reared up to paw at both of them, whining anxiously.

'Very well,' Gil said gently, his heart knotted in sympathy. 'Not that. Come to bed, sweetheart, and sleep on it. Things may look different in the morning.'

For a moment he thought she would speak; then she turned obediently and moved on through the bounding shadows towards the other door, the dog adhering to her skirts. He followed, riven with anxiety. In the eighteen months since he had first met her he had grown used to her companionship, to her – Yes, he thought, her friendship, she is my good friend as well as my lover and spouse. It put the whole world out of frame if that conjunction did not agree, and he did not know how to put it right.

Chapter Eight

'I thought we would come to visit anyway,' said Alys. 'It's company for everyone.'

'I'm right pleased to see you,' said Kate, looking hard at her face. What did she see? Alys wondered. Was it all there to read in her eyes? 'Babb, will you tell the kitchen?'

They had risen in the morning to the news, brought in by the men who had fetched the water, that the bellman was crying the quest on Danny Gibson put off for two days. Sir Thomas's rheum must be worse, Gil had speculated. So after hearing Mass and praying for her mother and everyone else who should be remembered on All Souls' Day, none of which helped the turmoil in her head, Alys had gathered up John and his nurse and made for Morison's Yard.

'Onnyanny!' announced John behind her from Nancy's arms. 'Onny*anny*!'

'Ysonde and Wynliane,' she corrected. 'Are the girls upstairs?'

Kate laughed, shook her head, and reached for her crutches. 'We're all going out into the garden for some fresh air. Nan took the girls down first, and we were about to follow.'

Alys looked about the hall, and realized that Mysie was wrapped in a huge striped plaid and holding Edward bundled in a sheepskin. Kate herself was also warmly clad.

'Onnyanny!'

'We'll just get you down these steps, my doo,' said Babb, returning from the kitchen door. 'Do you lassies want to take they bairns down the garden first?'

Mysie, taking the hint, set off with Nancy. As they crossed the yard John could be heard remarking, 'Baba. Onnyanny baba.' One arm in its bright red sleeve emerged from Nancy's plaid and gestured at Edward.

Maister Morison's property, like all the other tofts on the east side of the High Street, was much longer than it was wide and sloped down towards the mill-burn, divided from its neighbours by neat whitewashed fences of split palings shoulder-high on either side. Beyond the yard, past the barn and cart-shed which belonged to the business, past the kaleyard where hens pecked about among the autumnal plants and the kale waited for its first frost, they reached the little pleasure-garden. The low box hedges enclosed only well-dug earth at this time of year, the grassy paths bare of daisies or buttercups, but the spot was sheltered and in the thin sunshine warm enough to sit in. By the time Kate and Alys reached it, Wynliane and Ysonde had borne John off to take part in their game, the three nursemaids had tipped all three benches upright and already had their heads together discussing diet and feeding, and Edward was awake and happy to be handed over to receive attention from his mother and godmother.

'Has Gil learned anything more?' Kate asked, unwrapping her son a little. Babb surveyed the garden, checked that her mistress wanted nothing more, and strode off towards the house.

'I don't think so,' said Alys, relieved to be discussing this rather than her own affairs. 'He spoke with your neighbour's eldest son,' she pointed unobtrusively towards the Renfrew house, and Kate nodded approval of the ellipsis, 'who thought the poison might have been meant for his father, and that any of the household might be responsible.'

'No help,' said Kate, and made kissing noises at Edward. 'None of them had the chance to put it in place,

I'd have thought.' She grimaced, then smiled reassuringly at the baby. 'I'd like to get it cleared up, it's worrying Augie. He's hardly slept, these two nights.'

And nor did I last night, thought Alys, too busy thinking about – No, put it out of your mind, don't – The images came hurtling back to confront her, and she drew a shivering breath. Meg struggling with her mother and the two midwives, the dirt and smells and indignity, the screaming and pain –

A sermon she had once read listed the five dangers to the soul newly freed from the body, *Demons, punishment, the remnants of sin, doubt of the way and shrieking.* She felt she understood the last one now.

'I spoke to my lassies again, did Gil say?' Kate said, holding her son upright. Inside the swaddling bands and the multiple woollen wrappings his legs kicked against her knees. 'No, it's since I saw him. Stand up, wee mannie, stand up. *What* a clever boy! They had another thing to say about – about the lass next door.'

Alys made an enquiring noise, not trusting her voice.

'They both said, when she crossed the kitchen,' Kate recalled, 'and went on to the stair, she was just behind Andrew Hamilton.'

'Andrew – the wright? Or his son?'said Alys, startled.

'Oh, the boy, I'd think,' said Kate, eyes dancing. 'I doubt my lassies noticed the carpenter, he's away too old for them. Young Andrew's a likely laddie, he'll disturb a few folk's dreams when he gets his growth, and these two are no so much older than he is.'

'What was he doing in the kitchen?' Alys wondered.

'Likely went out to the privy. He'd come back in by the kitchen to see about Ursel's gingerbread, I've no doubt. Which reminds me, Ursel said there was marchpane fancies, tell Gil, but the laddie who died would have none of them. Quite sharp in refusing, he was.'

'And yet he smelled of almonds when he was stricken down,' said Alys. 'That must be the poison right enough.

Gil has learned that it might have been made from nuts, almonds I suppose. I never heard of such a thing.'

'Nor did I.' Kate bounced her son, who blew bubbles at her. 'A bababa! A bababa, then!'

'Did your lassies notice whether Nanty Bothwell followed Agnes?'

'Isa didn't notice. Mina said he did, but that it was a good bit after. I think since Bowster found the two of them talking it can't have been that long. Long enough no to be obvious, I suppose.'

'And Andrew Hamilton was ahead of them on the stair,' said Alys thoughtfully. 'So did he hear what she said to Bothwell?'

'We could ask him,' said Kate. 'It might help Gil.'

They looked at one another.

'Will you call at the house,' Kate went on, 'or will I send John to get him round here just now? He's more like to tell us what he heard if his mother isn't listening.'

'His mother was at the gossip-ale last night, and past hearing anything much when I saw her. I'd think she had a sore head today.'

'Yes, Babb told me she snored all afternoon at mine. Right, then. If you step up into the yard you'll likely find John Paterson.'

The steward's nephew was very willing to leave his task and go to look for Andrew Hamilton, but warned Alys shyly it might take some time to find him.

'See, mem, I've no notion where they're working the now,' he admitted. 'I'd heard they'd finished one task, but there's two more places I could look.'

'Then go and look, if you will,' said Alys, and returned to report this to Kate, who was unfastening her gown preparatory to feeding Edward.

'It's worth the try,' Kate said, applying her son to her breast. 'There's a clever boy!' She looked up, and studied Alys's face again. 'Had Meg a bad time of it?' she asked. 'The word that reached me wasny good.'

'She did.' Suddenly Alys was back in that space between

the bed and the window, Meg's screams echoing in her ears while the other women knelt doing dreadful things –

'Alys.' Kate's hand reached across the guzzling baby to clamp down on hers. 'Alys, how much did you see?' She hesitated, unwilling to put it into words. 'Screaming and pain and blood?' She nodded in relief. 'Look. Never let it worry you. It's not that bad. You forget, Alys.'

'How?' she burst out. 'How can you forget that?'

'When you've a new baby,' Kate declared, 'you'll forget your own name. I think nursing rots the brain,' she added, looking down at Edward. 'No, the recollection of the crying-time vanishes away immediately. Ask Meg about hers and see what she says. Mother and Margaret both promised me, it would be bad at the time but you forget afterwards, because the bairn's such a delight, and do you know, they were right.' She smiled anxiously into Alys's face, and shook the hand she held gently. 'Never fear, lassie. My mother's right about most things.'

'That's true,' said Alys, mustering a shaky smile.

'Put it out of your mind just now. You're not . . .?'

She shook her head, trying to control the turmoil of feelings in her body.

'Believe it, Kate, you'll be first to hear after Gil and my father,' she said, 'if I ever –'

'Baby Floris is getting fed,' announced Ysonde, materializing beside them. 'Wynliane, Baby Floris is –'

'No need to tell all the neighbours,' said Kate, laughing, as Wynliane hurried to join her sister. The two girls hung cooing over the baby, who rolled his eyes at them and redoubled his efforts, possibly in case of interruption. Alys looked about her.

'Where is John?' she asked.

'In bed,' said Ysonde. 'It was his bedtime.' She pointed at the further box hedges. 'We made him a wee bed down there in among the hedge.'

'Is he there now?' Alys rose and went to look. There was no sign of the little boy. 'Ysonde, he isn't here. Where can he be?'

'He must have runned away,' said Ysonde. 'He's a naughty boy.'

'I don't see him.' Alys stared about the garden, but saw no sign of a bright red tunic.

'Ysonde, go and help Mistress Alys find John,' prompted Kate. 'Both of you. Nancy,' she called, 'where did John go?'

The cluster of women broke open, and three faces turned towards them. Nan, the older woman, was the first to realize what was being said, and got quickly to her feet.

'Can he get through the fence?' she asked. 'A limber wee laddie like that, he'd get in anywhere.' She turned toward the nearest of the neat fences which lined the long boundary.

'The mill-burn!' exclaimed Alys, her heart leaping into her throat. 'Could he –?'

Edward screamed indignantly as Kate sat up straighter. She hastily shifted her hold on him, and he fell silent and resumed his meal.

'Alys, go out and look on the path,' she recommended. 'It's so muddy down there you'll see his wee footprints easily if he's got out. Nancy, Mysie, go and look in the kaleyard and then up in the yard, ask the men if they've seen him.'

'Would he go so far?' Alys asked, hurrying down to the gate. 'When did we – when did you see him, Ysonde?'

'Last night,' said Ysonde. 'It was his bedtime, I telled you.'

'No, my lassie, not in your game,' said Kate. 'John might have run somewhere he shouldn't be and we need to find him. How long ago was he here?'

'Just a wee bit ago,' offered Wynliane. 'He was being our wee boy.' She looked about. 'Could he be hiding under the hedges?'

'Maybe you should look,' suggested Kate, and the two girls began to scurry round, bending to look under the little box hedges and calling 'John, John!'

'There's no gaps in this bit fence,' said Nan to Alys as she struggled with the gate. 'I'd say he's no out there, mistress, but you have to check.' She hurried past, scanning the close-set palings. Alys stepped out on to the path which ran along the bank of the mill-burn, past the ends of the long narrow properties whose frontage was on the High Street. No small red-tunicked person was visible, no prints of the little leather shoes of which John was so proud showed up in the muddy, much-trodden surface. She looked up and down, saw a pair of workmen approaching, a woman with a basket of washing coming the other way. No sign of John, and surely if they had seen him they would wave, or shout, or –

'Mistress!' It was Nan's voice, urgent. 'He's next door. In the physic garden.'

She turned and ran to the foot of the Renfrews' garden. There was a gate, much like the Morisons' gate, but little used. She wrestled with its latch, struggled to drag it through the mud, squeezed through into the garden, past a barrel standing just inside the fence.

'John?' she called. 'Where's John? Come to Mammy Alys!'

No answer.

'He's yonder, mem, I can see him,' said Nan, her head just visible. She put an arm over the fence to point up the slope. 'Yonder, beyond the peas or whatever that is.'

The red tunic was visible, through the dried stems on the trellis. Not peas, surely, something more medicinal. She hurried up the path, past the midden. The Renfrews had been poisoning rats, there was a little heap of the creatures with a dead crow next them. Briefly aware of relief that John had not found that, she went on. In Kate's garden there were voices, which must be Mysie and Nancy returning.

'The men haveny seen him, my leddy.'

'We've found him. He's next door in the physic garden.'

'Our Lady save us, what will he be at? There's all sorts there he could put in his mouth!'

'What's he eating?'

153

She rounded the trellis, and the same question hit her like a flung stone. John sat on the ground, beaming up at her, his mouth smeared with fragments of something, brighter red than his little woollen tunic. He held out his hand, showing more crushed berries.

'Morple,' he said happily.

She knelt beside him in the earth, alarm surging up through her body, tightening her chest. With shaking hands she persuaded his mouth open, raking inside with an experienced finger, extracting broken fragments of fruit. He objected, rearing backwards, pushing at her hand, but did not bite.

'What is John eating?' she asked him. 'That's not good, John. Bad berries.'

'Goo' bez,' he contradicted, opening and closing his fat little hand on the pulpy mass. She scraped them off his palm, and scooped him up, looking round.

'Where did you get the berries, John? Show me.' Her heart was hammering as if it would leap out of her mouth. What the fruit was poisonous? What if he– how could she face her father? How could she face the harper, the boy's father?

'Morple,' he said again.

There was nothing with berries on it where he pointed. She set him on the ground again, saying, 'Show me, John. Where were the berries?'

He looked round him, up at her, and round the garden again. More voices over the fence, men's voices. *Have you got him? Aye, there he's over the fence in the physic garden. Christ aid, what's he found there?* She ignored them, intent on the child.

After a moment John trotted off towards a shaded corner by a laurel bush. Not the laurel, she thought, please blessed Mary I beg of you, not the laurel!

They'll eat anything at that age, said the voices over the fence. *My cousin lost one afore he was two, from eating unripe elderberries. What's the bairn got?*

'Bez,' said John happily. He squatted down to gather more, and held up a bright red berry between thumb and forefinger. 'Morple, pease?'

She stared at the patch of ground where he sat. Dark oval leaves flopped this way and that, and above them little stems nodded, each bearing a curve of bright berries. Not the laurel, but nearly as bad. How many had he eaten? How many would it take to –

She found she was running towards the gate, the child in her arms, wiping fragments of berries off her hands on his back and shoulders. He was struggling, and exclaiming, 'No! No! Want bez!' and the gate seemed to be getting no closer, as if she was running on the spot. Her mind was whirling round and round like a squirrel in a cage. What was the treatment? Was there an antidote? How many had he swallowed?

Nan was at her side, offering to take the boy from her. She clutched him closer, despite his indignant cries, and tried to run faster.

'What was it? What had he got at, mem?'

She stared, open-mouthed, over John's dark curls. Her Scots had deserted her.

'*Muguet*,' she said. '*Muguet des bois*. Little white – scented – I don't know –'

They were in Kate's garden, and Mysie was wailing and Nancy was hiccuping in shock. Edward was screaming, the two little girls were sobbing, everyone seemed to be crying except herself and Kate and Nan, but a ring of silent, appalled men stared at the scene. She set John down on the bench, and he pushed away from her, red-faced and cross.

'Want bez,' he reiterated. 'Mine bez. Now!'

'He had eaten berries of *muguet*,' she said to Kate, still unable to find the Scots word. 'I don't know how many but it is poisonous. We should make him vomit, we should –'

'Right,' said Nan practically, seized the boy and pushed a finger down his throat. He screamed angrily at her, but

155

did no more than hiccup and scream again when she withdrew the finger. Her next attempt obtained only furious roaring, which escalated rapidly into a full-blown tantrum.

'He's no having any,' said one of the men. 'I doubt, I doubt –'

'May lilies,' said Kate suddenly over her son's screaming. 'Lily of the vale, Our Lady's Tears.' She was shaking, but gathered her stepdaughters to her. 'Come, come, lassies, no need to cry. You wereny to know he'd run off.' She handed the baby to an awed Wynliane. 'Can you stop Edward, I mean Floris from crying for me? Andy, get the men back to work, there's nothing for them to do here.'

'He'll no throw it up,' said Nan despairingly, looking down at the roaring child in her arms. 'Should we try salt in water, mem?'

'I don't like his colour,' said Alys. 'He's gone very pale if that's a tantrum. And he's slavering.'

'Has he vomited?' A new voice. Alys looked round sharply, and found Grace Gordon at her elbow, her apron full of crockery. She seemed out of breath. 'Has he vomited?' she repeated.

'No, we can't make him –'

Without comment Grace set down the things she carried on the bench beside Kate, poured water and a few drops of something into a small beaker, added a single drop of something else, advanced on the child still roaring in Nan's arms. Mysie had stopped weeping and she and Nancy were clinging together staring. Edward was still crying.

'Had you cleared his mouth?'

'Yes, yes, I –'

'Hold his head, then,' Grace directed. Alys obeyed, and the entire contents of the beaker vanished into the square scarlet mouth. John choked, spluttered, began to cry rather than roar. Grace watched him tensely until he suddenly wailed in distress, dribbled at the mouth again and was

156

very sick. Nan tipped him expertly forward, and Grace inspected the results in the grass.

'Only some fragments,' she said dubiously. 'Is he finished, do you think? He needs to empty his wee wame.'

'No, there's more,' said Nan as the child wailed again.

Grace stepped back, and said to Alys, 'What has he eaten today?'

'Bread, porridge,' said Alys shakily, trying to recall. 'Nancy, what did he eat?'

'Two raisins,' said Nancy. 'An apple. Or was that last night? Oh, mem, I'll never forgive mysel!' Her face crumpled again, and she scrubbed at her eyes with her sleeve.

'Bread and porridge,' repeated Grace, bending to study the second instalment. 'I think that's most of it, then, and the apple, and it looks as if he'd only swallowed one or two fragments of the berries.' She broke off a twig of box from the nearest hedge and poked at the mess on the grass. 'Good.'

John was still crying, though the sobs were slower now.

'He's getting sleepy,' said Nan, wiping the child's mouth. Grace straightened up and came to check his pulse, then tilted up his head and raised one heavy eyelid to study his eye.

'Not bad,' she said. 'The pupil is enlarged but not greatly, the pulse is steady considering how distressed he is. Poisoning progresses rapidly in such a small form, but so does the antidote. I think we've caught it in time.'

'You mean he's safe?' demanded Nancy through her tears. 'Oh, is he safe, mem?'

'He must be watched,' said Grace, 'for the headache, cold sweats, pains in his belly. I'll give you something for him in case that happens. But if he sleeps naturally he should be safe.'

Alys crossed herself, tears starting to her eyes. Nancy dropped to her knees on the cold ground, snatching out her beads. Mysie imitated her, and they set up a murmuring of heartfelt thanksgiving, broken by Nancy's occasional sobs. Nan made her way to a bench and sat down on it, rather heavily, one hand going up to stroke the drowsy child's dark curls.

'What did you give him?' Alys asked anxiously, thinking of a candle to St John. The boy's weight in wax, or even double –

'A little ipecac, to induce vomiting, always the best beginning in a case of poisoning in a child,' said Grace with some hesitation, as if she was translating the comments out of one or more other languages, 'and to control the heartbeat a drop of fever-bark tincture, a valuable specific against the effects of May lily or foxglove.' She felt the child's pulse again. 'I wonder – maybe another drop of that the now, to be certain.'

'Christ and His saints be thanked that you came to our aid,' said Alys fervently.

'Thanks be to Our Lady your woman fetched me.'

'Fetched you?' said Kate. 'I was about to ask what brought you. I've never been so relieved to see anyone, Grace. Who fetched you?'

Grace paused in measuring the water for the dose.

'It was a woman,' she said blankly. 'Did you not send her? I was in my chamber, and she came in and said the boy had eaten berries of May lilies and needed my help. Is she not one of your women?'

'We'd had no time to think of sending for anyone,' said Kate. 'What like woman? You're sure it wasny one of the men?'

'No, it was a woman. Tall, dark hair worn loose, a checked gown,' said Grace. 'I took her for an Erschewoman. She made it plain it was urgent. So I gathered the remedies I needed and ran down the garden and in by the gate there.' She turned to administer her prescription, but at the look which Kate and Alys exchanged she halted. 'What have I said?'

* * *

158

'It sounds like Ealasaidh,' said Kate.

'But how can it have been? She is in Fife, I think, and the last I heard she was well.' Alys shivered, and clasped her hands closer round the beaker of spiced ale, grateful for its warmth. 'To think of what word I might have had to send her –'

Dinner was over, a subdued meal at which Alys had been unable to swallow more than a mouthful. Both Wynliane and Ysonde, standing at the table beside Kate, had had to be coaxed to eat, and Ysonde had suddenly burst out with, 'John might have died! Of poison berries!'

'Yes, but he didn't,' said Kate, 'and we're going to pray for Mistress Gordon all our days, aren't we? She saved him.'

Grace had gone back to the Renfrew house, matter-of-factly brushing off Alys's fervent thanks. On her advice, John had been watched carefully until the meal was ended, but he had slept heavily in a nest of plaids in one of the window bays, and had not woken when Nancy lifted him to carry him home. It seemed to be a natural sleep; his colour was good, his skin dry and neither cold nor hot.

'Don't think of it,' said Kate firmly now. 'John is safe, and home in his own crib, thanks be to God, and we've all learned a valuable lesson. I'll have Andy secure the fence before nightfall, and Nancy and Mysie both will keep a closer eye on the bairns from now on. But I don't mean,' she went on, returning to her point, 'that it was Ealasaidh herself. I think it must have been her fetch. Danger to the boy would be enough to summon someone like her. She's an Erschewoman, after all, as Grace said. They can do strange things.'

Alys eyed her warily. 'Gil has mentioned such things too,' she said. 'I find it – how can a living person be a ghost? And how would such a ghost know that Grace was the one to tell?'

Kate shook her head. 'As well explain one as the other,' she observed. 'Whatever happened, the boy is unharmed, we'll both be grateful to Grace Gordon all our days, and there's no sign of whatever woman it was on the rest of the High Street.'

Questioning the men in the yard and Maister Syme who was in the shop next door had elicited no sighting of a woman such as Grace described. They could not work out how the visitant had reached Grace's chamber without being seen by someone, the more so since the Renfrew house was busy with company as Meg's contemporaries called to congratulate her and admire the baby and the maidservants came and went with refreshments.

In the middle of their enquiry, John Paterson had returned, somewhat chagrined to discover he had missed the excitement, with the news that he had found Andrew Hamilton, working on a roof at the college, but Andrew said he had already spoken to Maister Gil about it and couldny be spared from the task at hand if they were to finish afore dark.

'I wonder what Gil learned from Andrew,' Alys said, trying to distract herself.

'Likely he'll tell you later,' said Kate. 'Is there anyone else he's yet to speak to?'

'He mentioned Nell Wilkie this morning,' Alys recalled. 'And Nell's mother asked me to have a word with her too. She was still weeping, yesterday afternoon. I – I forgot about it,' she finished abruptly, remembering the occasion. Just before she – just before – Think about something else. Someone else's troubles are the best distraction, Mère Isabelle had always said. 'I could do that now, I suppose. She might say more to me than to Gil.'

'Poor girl,' said Kate. 'She seemed very troubled when – when it happened, and I'd not think Nancy Sproull would have much sympathy for that kind of distemper.'

They looked at one another.

'I wonder what she knows?' said Alys.

'Only one way to find out,' said Kate. Her eyes lit up. 'I could do with a diversion, after a morning like that, Alys. May I come too?'

160

'And we can call in at St Mary's,' said Alys, 'and give thanks for John's safety.'

Alys stepped in at the gates of Wilkie's dyeyard along the Gallowgate, Babb on her heels leading Kate's mule. Maister Wilkie and his men were dipping a batch of indigo, two men sweating at the winding-gear to raise the bolt of cloth from the vat and Maister Wilkie himself inspecting it critically as the blue colour developed in the air. The characteristic pungent smell of the dyestuff met them on the chilly breeze.

The dyeyard was set out much like Morison's Yard, with the house to one side, the working space to the other, succeeded by long open sheds where swathes of cloth hung drying under cover, and beyond them the garden where in the summer weld and rocket showed yellow flowers and now the broad leaves of next season's woad spread flat and green. More things laid out invitingly for little boys –

Alys nodded to the dyers, turned towards the house and rattled at the pin by the latch. The maidservant who came to the door looked doubtful when she asked for Nell.

'I don't know about that,' she said. 'The lassie's hardly ceased weeping since they cam home on Hallowe'en. Maybe you'd speak wi the mistress first, only she's no very good the day. Will you come in, my leddy, mem, and I'll fetch her?'

It was hardly surprising if Nancy Sproull was suffering, thought Alys, agreeing to the suggestion. Babb assisted Kate to dismount and handed her the crutches, then strode off to the kitchen, one of the men ran to take the mule, and the servant led them through the house, saying hopefully, 'What was it happened? Is that right that Nanty Bothwell's pysont the whole of the mummers, or is it just Dan Gibson that's deid?'

'It's just the one man that died,' Alys assured her, seeing Kate's grim look. 'Is Mistress Sproull in her own

161

chamber, Sibby? Will we see ourselves there and save your feet?'

'No, no, I'll put you in the hall, for the mistress is in the kitchen, harrying the supper,' said the woman, clearly reluctant to be parted from a source of information. 'And what was it happened, then? Did he fall down dead in a moment, or was his belly afflicted first, or what? They're saying the corp looks quite natural-like, as if he never felt a thing. And the quest on him's put off till Monday, that should be a thing to hear!'

'Very likely,' said Alys, thinking that if this was one of her servants she would keep her home on Monday. 'How is Nell?'

'Still weeping, like I said.' Sibby paused in the act of setting a chair for Kate as her mistress came into the hall. 'Mistress? Here's Lady Kate and Mistress Mason from the High Street.'

'Och, Kate,' said Nancy. 'You shouldny ha bothered. How are you, my lassie? Are you recovered fro the fright yet? Sibby, fetch us a cup of ale, lass.'

'I'll feel the better for knowing who slew the lad,' said Kate briskly. 'And how are you, Nancy? How's Nell?'

'Oh, that lassie,' said Nancy, putting a hand to her head. She drew up another chair and sat down opposite them, a pretty woman not yet forty, still slender, the dark-lashed eyes shadowed today. 'She's in her chamber still, would you credit it, hasny left it since we cam home from your house. If I hadny sic a headache I'd have her out of there, though to be fair she's been busy at her sewing. Aye weeping, picked at her dinner which we put on a tray – she must be right sharp-set by now, the silly lassie. What it's about she'll no say, but it canny be Danny Gibson, her faither would never hear of her looking at a journeyman that young.'

Kate and Alys exchanged a glance, but neither commented.

'Has Agnes Renfrew been by?' Alys asked.

Nancy shook her head, and winced.

162

'I'd not have looked for her, either,' she said sourly. 'It's all one way wi that one. Nell's aye ready at her bidding, but she'll not go out her road to help Nell.'

'It's a strange household,' said Kate speculatively. 'I'm not sure any one of them has any love for another.'

'A true word,' agreed Nancy. 'Agnes isny even that civil to Meg, the bonnie soul. Complaining that day when she fetched her cushion to her, of having to seek it all over the house, when Meg had told her where it was exact. All Sibella Bairdie's fault, it was. If she'd gone her time wi her first bairn, Renfrew would never ha turned against her, and they'd ha reared the family in love and friendship as Holy Kirk teaches us. And here's Dod and me only raised the one, for all our prayers, and Frankie got that daftheid Nicol, and then Eleanor, sour as verjuice, and Robert and Agnes that would neither of them lift a hand to save you if you were drowning.'

'Is Nicol so daft?' Kate wondered. 'He's come home with a bonnie wife. Grace Gordon's a clever woman,' her eyes flicked to Alys for a brief moment, 'and wise with it.'

'I'll grant you that,' agreed Nancy. 'How a fellow like that managed to get himself such a wife I've no notion. Mind you, she lost the bairn.'

'Yes, poor soul,' agreed Kate, 'and no luck with another one yet, she tells me.'

Nancy laughed shortly. 'By what Dod says,' she divulged, 'as soon as Grace is howding, Frankie plans to pack Nicol off overseas again, and keep her here at his side, seeing what a good hand she is with the sweetmeats. That way he can rear the bairn himself.'

'He will send his son away?' Alys asked.

'Oh, aye. He sent the lad to the Low Countries to get him out the way in the first place. I heard he wasny best pleased when he turned up again, and I think they've had one or two shouting matches since then.' She turned as Sibby came in with the jug of ale and a handful of beakers. 'Is that lass of ours in her chamber yet, Sibby?'

'She is,' agreed the woman.

163

'Shall I go to her?' Alys suggested. 'She might talk to me. And would Sibby fetch her something to eat?'

'Aye, and you're a lass wi some sense,' said Nancy, as she had done before. 'See what you can make of her, my dear, for I canny tell what ails her.'

Nell was seated by the window in her chamber, a pile of sewing at her side, her beads in her hand. When the door opened she looked up wearily, obviously expecting her mother or Sibby; at the sight of Alys her expression lightened, and she mustered a smile from somewhere.

'May I come in?' Alys did not wait for the answer, but crossed the room to kiss the other girl in greeting. 'Are you not well? Your mother says you've not eaten today.'

Nell's colour rose. She was fully dressed but dishevelled and uncombed, and she had obviously been weeping.

'I'm well,' she said. 'I just didny – I wasny hungry. Is there – is there any word from the Renfrews' house?'

'Meg is safe delivered, yesterday evening,' Alys said, aware of those images stirring again in her memory. Don't think of it, don't think of it. 'Agnes has a wee sister.'

'My mammy said that.' Nell sounded approving, but there was no smile at the thought. 'How is she the day? And – did you see Agnes?'

'Not to talk to, for she was not at the gossip-ale,' Alys pointed out.

'I suppose.' Nell looked round, rose and fetched a stool for her guest, then flinched, visibly bracing herself as the door was flung open, and the maidservant entered with a platter and a jug.

'I hear it's a lassie at the Renfrew house,' said the woman, setting the platter down on a kist by the door. 'No doubt her man would rather a son. Mind, he's no that well pleased wi the sons he has, so what he'd want wi another is anybody's guess, but some folks is never satisfied wi what they've got. And had she an easy time of it? The mistress never said.'

'No,' said Alys. Don't think of it –

'Small wonder at that,' said Sibby in satisfaction, 'seeing the way she was frighted into it wi Nanty Bothwell murdering a man in front of her.'

'That will do, Sibby,' said Nell sharply. 'Away back to the kitchen and let us talk.'

'Hark at you!' said Sibby, and left the room, closing the door ostentatiously. Nell made a face.

'She's been wi us a long time,' she said, in partial apology. Alys rose and fetched the platter, which held oatcakes smeared with green cheese, and one apple cut in quarters.

'Eat something, Nell,' she coaxed. 'You'll feel more like yourself. What is it troubling you? Will you speak of it?'

'You saw it too,' Nell said. 'You were there on the day. And the wee lassies and all.'

'Gil got the lassies out of the chamber in time,' Alys said. 'I asked my good-sister – they were not troubled. The wee one was cross because she never saw the end of the play. Is it that troubles you?'

'Aye,' said Nell unconvincingly. 'What a thing to happen afore them.'

'Did you know Danny Gibson?'

'No.' The other girl turned her face away. Alys studied her carefully. She was acquainted with her, as she was with most of the women on the High Street, but though they were close in age she did not know her well. She was taller and slimmer than Agnes Renfrew, with oak-brown hair which fell in smooth waves round her shoulders when it was tended. Now it was tangled and untidy and the grey eyes which were Nell's best feature were swollen with weeping. But was it grief, Alys wondered, or something else which made her weep?

'It's a dreadful thing, for a young man to be struck down in the midst of his fellows like that,' she observed, 'but it happens often enough. Folk fall sick, or an injury poisons the blood. Death can strike at any of us, as God wills it.'

'Amen,' agreed Nell in a small voice, and crossed herself.

165

'Is it Maister Bothwell?' Alys asked. 'Held in the Tolbooth by the Serjeant. Is that what troubles you?'

'Would it not trouble anybody,' Nell said, with an assumption of more spirit, 'a bonnie fellow like that to be taken up for murder. Especial when he –'

'When he what?' prompted Alys. Nell shook her head. 'When he never meant to? Is that what you were going to say?'

'Well, a course he never meant to!' said Nell. 'They're – they were good friends, him and Danny Gibson! Poor fellow,' she turned her face away again, 'lying there in the Tolbooth and thinking on his friend's death.'

'Your sympathy does you credit,' said Alys gently. 'Would it help you to pray for him?'

'I've done little else the day,' admitted Nell, 'but pray for him and Agnes and –'

'Why Agnes? You think she needs your prayers? I'd have thought,' she kept her tone light, 'that now she's rid of one sweetheart she can just take the other, and no need to decide between the two of them.'

'It's no that way,' Nell said, and sniffled.

'Which one did she favour?'

'Neither of them!' Nell rubbed at her eyes with her sleeve. 'She just likes having the two of them on a string, when there's folk in Glasgow would be glad to call either of them –'

'Which is it you like?' Alys asked, with a sinking heart.

'I never meant myself!' said Nell quickly.

'That would be a wonder, two well-favoured young men like that. Is it Nanty Bothwell?' After a moment Nell sniffled again, and nodded. 'He'd be a good choice, he's a good worker and has his own business, if only we can get this charge of murder dealt with.'

'He's a bonnie fellow,' Nell repeated, and sighed heavily, 'but he's never looked my way, he can only see Agnes. And how could he – Serjeant Anderson's decided he's guilty, you could see that when he took him away!'

'Serjeant Anderson is not the whole of the law,' said Alys. 'Nell, can you tell me anything about that flask? It seems it was the wrong one, but we can't find out how it came into Nanty Bothwell's hand. Did Agnes fetch it for him?'

'Will he not say?'

'He claims it was one of his own, but all the ones he had are accounted for, and so are the ones Wat Forrest took. It must have come from the Renfrew house, though Maister Renfrew denies it.'

'He would, would Maister Renfrew,' said Nell. 'Agnes aye says her father likes nothing to stir in his house without he knows of it. It's one of her chiefest pleasures to balk him in that.'

'So she fetched Nanty the flask when he asked her to find him one.'

Nell looked at her and nodded. 'But she never knew what was in it,' she said earnestly. 'She said, she thought it was her father's drops, that he takes for his heart. She never thought it was poison. She was as stricken as any of us when Danny fell.'

'Where did she get it from? Was it in her father's workroom?'

'She never said. We never spoke of it, till after – after – and then we hardly had time for more than a couple of words, what wi Meg –'

She turned her face away again, rubbing at her eyes. Alys sat looking at her, considering what to do next.

'I wonder,' she said, half aloud, 'why Agnes has not come forward to show the young man innocent.'

'If she'd spoken in front of the Serjeant,' objected Nell, 'he'd ha taken her off in chains instead of Nanty.' There was a pause, in which she seemed to go back over the conversation. 'You said, *If we can get this charge dealt with.* Does that mean Maister Cunningham's looking into it, the way he did when Maister Morison –'

'Yes,' said Alys.

'Then have you never asked her about it?'

'Gil asked her last night,' said Alys. 'She denied all. Her father was there,' she added.

'She'd never admit it afore him,' said Nell, still thinking. 'Alys, does your man think Na – Maister Bothwell's innocent?'

'He thinks it was an accident,' said Alys carefully, 'and so do I. He gave Danny the poison, we all saw that, but we both think he never knew it was there.'

'And he's never said how he came by the flask,' said Nell. Alys waited, and the other girl smiled crookedly. 'He's protecting her, I suppose. He'll risk hanging, rather than get her into trouble. Well, I'm no such a fool. If we can get Agnes to come forward, Maister Bothwell will be safe, is that right?'

'It depends on the Provost,' Alys pointed out, 'but I think Sir Thomas will see that.'

Almost unconsciously, Nell reached for an oatcake and bit into it.

'D'you think maybe I should call on her?' she said.

Chapter Nine

Gil's reaction to the news of the postponed quest had been mostly relief. He did not feel like dealing with Sir Thomas's irritated questions. He had slept badly, aware of Alys lying rigid beside him, but when he had asked her again, softly, if she wished to talk she had pretended to be asleep. Later he thought she was weeping.

'Sir Thomas's rheum must be worse,' he said as they sat down to their porridge.

'It gives you two extra days to make a case for young Bothwell,' said Maistre Pierre. 'What will you do, do you think?'

'Pray,' said Gil succinctly. 'Call on my uncle, perhaps call on the Renfrew household. What about you?'

'We go to hear Mass at Greyfriars,' said Maistre Pierre.

'So should I,' he said guiltily, recognizing the date. All Souls' Day, the day when one recalled the faithful departed, a day for praying for those one had lost. 'Maybe I should do that before I call on the Renfrews.'

'They likely hear Mass as well,' said Maistre Pierre.

The High Mass at Blackfriars, the university church, was soothingly familiar. The building itself, the processing canons and members of the university, the young voices of the students' choir, the incense rising blue from the swinging censers, were all just as they had been when Gil was a student there himself. He found a pillar to lean against and let the chant wash over him, trying to call up the faces of his father and brothers, the sister who had died young, his grandparents, the other people to whom he owed a duty of prayer. The man whose death he had uncovered in Perth last August. Danny Gibson, still waiting for burial. Most of them remained stubbornly invisible, though oddly he had a clear image of Ealasaidh McIan, sister of the harper, aunt to young John. She was in good health the last he had heard of her, only a month or so ago, but now she seemed to be trying to tell him something. *The boy*, she said, over and over. *Look to the boy*. We keep him safe, he answered her, but she did not seem to hear him.

'Gil?'

He opened his eyes. Standing beside him was his friend Nick Kennedy, Junior Regent in the faculty of Arts, expert on the writings of Peter of Spain and author of a book on the subject which, if he ever finished it, would make his name and that of his university known across Europe. There was a wide grin on his dark-browed face. Behind him the service seemed to be over, the Dominicans processing back into the enclosed part of the convent, singing as they went.

'You were well away,' said Nick. 'Come and have some Malvoisie. John Shaw wants the barrel finished, there's a new one due in a day or two and he needs the room.'

'I need to pick up the dog – I left him at the west door.'

The Malvoisie was golden and tempting. Seated in Maister Kennedy's chamber in the shabby university building, Socrates lying on his feet, Gil accepted the glass his friend handed him and said, 'How's Peter of Spain?'

'Stuck fast,' said Nick, grimacing. 'I need a sight of one of Hermannus Petrus' sermons. I've heard William Elphinstone has a copy at Aberdeen, but he's no wrote back to me yet.' He sat down, looking at Gil with some concern. 'And how's yourself? How's Mistress Alys and the wee laddie?'

'The boy's fine. So is Alys.'

Nick's scrutiny intensified.

'Liar,' he said after a moment. 'Have you quarrelled?'

'My business if we have, surely?' said Gil a little stiffly.

'No if your friends are concerned for you both. Is it a quarrel?'

'No.' The dog lifted his head to look at him. Nick waited, and he found himself saying, 'I'm not sure what it is. Something has upset her, but she won't talk to me about it.'

'Does she need to?' Nick wondered, and Gil suddenly recalled that his friend was priested. 'Why should she talk to you about it?'

'Because we usually do,' he said. 'No, Nick, I'm not one of your students, you're not confessing me.'

'I'm not offering to. Was it something you did?'

'No, it wasn't – at least, she says not. Nick, leave it.'

'Do you know what it might be?'

'She was at the Renfrews' house. It seems as if she witnessed the birth. Kate thinks it might be that.'

'Oh. Women's business.' Maister Kennedy subsided, and contemplated his glass of Malvoisie for a short time. 'Did Lady Kate say aught else?'

'She said,' admitted Gil reluctantly, 'that Alys might not let me help. That it might need another woman rather than a man.'

'That's a true word,' said his friend. 'She's a wise woman, your sister. Take her advice, Gil. Leave it to the women and keep your distance. Would you talk to your wife if you'd trouble wi your engyne, after all?' He jerked an expressive thumb. *The blaes, the spaes and the burning pintle*, thought Gil, and found his face burning.

'She'd hardly miss noticing it if I did,' he protested. Socrates looked up again, and beat his tail on the floor.

'Aye, I'm glad to hear it, but would you discuss it?' Maister Kennedy tossed off the remaining wine in his glass and reached for the jug. 'Think on it, Gil. Now tell me what's to do wi this mummer that died on Hallowe'en. What happened? Whose doing was it?'

* * *

Andrew Hamilton the younger was where Maister Kennedy had said he would be, some way up in the roof of the college dining hall, helping his father to assemble a tenon joint the size of his own head. Gil stood watching as the boy steadied the great oak beam, calling directions with aplomb to the two men on the ropes below him, and his father stood by with the maul ready to strike when the joint married.

'North a bit,' said Andrew. 'South a wee bit. An inch lower – *now!*'

The maul struck, the joint slid home.

'Is that her?' said the older Hamilton. He bent to feel at the smoothed surfaces of the timbers, and nodded. 'Aye, she'll do at that. Good work. We'll have the pegs in now, Drew.'

Father and son, working together, pinned the joint with the three great oak pegs, each thicker than a man's thumb, two struck in from one side, one from the other. Socrates flinched at the banging and leaned hard against his master's knee. The two journeymen had glanced at Gil, but they were obviously used to being watched while they worked and paid him no more attention until he went forward to call up into the rafters, 'Maister Hamilton?'

'Aye?' The wright peered down at him. 'Who is it? Oh, it's you, Maister Cunningham. Good day to ye.'

'And to you, sir. Might I have a word wi young Andrew?'

'Wi him?' Hamilton looked round and jerked his head at his son. 'Aye, we're done for the moment here. Away down, Drew, and see what Maister Cunningham wants.'

The boy set down his own maul and obeyed, descending the ladder with what seemed like reluctance. He must think it's about that glass of Dutch spirits, thought Gil with sudden perception.

'Aye, maister?' said Andrew, reaching the ground. Then, possibly hoping to pre-empt a scolding, 'That was a terrible thing to happen at the play. Is Lady Kate recovered from the fright?'

172

'She's well, thank you,' said Gil, looking at the boy. He was just beginning to get his growth, and his feet and hands seemed much too big for him. 'I was going to ask you about the play. I hope maybe you heard something when you were there that might help me.'

'Me?' said Andrew warily. 'What kind of thing?'

'Did you hear Nanty Bothwell talking on the stair to Agnes Renfrew?'

'When would that be?' prevaricated Andrew. 'She never got a word wi him, he was all tied up and sitting wi two fellows guarding him. Agnes never went near him.'

'Not then. Before the play,' said Gil. Andrew looked at him under brows which were beginning to lower like his father's. 'On the kitchen stair.'

'Oh.' The boy looked down, and fidgeted one foot across the scuffed floorboards. 'I don't know about that. Was Agnes on the stair?'

'You know fine she was,' said Gil. 'She came up the stair just behind you, and Nanty Bothwell followed her. So did you hear them?'

'No – no really,' protested Andrew. 'I mean, I wasny listening. I wasny trying to hear.'

'I'm sure you weren't, Andrew. But it's a choice between getting Agnes into trouble with her father, or letting Nanty Bothwell hang. Because he will hang, if we don't find out where that other flask came from. So if you did hear anything at all, quite by accident, we need to know what they said.'

'I don't see that,' said Andrew. 'Besides –' He broke off.

'She gave him the flask, didn't she?' said Gil.

'Well, if you're as sure, why are you asking me?' Gil made no answer. Andrew slid a glance at him, and looked down at his feet again. Socrates stepped forward, his claws tapping on the planks, and Andrew scratched behind the dog's soft ears. 'Maybe she did,' he said after a moment. 'I never saw, for they were further down, round the turn of the stair. I only heard them. I couldny tell what they had.'

'What did you hear?'

173

'Well, he said – Nanty Bothwell said – *Did you get it?* and then he said, *Here, what's this?* As if it was something unexpected, you ken?' Gil nodded. 'And then she said, *He'd locked his workroom, I had to take what I could find.* And then I heard someone else coming up the stair, so I went on up, for I didny want to be found eavesdropping.'

'He'd locked his workroom,' Gil repeated. 'I suppose that means her father.'

Andrew shrugged. 'She never said.'

Outside the college Gil paused to consider matters, reflecting gratefully on the value of scholarly discussion. It was mid-morning, the street still busy with people going out to hear Mass or fetch in the day's marketing. He was guiltily aware that his uncle would take mild offence if he did not report the news of the last two days in person, and aware also of the paperwork still waiting for him at home, which he had not touched for several days, and after weighing up the relative merits of dealing with either of these and tackling an interview with Agnes Renfrew, with or without her father, he decided that nothing untoward would happen if he let Agnes wait.

A further hour's discussion with his uncle, in his chamber in the Consistory Tower, proved very soothing. Much refreshed, he went home for dinner, where he and Catherine dined in splendour at the top of the table, exchanging stately French compliments, and the rest of the household discussed Nanty Bothwell's chances. Over a dish of applemoy Catherine directed the conversation to a point where she could remark, with her usual formality:

'Madame your wife seems discomposed just now.'

'She is,' Gil agreed, and explained briefly, though he suspected she knew the reason.

She nodded, spooning the soft sweet concoction, and finally said, 'One must accept one's lot, however difficult it seems, and conduct oneself in accordance with one's duty, with the help of God and Our Lady. I will speak to her.'

'I wouldn't ask her to do anything she found –' Gil began, and checked, groping for a word.

She waited until she saw he would not finish the sentence, and said firmly, 'The duty of a married woman is quite clear, whatever her husband's nature. The fact that he is a considerate man does not free his wife from her obligations.'

Gil, torn between amazement at the implicit compliment, dislike of the word *obligation* in this context and embarrassment at discussing such a subject with Catherine, simply swallowed and gaped at her. She smiled slightly, and put a hand on his sleeve.

'Return to your duties, *maistre*, and let the women deal with women's matters.'

When the dinner was cleared he repaired obediently to his closet. It was a little panelled chamber at the far end of their lodging, beyond the bedchamber, a small comfortable space fitted with a desk and shelves, with his gowns hung on a row of pegs behind the door and his books arranged where he could reach them easily. The report for Robert Blacader was the most pressing item; he applied himself to that, vaguely aware at one point of a disturbance in the main part of the house, women exclaiming and someone weeping. He paused to listen, decided that if he was needed they would send for him, and addressed himself to the report again. Within another couple of hours it was complete. He made a fair copy, with the usual formal salutations at beginning and end, folded the letter, addressed it, sealed it, and put it on his writing-desk to take up to the Castle later for despatch. After that he tidied up the papers he had used for reference, and looked briefly at the ceiling. The painted vines wriggling along the beams overhead did not offer inspiration, and he had to accept the fact: nothing stood between him and a further interview with Agnes Renfrew.

This turned out to be not quite the case.

In Maister Renfrew's shop there was only young Robert, who looked up when the little bells rang on the door, and looked sourly at Gil.

'Aye, maister?' he said. 'And how can I help you?'

'I don't expect you can,' said Gil, disliking the tone of the question, 'seeing it's your sister I want to speak to. Is she home?'

'Why would she not be?' Robert reached under the counter and produced a marchpane cherry, which he popped into his mouth. 'Still sulking in her chamber.'

'Might I get a word with her, then?'

Robert shrugged, chewing with evident pleasure. 'Hardly for me to say, maister. You'll need to wait for the old man. He's gone to hear Mass at Blackfriars, he'll be a wee while. And Jimmy's taken Eleanor down to St Mary's Kirk, though why you'd take such a sour creature anywhere I don't see.'

'Is none of the other women home?'

'Well, Meg's no likely to be anywhere else, and I've no notion where Grace might be. Pursuing this invisible Erschewoman round Glasgow, maybe.'

What Erschewoman? Gil wondered fleetingly, but his chief reaction was irritation.

'Robert, I need a word with your sister,' he persisted. 'Will you send for her, please?'

'What's it about, anyway? She's in enough trouble wi the men she's spoken to already, what wi one of them slaying the other, I don't know that I want her talking to any more fellows.'

Slightly winded by this impertinence, Gil paused to assemble a reply of any sort, and Robert smiled at him, peered under the counter, and produced another marchpane cherry.

'So you'd best wait and speak to my faither,' he suggested, and bit into the sweetmeat.

The smile vanished. With an expression of horror he spat the morsel into his hand, stared at it, stared at Gil.

'Pyson!' he exclaimed. 'I'm pysont!'

Appalled, Gil sprang to the door that led into the house, flung it open and shouted into the hall beyond it, 'Help here! Help in the shop, and quickly!' He turned back, glancing about the shop for water to rinse out Robert's mouth, and found the young man grinning triumphantly.

'Hunt the gowk!' he said, beginning to laugh, slapping his thigh with his other hand. 'Your face, man! Your face when I said pyson!' He put the broken sweetmeat into his mouth, still laughing, wiped at his eyes, chewed, and assumed the same horrified expression. Gil stood watching impassively as he spat the chewed mess out again, while hurrying feet approached through the house.

'What's amiss?' demanded Grace Gordon, appearing in the doorway, looking from Gil to her brother-in-law. 'Who called for help?'

'I did,' said Gil, 'but it was a false alarm. Robert was playing the fool.'

'No, I'm pysont,' said Robert faintly. He was still standing, looking horrified, staring at the pulped stuff on his palm. The smell of almonds reached Gil. 'I'm pysont, Grace. It was in the cherry.'

'The cherry?' she repeated, looking back and forth between the two men.

'The marchpane cherry he ate a moment since,' said Gil.

'What's ado here? Is this a joke or no, Robert?'

'He claimed he'd been poisoned,' Gil said, 'and then fell about laughing.'

'Robert, you're a fool! It's no a subject for joking on.'

'I'm no joking now,' he said, and sat down shakily on the stool beside him. 'I'm done for, Grace. Who's pysont me, in Christ's name? Call a priest, quickly.'

'Are you serious?' She stared at him.

'Aye, I'm serious. I'm a deid man, Grace, like Danny Gibson, and the same way.'

'I think maybe he is serious,' said Gil, in chill realization.

'But what –?' She stepped round the counter to Robert,

177

touched his face and hands, sniffed at his mouth. 'Oh, Body of Christ, he is serious. How did it happen?'

'It's truth, right enough.' Robert grasped her wrist. 'It was in the cherry, I tellt you. I can taste it, burning my tongue. It's –'

'Rinse it out with this,' said Gil, handing him a beaker of water from the bucket behind the inner door. 'Quickly, now.'

Robert took the beaker, rinsed his mouth and spat, but said, 'Too late, away too late. If it slew Danny with just a drop, that he never swallowed –' He was breathing heavily now, his face reddening. 'Grace, Meg's bairn can have all I have to leave. Will you see to it? And – and my soul to Almighty God, is that what I should say?'

Grace crossed herself, and said, 'We need to get you within, my laddie, maybe to your bed. Maister Cunningham, would you step out and summon a priest to him? Or no – go through the house and shout again, I'll need a hand.'

She looked anxiously down at her brother-in-law, who was wilting visibly, his breathing harsh and rapid. A shudder shook him as they watched. Gil turned to obey, just as the shop door opened with its cheerful jingle of little bells and first Maister Renfrew entered and then James Syme and his wife.

'What are you at now, Robert?' demanded Renfrew, glaring across the counter at his son. 'Get on your feet and serve the – oh, it's you, is it? And Grace, I want you –'

'No the now, sir,' said Grace, on an odd warning note. At the same moment Robert raised his head and said gasping:

'Faither, I'm pysont. I – I canny –'

He slid from the stool, and Grace caught him and lowered him to the floor. Renfrew exclaimed in alarm, Syme hurried past him to help Grace, and Eleanor uttered a short scream.

'Pysont? How – who? Who'd pyson you, Robert?'

'He is took very bad, Frankie,' said Syme, looking up, 'and I fear it's the same as poor Gibson.'

'The same as – What have you done?' demanded Renfrew, seizing the front of Gil's gown. 'What did you give him? Why my laddie?'

Gil stepped back, catching Renfrew's wrist to hold him off, saying stiffly, 'See to your son, maister, he needs your help. I'm away out to call a priest to him.'

'No, you'll stay here where I can –'

'Who'd pyson our Robert?' demanded Eleanor again. She began to giggle wildly. 'It canny be Nanty Bothwell this time, he's still locked away. There's someone going about Glasgow poisoning laddies.'

'Aye, Maister Cunningham, a priest as quick's you like,' said Grace, helping Syme to lift Robert. 'Frankie, if you'll leave that and take his feet, we can get him ben the house to his own bed, or at least more comfortable than this.'

Blackfriars Kirk was closest, and one of the Dominicans easily summoned. Returning on the heels of Father James, Gil found the Renfrew household swirling with fright like a spilled beehive. Several maidservants were weeping in a huddle in the shop, while Renfrew and his partner ran to and fro arguing over treatment, and in a room that looked on the dreary November garden Grace knelt by the stricken Robert, tilting tiny sips of almond milk into his mouth with encouraging words. Eleanor stood beside her with a hand over her mouth, still gulping and giggling in that uncontrolled way, and as Gil followed the priest through from the hall Agnes appeared at a further door, saying:

'Meg wants to know what –' She broke off, and stared. 'What's going on,' she finished, her eyes fixed on her brother. 'Is Robert –'

'Robert's been poisoned,' said Grace, rising to let Father James take her place. 'Eleanor, stop that noise.' She shook the other woman by the shoulders, and when that had no effect dealt her a sharp slap. Eleanor swayed back, gasping, and Agnes clapped her hands and said brightly:

'Robert? So it can't have been Nanty on Hallowe'en, after all!'

'The cataplasm never helped last time,' said Syme, speaking over his shoulder as he returned from the shop. 'Better something cold and moist like this, Frankie, if he'll swallow it.'

'Agnes!' said Eleanor, apparently recovering her wits. 'Robert's like to die! Is that how you hear the news?'

'Serve him right,' said Agnes. She turned away, vanishing into the house, and Father James began the familiar quick murmur of the final questions, the prompts to the dying to confess sins and profess belief. Gil, watching, thought the young man stretched on the bench, his doublet unlaced, his head pillowed on his own short gown, was beyond hearing the priest's voice, but the form of the questions assumed the answers, and absolution would be delivered, which must comfort the family. Eleanor had retired to a stool on the other side of the chamber and was watching, dry-eyed, her face pinched and white. Syme, a beaker in his hand, was looking at his wife, deep compassion in his face; Renfrew appeared from the shop with a heavy step and stood numbly glowering at the scene with an expression of dull rage. Gil suddenly recognized that his own dominant emotion was a matching rage, tempered by guilt; the boy had been murdered before his eyes, like Danny Gibson, and he had been able to do nothing to prevent it.

'What did he take?' Grace asked quietly. 'What was it?'

'As he said,' Gil answered. 'When I came into the shop he was eating a marchpane cherry from under the counter. We spoke, and then he took another one.' He grimaced. 'He bit into it, and pretended it was poisoned, so I called for help, and he laughed and ate the thing. And then he said it really was poisoned.' He considered Robert's scarlet, unconscious face. 'If we'd believed him straight way, would it have made a difference?'

'No,' she said promptly. 'If a few drops on his skin slew the other man, then swallowing it would kill this

180

time, no matter what antidote –' She bit her lip and turned away.

'I wonder why he never noticed it at the first bite,' said Gil thoughtfully.

Father James withdrew his fingers from the pulse in Robert's throat, bent his head, crossed himself, and began the prayers for the dead. Eleanor and her husband both knelt to join in. Maister Renfrew muttered briefly, signed himself, and crossed the room to demand of Grace in a furious undertone, 'Where's that daftheid Nicol?'

'In his bed,' she said, looking directly at him. 'As you should ken, sir. He's hardly moved this day. You'll not blame him for this.'

'Have I said I did?' he said jeeringly. 'And you, Gil Cunningham, wi your daft notions about my family. Did you pyson my laddie to prove your point?'

'If you say that again,' Gil said levelly, 'I'll have you for slander. I watched Robert eat the sweetmeat, I called for help when he said it was poisoned, he admitted he was joking and then found it truly was poisoned. I'll swear that on anything you like to name, and Mistress Grace here will bear me out so far as she heard it.'

'He said, *I'm no joking now*,' she recalled. 'Poor laddie. Frankie, I'm right sorry for this. He was a likely boy, and a – a – He was a likely boy,' she said again.

Renfrew grunted, and said to Gil, 'And what brought you here anyway? I can do without you underfoot now, I'll tell you.'

Gil dragged the reason for his presence with difficulty from the back of his mind, opened his mouth, and closed it again.

'I still need a word with your daughter Agnes,' he said after a moment. 'I've found a bit more evidence, and I need her story about it.'

'Evidence of what?' demanded Renfrew. 'If you're still at this tale of my lassie helping young Bothwell to pyson his rival, you can put it out your head, I'll not hear a word of it.'

181

'I think it was an accident,' said Gil patiently, 'and I want her version of what I've learned. It's more important now than ever –'

'What, d'ye think she's pysont her brother and all?'

'Agnes?' said Grace sharply, and then, 'Maister Cunningham, this is surely no the time for yon kind of questions –'

'No, and it'll never be the time,' said Renfrew, 'and you can just leave my house afore I put you out myself.'

'My son, this is not the way to conduct yourself before the dead,' said Father James, getting to his feet. He was nearly as tall as Gil, with shaggy dark hair which he pushed out of his eyes now to peer round the group. 'What came to the poor boy? He was far gone when I reached him. Are you saying he was poisoned?'

'Aye, pysont,' said Renfrew angrily, and dashed tears from his eyes. 'My bonnie laddie lost to me, and I'm left wi that daftheid above stairs, wi his cantrips and excesses and his names for everything, and if I catch the one that did it –'

'Have you raised the hue and cry?' prompted the Dominican. 'Has the Serjeant been sent for? I know you, maister,' he bowed to Gil, who acknowledged this, 'you're Chancellor Blacader's quaestor, can you set matters in motion?'

'Maister Renfrew won't have it,' said Gil, with faint malice. Across the room a shadow moved, as if someone had passed the doorway.

'I'll go for the Serjeant,' said Syme. He met his partner's eye. 'He must be told, Frankie. Unless it's an accident, it must be murder, and how would strong pyson get into a marchpane cherry by accident?'

'Syme,' said Eleanor through tears, and put her hand out. 'Don't – don't leave me –'

He turned to her, took the hand and patted it reassuringly.

'I'll not be long,' he promised her. 'Stay with our goodsister the now, mistress.'

182

He strode out of the open door. His footsteps did not check; whoever had cast that shadow must have moved on. For a moment everyone in the chamber stood as if turned to stone; then Father James said, 'Not for us to question the ways of Heaven, my son. If this poor boy was poisoned, and deliberately, the miscreant must be found, but your chief duty to your son now is to pray for the remission of his sins, to shorten his time in Purgatory.'

'No, it's to find who sent him there and see them hang for it,' said Renfrew. He jerked his head at his older daughter, who was now sitting weeping quietly. 'I've no doubt she could do wi your comfort the now, though why she's bubbling like that, when she never had a civil word for the laddie when he was alive, is more than I can tell you. As for you,' he said angrily to Gil, 'come and show me these cherries you say slew my boy.'

The three maidservants were still in the shop, staring nervously about them. The oldest bobbed a curtsy as her master entered, saying, 'Is he – is the laddie –?'

'Dead,' said Renfrew curtly, at which they all crossed themselves and one began weeping again. Renfrew snarled and ordered them out, then stopped them to ask whether they had touched anything.

'No likely,' said the third one, sniffing dolefully, 'if something in here slew the poor laddie, that knew what was here, we'd no ken what was pyson and what wasny.'

'Mind your tongue, Jess,' said her master, 'and get back to your duties, the whole parcel of ye. Now, maister, where was these cherries?'

'Cherries?' The weeping girl stopped in the doorway, looking back. 'Was it cherries that slew the poor laddie?'

'So it's claimed,' said Renfrew, peering under the counter. 'Was it these?' He lifted a small box, the kind of woven chip box commonly used to hold sweetmeats. Gil took it from him. It was more than half empty, holding five marchpane cherries and a scattering of the sugar they had been rolled in before they were boxed up.

'They look no different from the usual,' said Renfrew. He looked up. 'Here, Babtie, what are you standing about for? Get to your duties.'

'Was the cherries pysont?' asked Babtie faintly. 'Oh, maister, never say so!'

'Did you eat one?' asked Gil.

'We all did,' she confessed, twisting her hands in her apron. 'We thought no – we thought – cherries is cherries, no like all the other things in the shop –'

'Well, that'll learn you no to steal from your maister,' said Renfrew. 'And Jess saying you'd touched nothing, I canny believe a word you women say.'

'Robert ate one without harm,' Gil said. 'It was the second one which killed him. They may not all be poisoned.'

'But they might be,' said Babtie. 'Oh, maister – oh, what will I do –'

'You'll go and get on wi your duties,' said Renfrew, 'for if the one you stole was pysont you'd be on the floor by now. Get away with you, lassie! What a tirravee about nothing, and my laddie lying there dead!'

The woman turned away, moving like a sleepwalker, and disappeared into the depths of the house. Renfrew snorted.

'She's frightened,' Gil said.

'She's a fool, and a thief,' said Renfrew.

Gil looked down at the cherries, tightening his mouth on a comment. 'How are these things made?' he asked instead.

'My daughters make them. Dried cherries, I suppose, crystallized, and then stuffed with marchpane.'

'Yes.' Gil tilted the box so that the cherries rolled around. 'Look at this. These four are the same as one another, but this one –' He looked round. 'I'd rather not touch it. Is there a stick, or something?'

'Here.' Renfrew led him into the workroom. Searching briefly in a jar of instruments on the bench by the window, he handed Gil a small pair of tongs and a copper rod.

'What have you spied? They all come out different, you'll realize, for that all cherries is different and takes a different quantity of marchpane to fill them.'

'It isn't that,' said Gil. 'See this.' He turned the sweetmeat, gripped it carefully with the tongs, and pointed. 'The marchpane in the others is smooth, this one looks as if it's been . . .' He paused, searching for a word. 'Reworked,' he finished. 'As if the marchpane has been broken open and mended again. Or perhaps . . .' He paused again, and Renfrew snorted.

'Or there's been mice at it, or a cockatrice has laid an egg in it,' he said sourly.

'Not a cockatrice,' said Gil thoughtfully, 'but – may I have a wee fine knife, maister, and a dish of some sort?'

'What are you after?' demanded Renfrew. 'I've matters to see to, maister. I can't be standing about here watching you learn yoursel potyngary.'

Gil ignored this, accepted the implements the older man handed him, transferred the suspect sweetmeat to the pottery dish, and sliced it carefully in two. The halves fell apart, mirror images, the dark flesh of the cherry cupping the round ball of marchpane with the small, milky, oozing patch at its centre. The apothecary stared grimly at it.

'Not a cockatrice,' said Gil again, 'but a rod like this one, I'd say, used to make a hole in the marchpane, then a drop of the poison placed into the hole and the marchpane mended over the top of it. That would be how Robert could take one bite with no harm,' he realized. 'The poison must have been in the other half of the marchpane. Do you see?'

'Aye,' said Maister Renfrew after a moment. 'I see.' He moved away from Gil and sat down on a stool at the end of the workbench. 'I see plenty,' he said. 'Which of them can it have been? And was it meant for my laddie indeed? He'd a right sweet tooth, a box of those things left open under the bench wouldny be safe from him. No that he'd have taken a fresh box from the stock,' he added defensively. Gil nodded, in complete disbelief of the encomium.

185

'Aye, I'll accept this as evidence, maister. It tells me clear enough, there's someone in my household willing to use pyson on another.' He turned his face away.

'One of your household,' said Gil with considerable sympathy, 'and aimed at your son. Who dislikes him that much?'

'You expect me to answer that?'

'And what was the poison, do you suppose?'Gil persisted. Renfrew shook his head without looking round. 'Maister Syme said it looked to be the same as what killed Danny Gibson. Wat Forrest thinks that might be something made from almonds, but he doesn't know any more than that.'

'Almonds?' The other man visibly pulled himself together, to attend to the conversation. 'And here was Grace giving the laddie almond milk? Well, he'd got his death long before we bore him through to the house. I never heard of a pyson made wi almonds.'

'So everyone says,' Gil commented. He looked at the evidence on the bench, and then at Renfrew's back, still resolutely turned.

'Well, well.' A loud voice, a loud tread. Serjeant Anderson, entering by the house door, stepping into the shop and across to the workroom. 'Aye, Maister Renfrew. I hear there's been a murder. More pyson, is it? And you couldny save your own neither? Well, man, I'm sorry to hear it, sorry for your loss,' he added more civilly. 'And you again, Maister Cunningham. I suppose it's no wonder I'm aye finding you where there's been a murder, but you'd have to admit it doesny look good.'

'Serjeant.' Renfrew got to his feet. He seemed to have aged by twenty years since he had returned from hearing Mass. 'He's ben the house. Come and see him.'

'I'll hear what you've to tell me first,' said the Serjeant, tucking his thumbs into his belt. 'And you, Maister Cunningham. I'm told you were present when the dead man took the pyson.'

186

'We've just now uncovered how it was ministered,' said Renfrew. 'Look here.'

Gil allowed him to expound the poisoning method as if it was his discovery, only relieved that he had accepted the idea. The Serjeant listened, and peered suspiciously at the drop of milky fluid oozing from the centre of the ball of marchpane.

'And it slew him the same way as poor Danny Gibson?' he said. 'Danny never ate any marchpane cherries, did he?'

'No,' said Gil. 'Danny's friends say he couldn't abide nuts, even almonds.'

'Aye,' said the Serjeant. 'So it was maybe the same pyson, but it likely wasny the same person, if the way it was ministered differs like this. Well, we ken that, seeing Nanty Bothwell's still in chains up the Castle, he couldny ha been down here pysoning expensive kickshawses.'

'He could ha made it up earlier,' said Renfrew rather desperately. 'He could ha left them there, and my laddie only now found them. Or his sister – ask at her, Serjeant, whether she slipped in here and put them ready to his hand.'

'Aye, right,' said the Serjeant. 'Now, maister, tell me what transpired when the laddie took the pyson.'

Gil gave him as clear an account as he could of what had passed. The Serjeant listened attentively, inspected the shelf under the counter where the box had been placed, and asked where Gil had been standing when Grace Gordon entered the shop.

'Aye, aye,' he said, scanning the unswept floorboards as if he expected to find footprints on them, 'that's clear enough, maister. And now I'll see the corp, if you please.'

Flinching at the term, Renfrew led him into the house. Gil followed slowly, and was completely unsurprised to encounter Alys in the shadowy hall.

'Gil,' she said, coming to tuck her hand in his. 'How terrible a thing for the family.'

She sounded very weary, but entirely herself. He kissed the high narrow bridge of her nose, feeling that the world had suddenly come straight round him.

'Who have you spoken to?' he asked quietly.

'Agnes. She denies all. Nell Wilkie is with her now, but she may not stay long. I think she is quite dismayed by Agnes's attitude.'

'Do they know what has happened?' He nodded towards the door of the chamber where the Serjeant could be heard questioning Grace.

'Yes,' she said baldly.

'How did she take the news?'

She was silent a moment. 'Agnes seemed pleased that her brother is dead. I was quite shocked. She said *Serve him right*, and would not pray for him, though Nell did. And then I asked her about the flask, and Nell reminded her of what she told her on the day, in Kate's house I mean, about thinking it was her father's drops for his heart. She denied all, laughed in Nell's face, said she must be imagining things. We tried to show her that it would save Bothwell's life if she came forward, but she said, *Why should I get into trouble to save him?* Poor Nell is quite distressed. She favours Bothwell herself.'

'Unpleasant,' said Gil, tightening his clasp on her hand. She returned the grip, and leaned her head against his arm for a moment. 'Alys, I think you might look in at the kitchen.'

'The kitchen? Why?'

Chapter Ten

'I'm staying here no longer than I have to,' declared the woman with the knife. 'I'll be away as soon as my term's up. But I suppose there's our supper to see to, even if they're no wanting to eat in there the night.' She rolled back the striped sleeves of her kirtle and bent to hack savagely at a turnip on the board before her, the little cubes flying from under her blade.

'Indeed,' said Alys, 'Your mistress must eat, for her baby's sake, but the rest of the household is in a great upset.'

'No blame to you for that, either, Elspet,' said Isa from her position by the charcoal range. 'There's none of us happy under this roof, even if we areny pysont.'

'How so?' said Alys innocently. 'It's a wealthy household, I'd have thought you'd be well suited here.'

She was seated by the hearth in the kitchen of the Renfrew house, a commodious limewashed structure across the cobbled yard from the back door, its nearest wall a sensible three paces from the house in case of fire. There was little bacon hung from the rafters so close to pig-killing time, but an array of well-scoured metal pans stood on a rack near the fire and the tin-glazed crocks on the shelf by the range glowed yellow in the shadows. She had been welcomed in and offered refreshment, plied with anxious questions, allowed to explain how Robert had died and that nobody else was in danger. She was guiltily aware that she was in another woman's kitchen, gossiping with her servants, but the chance to ask questions was too valuable to pass up.

The two much younger girls in the corner, still pallid and tearstained despite her reassurances, shook their heads now at her comment and Elspet said, 'Oh, there's aye enough to eat, the mistress is well taught, for all she's young, and runs a good house. But the maister's an ill-tempered man and the young ones are no better, aye quarrelling and disputing, carping and criticizing. It's no a happy house.'

'Do they not agree well?' Alys said. She bent to put her ale-cup on the flagstones beside her stool. 'Brothers and sisters often argue, I believe,' she added. 'I have none.'

'There's squabbles,' said Elspet, attacking another turnip, 'and there's the kind of thing we get in this house, and they're no the same thing. And there's what you heard, Isa, and all.'

'There is,' agreed Isa. She turned from the pot she was stirring and gestured with a dripping spoon. 'Wi these ears I heard her. *I'll pay you for that, Robert*, she says, *if it's the last thing I do*. What way's that for a decent lassie to talk to her brother?'

'And she did,' said Elspet. She scraped the heap of yellow cubes into a bowl beside her and reached across the table for a bunch of carrots. 'Pay him, I mean. Or someone did.'

'Surely no!' protested one of the two in the corner. Her name was Babtie, Alys thought.

'Oh, aye,' said the other one darkly. 'I'd put nothing past her.' She bared her arm above the elbow, to show an array of many-coloured bruises. 'See these? That's from I lost a bunch of ribbons off her blue gown, that one's from when I washed her hair last and got soap in her eye –'

'There was the time Robert stole her billy-doo,' said Elspet. 'God send him rest,' she added perfunctorily. 'Aye, a billy-doo. From young Walkinshaw, it was.' Alys, who had been pursued by Robert Walkinshaw before she met Gil, pulled a face. 'Read it out afore the family at dinner, though she tried to stop him, and laughed when she swore she'd be even. And do you ken what she did, mem?' Alys

190

shook her head. 'She cut the codpiece out of all his hose, every pair he had, and threw them in the pigsty. He'd to wear his faither's for a week, and the maister doesny favour joined hose, being the age he is. You should ha heard what young Robert had to say about that.'

'Aye, but,' said Babtie. 'That's different. Putting pyson for someone, for your own brother, that's no – that's no . . .' She paused, unable to find a word.

'It cannot have been Agnes, surely,' said Alys. 'Could she do such a thing? Put poison in the sweetmeat so it would not be noticed?'

'It's Agnes and Eleanor makes those cherries,' said Isa. 'Eleanor's hardly been round the house the last couple of days, except she's been talking wi the mistress, so it won't have been her. It would take our fine lassie no time at all to pyson one or two out of a box and put it where she'd know he'd get them.'

'And where anyone else would –' put in Babtie, shivering.

'Like we did,' agreed Isa grimly. 'I'm away at the term too, Babtie, I'm no staying in a place where pysons is left lying about for anyone to lift by accident.'

'But I believe her father keeps his workroom locked when he isn't there,' said Alys. 'She would hardly work at such a thing under his eye. And how would she come by the poison?'

'Made it up hersel, most like,' said Elspet. 'I'd put noth-ing past that one.'

Not if it must be distilled, thought Alys, that would cer-tainly have been noticed.

'She found some somewhere in the house on Hallowe'en,' she observed, 'for she fetched it next door to Nanty Bothwell. Did any of you see her that day?'

Heads were shaken, regretfully.

'We were all in here,' said Isa, 'seeing they was all out, the mistress had said we could have a wee bit extra to wir dinner, and take the rest of the day. Then they come back early, and her groaning,' she added darkly.

Don't think about it –

'She'd likely have it hid in her chamber,' said the bruised girl. 'She works in there often enough, likely she brewed it there and all. She'll carry all she wants up there, and scold at me for disturbing her when I go in for something out my own scrip under the bed, and then there's another tray of kickshawses drying by the window, and I've to sleep in there wi the smell of them driving me wild.' She sniffled again, and rolled down her sleeve.

Isa gave her a hard look, and said, 'If you're feeling more like the thing, Jess, you can fetch me in a pail of water.'

'But surely, she can't have been working like that lately?' Alys wondered.

'Oh, aye,' said Jess. 'Just yesterday, she was.' She got reluctantly to her feet. 'After her wee sister was born, when I went to call her to see the bairn washed and wrapped, did I no get my head in my hands, only for opening the door. That's likely when she was preparing what slew her brother.'

'Never say it!' said Isa, crossing herself. 'And sitting in at the supper-table last night, making up to her daddy like a good daughter.'

That cannot be right, thought Alys. The timing is wrong, and she would hardly work a distillation in her own chamber.

'But is that how they are all the time?' she asked. 'Such vindictiveness and ill feeling.'

'Aye,' said Babtie baldly.

Jess paused on her way across the kitchen and said, 'It's those two's aye been the worst. Eleanor's no as bad, and that Nicol,' she giggled suddenly, 'he's aye a laugh, he's no got the same temper as the rest.'

'Och, you're sweet on him,' said Babtie.

'You never heard him the night they came home, like I did,' said Isa. 'Him and his father, going at it like the Stewarts and the Douglases.'

192

'The very night they came home?' repeated Alys, making round eyes.

'Aye. All seated round the supper-table, wi their baggage still lying in the hall, shouting about whether Nicol had any right to expect a place in the business, what his bairn could inherit – and the mistress half in tears, and Mistress Grace white as new milk, she was that tired wi the journey. And then she miscarried that same night, the poor soul.'

'Oh, how sad,' said Alys. That was what Kate told me, she thought. And how interesting that Grace gets her title when Eleanor does not.

'She's never taken again yet,' said Elspet. 'It's a crying shame, that. She's a good woman.'

'Aye, but what sort a bairn would that Nicol get?' objected Babtie.

'You speak civil of your maister's son,' ordered Elspet.

'But Mistress Grace being as wise hersel,' said Isa, 'you'd think it would even out, surely? And you'd think and all, she'd know of a pill or a 'lixir or the like would help her to what she wants. Or the maister, even, given the way he values her, he ought to know something would help. Aye asking her advice, he is.'

'She is wise indeed,' said Alys.

'She couldny save Robert, just the same, Our Lady succour him,' said Elspet, slicing white discs of carrot. 'She was running up and down from her own chamber, wi almond milk and all what, but it never helped the laddie.'

'She saved our John,' said Alys, and crossed herself quickly at the thought of the morning's disruption. 'She knew exactly what to do for him.'

'Oh, mem, I'd forgot that,' said Isa, 'what wi the rest of the day. How is your wee one? Did you ever find that Erschewoman? I tell you, I was working in the hall at the time, taking the dust off the panelling, to be handy for the door when the mistress's gossips came calling, and the first I knew was Mistress Grace ran down the stair wi her apron full of crocks, and out the back way and down the garden. I never saw any Erschewoman or anyone else come through the hall.'

'No,' said Alys. 'Nor did anyone. It's – it's very strange.'

'Here, Isa, look yonder,' said Elspet, on a warning note, looking out of the window into the yard.

Isa craned to see, and exclaimed in annoyance. 'What's that lassie up to? Is that one of John Anderson's constables she's daffing wi?' She stepped quickly to the door. 'Jess! Come in here now wi that water!'

Alys got to her feet. 'He will wish to speak to you all,' she said. 'I should leave. Thank you for the ale –'

'Speak to us?' said Babtie on a rising squeak. 'What for? We've never done anything!'

The three women still in the kitchen seemed almost to draw together, though they did not move. Jess's wooden soles clopped on the cobbles and she appeared in the doorway, the burly blue-gowned form of one of the constables looming behind her.

'That's her,' she said. 'That's Isa that heard her say it!'

Back in the house, Alys paused in the hall. She could hear the Serjeant in the room where Robert had died, still asking questions; Gil was there too, putting in the occasional word. She curbed her wish to hurry to his side and considered what she might usefully do now. She had no wish to speak to Agnes again, though poor Nell must still be with her since it was beginning to grow dark and there was nobody to walk her home. Perhaps Meg could tell me something useful, she thought reluctantly.

'What's ado?' asked Nicol Renfrew in the doorway from the stair. 'The house is full of constables, all asking questions. Who's that? Oh, it's you. Gil Cunningham's wee wife.' He giggled sleepily, and slouched forward through the shadows. 'How are you the day, mistress?'

'Do you know your brother is dead?' she asked directly.

'Oh, aye, Grace told me. Are they all in there?' He ambled towards the open door. Alys followed him. 'And

194

there's the Serjeant. Are you come to arrest us all, Serjeant?'

Within the room, Serjeant Anderson was interrogating Maister Syme about whether marchpane cherries habitually lay about the shop. Give the man his due, Alys thought, he was asking the right kind of questions, perhaps because whatever conclusion he reached would offend Maister Renfrew, who was standing over the settle, his beads clenched in his hand, his colour ominously high. Gil was over by the wall, listening, though he met her eyes and smiled as she entered, and there was a Dominican priest talking to Eleanor; there was no sign of Grace.

'Where have you been all day?' Maister Renfrew demanded of Nicol. 'Here's Robert dead of pyson and none to lift a hand to prevent it –'

'Pyson?' said Nicol with interest. He looked at his brother's body. 'Better have him out of here, Faither, or he'll set afore he's washed.'

'Is that all you've to say, you daftheid? Where have you been, anyway?'

'I've been a wonderful journey.' Nicol waved a hand in a wide gesture, and Serjeant Anderson swayed back to avoid being slapped. 'Three times round the world, met Agnes in Rome and Grace in Constantinople, and that mad Italian in his strange new world, and then back across the Dow Hill. Is there aught to eat in the house? I'm famished.'

'Can you make marchpane cherries?' asked the Serjeant.

'Me?' Nicol giggled again. 'No, I leave that to my wife. And the putting pyson in them.' The Serjeant looked sharply at him. 'Grace told me,' he added. 'A bad business, Faither, for the both of us, and for you, Jimmy, but we'll no talk of it now wi so many present.'

The Serjeant grunted, and returned his attention to Maister Syme.

'It's a habit of the young man's,' Syme pronounced, with that air of sharing a secret, 'I mean it's aye been a habit, if a box of sweetmeats gets broken, he'd eat the dainties himself, rather than save the box and perhaps put two such together and sell one complete. I've mentioned it a time or two,' he admitted, 'but Robert never desisted.'

'Aye,' said the Serjeant. 'Young men will aye have their cantrips.' Syme's offended expression suggested that he possessed none. 'And who knew of this, maister?'

'All his family,' said Syme steadily, 'but also anyone that came into the shop while Robert was there could observe him, and a few of those might have heard me mention it to him.'

'Aye,' said the Serjeant again. He looked round as his constables entered. 'Well, lads?'

The one who had been in the kitchen nodded significantly. What had he learned? Alys wondered. Their superior acknowledged the nod and went back to Syme.

'And who makes all these kickshawses?' he asked.

'My wife,' said Syme, 'her sister, her good-sister. All three of them's right good at the fancy work –'

'And does each one have her speciality? What do you make best, mistress?'

'I made those marchpane cherries,' admitted Eleanor wearily. 'But I never put aught in them but dried cherries and marchpane. And as for harming my brother, I'd never – I'd never – Oh, he was the dearest wee boy!' she burst out, tears springing to her eyes, and Father James patted her hand. 'I canny believe it!'

'Well, well,' said the Serjeant, with a certain rough sympathy. He turned to his men again, and Syme hurried across the room to his wife. Alys watched, wishing she was closer, as the constables conveyed some information to the Serjeant's ear.

'Right, lads,' said Serjeant Anderson. 'I think that's all we need to know. Away and take her up, and you'll no accept any marchpane cherries off her.'

'Who?'demanded Eleanor as the two constables left the room.

'Take who up?' exclaimed her father at the same time. 'Her? Who – not – not Grace?'

'Your daughter Agnes,' said the Serjeant with satisfaction. 'She was heard to say she'd get back at her brother, and she'd the means and the chance to put the dainties where he'd find them.'

'Agnes?' said Nicol, interested. 'I'd never have thought she'd do that. Senna in his porridge maybe, but no pyson. She must dislike him worse than I thought.'

'Agnes?' said Eleanor at the same moment, but not as if she disbelieved it. She looked up at her husband, and he put a hand on her shoulder.

'No!' said Renfrew. 'No, Serjeant, no my wee lassie! You canny mean it!'

'Oh, I do,' said Serjeant Anderson. 'And I'm wondering if she's responsible for what came to Danny Gibson after all.' He smiled kindly at Gil. 'There you are, Maister Cunningham, two deaths sorted and the miscreant taken up, all in less than half an hour.'

What was that line in the play? Alys thought. *I'll rug you down in inches In less than half an hour.* Gil returned the smile with the politeness which meant he was deeply annoyed.

'Sir Thomas will be impressed,' he said.

'We should have some light in here,' said Syme anxiously. He looked at Alys. 'Could I trouble you to call for candles, mistress? It would –'

She nodded, and stepped out into the hall, closing the door behind her and wondering whether to go out to the kitchen for lights. Overhead, suddenly, there was screaming, exclamations, running feet, loud voices. The two constables seemed to be having some difficulty with their capture. In the same moment she realized that the two younger maidservants were by the door which led out to the kitchen, clinging together and staring at the ceiling.

'No!' shrieked Agnes overhead. 'It was nothing to do wi me! Get your hands off me! My faither will –'

'What in Our Lady's name are you doing?' Grace's voice.

'Ah, you wee bitch! Mind her claws, Willie.'

'Oh, mem!' said Babtie. 'What are they doing? Are they taking her up for it?'

'A course they are!' said Jess scornfully. 'What else d'you think? Even if Isa wouldny tell them what she heard, I let them know it plain enough. Proof positive, that is.'

'We need lights in the chamber yonder,' said Alys. 'Will one of you fetch candles?'

'They're here, mem,' said Babtie. She crossed the chamber to the plate-cupboard and lifted two candles from the box on its lower shelf, a small two-branched pricket-holder from the upper shelf. Fitting them together she struck a light and lit the candles, their small flames blossoming in the suddenly darkened room. As she returned, the thumping and shouting overhead moved on to the stairs, the newel-post rocking in the approaching light. Booted feet appeared round the turn of the stair, stamping uncertainly, and then Agnes's skirts and the rest of her person, writhing as she attempted to free herself from the grip of the two men. They all lurched gasping off the stair on to the flagged floor of the hall.

'It's nothing to do wi me!' Agnes shrieked again. Behind her, Grace descended quietly, dismay in her face, and a frightened Nell Wilkie appeared at her back. 'My faither will stop you!' Agnes persisted. 'Daddy, tell them! Make them let go!'

'Ah, shut your noise,' said one of the men, the one with the scratched face. 'This way, and we'll see what your daddy says.'

'Why have they taken her? Have they proof of any sort?' Grace said quietly.

'Circumstantial only,' said Alys. 'Is Meg –?'

'Her mother's wi her.'

Alys took the candles from Babtie and followed the constables into the chamber, Grace at her shoulder, aware that the two maidservants were following them. Nell hurried after, clearly unwilling to be alone.

It was already a complex and noisy scene. Agnes was appealing again to her father, Eleanor was on her feet sobbing on Syme's shoulder, Nicol was leaning against the wall beside Gil and giggling foolishly, and Maister Renfrew, his face alarmingly dark in the dim light, was arguing with the Serjeant, who alternately answered him and conjured Agnes to admit her guilt. By the settle, in deep bell-like tones, the Dominican priest whose name Alys had not caught was reciting prayers for the dead and intercessions for the bereaved and the guilty, a grace she felt they could have done without at this moment. Babtie slipped in behind her, shrinking against the door where she obviously hoped to be unnoticed, staring round-eyed at Robert's body. Jess followed, gazing triumphantly at the struggling prisoner, and Nell Wilkie peeped timidly round the door.

'It wasny me!' repeated Agnes. 'Where's Grace, she'll tell you, where's –' She twisted round to see who else was in the room, and froze briefly, staring at the group by the door. 'It was you!' she exclaimed in fury.

Next to Alys, Grace jerked as if she had been struck by an arrow. She turned to look at the other woman, and then over her shoulder at the two maidservants, who were staring back at Agnes, open-mouthed.

'Who?' demanded Renfrew. 'What are you saying, Agnes? It was never Grace!'

'It was you!' Agnes said again. 'You, Jess Dickson!' She glared from one to the other of the men that held her, her eyes glittering. 'Take her, no me. It was her poisoned my brother, she did it.'

'No I never!' Jess looked round her, alarmed, and edged towards the door. 'How would I pyson anybody?'

'Aye, hold the lassie!' ordered Renfrew. Alys met Gil's eyes across the chamber. Even in that light, she could tell that he was as startled as she was.

The Serjeant sighed. 'We'll just take them both,' he said resignedly. 'Hold her and all, lads.'

* * *

'But why can they not release my brother?' asked Christian Bothwell heatedly. 'If she's poisoned one man, she's poisoned another, surely?'

'The Provost must decide,' said Gil, with sympathy, 'and he's abed with the rheum. It could still have been a matter of conspiracy between them, you must see that –'

'Never! No my brother!'

'I realize it's not in his nature, but the law takes no account of such things.'

'The law is a fool,' said Mistress Bothwell.

They were standing in the street, where she had caught up with them on their way home after seeing a tearful Nell Wilkie back to the dyeyard. The news of Robert Renfrew's death and his sister's arrest had obviously spread rapidly in the lower town, and she was certain Gil could now secure her brother's release.

'This is not the place to discuss it,' said Alys. 'Will you not come home with us just now? If you could persuade your brother to confess where he came by the flask he used, it would help him. It would help us too.'

'He'll not hear me,' said Mistress Bothwell, wringing a fold of her plaid in her hands. In the torchlight her face was pinched and her eyes huge and dark. 'I got in to see him yesterday, afore they moved him to the Castle, but he'd not admit it was other than one of ours, I asked him where he'd got it and he never answered –'

'He might tell us more when he knows Agnes has been taken up,' Gil observed.

She shook her head. 'No, if he's decided to protect her he'll not change his mind.' She scrubbed at her eyes with the back of her wrist. 'I canny bear it if I'm to see him hang, only for the sake of a vicious wee trollop like Agnes Renfrew.'

'Come back with us,' said Alys again, 'and at least have some company for the evening.'

She shook her head again. 'My thanks, lassie, I'm bidden to the Forrests for my supper. It's right kind of them, considering. And kind of you, too.' She looked up at Gil. 'So you'll not see Nanty released?'

'I've no authority,' he said with reluctance. 'I'd like nothing better, but the Provost makes his own decisions. He'll not rise from his bed to question Agnes, I suspect, and he won't release your brother till he has good reason.'

'Is there more you need to know?' she asked directly. 'Can I find anything for you?'

'I still haven't learned what the poison is or where it came from,' said Gil. 'Anything you can think of that might help me to that would be valuable.'

'Aye, I can see that.' She gathered her plaid round her, preparing to walk on up the High Street. 'I could – I'll think on it more. I suppose Agnes isn't saying anything that will help?'

'She still denied everything, even when they put the chains on her,' said Alys. She turned to put the platter of roast meat on the plate-cupboard where it would not tempt Socrates. Gil watched appreciatively as the high delicate bridge of her nose was outlined for a moment against the candlelight gleaming on the plate. Turning back she looked briefly down the table as she had been doing all evening to make sure John was safe on his nurse's knee, and lifted the serving-spoon before her. 'Catherine, may I help you to the applemoy?'

'It is unbelievable,' said Maistre Pierre.

'On the contrary,' said Gil, 'I find it all too believable, and what Alys learned in the kitchen bears me out.'

'But whether you find it believable, Gilbert,' said Maistre Pierre, 'do you think she did poison her brother? Or was it the maidservant as she claimed?'

'She accused the girl out of spite,' said Alys. 'When she recognized who had set the constables on to her. She is very vindictive.'

'*Never yet I knouste non Louesomer in londe*,' observed Gil, with irony.

'So not the maidservant but the mistress.'

'Her father thinks she did,' said Alys.

'He looked as though he would have a seizure when he saw her manacled,' said Gil. 'I was glad when Grace reminded him to take his drops, though they didn't seem to help much.'

'It seems to me,' said Alys slowly, 'it could have been any of them. Agnes is likely, I admit, but as we found last night, they all have as much reason as she does to poison Robert, they all have the knowledge, and the method was open to any of them. Or to anyone else who recognized the possibility.'

'Except for Nanty Bothwell,' said Gil.

'Unless he had prepared the things earlier and left them in place,' Maistre Pierre said, 'and it only now came to light. But why would he poison Robert Renfrew if he had a notion for Agnes?'

'To gain favour with her?' suggested Gil.

'It might work,' said Alys critically, 'but it would be out of character. None of his friends could believe it of him, that he might poison his rival, and it makes even less sense to poison his sweetheart's brother. It was her father who objected to her choice of sweetheart, not her brother.'

'And at the rate Robert ate the things, if they were left before the play on Thursday I'd have thought he would reach a poisoned one sooner than this. No, I think we can probably discount Bothwell,' Gil agreed. 'Which only leaves us the entire family. And the maidservant.'

'Da Gil!' said a forceful voice at his side. He looked down, to find John, who would usually have been in bed by suppertime, beaming at him under dark curls full of green sauce. Socrates reached an enquiring muzzle and licked the boy's ear.

'What a sight you are,' Gil said, pushing the dog away and lifting John on to his knee. 'He seems well enough now, after his misadventure.'

'I think he's unharmed,' said Alys. 'He slept all afternoon, Nancy told me. Only the adults were afflicted. I thought this morning I would never recover from the fright, and poor Nancy is consumed by guilt.'

'He will be guarded more carefully now,' observed Catherine.

'Poon,' said John, seizing Gil's spoon.

'It seems to me,' continued Catherine, laying her own spoon in her plate, 'that the key to the question is, what is the source of the poison.'

'I think so too, madame,' Gil agreed. 'Whoever poisoned the cherries must at least have had access to the same stuff that killed Danny Gibson, whether or not it was the same person.' He wrestled the spoon back and silenced the shouts of indignation by using it to offer John a mouthful of applemoy.

'But is that sufficient reason to kill her brother?' said Maistre Pierre disapprovingly.

Gil suddenly recalled his sister Dorothea, of all people, a year ago in this hall saying, *You don't need a sensible reason to want to kill a brother, just a strong one.* He repeated the remark, and Alys nodded.

'And Agnes's reasons were strong,' she said. 'But were anyone else's as strong?'

'Poj!' said John, reaching out to Gil's plate. Gil checked the sticky little paws and gave the boy another spoonful.

'It isn't porridge, John,' he said. 'It's applemoy. Nancy,' he called down the table, 'bring me his wee dish.'

'Moy?'

'He never grasps the whole word, does he?' Gil said. 'Thank you, Nancy. You're a good lass.' Nancy gave him a watery smile, bobbed and went back to her own seat. 'We should call you Tuttivillus, wee man.'

'Have you still the list you made, *ma mie*?' Catherine asked Alys. 'You should study it after supper. It might prove of value.'

'It was certainly no accident, by what you say,' said Maistre Pierre. 'The sweetmeats were deliberately poisoned. Could they have been intended for someone else?' He turned his head. 'Is that someone at the door? Who would come calling at this hour?'

'Syme,' guessed Gil, as his father-in-law rose. 'He's the most likely.'

He was right. Admitted in a flurry of apologies for disturbing their supper, James Syme bowed to the company, refused a seat at the table, and begged a word with Gil when he was free.

'I'm about done here,' Gil said, 'if Pierre will excuse me. John, go to Mammy Alys.'

'Take dish,' ordered John, sliding to the floor.

Gil obediently handed him the little painted plate with its mound of applemoy, and he pattered round the table to Alys. Gil rose, wiping food from his person, and Maistre Pierre said, 'Go above to my closet, if you wish.'

Seated in his father-in-law's comfortable panelled closet, with its shelf of books, its jug of Malvoisie left ready, Alys's sewing lying on the windowsill, Gil handed Syme a glass of the golden wine and studied the man.

'A bad business,' he said, with genuine if conventional sympathy.

'Oh!' Syme shook his yellow head. 'My – my wife's at her wits' end, poor lass. She's howding, you ken,' he divulged, with that air of imparting a secret, though the whole of Glasgow could recognize this one, Gil thought. 'It makes her easy upset. But I said I'd come out and ask you –' he paused, biting his lip – 'ask you what you thought in the case. Is my good-sister guilty, do you think, Maister Cunningham, or the girl Jess, or is my wife right that it must ha been some other enemy of the family?'

'What do you think?' Gil returned the question.

Syme threw him a hunted look, but considered his answer with care. 'If Agnes hadny named her, I'd never ha thought of Jess. She's a cheery wee soul, but not clever. I would never ha thought she'd do such a thing on her own. But I can see why John Anderson took Agnes up for it,' he admitted. 'She's the means for it, since she makes many of

204

the dainties we sell, and she'd know how to – to – it was right defty, what you described, the way the stuff had been put in the marchpane and then covered over. I can roll pills wi the best, but I'd not manage that, nor would Nicol I'd say. Agnes is neat-fingered, like Frankie and my wife.'

'Go on,' said Gil.

Syme looked at the candlelight reflected on his glass and said, 'As for why she'd do such a thing, there's never been any love lost between her and her brother. But in that family it means little, maister.' He smiled sourly. 'I don't think they know what the word means. Love, I mean. The tales I could – well, never mind that. The point is, why pick on Agnes when it might as well be any of the family or none?'

'Was her chamber searched?' Gil asked.

'Aye, the Serjeant and I searched it after they'd taken her up. We never found any sign she'd been working wi sweetmeats there, but then she's been trained to clean up after hersel, like any good worker. There was no sign of the poison either, not in Agnes's goods nor in the lassie Jess's scrip.'

'Interesting,' said Gil. 'How did her father take that?'

'I'm not right sure he took it in.'

'Could it have been any of the rest of the family?' Gil asked, without inflection. Syme shook his head. 'Why would anyone want to kill Robert, do you think?'

Syme looked uncomfortable. 'He's never – he's no that easy to get on wi,' he revealed unnecessarily. 'I was Frankie's prentice, and then his journeyman, till he took me into partnership, so I've watched the laddie growing up, and I've wondered, lately, about the future of the business.'

'In what way?' Gil prompted, when he paused.

'Well, it seemed likely Frankie would take the boy into the partnership too, and I'm junior partner, I'd be able to say nothing on that, the way the papers were drawn up. And he's aye been wilful, steering, fond of his own way, and his manner no always what would be best for a man dealing wi folk across a counter.' Syme turned his glass in his hand, then took a sip from it. 'Well enough for me, I could always sell out, assuming I could find the money, and move elsewhere. But Frankie would have to live wi it, and wi the boy's prying and spying. No that I've discussed it wi him, you understand.'

'What about Nicol?' Gil asked. 'And Mistress Grace? How did they get on with him?'

'You've seen them,' said Syme awkwardly. 'Nicol just laughs when his brother digs at him. Robert's aye been civil to Grace, and she to him, I'll say that for him. She's a remarkable woman, is Grace.'

Gil sat for a moment, absorbing this, and then said, 'How long a task would it be, would you think, to –' he hesitated for a word – 'treat two of the marchpane cherries like that?'

'Maybe a quarter hour, once you had all the materials to hand, for someone used to making the things. Not more than half an hour, at any rate.'

'And when were the marchpane cherries put under the counter, do you think? Would it have been easy done?'

'Robert finished a box of apricot lozenges that he said the mice had been at, yesterday after dinnertime,' said Syme reflectively. 'He'd to do without after that, for I was in the shop and watching him. I'd say there was nothing under the counter the rest of the day, nor first thing this morning.' He shut his eyes to recall more clearly. 'Today in the time afore dinner we'd a bit of custom, a few folk calling to talk about the mummer or congratulate Frankie, Agnes and Grace was both through the shop passing the time of day, and Robert was out at the door a lot, crying a barrel of spectacles your good-brother fetched to us last week.' He grimaced. 'I said it was unwise, but he would go ahead, and the chaffing and japing it earned us, well! Then we'd the upset about your wee laddie.' He opened his eyes to look at Gil. 'Was that him up at the table now? He's recovered well, whatever it was he took, Christ and His saints be praised for it.'

'He's well,' agreed Gil, 'and we owe Mistress Grace a debt for life.'

'And we were all in and out,' continued Syme, nodding agreement, 'looking up and down the street for this Erschewoman Grace says called her to help. I suppose in all that time there would have been opportunity for someone to put the box where you found it, but I never saw such a thing when we locked up for dinnertime, and Robert, Our Lady send him grace, was never eating at anything. Which he would have been if it was there.'

'So it probably wasn't there,' agreed Gil. 'And over the dinner-hour? Where was everyone? Where did you eat your own dinner?'

'With the family,' said Syme modestly. 'It shortens the time I'm away from the business, and eases the burden on my wife just now.'

'So was everyone there?'

'Not everyone. Nicol was absent, and Mistress Mathieson herself a course, and I believe her mother ate with her, the two of them off a tray. Robert and myself went through to the dining-chamber when we closed the shop, and Agnes came down from above, and Frankie from somewhere about the house, and Grace, and then Frankie gave thanks for the food and we sat to eat. The family eats separate from the household,' he divulged, with a return to his usual manner, 'Frankie hasn't held by the old ways like your good-father here.'

'Where was Nicol?' Gil asked. 'Was he ill? Mistress Grace said he was abed, but he seemed well enough when he came down.'

Syme hesitated, his expression disapproving.

'You'd best ask Nicol himself about that,' he said at last. 'I'll not – no. It's for him to tell you, if he will.'

Tell me what? Gil wondered. What had Nicol meant with his talk of a journey? Where had he been?

'And was that the order that you gathered?' he said aloud. 'You and Robert, and then Agnes, and Frankie, and Grace?' Syme nodded. 'And your wife?'

'She'd spent the morning by the fire in our own house, stitching at bairn-clouts,' said Syme, his face softening again. 'I think she'd never moved. When I'd eaten my dinner, I went home to take her down to St Mary's Kirk, to hear Mass where her own mother liked to hear it, and she nearly fell when she stood up, her legs were that stiff.'

Gil nodded. The man was a partial witness, of course, but he could check later, perhaps with the servant, and meantime it did seem as if he could leave Eleanor out of the matter. Which left –

'Mistress Mathieson,' he said. 'Your good-mother, I mean. Is she capable of –'

'No,' said Syme firmly. 'Even if she could rise from her bed, which I doubt, she'd a right bad time of it, it seems – even if she rose, as I say, she's neither the skill nor the ability to concoct sic a thing. She might put it in place, but she'd have to get someone else to make it for her.'

'Her mother?' Syme shook his head. 'And nobody suggested the other apothecaries – Wat and Adam, or Mistress Bothwell.' Another shake of the head, an impatient exclamation. 'No, I agree. But that leaves us with,' Gil counted them off on his fingers, 'Agnes, her father and Mistress Grace. If Frankie Renfrew poisoned his son, he put up a very good act this afternoon, and Mistress Grace tried as much as you did to help him.'

'Aye, but she would anyway,' said Syme without thinking. 'I mean,' he elaborated, 'she's a clever woman, if she'd been the one to put the stuff there in secret, she'd see she'd have to dissemble.' He put a hand over his eyes. 'Our Lady save me, what am I saying here?'

'I agree,' said Gil again. 'So unless it was you –' Syme snatched the hand away to stare at him, then realized Gil was not serious – 'we are forced to assume it was Agnes.'

'Aye, I see your reasoning. You make it very clear.' Syme sagged in his chair, and swallowed the remaining wine in his glass. 'It's as much like the way we'd think through a case. Is it this, is it that, using one argument or another to discard till you're left with a single – well.'

'The other thing I'd like to know,' said Gil, 'which might have some bearing on it all, is where the poison came from.'

'Where it came from? Have you never sorted that out yet?' Syme shook his head. 'I suppose it's only been two days. What did Wat and Adam learn?'

'Wat thought it might be made from almonds. He found a scrap of nutmeat at the bottom of the flask.'

'From almonds? I never heard of a poison made from almonds,' said Syme, as everyone else had done. He paused, however, and said after a moment, 'You could ask at Nicol. He knows some surprising things, though whether he'll tell you is another matter.'

'Nicol? Yes, of course, he studied with a Saracen in the Low Countries. I suppose if it exists the Saracens will have heard of it.'

'Oh, you can be sure.' Syme set his glass down, and began to gather himself together. 'I'm right grateful to you, maister. It's no great comfort, I'll admit, but what you say has clarified my mind. Now I have to bring my wife to accept it, if I can.'

'It must be hard for her,' said Gil. 'But I'd not thought she had much affection for her brother, or for her sister.'

'I think that makes it all the harder,' said Syme.

'He's a good man and a wise one, for all his irritating ways,' Gil commented, when he had returned to the hall after seeing Syme out to the street, and recounted the gist of the conversation. 'Eleanor Renfrew has done better than she realizes yet.'

'I think she's beginning to see it,' said Alys.

'Perhaps.' Gil sat down on the settle beside her and sighed. 'This is difficult. I feel I ought to act in the matter

209

of Robert's death, but I've no idea what to do next. I suppose I can hardly call on Nicol at this time.'

'He would have no objection,' surmised Maistre Pierre.

'So it could have been Agnes, with or without Jess,' said Alys, 'but Maister Renfrew or Grace would have had as much chance to place the box of sweetmeats.'

'So would Nicol. I wonder if he really was in his bed all day? But he seems not to want a place in the business, which removes one reason for disposing of his brother, and he seemed to find Robert more amusing than annoying. Hardly worth the risk of poisoning him, at any rate.'

'He might dissemble,' said Maistre Pierre.

'Could he?' said Alys.

'Probably not. And I'd think Eleanor could have done it, but she would have had to pick her moment so as not to be seen.'

'But she would know when the family would be at dinner and the shop would be empty,' Alys pointed out, 'and she could just walk into the house. And we have to consider Syme himself, of course.'

'We do. I think he was telling the truth, but he did dislike Robert.'

'That much?' queried Alys.

Gil sighed again. 'Poison is a hidden crime, I suppose it might go with hidden passions. If we ignore the idea of a stranger for the moment, we have,' he counted, 'seven people, no eight, close enough to Robert and with access to the house and the shop to have put the sweetmeats there for him.'

'But Mistress Baillie or Meg would have to procure the poison from somewhere else,' Alys objected, 'and from someone else.'

'And if they got it in Glasgow,' contributed her father, 'whoever provided it is not saying.'

'So we're left with Renfrew himself, Agnes, Nicol and Grace, Eleanor and Syme. We're going round in circles.'

'Indeed,' said Maistre Pierre gloomily, 'we have one corpse whom nobody disliked, and we find nobody we can plausibly suspect of killing him on purpose, and another who was widely disliked, and far too many people to suspect. If you call on Nicol, I come too, and pay my respects to the dead. And you, *ma fille*?'

'No,' she said reluctantly, 'I have things to do here in the house.'

Chapter Eleven

Nicol, surprisingly, was acting the part of his father's elder son with some aplomb. Robert's body was already washed and shrouded, laid out on a black-draped trestle in the same room where he had died, with a branch of candles either side of his head. When Gil and his father-in-law were shown in, by a sniffling maidservant, an older woman, Nicol welcomed them and handed each a brimming glass.

'To drink to his memory,' he said.

'Usquebae,' said Maistre Pierre, accepting his glass with reluctance, and went forward to commiserate with Maister Renfrew who was standing bleakly at the foot of the bier, surrounded by his friends of the burgh council. Gil stayed beside Nicol.

'I think maybe your father would rather not speak to me just now,' he said.

'More than likely,' agreed Nicol, and paused to greet another guest. 'Christ aid us, we're a bigger draw than the sheep wi two heads at St Mungo's Fair. You're no drinking your aquavit.'

'No.' Gil set the glass down untouched beside the others. 'Nicol, there's a couple things I'd like to ask you.'

'Is there, now?' Nicol looked at him sideways. 'But will I like to answer them, man?'

'You won't know that till I ask you,' Gil pointed out.

'That's a true word,' agreed Nicol, seeming much struck by the argument. 'Well, ask away.' He glanced over at the group by the bier. 'They'll no hear us.'

212

'The poison,' Gil said, keeping his voice low.

'No idea,' said Nicol promptly.

'No idea of what? Of what it is, or where it came from?'

'Neither.' Nicol looked past him as the door opened, and another member of the council entered with his face solemnly arranged. 'Maister Walkinshaw, it's right good of you. Aye, a sad loss to my faither. Hae a glass in the lad's memory, will you? Aye, he's yonder, looking the picture of health, save that he's deid.'

'Syme thought you might know what it was,' Gil said, as Clement Walkinshaw sailed past him, wearing a fortune in black velvet and sipping usquebae.

Nicol gave him a sharp look. 'Did he, now?'

'On account of your studies abroad,' Gil persisted. 'He thought your Saracen master might have met such a thing.'

'Oh,' said Nicol vaguely. He appeared to give it some thought, but shook his head. 'No, I canny mind that he mentioned it to me.'

'If you think of anything,' said Gil, 'I'd be pleased to know of it.'

'You'd be amazed at what I think of, times,' said Nicol with a happy smile. Gil eyed him with a feeling of bafflement. He seemed about to go off into one of his strange moods again, and there was still a question for him.

'Where were you the most of the day?' he asked, in fading hopes of an answer.

Nicol giggled. 'I was away a journey,' he claimed, as he had done earlier. 'Sic dreams as I had. You should try it yourself sometime.'

'Try what?' Was this connected with Syme's cryptic remark?

'Your wee wife kens.' Another giggle, a sly sideways look. 'Though I think it never took her as far,' Nicol added, on consideration.

'Right.' He could ask Alys later, then. 'How is your good-mother? How has she taken this?'

213

'None too well,' Nicol admitted, sobering. 'Poor lass, it's a shock to her, and her new delivered. She'd a liking for Agnes and Robert both, for all the business wi the gloves, being a gentle soul hersel and no too far from them in age. Her mammy tells me she keeps saying how she canny believe it.'

'Could I get a word with her, do you suppose?'

'Wi Meg?' Nicol looked surprised. 'What way would you – aye, very likely. Isa,' he said to the maidservant, as she opened the door to admit another mourner, 'see if my minnie would gie Maister Cunningham a word, will you, lass?'

Gil was aware that it was unusual for a man not related to her to visit a new mother this soon after the birth, but nearly half an hour later, the time it must have taken to spread the embroidered counterpane and pillow-bere, dress the cradle and get the new mother back into her bed attired in the blue satin wrapper with the gold cords, he found himself offering mingled congratulations and con-dolences to Meg and her mother.

'Aye, it's a sair business,' sighed Mistress Baillie, patting her daughter's shoulder. 'It was dreadful to hear the word that Robert was dead, and then when they came up to take Agnes away –'

'Don't, Mammy,' said Meg. She was propped on several pillows, the cover on the topmost embroidered with bees as big as Gil's thumb; in the candlelight she looked weary.

'And to think she might have found the stuff here in the house,' pursued Mistress Baillie. 'I was never skilled in stillroom work, maister, and nor's my lass here, and I was never so glad of it as now. To be connected wi such a –'

'Mammy, please!'

'But I hear you've a daughter,' Gil prompted. This got him identical proud smiles, and Mistress Baillie rose and went to peer into the cradle, shielding the candle with her hand. He followed, and having been well brought up duti-fully admired the crumpled red creature inside, claimed it resembled its grandmother, tucked a silver coin into one of the little hands with its exquisite fingernails, and eventually led the conversation round to the morning's visitors. They were quite happy to list all the gossips who had called to admire wee Marion, and too much of the conversation which had gone on over the cradle; it became obvious that Agnes had not shown her face, though Grace had been there for part of the morning.

'And Mistress Eleanor?' he asked.

'She was here yestreen,' Mistress Baillie assured him. 'As soon as my lass was fit to be seen, Eleanor was here, wasn't she? And right pleased at her wee sister, too. She's in hopes that the two bairns will play thegither when they're older.'

'For all that hers will be wee Marion's niece or nephew,' said Meg, half laughing. 'I was glad to see her, too. And then when she came up to me the day –' Ready tears started to her eyes, and she turned her face away from the light.

'Hard to say which of them was the more grieved,' confided Mistress Baillie to Gil. 'Weeping in each other's arms, they were, I'd to fetch Grace to dose them both. And such news as Grace brought – saying the poor laddie left his goods to wee Marion with his dying breath – I tell you, maister, I wept myself.'

Gil nodded. 'I heard him too,' he said, 'if ever you need a witness.'

'Oh, it'll not come to that,' said Mistress Baillie. 'And you've had a wee sleep since then, haven't you, my lass? So you'll be ready when the bairn wakes for her supper. You've her to think on now, you need to put your own cares aside or you'll turn your milk.'

'And I should go and let you rest,' said Gil, rising. 'I'm right grateful for your time, both of you – all three of you,' he corrected, glancing at the cradle.

Meg laughed again, wiping her tears.

'Maybe next time you see her Marion might have her eyes open,' she offered.

* * *

215

'Interesting,' said Maistre Pierre.

'Very,' said Gil. 'The women of the household have reacted quite differently from the men.'

He held his lantern down to see the roadway, and turned for home. His father-in-law fell into step beside him, his own lantern bobbing at his side.

'The father presents a convincing image of grief,' he observed, 'but I should say his first emotion was anger.'

'With whom?'

The lantern swung wildly as Maistre Pierre spread his hands and shrugged. 'That was not clear. Fortune, Almighty God, the boy himself perhaps.'

'His daughter?' Gil stepped aside to let a group of cheerful journeymen pass.

'Yes, certainly, it seems by the way the man is speaking that he believes both her and the maidservant to be guilty. He did not defend her, you understand, when Maister Wilkie remarked on ingratitude.'

'Poor devil,' said Gil. He turned in at their own pend, but paused, listening, while their shadows jumped on the walls and the roof-beams which supported the floor of Gil's own closet overhead. 'Was that –?'

'Someone called your name.' Maistre Pierre was still out in the street, peering uphill. 'It is two people, I think. Hello? Who calls?'

'Peter.' A man's voice. 'It's me – Adam Forrest.'

'Is Maister Cunningham there?' Mistress Bothwell sounded out of breath. 'I thought I saw him.'

This time she was persuaded into the house, Adam watchful at her side, both trying to explain their errand. Lighting more candles in the hall, Maistre Pierre said soothingly, 'Yes, yes, I can hear something has come to mind, but one of you must tell us, rather than both at once. Will you have some wine? Ale, a drop of aquavit against the cold?'

'We've but now eaten,' said Adam. 'Christian, it's your tale. You make it clear.'

She nodded, and sat down at Gil's gesture, pushing her plaid back from her shoulders.

'It came to me of a sudden,' she said. 'You're still looking to know what the poison was that – that –' She bit her lip, and Gil nodded in sympathy. 'Nanty and I have kin in Edinburgh, maister, a cousin of our faither's that's a potyngar in the Canongate. We don't get on, but kin is kin, and it came to me that Ninian Bothwell might answer your question, seeing we've about exhausted the resource of Glasgow.' She glanced at Adam, and they exchanged rueful smiles.

'The man himself, or another of the craft in Edinburgh,' Adam expanded.

'A good thought,' Gil said. 'Do you have his direction? We could send –'

'I've done better than that.' She unbuttoned the tight old-fashioned cuff of her gown, and drew from her sleeve a folded paper. 'I've writ him a letter, begging his aid for kin's sake and putting a *descriptio* of the substance to him, with Wat and Adam's help. And its effects as well,' she added. 'It's took us the most of the evening.'

'Indeed, a good thought,' said Alys, coming forward from the stairs. Gil looked at her carefully; she seemed to have been crying, but avoided his eye. Instead she embraced Mistress Bothwell and nodded to Adam, saying, 'How will you send it?'

'That's why I was right glad to see you turn in at the door here,' said Mistress Bothwell earnestly. 'We could hire a man to take it, but I wondered if maybe you'd have a likely fellow about you that we could trust better with such an errand.'

'Two days at least, to get to Edinburgh and back this time of year,' said Gil thoughtfully. 'And the wait for a reply.'

'I cannot spare Luke or Thomas so long,' said Maistre Pierre. 'We must get on while the weather holds. Would your uncle lend Tam again?'

'He might, but I think the Provost would send it for us, as an official errand, which would be faster. I can ask him in the morning, first thing.'

Mistress Bothwell sighed in relief. 'I hoped you'd say aye to it.' She held the letter out. 'My thanks on this, maister.'

'If it helps the case,' Gil said, checking that the direction was clear and the seal secure. 'I take it you've got no further in proving the stuff, Adam?'

'We've a list this long of what it isny,' said Adam, grimacing. 'It's held us back in the work of the shop, no that that's a consideration when Nanty's life's at stake, but the two of us has thought of little else for the last few days, and Barbara as well.'

'It was Barbara encouraged me to write the letter,' said Mistress Bothwell. 'She's a good woman.' Beside her, Alys murmured agreement.

'Were you at Frankie's the now?' Adam asked. 'How are they all? We'd heard nothing of their trouble till Christian came up the road at suppertime. Wat and I will have to call in the morning to condole.'

'Frankie is much shaken, as you would expect,' said Maistre Pierre. 'We were just saying as we came home that he seems to believe his daughter guilty.'

'So likely would the half of Glasgow,' said Mistress Bothwell grimly.

'And Nicol?'

Maistre Pierre grimaced. 'I had a word with him, after you left the room,' he said to Gil. 'He was not sober, I should say. I asked him what he would do now, would he take up his brother's place in the business, and he said, on the contrary, he was the more determined to go back to Middelburgh.'

'It might just be his imagining,' Gil said. 'I asked him where he was all day, and he talked about a journey again, though his wife said he was abed.'

'Ah.' Adam Forrest exchanged a glance with Mistress Bothwell. 'He must be still taking the stuff.'

'I'm sorry to hear it,' she said.

'Taking what?' Gil questioned.

Adam looked disapproving. 'Hemp. At least, a dose made from – it's an intoxicant, a relaxant, it calms the system but confuses the mind, it prompts strange dreams.'

'It's right good for a vicious horse,' supplied Mistress Bothwell. 'I suppose the beasts willny be troubled by dreams.'

'My mother's groom puts hemp seeds in horse tonic,' Gil recalled. 'Now I think of it, there were folk that used it when I was in Paris. They would burn it and drink the smoke. One fellow swore it was better than wine for easing the mind of troubles. But I thought the hemp we grow here doesn't have the same properties.'

'No, potyngar's hemp has to be imported,' Adam said. 'It comes from Araby, in the long run. And there's some even stronger stuff, not the leaf but a resin of some sort, I think they call *charas*, we've had the dried leaf in the shop but never that. I've heard it's put up in wee leather bags, and you make a drink of it or burn it.'

'Oh!' said Alys suddenly, and then, 'Could that be what his drops are?'

'Very like,' agreed Adam, sounding struck by the idea.

'He said I should ask you about it,' Gil said to Alys, and she blushed darkly in the candlelight. 'He's by far calmer than when we were boys. Do you remember him at school, Adam? Who could have prescribed it to him, would you think? '

'His father, most likely,' suggested Adam. 'I'd say it might help with his twitching and his odd ways, so if Frankie got his hands on some of the stuff, he might try if it worked.' He pulled a face. 'But it looks to me as if Nicol uses far more than he needs.'

'Always the danger, with such a drug,' observed Mistress Bothwell. She drew her plaid up over her shoulders again. 'I must get home, Adam. There's as much to be done in the morning, and food to take in for my brother and all. Will you get that letter away, do you think, maister?'

'I'll speak to Sir Thomas first thing,' said Gil.

Having seen the callers across the yard, Maistre Pierre extinguished his lantern and began barring the door, saying, 'So have you had a profitable evening, *ma mie*? And how is John? What was this about a strange woman who fetched Mistress Grace?'

'No,' said Alys. 'Catherine wished to talk to me. John is well, and sound asleep in his own cradle, and Nancy is recovering from her fright, poor girl, and will keep a closer eye on him from now on. As for who fetched Grace, I think we may never know. There was no such woman in the house, or on the High Street, today. Kate thinks it was Ealasaidh's fetch.'

'I think it more than likely,' said Gil. 'I have heard of such things. Ealasaidh herself may know nothing of the matter when we speak to her next.'

'Do you tell me?' said Maistre Pierre. 'Extraordinary! But then, she is an extraordinary woman,' he added thoughtfully.

'I don't know,' said Sir Thomas, 'I take my eye off the burgh for a day and what happens? Another pysoning, Frankie Renfrew's lassie in the Tolbooth, John Anderson saying he's done your work for you –'

'Is he now?' said Gil politely, suppressing fury. Sir Thomas blew his nose and dabbed at the organ cautiously with his handkerchief.

'So tell me the tale yoursel, Gilbert, till I understand what's going on.'

Gil summarized the events surrounding Robert Renfrew's death, as carefully as he might. Sir Thomas listened, blowing his nose from time to time and fidgeting with the papers before him. His clerk, Walter, sat at the end of the end of the table, his pen squeaking as he copied something into a great book.

'No that clear,' said Sir Thomas when Gil had finished. He shook his head. 'No that clear. The lassie was heard to say she'd get him for something, and she rejoiced when he was dead. What a way for a Christian lassie to behave! Frankie's a worthy member of the council, but I'd no wed any of his bairns to any I cared for. But that doesny say she gave her brother the pyson. As for taking up the maid-servant, only because the lassie accused her, I'm no convinced. What do you say, Gil?'

'I'd say Agnes was the likeliest, but it's all very circumstantial,' agreed Gil. 'It's the poison still worries me. It seems the girl's chamber was searched, and no sign found either of poison or of her working with the sweetmeats. If it was the same stuff that killed Danny Gibson, which nobody in Glasgow seems to recognize, then where did it come from?'

Sir Thomas dabbed at his scarlet nose.

'Maybe this letter I've sent away for you will get us some result. Or maybe all the potyngars in Glasgow are in it thegither,' he suggested gloomily. 'Did John Anderson question the rest of the household? Did he search the shop and the house, or only the lassie's chamber?' He read the answer in Gil's face, and grunted. 'And how does it connect wi the other death, other than it was the same stuff that slew both?'

'Have you questioned Nanty Bothwell yet?'

'I have not. That's for the day, St Thomas help me. Standing in a cold cell, watching Andro wi the pilliwinks and thinking what to ask next, it's like to bring on a lung-fever. Confound this rheum!'

'I've an idea about that,' Gil offered.

Nanty Bothwell was sitting on the bench in his damp cell, staring blankly at the chain which led from his ankle-iron to a hasp in the wall. He looked up when the captain of the guard unlocked the door, and got to his feet.

'Provost,' he said, with a nervous bob of a bow which made the chain clink. 'Maister Cunningham. What – can you tell me how's my sister?'

'Well enough,' said Gil, 'considering she's worried sick for her brother.'

'Never mind that,' said Sir Thomas, and blew his nose again. 'We've taken up your accomplice now, Nanty Bothwell –'

'Accomplice?' he said sharply. 'What accomplice?'

'– for she's used the the same pyson to slay Robert Renfrew, which is –'

'*What?*'

'Robert was poisoned yesterday,' said Gil, 'by what seems like the same stuff that killed Danny Gibson, hidden in a marchpane cherry.'

'In a marchpane *cherry*?'

'Clearly Agnes Renfrew's work,' said Sir Thomas, 'and the Serjeant very properly –'

'Or the girl Jess Dickson,' Gil put in.

'Jess Dickson? Who's she? It canny be Agnes. How'd you make out it was Agnes?'

'It's certainly someone skilled in potyngary work,' Gil said, 'and Agnes had the chance to do it and to use the same poison as before.'

'But she'd no – she never knew – she'd no idea –' Bothwell bit off his words.

'No idea?' Gil repeated. 'No idea what it was?'

'If she'd no idea, how come she used it on her brother?' demanded the Provost. 'Where did she get it, anyway? Did you supply it to her?'

'No! No, I –'

'Either you gave it to her,' Gil said, 'or she gave it to you. One or the other, Nanty. '

'Maybe we both got it from the same place,' Bothwell offered desperately.

The Provost pounced. 'And where was that, then? The lassie Dickson?'

'I don't know!'

'You don't know? You don't remember how you got something that fatal?' Sir Thomas blew his nose, with some diminution of his authority, and declared, 'If there's someone running about Glasgow purveying pyson that slays a man in minutes, I want to find him and stop him. Or her,' he added scrupulously. 'So out with it, my lad, who gave you that flask and the stuff in it, or did you brew it up and supply it to Agnes Renfrew for the slaying of her brother? Was that your aim all along?'

'I think Agnes brewed it and gave it to him,' said Gil. 'Is that right, Nanty?'

'No! I told you, she'd no idea!'

'The lassie's made a fool of him as well as her brother,' said Sir Thomas.

'No, she – she never –' Bothwell swallowed, looking from one to the other in the grey light. 'It wasny like that. We never –'

'Never what?' prompted Gil.

'We neither of us knew what was in the flask. It was just something she found.'

'Found where? Let's have the story, my lad,' said Sir Thomas. 'And be quick about it, so I can get out of here. It's ower cold for a man wi the rheum.'

Bothwell sighed. 'We'd no conspiracy,' he said, 'I swear it. Only I forgot the flask I should ha carried, wi the stuff that smokes when you draw the stopper, and when I saw Agnes in the yard, on her way back to her own house, I asked her if she'd fetch me one of the wee painted ones from her father's workroom. She brought me that one, but she never said where it was from, only that her father had locked his workroom. We – we thought it was almond milk, it looked – it smelled – when Danny fell down, I'll never forget –' He stared at Gil. 'I'll swear it's the truth on anything you mention, maister. Agnes never knew it was pyson when she gave it to me.'

'Why not tell us this earlier?' Gil asked.

'He's only just now made it up,' said Sir Thomas.

'No, it's the truth,' said Bothwell earnestly. 'I never – I didny want to bring the lassie into trouble.'

'Hah!' said Sir Thomas explosively. 'She's done that for herself, wi none of your help.'

223

'I canny believe it,' said Bothwell. 'Why would she do that? Surely it's been this lassie Jess, or another of the family – or some kind of an accident, maybe? Or that Grace? She's a wise woman.'

'Too wise to go about poisoning her brother-in-law,' Gil said.

'Hah!' said Sir Thomas again. 'I'm away back to my fireside. I'll leave you to it, Gil. Andro! Here and let me out!'

As the key turned in the lock again behind the Provost Gil said, 'Is that the plain tale? And the whole one?'

'Aye.'

Gil waited, unmoving. After a long moment the other man turned his head away.

'I canny believe it,' he said again. 'She's such a bonnie wee thing, wi such taking ways. How would she – and why? What way would she kill her own brother?' Another pause. 'And do you – I canny – do you suppose she kent fine all along what it was? That she kent what she'd got in that flask?'

'I don't know,' said Gil. 'What do you think?'

'I canny believe it of her,' said Bothwell, shaking his head. 'And yet –' He laughed, without humour. 'Chrissie would say she tellt me. We'd words a few times, about my looking towards that family.'

'What did Agnes say when she brought you the flask?' Gil asked.

'I don't recall right.' Bothwell thought for a moment. 'We were on the stair up from the kitchen, and she handed me the thing and said, her father had locked his workroom, she'd to take what she could get. I smelled at it, just at the flask, I never unstopped it, you ken, and I said, *What is it*, and she says, *It looks like almond milk.* Which I thought nothing of at the time, but it came to me sometime yesterday, who keeps almond milk lying about in a wee flask? The kitchen has it in a bowl or a jug, no in a tottie wee flask.' He held up fingers and thumb to show the measure of the object. 'Then I wondered if maybe she'd put it up especial to bring me.'

'If she put it up for you, she knew what it was,' said Gil, 'or else she was very neat about it, for it seems even a drop on her skin would have killed her like Danny Gibson. She didn't say?'

'We'd no more conversation.' Bothwell sighed. 'Tammas Bowster came up the stair and was on to me for upsetting Danny and the company just then, what would it do to the play, and Agnes says, *I've saved your play*, and off she went up the stair to her minnie wi the cushion.' He looked anxiously at Gil in the dim light. 'Has she no tellt you about it?'

'She denied any connection with it,' Gil said. 'She's not been questioned yet since the Serjeant took her up. She might change her tune once Sir Thomas gets to work on her.'

Bothwell winced at the thought, but said helplessly, 'I still canny believe it. It's all tapsalteerie in my head, Maister Cunningham. And Danny's dead, and now young Robert, though there's no many will shed a tear for him. I keep hoping I'll wake up.'

Sir Thomas, huddled over his brazier again, sniffed gloomily and agreed with Gil.

'If he's telling us the truth, which is aye the question,' he qualified, 'then the lassie never knew what she'd gied him on Hallowe'en, that was Thursday. But having seen it was lethal she knew to go back to get some more on Friday to use it on Saturday, so there must ha been more of it. The question is, where? Is it somewhere in the house?'

'It's the place to start, at least,' Gil said. 'Otherwise it's search the whole of Glasgow, wi the entire Gallowgate bringing us flasks of one shape or another for the reward. And what about Agnes and the maidservant? Has either girl anything useful to say?'

'They're both swearing they've nothing to do with it. I've no palate for a long stand down in the questioning-chamber,' said Sir Thomas, sniffing again. 'It's gey cold down there, even wi the fire to heat the pincers, but I'd as soon have the quest on Robert Renfrew the morn as well as Danny Gibson, get them both out the way.'

'It's a bit –' began Gil, but the Provost dabbed his nose and went on, ignoring him:

'Seems to me whichever lassie's guilty, she'll talk faster if we have the evidence to show her, so I'll have you and Andro go and search the Renfrew house yoursels, Gil, and make a thorough job of it. And maybe question the rest of the household while you're about it. If John Anderson can do your work, you can do his,' he added sourly.

'You might as well have gone home for your dinner, for all the good that's done you,' said Grace Gordon with quiet sympathy.

'It had to be done, just the same,' said Gil, setting a stool for her. She sat down and looked up at him, folding her hands in her lap.

'Aye, I see that,' she agreed, 'and though Frankie may not say it I will: it was good of you to make so much effort no to distress Meg. You were doing fine up till the man wanted to see into the cradle.'

Gil grimaced. Young Mistress Mathieson had accepted his careful explanation of the need to search her chamber, and risen from her bed willingly enough, to sit clasping her swaddled infant with her mother on guard at her side. It was only when Andro had begun poking in the embroidered coverings of the cradle that she had grasped the reality of their intent.

'I think what owerset her was that you might suspect her of hiding such a nasty thing among her bairn's bedding,' added Grace. 'Will you not sit down, sir? It's a long way up to see your face, I'll get a kink in my neck.'

'Is she calmer now?' Gil asked. He sat down facing her, and drew his tablets from his sleeve.

'Aye, she was asleep when I looked in on her. Now, what is it you're to ask us all? Am I the first?'

'I've spoken to Maister Renfrew.' Gil paused, assembling his thoughts. 'We've gone through the house,' he said, and she nodded, with a wry smile, 'and found nothing that tells us aught about how Agnes came by the poison, either on Thursday or later. Can you shed any light on the question?'

'What, you think I've been handing poisons out to the half of Glasgow?' She met his eye, an ironic amusement gleaming in her expression. 'I've no notion how Agnes got her hands on the stuff, maister. Do you know what it is yet?'

'I do not. Have you no idea yourself?'

'I've no suggestions to make, maister. It's in none of Frankie's books.'

'Could it be something she brewed herself? Her father says not, but I think he underestimates her.'

'I think he does and all.' She considered the question. 'She could have done, but if she had, you'd not find a trace of her working. Jess might have something to tell you about that, if you're present when the Provost questions her, poor lass.'

Gil nodded, thinking of what Alys had reported yesterday. 'If Agnes did make the stuff up, does she have anywhere particular she might hide it?'

'I'd not know if she did,' Grace pointed out. She pulled the corners of her mouth down in a rueful grimace. 'The likeliest to know where she hid her secrets was her brother Robert, aye spying on her and the rest of the household. Yet another reason for her to have poisoned him, if it was her that did it.'

'No love lost between them, then.'

'Not atween any of them,' she assured him. 'I never knew sic a family. I'll be glad to take Nicol away from them and back to Middelburgh.'

'What, are you leaving Glasgow? Is Nicol not to stay and take a part in the business?' Gil asked innocently, although Maister Renfrew had already expressed himself forcefully on this subject.

Grace shook her head. 'It doesny seem like it. They'll never agree, him and his father, and Frankie has sic an opinion of Nicol I'd not want him to stay in the same house.' She studied Gil carefully with those light grey eyes. 'You were boys wi him, maister, I've no doubt you'll understand me when I say Nicol's no daftheid, he's a clever man and a good one, but he needs to be among folk who think well of him, if he's to do well himself. If he's abused and made a fool of, he gets – he gets foolish.'

Gil thought of Nicol Renfrew as a boy, and nodded.

'He's calmer by far than he was,' he observed. 'Is it something he's taking, or is he just grown out of his trouble?'

She opened her mouth to answer, checked, and finally said, 'Both, maybe. He has drops to take, that our maister in Middelburgh ordered for him, and Frankie makes up now. They help him greatly, but I think when I met him he was already better by far than he'd been, by what Eleanor and Agnes has told me.'

'So he had taken a dose yesterday, had he?'

'Yes,' she said. Another check, and then she continued, 'So he slept the entire day. He was newly wakened when I went up and told him his brother was deid.'

'Could he have poisoned Robert, do you think? Or supplied Agnes with the poison?'

Her eyes sharpened on his. After a moment she said, 'It would be not at all like the man I know. He and Robert got on well enough, at least,' she corrected herself, 'Nicol did no more than laugh at Robert's ways. The craft is for heal-ing, not for harm, maister, and Nicol holds that as strongly as any. As for Agnes asking him for it, she'd as soon ask the man in the moon, I'd have thought.'

'Anyone else in the household?' he asked, without much hope.

She considered the question, but shook her head. 'None is more like than another, and some less.' She smiled wryly. 'The girl Jess, or Meg and her minnie, for instance. Unless you think Meg poisoned the laddie in the expectation he'd leave his goods to wee Marion.' She closed her eyes, and her mouth twisted again. 'Poor laddie, I can hear him saying it yet.'

'Had he much to leave?' Gil asked.

'At that age? They spend it as soon as make it. We'll likely sell his clothes on, and Meg can save the coin for the bairn along wi his prayer-book and his Sunday beads. If it comes to more than a few merks I'll be much surprised. Did you not search his kist?'

'Andro did that. He reports there was no pig of poison hidden among the laddie's clean drawers.' Only some grubby woodcuts, enough to make Andro's eyes pop but nothing to what Gil had encountered in Paris. Those, he suspected, were now in Andro's doublet, and unlikely to reach the Provost's desk.

Grace seemed to relax faintly. He considered her position again, the hands folded on her lap, her shoulders back, her head in its Sunday wrappings of velvet and linen poised on her elegant neck. She had not moved her hands since she sat down. He had thought he saw simply her native stillness and calm, but now it seemed as if she was on the defensive. In defence of what, he wondered, or of whom? Was she relieved to hear there was nothing there, or to hear that Andro had missed something she knew was hidden? Or did she know about the woodcuts? Surely not, he thought, and briefly considered Alys's probable reaction to such things. It was unlikely to be the most predictable one, but – He shook his head, and realized that he was becoming distracted from the point at issue, which was the questioning of Grace Gordon.

'You're tired, man,' she said. 'Have you eaten? Frankie refused to have you at the table, but I bade the kitchen –'

'My thanks for that. They gave us bread and cheese and ale,' he said. 'Mistress Grace, it's gey strange to me that Agnes – or anyone else –' he added scrupulously, 'could have contrived these poisoned sweetmeats without being seen at work.'

She considered this point.

'If it was on Friday,' she said slowly, 'or yesterday morn, the lassie kept her chamber the whole time. I spoke to her through the door a couple of times, but she'd have no company, nor be any help about the house. Whether Jess saw anything, you could ask her, but the thing is Agnes's chamber is the inmost of that set so unless anyone entered to speak wi her she'd have privacy for whatever she wished to do.'

Gil nodded. He had now discovered that Agnes's chamber was reached through Maister Renfrew's own bedchamber, a very proper way to lodge a daughter.

'And you've no idea where the stuff came from,' he said, without much hope.

She shook her head. 'I canny help you there, maister.' She tilted her head, and a corner of her black velvet veil slid back across the shoulder of her gown. In its shadow there was a fresh love-bite, dark against the white skin of her neck. 'Is that it? Are you done wi me?'

'For now.'

She rose, shaking out her grey silk skirts, and paused to ask with concern, 'How's your wee laddie? Did he sleep it off?'

'He's well.' Gil had risen likewise. 'Chattering away and eating his porridge when I saw him. We're grateful to you for ever.' She shook her head, making light of the matter. 'When will you leave?'

'Not for a day or two yet. There's still things to see to wi Frankie.'

'As soon as that?'

'Aye, or sooner,' said Nicol. 'If it was for me to say I'd be down the river on this tide, but Grace wants to take her gear back wi her, and she's still in hopes we can get Frankie to agree . . .' He paused, and giggled. 'You've no need to hear all the business of the family.'

'I need to hear enough of it to determine how Robert died,' Gil said.

Nicol looked at him in faint surprise.

'He died of taking poison in a marchpane cherry,' he said. 'You were there, man, you saw more than I did.'

'I need to find out how the cherry came to be poisoned.'

'Why? It's done, and Agnes taken up for it.' He giggled again. 'She'll not poison anyone else now, that's certain.'

'Are you sure of that?' Gil asked. 'Where did she get the poison?'

Nicol shrugged. 'Out of an apple, for all I ken. Or the Deil himsel popped up in the shop and offered it to her. Maybe Frankie's trying to rid himsel of all my minnie's bairns, and I need to watch mysel.'

Gil stared at him. This was one interpretation he had not thought of. After a moment he set the idea aside to think on later, and said, 'How will you live, if you go back to the Low Countries?'

'Set up as potyngars,' Nicol said promptly. 'It's what we do, both Grace and me, and we know all kind of ways to get supplies you never heard of. I might,' he added, considering the matter, 'come to an agreement wi Wat Forrest to send some of it on. I should think he'd be glad of it. A good source of *materia medica*'s worth a second income, so it is.'

'So your father won't have you back in the business?' Gil said cautiously.

'He'd sooner have wee Marion.' Nicol considered this too. 'Much sooner,' he added, grinning. 'And if you're wondering, he says I'm to have no more share out of it either, I had my portion when I went overseas, and he's had his will drawn up and signed and sealed declaring as much. So I'd be daft even to dream of poisoning Frankie, for all it's a bonnie thought.'

'You're not daft, Nicol,' said Gil firmly. 'So what is it Grace is hoping to persuade your father to?'

Nicol shrugged again. 'She's got the notion he might let us have a bit more coin. I don't see it mysel, unless as a payment to go away and no come back, but you never know.'

'Stranger things have happened,' Gil said, though privately he agreed with Nicol. Maister Renfrew had presented a slightly different view of the situation when he interviewed him earlier.

'That daftheid!' he had said explosively. 'He's after me to let him into the partnership, he's wanting an allowance off the business, he's –' He ended with a snarling sound.

'You won't consider it even now?' Gil had asked. 'I'd have thought you'd want one of your sons in the business.'

'Hah!' said Renfrew. 'And my boy not buried yet!'

Chapter Twelve

Making his way up the High Street in the November dawn with the dog loping at his heels, Gil felt he was no closer to learning what had distressed his wife. Her long talk on All Souls' Day with Catherine, her nurse, governess, duenna, had left her very tearful but still unable to explain why. Anxious questions had got him the assurance that it was nothing he had done or said, nothing he could help with. He would have been more able to believe her if she had not spent the past three nights lying rigid with her back to him, refusing any overtures he made.

'Aye, Gil,' said a voice in his ear. He looked up, startled, to find Nicol Renfrew beside him, Socrates nosing his hand in greeting. That aimless, heavy-eyed grin lit the round face. 'You were thinking, I can see that. Not a good idea, thinking, man. It makes your head ache. If you think too much it rots your brain.'

'Is that so?' Gil fell into step with the other man. 'Where did you learn that?'

'Oh, in the Low Countries. They all say that there. I'll prove it, too,' added Nicol, waving his arm largely and just missing a woman with a bucket of water. She shouted at him, but he appeared not to hear her. 'I'd a dream last night, all because I was thinking too much yesterday.'

'Is that right?' Gil asked, hoping he was not to be regaled with an account of the dream. The hope was false; Nicol launched into a complex, rambling narrative involving his father, someone called Lord Simon who might have been another painted flask, Grace, and an extra hand, though whose that might be was not clear. Gil strode on up the High Street in the grey daylight, nodding at intervals, while Nicol expounded the different forms these elements had taken in the course of the night.

'You're not listening, are you, Gil?' he said suddenly. 'No that I'd blame you,' he added, giggling, 'it's a daft tale and I'm daft to heed it, but it's no good manners no to listen when someone talks to you.'

'That's true,' agreed Gil resignedly, 'and I was listening. Your father had just given you a hand to compound something.'

'Aye, but it was all of wood. And it's no use now, anyway.' Nicol waved happily at the man on duty at the Castle gate as they passed into the courtyard. 'Are you here for these quests, on Danny Gibson and our Robert? Have they set Nanty free yet?'

'No,' said Gil. 'I can't get at the truth. I think your sister Agnes fetched Allan Leaf to Augie's house for him, but she won't admit it, nor anything else, and he claims she never said where she found it.'

'No, she wouldny,' agreed Nicol. 'She might now, if the Provost uses his thumbscrews.' He looked round vaguely, and flourished his arm again. 'See, there's Robert and poor Danny waiting for us, all under a cloth of state and attended by armed men. No, it's no armed men, it's just Tammas Sproull.'

Gil, who had already noticed the corpses, laid out under a striped awning in case of rain and guarded by one of the constables, gave him no answer but went to turn back the linen cloth and look at the young mummer. After four days the body was beginning to smell, but the expression had relaxed and was remote and peaceful, the face pitifully young. Socrates put a paw on the edge of the bier and stood up to sniff with interest.

'Looks like he's asleep, don't he no?' said Tammas gloomily. Gil nodded, muttered a brief prayer, then looked similarly at Robert Renfrew, who really might have been asleep, a surprisingly healthy colour in his face, his expression one of faint surprise. After a moment Gil snapped his fingers to the dog, crossed the courtyard and climbed the steps into the Castle hall. Here, early though it was, a good crowd had gathered for the entertainment.

'There's Wat and Adam,' said Nicol, still behind him and pointing largely, 'and Christian with them, the poor soul. And all the mummers over there, see them, and Andrew Hamilton and Dod Wilkie. And here's Augie just come in the door. We're all gathered for Danny, though there's only me and yoursel for Robert.'

Gil made his way through the gathering towards the Forrest brothers. Nicol gangled after him, grinning at one or two people who spoke to him, but it was not till Morison caught up with them, nodded to Gil, clapped the other man's shoulder and said solemnly, 'Good day to you, Nicol. I'm right sorry about the news, man,' that the tenor of the other remarks reached Gil. He turned to stare.

'Your father?' he said. 'What's happened?'

'He's deid,' said Nicol cheerfully. 'I'm rid of him at last, and none of my doing either. We found him cold in his bed,' he elaborated, and giggled. 'So I had wine instead of ale to my porridge, to toast my fortune.'

'Dead in his – What from?' Gil closed his mouth, swallowed, and said more carefully, 'I'm right sorry to hear that, Nicol. Do you ken what killed him?'

Nicol shrugged. 'Never a notion,' he said offhandedly, 'unless it was my prayers, man, and they never worked before this, so why now? Or maybe it was grief for Robert, since I'd say he was the only one of us that was grieved.'

Gil exchanged glances with Morison, who seemed winded by amazement.

'When was this?' he asked. 'When did you discover him? Should you be here, man? There must be all to see to at home.'

'Och, there's only Christ and His saints ken when it happened,' said Nicol, taking these in order. 'Last night, for certain, he was stiff by the time I saw him. One of the maidservants came to let Grace know it when he never came down at his usual time, and I went to his chamber, and there he was. And some one of us had to come out the now,' he pointed out, 'to see poor Danny done right, and Jimmy's better than me for seeing to what's needed. No to mention Eleanor came to the house and took the hysterics when she heard the news, so Jimmy would stay wi her.'

'Word reached us just as I left to come up the brae,' said Morison, finding his tongue. 'It seems it was a natural enough death, by what they're saying.'

'Oh, aye,' agreed Nicol cheerfully. 'He was fine last night. Well, no to say fine,' he qualified, 'but fit enough.'

Gil looked about him, wondering what best to do next, aware of Socrates staring anxiously up at his face. It was likely that the Provost would want his evidence at the quest; it was also possible that the Renfrew family would not let him into the dead man's chamber, particularly since the body would not have been properly laid out yet.

'Did you notice anything strange about him?' he asked, without much hope. 'Was his chamber just as usual? Did he seem – peaceful, or as if it was easy?'

Nicol shrugged again. 'I couldny say,' he admitted. 'I've never been in his chamber for ten year, no since he last beat me, afore I went to the Low Countries. It was all neat, just as it used to be, and nothing out of place. And he looked peaceful enough, just like poor Danny there or Robert.'

'No sign that he'd eaten or drunk anything before he died?'

'Oh, aye. He'd had his supper wi the rest of us,' said Nicol helpfully, 'and we all had cakes and buttered ale afore bed, and there would be oatcakes and cheese in the dole-cupboard like there aye is.'

'Here is the Provost,' put in Morison. 'And young Bothwell. Ah, poor laddie, they have questioned him.'

Bothwell, hustled into the hall by two of the Castle men-at-arms, was manacled, and his hands were bloody. He almost fell at the step up on to the dais; his sister cried out in pity, and he turned a bruised face towards her.

236

Thumbscrews, thought Gil, and a beating. Sir Thomas must have decided to risk the chill of the torture chamber after all. Bothwell was placed against the wall under guard, the Provost made his way to his great chair, and his clerk hurried in behind him with an armful of parchments and took up position at the other end of the table. The Serjeant, brandishing the burgh mace, bawled the order for silence, and the quest began.

'We've two to deal wi,' announced Sir Thomas, 'but the one assize can do for both. We'll just take them in order as they happened, Danny Gibson first. Who's here to identify the laddie?'

It was clear that the Provost's rheum was no better, and he was inclined to be even more short-tempered than usual. He dealt ruthlessly with the business of identifying the corpse and choosing an assize, despatched its fifteen members outside to inspect Danny Gibson and agree that there was no visible sign of the cause of death, and summoned Morison to describe the event, all between loud trumpetings into another handkerchief. Gil caught his eye at one point, but received only an irritable shake of the head.

'And then he fell down,' ended Morison, 'and we – all the potyngars went to see if they could help, and then he died.'

'Aye, he would,' said someone at the back of the hall, and one or two people laughed. Sir Thomas glared round, and the laughter subsided.

'We'll ha none of that. This is a serious matter,' said the Provost. 'Who attended him? Is any of the – aye, Maister Forrest, come and let us hear what he died of.'

'But we ken what he dee'd from,' objected one of the assize from within their roped-off enclosure. 'He was pysont by Nanty Bothwell, in a conspiracy wi the lassie Renfrew, as it's being said all round the town.'

'You be quiet and listen, Rab Sim, and let me ask the questions,' ordered Sir Thomas. 'Right, Wat, tell us what you saw, man.'

Wat Forrest recounted the signs he had observed on the dying man, agreed that it seemed like poison but not one that he knew of, and reported that the stuff in the flask appeared to be poison, also unidentified.

'So it might be what was in the flask killed Danny,' he said earnestly, 'but it might not.'

'Aye, but what was it if it wasny?' asked an assizer. 'What else could it be?'

Nanty Bothwell raised his head at that, but gave no other sign.

'A course it was in the flask,' said Rab Sim.

'Could a bin something he ate,' said another assizer. 'Was there a refreshment afore the play, maybe?'

'I told you to let me ask the questions,' said Sir Thomas irritably. 'Where's these mummers? Tammas Bowster, come and tell us what passed afore the play.'

'Does he ken it was the wrong flask?' asked Nicol in Gil's ear. 'Will Tammas tell him?'

'Likely.' Gil was watching the assize. It did not seem to him that they were hostile to Bothwell, but the evidence being put to them was not favourable. Bowster was now detailing the events in the kitchen, how the two young men had disagreed over Agnes Renfrew and how the refreshment handed round had been common to all.

'So there's your answer, Davie Johnson,' said Sir Thomas. 'They all shared the refreshment. It wasny in that, whatever slew the poor lad.'

'It might ha been a bad cake,' persisted Johnson.

Sir Thomas glared round the hall, ignoring this. 'Is any of the Renfrew household here?' His eye fell on Nicol. 'Is it just you? Where's Frankie?'

'He'll no be coming,' said Nicol, pushing forward to the edge of the dais. 'He's no able.' He gave Sir Thomas one of his sunny, heavy-eyed smiles, and the Provost stared at him in growing indignation until he realized what the bystanders were saying.

'Dead? Are you saying Frankie Renfrew's dead, man?'

'Aye, he's dead,' agreed Nicol. 'I found him.'

Sir Thomas looked briefly at Gil, then back at Nicol in some bafflement.

'I'm right sorry to hear it,' he said, 'for he'll be a sad miss in the burgh, but –'

'I'm no,' said Nicol. 'We'll none of us miss him in our house, save maybe wee Marion.'

'But we're here to deal wi Danny Gibson's death, and we'll get on wi that for now. Come up here, man and tell us what your sister Agnes has to do wi the matter.'

'Oh, she's nothing to do wi't,' said Nicol, stepping obediently on to the dais, 'for Frankie would never ha let either of them wed her. He's got other plans for her, seeing Adam didny want her to wife, being a man of good sense.' Adam Forrest went scarlet at this, and Nanty Bothwell looked up and stared at his sister. 'But I suppose those will come to naught now,' went on Nicol. 'There's none will want to wed her if she's to drown for poisoning Robert.'

'We're dealing wi Danny Gibson,' repeated Sir Thomas. 'If your sister's naught to do wi that, why were these two lads quarrelling over her in Maister Morison's kitchen?'

'I don't know,' said Nicol, 'for I wasny there, man, but maybe it was because Agnes fetched the flask to Nanty out of our house, that had the poison in it.'

Nanty Bothwell lunged forward exclaiming, 'No! No, it was nothing to do wi her, she never knew what it was!'

'You be quiet,' said one of his guards, and dragged him back to buffet him round the head. 'Stand there at peace now!'

Bothwell sagged against the wall, half-stunned, and Sir Thomas said over the sudden buzz of conversation, 'You're certain it came from your house?'

'Oh, aye.' Nicol smiled at him.

'How are you so sure it had the poison in it? Wat Forrest's just tellt us it might not.'

'Oh, aye, it might not,' agreed Nicol. 'But it might, too. Hard to say.'

Sir Thomas snarled faintly. 'Tell me a straight tale, man, and be quick about it.'

'It's no very straight,' said Nicol, shrugging again. 'Anyway she said she never. Just Gil Cunningham thought she did.'

Sir Thomas closed his eyes, rubbed his brow, and said wearily, 'Leave Maister Cunningham out of it and tell me what you know, Nicol Renfrew, till I see if it helps us any.'

'What I know? You mean all what I know? That's a lot, man,' objected Nicol.

'All that's to our purpose the now. About your sister Agnes and the flask.'

'Agnes and the flask?' repeated Nicol. 'She fetched it to him, since he'd forgot the one he should ha had. I never saw her fetch it, seeing I was in Augie's house at the time, but it's the flask that should ha held my father's drops for his heart, one of those that he keeps in his workroom. I saw it in our house just afore we left to see the play.'

'Those were never drops for the heart,' said Wat Forrest clearly.

Sir Thomas nodded at him, leaned back and spoke to his senior man-at-arms, then said to Nicol, 'Why are you so certain it was your sister fetched it?'

'Because he said so.' Nicol made one of his wide gestures in Gil's direction.

'Would it no be more likely Nanty Bothwell stole it out of your father's house?' demanded one of the assize. 'What's he say himself, anyway, Provost? Has he been put to the question?'

'I'm asking the questions,' said Sir Thomas. 'We'll have Anthony Bothwell's statement read out in a wee while. Nicol Renfrew, are you telling us your sister stole a flask of poison out of your father's workroom and gave it to one of her sweethearts to poison the other?'

Gil closed his eyes for a moment. Prompting the witness, he thought, is the presiding officer's prerogative.

'You're putting words into my mouth, Provost,' said Nicol, laughing indulgently. 'I'm saying Agnes fetched the

240

flask from our house, for I'd seen it there afore we came out, but where she found it or what she thought was in it I've no knowledge. Nor what Nanty Bothwell thought he'd do wi it.'

'Have you asked her if she'd done sic a thing?'

'We don't talk,' said Nicol simply. 'Besides, there's been all to do in our house these last days, what wi my minnie brought to bed and now the old man struck down. There's been more to think on than a silly lassie. You've more chance than I have, now she's locked up here.'

'What's a flask of poison doing lying about the house,' asked one of the assize, 'where a lassie can find it? That's no very good practice.'

'Oh, it wasny lying about,' objected Nicol, 'for it would all have run out if it was lying, and pysont the whole lot of us wi the foul airs. It was standing just where it ought to be when I saw it, all at peace on the shelf. Mind, I've no notion whether it was poison in it then,' he qualified.

This generated a three-cornered argument involving Sir Thomas, Nicol and the assize, who seemed unable to accept that any householder, much less an apothecary, could have a container in his house whose contents he could not identify at once. Gil, despite his several anxieties, found the exchange amusing, as did most of the women in the audience. Sir Thomas, eventually losing his temper, ordered the assize to leave the subject and attempted to get out of Nicol a statement of who might have filled up the flask. Finally he abandoned that too.

'Right, that'll do for that,' he said. 'Walter, let's have Bothwell's deposition, afore we're all demented wi this.'

Walter the clerk rose, selecting a sheet of parchment from the array before him, found his place and began in a clear monotone, 'Anthony Bothwell compearing, deponit that on All Hallows Eve in the year of Our Lord 1493, in acting of the play of Galossian . . .'

It was roughly what the man had said yesterday, Gil realized, tidied into continuous narrative in Walter's competent prose. The failure to bring the right flask, the statement about almond milk, were included. Whatever had prompted them to use the thumbscrews, Sir Thomas and Andrew had got no new facts out of Bothwell.

'I should not be here,' he muttered to Morison. 'I need to speak to Syme.'

'Never worry your head,' said Nicol at his other side. 'The auld man went quiet in his sleep. I'd say it was his heart, mysel, he would forget he was past fifty.'

And by now he would be washed and laid out, Gil recognized, as the assize began asking questions about Bothwell's statement. Was a third sudden death in the same group of people really something to look at closely, or was he being unduly suspicious?

'Can we no ask the lassie what it was she brought him?' asked one of the assize.

'She should be here by now,' said Sir Thomas irritably. 'Where's Andro got to?'

With the words, a door was flung open, raised voices reached them, and Agnes was hustled in shrieking furiously and striking out with her manacled hands at the two men-at-arms who gripped her shoulders. One of them contrived to get hold of her fetters and dragged her up on to the platform.

'Let me go, you villains!' she shouted. 'Let me go, afore my faither comes – he'll slay you, he'll have the law on you, he'll –'

'Be silent, lassie!' bawled Sir Thomas, and she stopped, open-mouthed, and stared at him. 'Your faither can be no help to you now.'

'Aye he can,' she protested. 'He'll get a man of law to speak for me –'

'Frankie Renfrew is deid,' said Sir Thomas.

Agnes went very still. She stared at the Provost for a moment, then turned her head and looked direct at her brother. She must have noticed him as she was dragged in, Gil realized. Again, she must be far less upset than she appeared to be, though that seemed to be changing now.

'Died in his sleep,' said Nicol cheerfully. 'Found this morning.'

Agnes swallowed. She had gone white, the blue eyes suddenly huge in her pinched face.

'Poison?' she said. 'Was it poison? It must ha been the same person as poisoned Robert, then.'

Sir Thomas looked at her, his eyes narrowed, then turned to Andro and conferred with him again. As the man made his way down off the dais and through the press of people, the Provost said, 'Right, lassie, what was this flask you brought out of your house to give Nanty Bothwell on Hallowe'en?'

'I never brought any flask,' said Agnes. She seemed to be trembling. 'It was nothing to do wi me. I've no idea what he's talking about.'

'It never flew from our house to Augie's,' observed Nicol. 'Somebody shifted it.'

'Maister Cunningham?' said Andro at Gil's shoulder.

'It's right hard to believe,' said James Syme. He was standing at the desk in the workroom, his hand on a stack of papers. He shook his head. 'I – I suppose it's grief that slew him, but he seemed stout enough last night. You'd never ha taken him for one to die of grief.'

'So Nicol said,' agreed Gil. 'Did anyone hear anything? He'd no chamber-fellows, no company?'

'It's a big enough house there's no need for the maister to share his chamber,' divulged Syme, with a flicker of his usual manner. 'And seeing Mistress Mathieson's lying apart the now, being new delivered, he'd be all his lone.' He looked intently at Gil. 'Is there any suspicion about his death, maister? Is that why you're here?'

'The Provost and I would both like to be sure there's no suspicion.'

'Oh,' said Syme slowly. He shuffled the papers into a neat stack and turned from the desk. 'You'll want a look at the chamber, then, for a start.'

'How have the women taken it?' Gil asked, following the man up the stair.

'Grace has been a marvel,' said Syme over his shoulder. 'My – my wife was that struck down, weeping fit to break her heart, poor lass, and her good-mother was right bad too, but Grace and Mistress Baillie atween them two got them calmed down and resting. Grace had some drops that worked a wee miracle.'

Did she, now? thought Gil.

'The women are little help,' Syme added, 'the maid-servants I mean, they were all in pieces already with the one lass being taken up alongside Agnes, they're useless the day, but Grace saw to getting him laid out, and we've taken Mistress Mathieson's opinion on the burial, and – we ordered as much in the way of mourning yesterday, you'll understand, for Robert, that it's no been a hard task for me the day.'

'How are matters left?' Gil asked. 'Who gets the business? I'd have thought you and Robert would be his heirs, by the way he talked, but he'll not have had time to change that since Saturday.'

'I've no a notion. I was looking for the will just the now. His share might be all left wi Mistress Mathieson.' Syme led the way through one of the well-furnished chambers Gil had seen before, and into the next. 'Here it's, maister. This is where we found him.'

The high tester-bed was stripped, the hangings gone, the woollen mattress bare and hauled up into a ridge to air. Pillows were stacked on the kist at the bed-foot, blankets of several colours were folded on a stool by the wall, and a red worsted counterpane lay forgotten in a heap beyond the bed-frame. There was nothing to be learned here, Gil recognized. Sighing, he looked about him.

'Did you see him before he was moved?'

'I did. Nicol came out to find me and break the word to my wife. He's a kind man, I think,' said Syme thoughtfully. 'I never understood Frankie's – well.'

'How was he lying? How did he look?'

Syme bent his mind to this.

'When I saw him,' he said with care, 'he was lying in his bed, on his back, with his mouth open and one hand here.' He pressed a hand to his chest, just below the windpipe. 'The bedclothes were flung back, but Nicol and Grace both had tried to find a heartbeat, likely that was their doing.'

'His legs?'

'Straight. One foot turned out a wee bit.' Syme eyed Gil. 'He'd gone quite peaceful, I'd say. He'd neither struggled nor voided. There was no blood, nor other signs.'

'But,' Gil prompted after a moment.

Syme shook his yellow head. 'I'd not like to start anything – anything –'

'But,' Gil said again.

'It was just –' He bit his lip. 'Just somehow awful like the way Robert looked, once we'd laid him out, and the way poor Gibson looked. And yet, one peaceful death's much the same as another, and those two slipped away easy enough at the very end. There's nothing to go on.'

'Nothing but an experienced man's feeling that something wasny right,' Gil said. He bent to look under the bed-frame. 'The jordan is missing. Had it been used? Has Mistress Grace taken it away to empty it?'

'Aye, likely. He'd voided urine in it, a reasonable quantity for a man his age, the colour what you'd expect considering his state of health.'

The apothecary's response to the question, Gil thought. He stood by the head of the bed and surveyed the chamber. There were two painted kists against one wall, the initials MM displayed in a wreath of daisies on each. The one at the bed-foot, he recalled, had Renfrew's initials. 'Most of us can find the jordan in the dark. Was there any sign that he'd tried to strike a light, maybe to get at his drops, to call for help?'

'Ah.' Syme considered. 'When I saw him, which was maybe half an hour after they'd found him, for I came straight away and left Nicol to bring my wife, when I saw him there was an empty candlestock on the dole-cupboard yonder, which was at the bedhead then. Grace must ha taken it for cleaning, like the jordan.'

'Empty. As if the candle had burnt out.' Gil moved to the dole-cupboard, a well-made piece whose spiral-turned legs matched the more massive posts of the bed. He lifted the neat brass latch and opened the little door to peer in at the empty platter.

'I suppose so.'

'What do they usually put in the dole-cupboard?' he asked. 'I think Nicol mentioned oatcakes and cheese.' His uncle's housekeeper Maggie had always left little sweet cakes and a cup of ale; he had encountered this more substantial dole first in his father-in-law's house, oatmeal bannocks and hard cheese, or sometimes a cold meat pasty, set ready to deal with night-time hunger in a household devoted to manual labour.

'When I was prentice here,' said Syme carefully, 'it was aye oatcakes and a finger of hard cheese. I've no notion whether Mistress Mathieson has changed that.'

Gil nodded, and lifted a few crumbs of oatcake from the platter. 'And was the wee flask of his drops anywhere?'

'No that I saw.' Syme looked about as Gil had done earlier. 'I wonder where Grace would have put his clothes from yesterday?'

'In the kist?' He nodded at the bed-foot.

Syme moved the stack of pillows on to the bed-frame and opened the painted lid. 'Indeed, aye.' He lifted the dead man's purse from a corner of the box and came to empty the contents out on to a flat portion of the mattress. 'This and that, his coin-purse, his beads, his tablets and seal.'

'And his drops.' Gil lifted the little flask and shook it, then drew the stopper and sniffed cautiously. 'It seems to have been the drops, right enough, but it's empty.' He offered the mouth of the flask to Syme, who sniffed with equal caution and nodded.

'That's his drops. Nothing odd about them, I'd say.'

'Did he ever keep a separate store of the remedy here in the chamber?'

'I wouldny know. You might ask at Mistress Mathieson, if she's fit to talk, or at Grace.'

Gil looked about him again, then moved around the room, bending to peer under the bed again, looking into the kist where Renfrew's clothes had been folded. His linen had been removed, presumably with the sheets from the bed, which would all be in the washhouse by now. There was no sign of anything untoward, other than Syme's unease and his own feeling that this death must be considered carefully.

'Might I see him?' he said.

Maister Francis Renfrew was laid out in the same chamber where his son had lain, washed and shrouded, candles burning at his head and feet. The maidservant Isa was on her knees in a corner of the chamber, her beads in her hand; she looked up when they entered, and rose, saying in some relief, 'Will I just get back to the kitchen now, Maister Jimmy? There's the dinner to see to, and Babtie no feeling too good again, no to mention the wash willny wait, it being Monday and the first wash of the month.'

'Aye, on you go, Isa,' said Syme, his felt hat held against his chest. 'I'll get someone to him. Thanks, lass.'

She bobbed briefly and slipped out of the room. Gil bent his head and offered a brief prayer, then drew back the shroud and studied the corpse. As Syme had said, there was nothing untoward to see; the face was a healthy colour, perhaps not as high a colour as the man had sometimes flown in life, and once the jaw softened and the mouth could be closed the expression would be as peaceful as Robert's. Gil bent to sniff at the cold lips, but there was no odour at all; reaching for the nearest candle, he held it to cast light into the dark cavern of the open mouth, without success. Resignedly he set the candle back in its place and inserted his forefinger, feeling cautiously round the stiffened tongue and behind the teeth. The cavity felt strange, and curiously much smaller than his own mouth

247

felt when he explored it. Many of the back teeth were missing.

'What are you *doing*?'

He looked up, to see Grace Gordon standing in the doorway, her light eyes wide with astonishment.

'Wondering what he ate last,' he said, returning to the task.

'Why?' She came forward into the room. 'What's it to you? Never tell me you think he was pysont!'

'I'm not easy in my mind.' Gil withdrew his finger and looked at it. The usual whitish material was caked under the nail, scraped from the dead man's teeth; there were some darker fragments lodged in it, which seemed to be crumbs of oatcake.

'He had oatcakes and cheese to his dole,' Grace agreed, still disapproving. Her voice was high and sharp with tension this morning. And small wonder, he reflected. 'He'd eaten them, it was all over his teeth, so I rinsed out his mouth. No sense in upsetting Meg further, if she felt equal to seeing him afore we can close his mouth, I thought.'

'A good thought,' said Syme solemnly. 'A right good thought.'

'You saw nothing out of the ordinary?' Gil asked.

'Beyond him being deid, you mean?' she responded, her tone acrid. 'No, I can't say that I did. He'd slept in his own bed, eaten his own dole, lit his own candle. There was no albarello of pyson in the chamber, no marchpane fancies. Are you thinking now it wasny Agnes that slew Robert?'

'No.' Gil drew back the shroud, looking down the length of Renfrew's body, flabby and blue-veined, with a paunch the man's garments had concealed in life. How undignified death is, he thought, stripping away all the defences we put in place. Is this how God and the saints see us?

'You might leave him some dignity,' said Grace, echoing his thoughts.

'I'd rather send him justice, if he should need it.'

'Justice? For Frankie?' she said bitterly. Syme looked at her in astonishment, but she turned to leave the room, just as Nicol slouched in from the hall.

'Aye, lass,' he said, putting an arm round her, and raised his eyebrows at Gil. 'Getting a word wi Frankie, are you, Gil?'

'He's looking for poison,' said Grace into his shoulder. 'He thinks it wasny Agnes slew Robert.'

'That's a pity,' said Nicol cheerfully, 'for it's just been determined up at the Castle that it was Agnes slew both Robert and Danny Gibson. I brought the lassie Jess down the road wi me.'

All three people in the room stared at him.

'Gibson as well?' said Syme at length. 'Have they let young Bothwell go?'

'They were just striking off his chains and all when I came away. I'd thought his sister was hoping to cure his hurts wi her tears.' He grinned. '*Unguentum Lacrimae*, how would that sell, would you say, Grace?'

'Is that right, d'you think, maister?' Syme said to Gil.

'It's the best we'll get,' he said. 'I'd thought Danny's death was an accident, myself, but I'd never ha hoped to convince the assize it was none of Bothwell's intent. Someone was right eloquent, I'd say.'

'It was the Provost,' said Nicol, without great interest. 'What do we need to see to here, Jimmy? If Gil's no wanting the corp, can we see to getting the old man buried along wi Robert? There's no denying it would be handier to put them both under at the one time.'

Syme swallowed this one with difficulty, and suggested, 'We'll need to send round word to his gossips. They'll want to drink to his memory, and that will have to be for this night. We'll no get the two of them buried afore the morn's morn, and it might need to be the day after. Wednesday, that would be.'

'The morn's morn,' repeated Nicol. 'Aye, I suppose Gerrit might wait so long. Grace?'

249

She looked steadily at him, and nodded.

'I'll get on wi packing,' she said.

'No, I'm no interested,' said Sir Thomas. 'If you've found nothing we can show an assize, and none of the household suspects poison, I'm no for opening it up. They've enough to bear for now, what wi this morning's work and the head of the house dead and all.'

'I think Syme is uneasy,' said Gil. 'He said the corp somehow resembled Robert's.'

'They're father and son,' said the Provost irritably. 'What else would they do but resemble one another?' He sat back in his great chair; Walter the clerk looked up briefly, then went back to his scratching pen. 'We'll take a look at this a moment, if we must. Was there any sign of poison in the chamber or elsewhere?'

'The house is full of poisons,' Gil observed. Sir Thomas grunted. 'There was no sign in the chamber, and no sign the man had taken poison, but then Robert shows no sign either by now, even the smell of almonds has left him.'

'Aye. Now who was in the house that might have ministered the stuff?'

'The maidservants.'

'No. No that lot.'

'No, I agree. Mistress Mathieson, who everyone says is not fit to leave her bed, though I've seen her up and seated in a chair. Her mother. Grace and Nicol. The man himself,' he added scrupulously, 'though if it was the same poison, he could never have taken it himself and then left all tidy. It works too fast.'

'Aye, and we don't know yet what it was. The messenger's no like to reach me afore this evening at the best, this time of year,' said the Provost, glancing at the dull window.

'And there was no sign of anything untoward in the bedchamber,' Gil reiterated.

Sir Thomas grunted again. 'And who of those might have a reason to kill Frankie Renfrew? The wife, I suppose, given that she'd sooner ha wedded Tammas Bowster, but you tell me she's not got the knowledge. The good-mother, who I met at Frankie's wedding,' he said unexpectedly. 'A woman of sense, I'd not put it past her to have the ability, and if she thought Frankie had slighted her bairn, I suppose she might. Did you get a word wi them?'

'I did, after I'd seen the corp,' said Gil. 'Mistress Mathieson is hardly able to speak from shock, poor woman. Her mother made more sense, but it seems the two of them were up most of the night with the baby, and the lassie called Babtie with them, so all three can speak for one another through the night. I saw the candles,' he added. 'Anyone can burn a candle down, but I thought they were speaking the truth.'

'Right,' said the Provost. 'And what of that daftheid and his wife? Did you ever hear sic a thing this morning? *Frankie's no able,*' he mimicked. '*We'll none of us miss him.* Hah! Did you say they were leaving Glasgow?'

'They have a passage booked from Dumbarton,' Gil said, 'sailing with the morning tide on Wednesday, assuming their dead can be in the ground by then.'

'M'hm.' Sir Thomas blew his nose and mopped it thoughtfully. 'They're not expecting to gain from the will, are they?'

'Renfrew made that very clear,' Gil said. 'Nicol has had his share from the business already, and he could expect nothing. I've no information about whether Renfrew altered his will since they came home,' he added, 'but he'd no chance to make a new one since Robert's death, so it all likely goes as you'd expect, the widow's third portion to Mistress Mathieson and the rest between Robert, Agnes and Eleanor, with whatever he thought proper to Syme as his partner. Oh, and the bairn must get a share.'

'They'll not be able to divide it, either,' said Sir Thomas, 'till the Justice Ayre deals with that wee wildcat Agnes. They might find her innocent, after all,' he said, shaking his head. 'You never can tell. But if Nicol's no expecting anything under the will, why would he poison his faither?'

'He's never liked him,' Gil said slowly. 'But he said to me, when he told me his father was dead, *I'm rid of him at last, and none of my doing either.* Coming from him, I'd take that as the truth.'

'And the wife, Grace Gordon, is that the name? What of her? She's a wise woman, it seems, but is she wise enough to poison her good-father and leave no traces?'

'It was her that cleared up, stripped the bed, washed the corp.'

'Aye, but what gain? What benefit to her from this death?'

Gil shook his head. He was still unconvinced, but he could not muster an argument to support his suspicions.

'She gains the return to the Low Countries, which he'd been trying to prevent, but since they must have had the passage booked already, that doesn't seem like a reason. They could well pack and leave without him knowing, in a house that size. I think she disliked him more than she let on, but that's not much of a reason either.'

'Aye.' Sir Thomas reached into his purse, produced a small box of ointment, and anointed the reddened area under his nose. Replacing the box, he said, 'This is all assuming it was the same poison, and it was left overnight. It could ha been that wildcat Agnes left it for him, though I think she was surprised by Nicol's news. Or it could ha been something else entirely. No, Gil, it's too wide open, it's like catching smoke. I'll ha none of this. The man died of grief, and that's that.'

'Packing?' repeated Alys, serving out stewed kale with caraways to go with the cold sliced mutton. 'So they are leaving immediately? Not even waiting to read Maister Renfrew's will?'

'And young Bothwell is set free?' said Maistre Pierre. 'That I am glad to hear.'

'It seems Agnes did herself no favours,' Gil said, 'denying everything and casting blame on Bothwell or on the girl Jess indiscriminately. The Provost was able to convince the assize she was to blame for Robert's death, and they decided on their own account to name her alone for Gibson. Bothwell may be liable for blood money, since he ministered the poison, but the Provost can consider that at more length. The man is free.'

'And so Frankie Renfrew is dead.' Maistre Pierre frowned. 'I wonder what will come to the business now? There is the young widow, and the daughter and her man, but if Nicol is to return to the Low Countries –'

'What troubles you, *maistre le notaire*?' asked Catherine. 'I think you are not convinced of the truth of something.'

Gil shook his head. 'You are perceptive, madame. I'm not . . .' He hesitated. 'I'm not convinced Renfrew's death is natural, but I can't see who could be responsible.'

'Then you must find out,' she said, and returned to her kale.

Chapter Thirteen

Sitting on his folded plaid on a damp bank on the Dow Hill, the dog ranging happily in the rough grass, Gil surveyed the burgh laid out before him in the afternoon light and considered three deaths.

Small birds scolded among the bushes as Socrates invaded their territory. Sounds drifted up from the town on the brisk wind, voices and hammering, the clack of the several mills downstream, a steady rasping from the sawpit at the foot of Andrew Hamilton's toft. Up to his right, the blond bulk of St Mungo's loomed against the grey sky, its narrow spire and lopsided towers familiar as a friend's face. The big houses of the Chanonry stood round it, their gardens sprawling down to the mill-burn dotted with autumn-leaved fruit trees and plots of dark green kale. A tumble of smaller cottages on the High Street led down the steep portion known as the Bell o' the Brae, their long narrow tofts built up with workshops and storage sheds. The university was easily picked out by its swarming students in their blue gowns, with what seemed to be a noisy game of football taking place on the Paradise Yard. Next to that, the Blackfriars' austere narrow kirk stood among the conventual buildings, and was succeeded, directly in front of him, by more big houses where the successful lived. He picked out Pierre's house, and Morison's Yard, and the Renfrew house next to it, the source of his present problems.

He cast his mind back over the past few days. The first death, the mummer's poisoning, he was fairly certain was an accident. The way both Bothwell and Agnes Renfrew had reacted made that clear. But who had the lethal little flask been intended for, if not for Danny Gibson? And where had Agnes found it? *He'd locked his workroom*, she had said, *I had to take what I could find.* Where would she look if her father's workroom was unavailable, and all the servants in the kitchen? He or the man Andro had searched the rest of the house; they had both found similar painted flasks, but the content of each was identifiable, though some they had had to refer to the helpful Syme or to Grace Gordon.

That flask, the one which Nicol called Allan Leaf, had gone to the Forrest brothers and so far as he knew was still in their possession. So Agnes must have found a further supply of the stuff, to concoct the sweetmeats which had killed her brother. Where? Or had she first located a larger quantity, and helped herself to what she needed each time? If the stuff killed on contact with the skin, she must either have been very lucky the first time or have known already what it was. And where was it stored?

That was the point they kept coming back to. What was the stuff, where did it come from, who knew about it? Presumably one person in the house did. Was that person still in the house? Still in the world? Could it have been Robert who brewed the poison, only to fall victim to it at his sister's hands? Could it have been Frankie's work?

And if Renfrew's death was not natural, how had it happened? He considered the scene in the stripped bedchamber this morning. Grace's motive seemed to be a good one, of sparing the young widow the distress of dealing with the task herself, but in doing so she had made a clean sweep of everything which might have indicated whether the man had died peacefully of a heart attack or not. You would hardly have known he had slept in that chamber, he reflected.

Below him, across the Molendinar, a figure in the garden of the Renfrew house was grappling with what seemed to be a barrel, twirling it on one end down the rough path towards the back gate. He watched, half attending. The chimney of the washhouse in the same garden was smoking briskly; the November wash must still be under way. Up and down the bank of the mill-burn other households seemed to have completed their wash, and linen was being spread out on dykes and hedges, bushes and greens, in the hope that this wind would continue. Likely the Renfrew household had been late starting, in the circumstances.

If Renfrew's death was not natural, who could be responsible? The figure with the barrel – was it Nicol? – had deposited the thing by the gate and was returning to the house. What about those two, he wondered, Nicol and Grace? Why had they come home? Why had they stayed so long when they were unwelcome? No, more logical to ask why Renfrew had made them stay so long when they were unwelcome. A man of contradictions, the apothecary, a man who wished to control everyone round him. Nicol would return to the Low Countries, presumably make a living there, his quiet, beautiful wife with him. They had planned to leave already, as he had told the Provost, why would they have to poison Frankie in order to get away?

Mistress Mathieson and her mother claimed not to have stillroom skills. Faced with something labelled as poison, one would hardly need stillroom skills to make use of it, but this stuff was dangerous, and an untrained person using it would put himself at serious risk. Or herself, he corrected, as the Provost had done. Would Renfrew have taken a wife who knew nothing about the work in the shop? Perhaps he planned to train her, he answered himself.

Who else was left? The servants, and Syme and his wife. The maidservants did not seem to him to be strong contenders, though of course they had access to all parts of the house while they were working, and whichever one it was who had come to tell Grace her master had not risen might have had the chance to remove whatever evidence

256

had been left before the rest of the household reached the chamber.

Across the burn, down in the Renfrew garden, Nicol appeared from the house with a box. It seemed to be heavy; when one of the women emerged from the washhouse to speak to him he lowered it to the ground. Gil watched idly as the two held some kind of discussion. Nicol's manner never related closely to his words, but the woman appeared to be telling him something she relished knowing. Then he spoke, and she seemed to take offence, swung round and hurried back into the washhouse. Nicol lifted the box, carried it to the gate and set it on top of the barrel. Then he let himself out of the garden, crossed the Molendinar by the nearest footbridge, and set off purposefully up on to the hill.

Who else? Yes, Syme and his wife. Always about the house, well able to leave a trap for Renfrew, both well placed to gain a great deal from the two deaths in the family. Both with the necessary knowledge. Either must be a good actor if guilty, he considered, recalling Eleanor's response to her brother's death. It did not seem to have occurred to either that the other might be guilty; perhaps they were in conspiracy. He thought about that for a moment, trying to imagine how one would discuss such a subject, broach the idea in the marriage-bed perhaps.

'I thought that was you, Gil Cunningham!'

He looked up, startled, to find Nicol Renfrew standing in front of him, face lit by that aimless grin.

'Did you, then?' he returned. Socrates loped over to inspect the newcomer.

'Aye, from yonder in our garden.' Nicol sat down beside him, without benefit of plaid or padding, and reached to scratch behind the dog's ears. Socrates accepted the attention, then wandered off again, nose down in the brown tussocks. 'Here, this grass is damp. And I wanted a word, so I cam up to find you.'

'Did you so?'

'Aye, and here I am.' Having found him, Nicol did not seem to be in a hurry to get the word. He fidgeted with his hands and feet for a space, while Gil sat silent. Eventually he observed, 'We're packing. Grace and me. It's surprising how much you collect thegither in six month or so.'

'Did you bring much with you when you came home?'

Nicol turned his head to look direct at him. 'Never say that, man. This is no my home. We're going home now.' He grinned again. 'Eleanor'll no have me under the same roof, and it has to be her and Jimmy dwelling in the house now, to keep Meg safe till she can wed Tammas Bowster.' He paused. 'Christ aid, I never tellt Tammas Frankie's deid.'

'He'll know by now,' Gil observed. 'I think the word is all over the town.'

'Aye, but better to hear it from a friend.'

'Why should you and Grace not stay in the house?'

'Because it has to be Eleanor and Jimmy.' Nicol struck his hands together. 'Strange to think Frankie sent me overseas to be rid of me, and here's me done better than he ever imagined, and here's him shrouded for burying.'

'How well have you done?' Gil asked.

'Well, I've wedded Grace,' Nicol pointed out, 'that Frankie never valued as he ought, and we've a partner in the Low Countries is waiting for us to come home and get on wi the business.'

'Have you now?' Even less reason for Nicol to poison his father, Gil thought.

'I have that. I'm a wealthy man, Gil Cunningham.'

'My congratulations,' Gil returned. There was another pause.

'That Isa,' said Nicol after a time. 'She wanted a word wi me the now. Said she had to tell me something.'

Gil made a questioning noise.

'She said the old man had a woman wi him in his bed last night.' Gil turned to stare at him. 'Aye, you may well gawp. How would she ken that, I asked her, seeing she slept in the kitchen where it's warm. His sheets, says she, my nose tellt me as soon as I surveyed the sheets. So what woman was it? I asked her. Neither Elspet nor me, she says, nor Jess for she joined us in the kitchen, and Babtie was wi the mistress all night. Fetched someone in off the streets, I'll wager he did, she says. So I bid her be silent. I wouldny mind if word of that got round Glasgow, it's no skin off my porridge, but if Eleanor heard her say sic a thing she'd be out on her arse and no waiting for the term of her hire. And Eleanor would take the hysterics again, which isny good for her bairn.' He looked at Gil, eyebrows raised. 'So what d'you make of that tale, eh?'

'There was no other sign,' said Gil slowly. 'Maister Syme detected nothing.'

'Nor did I,' admitted Nicol, 'but then I never passed the sheets under review. Frankie's maidenhead was never my concern.'

Gil thought about this.

'You were first to leave the house, when you went to fetch Syme,' he said. Nicol nodded. 'Was everything locked as usual?'

'Oh, aye. Just the way Frankie fastened all down at night.'

'So if your father fetched a woman in, he must have risen to let her out again, and returned to his bed. It might account for his heart giving out,' Gil added.

'Aye, it might that,' agreed Nicol with enthusiasm.

'But Mistress Mathieson and her mother and Babtie,' Gil said, thinking it out, 'were all in the chamber off the hall, one stair up, and awake much of the night they told me.' Nicol nodded again. 'Your father was in his bedchamber, on the floor above. Surely they'd have heard – voices, movement, anything –' Nicol grinned at that. 'And what about you and Mistress Grace? Did you hear nothing?'

'I'd hear nothing,' Nicol said cheerfully, 'seeing I slept like a log all night, and Grace beside me. And if the bairn was screaming, which I never heard neither, perhaps they'd not hear the houghmagandie over their heads.'

259

Perhaps not. Gil considered this.

'Had he done the like before?' he asked.

'How would I ken? Though I can tell you, if he did and Mistress Baillie learned of it,' Nicol grinned again, 'she'd have cut him into collops and served him for supper.'

'I'd agree there.'

They both looked out over the town for a space, Gil turning this new evidence over in his mind. If Isa was right, and the stains she had found were fresh, and resulted from –

'I did ask her,' said Nicol suddenly, 'if she was sure he'd had a woman wi him, if he'd no just, seeing he was with-out Meg –' He mimed crudely. 'No, she said, she's washed the family's sheets for twenty year, she kens the difference, there was two in that bed. I never knew you could tell that much from the wash, did you, Gil?'

'No,' he said, wondering which of the maidservants in Pierre's house knew the details of his own marriage.

'I'll not have you send the bellman round asking for her,' Nicol pursued. 'Same as I said to Isa, I'm no troubled myself but Eleanor wouldny care for it and Meg likewise, never mind it would sound right daft. *The woman that was wi Frankie Renfrew the night he died, speak wi his family. The reward is, we'll get the Serjeant to you.* No, I think we'd get no applicants.'

'You're probably right.' Gil shook his head. 'I can ask about if you like, Nicol, see if I can find her, though to tell truth it's not a trade where I've contacts –'

'I'm glad to hear it, man,' said Nicol, grinning again. Socrates appeared, and flung himself down at Gil's feet, his expression matching Nicol's. 'No, I think we leave it, for I canny see either how we learn more without discredit to the family.'

But that isn't justice, thought Gil.

'Alys might know,' he said. 'Or Mally Bowen. She must know likely names.'

'But would she keep the Serjeant out of it? Leave it, Gil. I tellt you for cause I'd not want you to think I left

260

Glasgow without telling you all I knew, but I think there's no more to be said on it.' Nicol got to his feet, rubbing the seat of his hose, and produced that annoying giggle again. 'I'm soaking wet. If Grace has packed all my hose I'll need to borrow some of wee Marion's tailclouts.'

Alys, kneeling at the prie-dieu which had once been her mother's, was having difficulty with her devotions.

Gil and her father had gone out after supper, once again, to offer sympathy at the Renfrew house, and she had retired to the bedchamber, intending to take prayerful stock of the past few days. She had offered all her usual petitions, and those which were appropriate for the apothecary's family, living or deceased. She had tried to put her own swirling fears and horrors into some sort of order, to offer them to Our Lady and St Catherine in the hope of lightening the burden or clearing her mind. Neither saint had helped. Instead she found herself thinking through her successive encounters with the Renfrew household, with the servants and Meg's mother as well as the family, Gil's latest piece of information tumbling among the words and images which succeeded one another in her head without order. Perhaps that was what she was supposed to think about?

Sighing, she cleared her mind and began from the start, from her first encounter with Eleanor and then Grace in Kate's new great chamber, the smell of paint and new wood about them. Carefully, as Mère Isabelle had taught her, she offered each person up, surrounding the image in her head with light, with the love of God even if not her own. It took time, and concentration. With her attention successively on each individual, she was faintly aware that the words and images, the odd facts were falling together in the background, that things glimpsed or half-spoken were beginning to shed light on one another or fit together to make another image. She persevered in her task, though the outline of that image began to frighten her. By the time she finished she was trembling. But she also knew what she must do, and that frightened her even more.

She rose from the little prayer-desk, stretched stiffened limbs and hugged herself, trying to still the trembling, thinking about how to proceed, wondering how her kind, civilized, considerate husband would react to what she was about to do. It was one thing to act independently of him, another entirely to act against his duty to his master the Archbishop. She had never seen him really angry, though her father had. Socrates came to her, pushed his nose under her elbow, waved his tail. She uncurled her arms and patted him, wondering how he would react if Gil struck her.

He would return soon. She moved into the outer chamber, where she lifted her plaid from its nail by the door and lit a lantern from the candle. The dog pricked his ears hopefully.

'Stay, Socrates,' she said, and extinguished the light.

'It's right kind in you,' said Grace Gordon, folding a fine linen shift. The candle flickered in the draught as the fabric swayed in her grasp. 'But you can see I'm a wee thing taigled here, Alys.'

'Can I help?' she offered.

Grace shook her head. 'I'm about done. I've been packing for most of a week,' she admitted.

'When did you book the passage?'

'As soon as Gerrit sent word he'd reached Dumbarton. Then he'd to loose his cargo and find another, but it seems that's mostly on board now. He'll wait till Wednesday for us, no longer.' Grace considered the box she was filling, lifted a pair of shoes and crammed them into a corner. 'I'm sorry to leave, in some ways. Meg is a dear soul, and I could learn to love Eleanor, I think, but she and me would never come to terms wi Nicol in the way, and my duty's to him.'

'Where are they both?' Alys asked.

'Meg and her mammy are below, with the bairn.' Grace gestured in the direction of the birthing-chamber. 'Eleanor went to lie down awhile. I hope she'll bear up, for her own bairn's sake.'

'But you lost yours,' said Alys. Grace looked up sharply at the words, her light gaze focusing on Alys's face. 'That must be a grief.'

'It is.' The other girl looked down at her packing, and pushed a bundle of stockings in at random.

'A great pity you've not taken again.'

'D'ye ken, if that's all you came for, Alys, I'd as soon you left, and let me get on.'

'No,' said Alys. 'I came to make sure you get away. I think you should leave Glasgow as soon as you can. Before the funeral, if it's possible.'

The stare was needle-sharp this time. 'Why? Why me?'

'You and Nicol both.'

'How so? Why would it be so important? What's it to you, anyway?'

'I think you need to know,' said Alys gently, 'that the Provost has learned what poison it was killed Danny Gibson and Robert.'

There was a small pause. 'Has he now? And what would it be?'

'Some kin of the Bothwells, an apothecary in Edinburgh,' Alys said, watching her carefully, 'has said it sounds to him like something brewed up from apple pips. The appearance and the action, he says, are very close.'

'Is that right?'

'And Gil will put everything together sooner or later.'

A wry smile. 'So how come you're so much faster than your man to come to conclusions?'

Alys shook her head. 'I had all the facts, I just needed to put them in the right order. He may have to guess some of it.'

'But suppose your conclusions are wrong, you've no got the facts in the right order?'

'Grace, when I mentioned apples, you looked at your workroom door.'

Grace was silent, while she folded a woollen kirtle and smoothed it into the box.

'Why are you doing this, Alys?' she asked at length.

'You saved John's life.'

That got her a hard look.

'The craft's for healing, no for killing,' the other girl repeated firmly. 'I did nothing more than my duty to them that taught me.'

Alys bit back the reply that rose to her lips, and said, 'You acted quickly, you knew what must be done, you reassured us. John's family and Kate's as well owe you a debt for ever. This is part of it, Grace.'

Another wry smile.

'I value it,' said Grace. 'Well, my quine, you've paid your debt. You should get home, afore your man leaves here and finds out what you're at.'

'He's just left,' said Nicol in the doorway. 'What's his wee wife here for?'

Grace looked round, her face suddenly vulnerable, and went to her husband. He took her hands in his, but stared blankly at Alys over her shoulder.

'What's she want?' he asked again, and then switched to something Alys thought must be Low Dutch, a strange hard language full of gutturals and half-familiar words. Grace answered him, he asked a question, she spoke at more length, urgently. His expression remained blank but his lanky body seemed to tense as he listened to her. Finally he mustered one of his happy grins.

'Aye, thanks indeed, mistress,' he said. 'But Grace is right, she's aye right, you need to get away now. Put up your plaid and I'll see you to your door.'

'I'd be grateful,' she admitted, rising. She was unused to being out in the burgh alone quite this late, and it had surprised her how the shadows had seemed to threaten her footsteps. 'I had a lantern.'

Grace put out her arms. *'Our dance is done, sister adew.* My thanks, lassie,' she said. 'I'll pray for you.'

'And I for you,' said Alys. 'God speed the journey.'

They embraced, and Nicol said impatiently, 'Come away, come away now, for we've other things to see to and all.'

Her head hurt. For what felt like years that was all she was aware of; then gradually she recognized that the world seemed to be rocking, and water slopped coldly quite close to her. There was a smell of fish, and it was dark, but the principal thing was still the headache.

Somebody groaned. After more years somebody else spoke, a voice she did not know. It seemed to be angry. Not Gil, but Gil was going to be angry –

Her head was really painful. She had not had a headache like this for a long time. She tried to put her hand up to her brow, but it would not move, because her wrists seemed to be fastened together. She tugged at the fastening, and groaned again.

Fresh air reached her face as her plaid was turned back. A gentle hand touched her cheek.

'Que passe?' she asked.

'Lie still,' said someone in horrible French.

'My head hurts,' she said.

'Yes. He hit you hard.'

'Hit me . . .?'

She opened her eyes. It was still nearly as dark as it was behind her eyelids, but after a moment she recognized a sky of black clouds, stars sailing between them. Water splashed again. A dark shape came closer to her, and she flinched.

'And forbye,' said the angry voice in Scots, more distantly, 'that's another groat ye're owing me, for we never contracted for more than the two o ye and yir goods, let alone if all yir baggage sinks the *Cuthbert* afore we reach Dumbarton– keep baling, mannie!'

'You'll get your extra,' said another voice. She knew it. It had promised to see her to her door, and then – and then –

'He hit me,' she said.

'He did,' agreed Grace in that badly accented French. 'He should never have done it. I'm truly sorry, my dear, after what you did for us.'

'Where are we?'

'Beyond Erskine, I think.'

'Erskine?' she repeated. 'What – where – are you taking me to –' She tried to rise, to sit up, to raise her head enough to see what was happening. A boat. They must be in a boat. That had been the boatman demanding money. Where were they taking her? Why was she here?

'Haud still!' ordered the Scots voice. 'We've no more than a handspan o freeboard, we'll ship half the Clyde if ye stot about like that!'

'Rest easy,' said Grace.

'Let me sit up!'

Grace bent to assist her, heaved her to a sitting position. Her head stabbed pain and the world swam round her, but when it steadied she was aware of the banks of the river sliding past her, bushes and reeds briefly lit by the lantern at the mast while the water chuckled and sparkled inches from her shoulder. Little birds stirred, fluttered, called alarm as the light passed their roosting-places. Somewhere a fox barked.

She seemed to be sitting on tarred canvas, and her feet were in water in the bottom of the boat. Before her the lantern-light glowed dark rust on the sail and outlined shapes below it, the baggage, the boatman at the tiller, a moving form which must be Nicol scooping water back into the river. She raised her bound hands to her brow, pressing the cords against her face.

'Why?' she asked simply.

'You're our insurance,' said Nicol. His accent was as bad as Grace's; she suddenly recognized Burgundian French.

'*Hein?*'

266

'He thinks he can bargain with your man,' Grace said. 'Use you as a token to pay for our safe passage.'

'But he –' She swallowed. 'He need not have known until after you had left Glasgow. I'd have said nothing.'

'Keep baling, maister,' ordered the boatman. '*Cuthbert*'s no accustomed to carrying boxes, she's better wi fish, and it makes her uneasy. Keep baling.'

Grace bent forward so her head was close to Alys's.

'Can you swim?' she ask quietly.

'No.'

'If I free you, you'll not try to get away? You could sit here on the bench at my side and be more comfortable.'

Bench? she wondered, and groped for the right word. Thwart, was it? Grace's French was like her own Scots, a second language, much used but not completely familiar. Concentrate on the situation, she told herself wearily.

'Where could I go?' she returned. Grace laughed faintly, produced her penknife and sawed through the cords at Alys's wrists. She flexed her fingers painfully, and accepted help to move on to the thwart with Grace, her head stabbing pain as she moved. The other girl opened huge wings which turned out to be a heavy cloak, and drew Alys to her side under it.

'The wind bites right through your plaid,' she said. 'It takes this boiled wool to keep it off. How is your head? How do you feel?'

'Confused.' Alys sat still, glad of the warmth but uncertain of the close contact. Through the headache she said, 'I still don't understand – what gain is it to bring me away like this? Surely it can only fetch Gil after me faster than ever?'

'You're our insurance,' said Nicol again. 'Even if he reaches Dumbarton before we sail, he'll let us go rather than see harm come to you, I'd say.'

She swallowed hard. What had Gil said about this man? What was the condition called? *Akrasia*, that was it, *Impotens sui*, the state of not having power over oneself, of being unpredictable, without moral judgement. What did he threaten?

'Nicol, you won't harm her,' said Grace. Was that anxiety in her tone?

'You don't know that,' said Nicol, giggling. 'And nor does Gil Cunningham.' He bent to his task again, and water splashed over the side. The river did seem to be sliding past very close to the topmost plank of the boat; there was a surprising amount of baggage piled in the midst of the little craft, and beyond it the boatman was now doing something mysterious with a rope. The sail flapped, their speed checked in the water, something swung. Water slopped and Nicol's activities with the baler redoubled, the sail filled again and the chorus of creaks began a different tune. Child of a western seaport, she understood enough about small boats to know that the wind was not completely favourable, that the set of the sail must be altered to make the most of it. They must have negotiated one of the bends in the river. On the Renfrewshire shore an owl screeched, and another answered.

'I wouldn't have told Gil,' she said quietly. 'And I don't think he knew about the apple-cheese or your workroom. It would take him a little time to come to the right answer. But now – your house is the second place he'll look for me when he finds I'm not at home, and Isa knew I'd been there. He'll pursue us to Dumbarton with all the speed he can make.'

'Isa also saw you leave,' said Grace, equally quietly. 'I don't know what my husband intends.' She sighed. 'Such a fright I had when he bore you in at the back gate. Then we had to fasten you on to the handcart, all among the luggage, and then we had the argument with this fisherman. I regret this. I really regret this.'

'What does your husband fear Gil will do?' she asked. Her hands seemed to be trembling again.

'Prevent us leaving. Take either of us up for Frankie's death.'

'Either of you?'

Grace's face turned towards her, a pale blurred oval in the lantern-light. Incongruously, there was a laugh in her voice. 'Either of us. And whichever he takes for it, he'd be wrong.'

Alys digested this.

'It was his heart, then?' she said.

'It was.'

'You're very sure.'

'I witnessed it.'

'You were there when he died. In his chamber, in the midnight.'

'He'd summoned me there.'

It was one thing, she discovered, to suspect something so dreadful, but quite another to have it confirmed. Appalled, Alys put a hand out, groped for Grace's, gripped it. The clasp was returned. 'How long?' she asked. 'How long had he been – been – imposing himself –'

'Five month. Any time he saw the opportunity. Any time his son was out of it with the drops, which seemed to happen more often lately. Sometimes in our own bed, wi Nicol drugged at my side.'

Please God and Christ and Our Lady and all the saints, she begged, send that Nicol could not hear their voices, above the increased creaking of the boat, the splash of the baling. And blessed Mary, forgive me that I complained of my own barrenness, when this was happening almost next door.

'What a blessing you have not conceived while you were in Glasgow.'

Another faint, bitter laugh. 'I made sure of that. And he never suspected.'

'He wished to – to replace the one you lost himself?'

'My God, you're fast. Yes, that was what he told me, time and time again. He'd make sure his heir was a Renfrew born. But that wasn't the worst of it.'

Alys made a small questioning noise, but the answer struck her almost at the same moment.

269

'The tisane,' she whispered. 'The night you came home.' Grace's hand tightened on hers, and she felt the movement as the other girl nodded. 'Ah, what wickedness! No wonder you –'

'Planned to poison him.' The words were almost inaudible.

The sail flapped. *Cuthbert* checked, lurched, rushed onward. Water gurgled very near her waist. Away to her left, on the Dunbartonshire shore, there were hoofbeats, several horses. A sliver of moon had risen, and slid out of the clouds occasionally.

'He'd sweetened it with sugar,' Grace said suddenly, softly, 'and put galangal and cloves and all sorts to it, to disguise the taste. If it hadny been for that I'd have recognized what he was about. I'll never be able to face cloves again.'

'I can see that.' Alys put her other arm about Grace under the cloak. They leaned together, sharing warmth. 'And then Agnes found the stuff you had prepared.'

'I thought I'd hidden it. She's always been one for prying and spying, though not as bad as her brother.' She checked. 'I always forget that my husband is her brother too. Not as bad as her brother Robert. She took the first batch I made, not knowing it for what it was I suppose, and gave it to the man Bothwell. I replaced it the next day.'

'The apple-cheese –'

'Yes. She must have borrowed what she needed, just the day after. I thought the flask had been moved, I thought I'd made more than there was left in it, but the past few days have been such a turmoil I wasn't certain. Then the boy – Robert – died, and I knew I was right.'

'Where was the flask when Gil searched the house?'

'In my purse, while I hoped the stopper was fast.'

'Where are we the now?' demanded Nicol suddenly from beyond the piled-up baggage.

'Kilpatrick's yonder,' said the boatman. 'And Bowling ayont it. We'll be at Dumbarton in a hauf an hour or so,

270

and you'll can gie me the extra two groats afore I set you ashore.'

'One groat,' said Nicol.

'Aye, well, that was afore you mentioned insurance,' said the boatman. 'Did you never think to ask if I spoke the French tongue? There's most mariners can manage a few words. I canny afford to insure my boatie, but I can get extra off you if you're taking me into danger, my lad. Two groats it is, or I'll not set you ashore.'

'We're no wanting to go ashore anyway,' said Nicol cheerfully. 'We're bound aboard the Dutchman that's lying off Dumbarton, *Sankt Nikolaas*.'

'Wherever I set you,' repeated the boatman doggedly, 'that's another two groats.'

'D'you reckon?' said Nicol.

There was a sudden movement aft of the pile of luggage. The boat rocked, Alys exclaimed in fright, the boatman cried out. There was a huge splash, and the boat lurched and sped on, lighter in the water. Someone shouted.

'Nicol!' exclaimed Grace, leaning forward as if she would rise. She recollected herself in time, and Nicol said lazily:

'Never fear, lass, I'm here.'

'Hi! Come about there!' floated after them, and more splashing. Nicol laughed.

'I'm no sailor,' he said, but hardly loud enough for the man to hear. 'I canny turn your wee boat.'

'Nicol!' said Grace on a note of panic. 'Fit deein, loon? What – what have you done?' she corrected herself in Scots.

'He'll no drown,' said Nicol. 'It's chest deep, no more. He can walk to Bowling.'

'But how do we – Nicol, we canny sail this boatie! How do we steer it? We'll run aground, we'll sink –'

The splashing and shouting was diminishing beyond him. Alys, rigid with fright, stared as Nicol, faintly outlined by the lantern, settled himself at the stern of the boat.

'It's the tiller steers it,' he remarked. The boat lurched, the sail flapped, and was corrected. 'Aye, like that. And

271

what wi the tide still running downriver, we'll likely no go aground afore we can see the *Sankt Nikolaas*. And how's our wee token doing,' he asked suddenly, 'our safe pass out o Scotland?'

'She's well enough,' said Grace. Alys could feel the effort it took for her to sound so calm. 'Nicol, how do we go aboard? We'll never – we canny –'

'Ach, Gerrit will send a boat to bring us in,' said Nicol easily. *Akrasia*, thought Alys, still staring at him, and began to recognize a real chance that she might not see Gil again.

The boatman had said it was half an hour to Dumbarton. It might have been a year, by the number of prayers Alys contrived to cram into the time. She sat tensely in the bow, not daring to draw out her beads, dredging her mind for all the travellers' supplications she could recall. Grace had scrambled over the baggage and was baling as Nicol had been, though there seemed to be less water coming aboard now. The lantern at the masthead flickered, but the river had widened, there were no banks or bushes to show up in the tiny light, only an endless running of water and the occasional ripple of a sandbank. Nicol failed to run them aground; the sliver of moon slid in and out of the clouds.

Blessed St Christopher, pray for us, she thought, send that we may not drown. Was that a voice across the water? She tilted her head to listen, and a seabird called, was answered, set up a whole flight of high anxious peep-peep-peepings which soared above their heads in the darkness. What had disturbed them?

That was certainly a voice. It seemed to be behind them. Who else could be out on the river in the midnight like this? Long after midnight, her rational mind answered. Sunrise was after seven o'clock just now, there was no sign of the dawn, but surely it must be getting on for Prime. Please God let the dawn come soon, I don't wish to drown in the dark – like the boatman, maybe. Did he find his way ashore?

'There's a light yonder,' said Grace. She twisted to look, and saw one, two, a handful of lights, some higher than others. Some of them rocked gently, and one low down was fixed and seemed bigger, as if it was a lit window rather than a lantern like the one at their mast. Beside it, behind it, a huge black bulk loomed against the stars: Dumbarton's great cloven rock, which guarded the Clyde.

'It's all the vessels in the roads off Dumbarton,' said Nicol happily, 'each one wi a star at its top. And yonder, I'd say, the baker getting the oven hot for the day's bread. The folk o Dumbarton'll no go hungry.' He shifted the tiller experimentally, and the boat rocked. 'I'm no wanting the sail now, I think.'

'He said low tide was about four of the clock,' said Grace doubtfully. 'Will we not run aground at low tide? We'll need the sail to take us to where the vessels are. We canny – we canny just go ashore and ask for aid. What if the boatman's reached the town ahead of us?'

What if he never came ashore? thought Alys.

'We're no going ashore,' Nicol said sweepingly. 'We'll find Gerrit, never fret, lass, and catch the day's tide. *At morn, when it is daylight, we'll do us into the wild flood.' Floris and Blanchflour* again, Alys recognized. Nicol laid a hand on one of the ropes beside him, and tugged at it. The sail shifted, spilled wind, the boat danced a little sideways.

'You'll have us aground,' said Grace on a high note. Alys realized the other girl was as frightened as she was. And beyond Nicol, was that a movement in the darkness? A flicker of light, something catching the starlight or the exiguous moon, a splash of oars? She stared into the night, heart hammering, half-certain she had imagined it. Could it be Gil?

Nicol suddenly tipped his head back and let out a great halloo which rebounded off the Rock and echoed across the river. There was a huge flapping and screaming, and Alys cried out in fear, cowering down in the boat, until she saw that it was a flock of seabirds startled by the noise, lifting up off the water. As the birds vanished into

273

the night a spark flared under the nearest of the riding-lights, and a surly voice demanded who called, in almost unintelligible Scots.

'*Cherche le Sankt Nikolaas,*' Nicol shouted.

'*Pas ici!*' retorted the surly voice. The light was extinguished.

'That's no very friendly,' said Nicol reproachfully. He must have tugged at the rope again, for the sail cracked, spilled wind, and the boat slipped sideways once more. There was a rasping from under the bottom, then a shuddering jolt and they stopped moving.

'We're aground!' said Grace.

'It wasny meant to do that,' said Nicol, and giggled. He put his head back and hallooed again, the sound echoing round them from the Rock.

'*Tais-toi!*' roared the near vessel. '*Faut dormir!*'

'Gerrit!' yelled Nicol.

Behind him, two boats appeared in the circle of their lantern. Alys stared as they slid closer, the men in them reaching for *Cuthbert*'s strakes. Grace turned her head and screamed, pointing, but one of the boats bumped alongside where there was still water under the stern, and two men scrambled over into a sudden fierce tangle with Nicol, and when Grace would have struck one over the head with the baler a third man seized her wrist.

Terrified, despising herself, Alys slid down into the bottom of the boat again, and was taken by surprise when a man climbed in over the prow, standing heavily on her wrist as he went. She managed not to cry out, and he trampled aft over the luggage to join in the fight. Waiting for the sea to come in and swamp everything, waiting to drown, Alys realized that *Cuthbert* no longer rocked on the water, must be well aground, that there must be sand or –

With the thought itself she had uncurled and was over the side, hauling wet skirts up out of her way, her feet in inches of lapping water, the sand under them firm enough to walk on. She looked about, located the light of the baker's window, crossed herself, seized her skirts again and set off away from the struggle.

There were other voices, other boats out on the water. Oars splashed rhythmically, lights showed and were concealed. She waded on, hoping that the water was not really deeper, hoping the sandbank ran to the shore or at least that no deep channel cut her off, hoping they had not noticed she was gone –

'Gerrit! *Par là! Attrape-elle!*'

She stumbled in a hollow in the sand, righted herself, waded further. The water was certainly deeper, and oars – no, feet, a bigger body than hers splashing through the shallows, came after her. She threw a glance over her shoulders, but could make out only bobbing lights in the dark. The baker's window seemed to be no nearer, and the sounds behind her were approaching fast –

She screamed as a hand fell on her shoulder, and another grabbed her arm in a punishing grip. A huge shape loomed over her, smelling of ships and stale spirits.

'*Waar komms du, ma fille?*' asked a deep cheerful voice. '*Dies ist niet goed. Par-là ist Tod.* Live is dis way. *Votr' mari ist hier.*'

Chapter Fourteen

Riding through the dark, as fast as one might with the lanterns held low, with two good men beside him and the horses shying at shadows and owls, Gil found his thoughts churning round and round in the events of the night.

He had been surprised, returning to the house with his father-in-law, not to find Alys waiting to hear what they had observed. (Though that was little enough, commented a small part of his mind now.) Seeing their lodging in darkness, he had assumed she must be abed already. He and Pierre had sat down to discuss the evening over a jug of ale without reaching any new conclusions, and he had made his way through the drawing-loft to join his wife, only to find the bed cold and empty, and an apologetic dog trying to explain that his mistress had gone out without him, and he needed to go down to the courtyard urgently.

Pierre and the maidservants had been as astonished as Gil. They had searched anxiously for Alys through the sprawling house, half-certain she had fallen on one of the stairs or fainted in a deserted storeroom; they had checked the garden, the bathhouse, the privy. Catherine, finally disturbed at her prayers, had not seen Alys since shortly after he and Pierre had left the house, but suggested that she might have gone to see Kate.

'She gains great comfort from talking to your sister, *maistre*,' she said formally to Gil. 'She may not have noticed how late it is. Or perhaps,' she added, 'she had more questions for the women at the apothecary's house.'

'But to go out alone!' worried Maistre Pierre. 'She never does so, not this late!'

'I'll step round to Kate's house now,' said Gil, 'and then try the Renfrew house. Though I'd have thought their woman would have said if she was there before we left.'

The dog at his heels, he made his way down the dark street. The torches on the house corners were burning low, but there was enough light to see by; at Morison's Yard he found the double gates barred, and scrambled up long enough to crane over them and check that the house was in darkness. It must be past eleven o'clock, small wonder they were all abed. Alys could not be here.

There were still lights in the Renfrew house. He banged on the shop door with the hilt of his dagger, and after a while a shutter opened overhead and Syme's voice said warily, 'Who's that at the door?'

'It's me, Gil Cunningham,' he said, stepping back to see the man as a dark shape leaning from the window. 'Has my wife been here?'

'Your *wife*?' Syme repeated. 'No that I ever – bide there and I'll ask.'

Gil stood on the doorstep, fidgeting, wondering where to seek next if there was no trace here. After a surprising length of time he heard the house door unbarred, and a streak of light fell out. He took one long step into the pend and found himself face to tearstained face with Eleanor Renfrew, fully clothed and holding a candle.

'She's not here,' she said. 'But nor is my fool of a brother nor his wife.'

'It's true,' agreed Syme behind her. 'Nicol and Mistress Grace are gone, and taken all their gear wi them. And afore the funeral, too! I can see no sign that Mistress Mason was here the day.'

'No sign,' Gil said blankly. 'Are you sure?'

'Sure enough,' said Eleanor. She peered at him over the candle, then stood back. 'Is she not at home? You'd best come in out the cold and make certain yoursel.'

'My wife has been here all day,' said Syme, putting a possessive hand on her shoulder, 'but maybe Mistress Mason wouldny disturb her if she was resting. I've not seen her myself.'

'Have you asked the servants if they saw her?' Gil demanded abruptly. 'Or Mistress Baillie? Or Mistress Grace?' At Grace's name the sense of Syme's first remark finally reached him. 'Grace and Nicol? Did you say they've left the house?'

'Taken their gear and gone, and my faither no buried yet,' Eleanor said, nodding. She looked like someone who had taken one blow too many to the head. 'It's like the bairns' rhyme, first one goes and then another. There's just me and wee Marion left of the family.' She giggled faintly, sounding very like her brother, and turned away to light the candles on the pricket-stand. The shadows retreated into the corners of the hall, and Syme said gently:

'And your good-mother, and me, lass. And your own bairn soon.'

'Alys has been here,' said Gil with certainty. Both Eleanor and her husband turned to look at him. He nodded at the plate-cupboard, where a candle-box and two wooden candlestocks stood waiting for whoever needed them. Next to them was a lantern, a square copper object with real glass windows and a trailing chain. 'That's our lantern. I know it well. Pierre has four like that which he brought from France.'

In the chamber which Nicol and his wife had occupied the hangings were still on the bed, the furnishings still in place, but kist and shelf were empty, no clothes hung on the pegs behind the door, a cavernous space under the bed spoke of items removed.

'You see?' said Eleanor triumphantly. 'I was right, they've left, and taken all wi them.' She stepped past him, holding her candle high, and the shadows bobbed as she crossed the room to open a further door. 'Even her work-room stripped bare, though gie her her due, she's left Frankie's glassware.'

'Workroom?' repeated Gil, following her, the dog's claws clicking at his heels. Andro had never mentioned a workroom; had he even searched it? 'This was Mistress Grace's workroom?'

'Oh, aye,' said Eleanor. 'See, Agnes and me lodged here afore I was wedded, and made use of the workroom for making of sweetmeats and the like, so we wereny under Frankie's feet. Which suited us just fine, I can tell you,' she added with a flicker of her usual manner. 'So Agnes being lodged in the main house, in the end chamber under Frankie's eye ever since I left, Meg put Nicol and Grace in here when they came home.'

Never say that, Nicol had said. Gil did not comment, but looked round the small closet in the candlelight. Bulbous glass gleamed, jars of glazed pottery caught the light, a microcosm of the workroom behind the shop. The brazier was cold. There was a lingering smell of –

Yes, of apples.

'Their passage was booked from Dumbarton,' he said over the sudden thumping of his heart. 'Do you know what vessel? How would they get there?'

'Surely by boat,' said Syme from the doorway. 'They had such a quantity of baggage, it would take two days to reach Dumbarton on a cart at this time of year.'

'They came upriver by boat in May,' said Eleanor, and giggled again. Socrates emerged from the workroom and cast about the main chamber, pausing at the bench with his long nose jammed against the cushion. He padded back to Gil's side and nudged his hand, whining faintly.

Syme, consigning his wife to the care of a weary Mistress Baillie, had accompanied him to the riverbank. They had gained little there; the fisher community, its hours dictated by the tides as much as by the daylight, was awake and stirring but the best information Gil could extract was of a great stushie two or three hours since, when Stockfish Tam's passengers, bound for Dumbarton, had turned up wi a great load of boxes and barrels on a handcart and an extra –

'An extra passenger?' he repeated, heart thumping again. 'Who was it, do you ken?'

His informant spat inaccurately in the direction of the river. 'Naw. Just I heard what he was telling them. More boxes than they'd tellt him, an extra chiel to carry, lucky if the boatie reached Partick. Mind, there was only the two of them standing there arguing,' he added.

'Did they –' Gil swallowed – 'did all go in the boat in the end?'

'There's the handcart yonder, standing empty. Once they'd agreed the extra groat,' said the man, grinning in the light of Gil's lantern, 'it all packed in right enough. They'll be past Renfrew by now, wi this wind, seeing they left just afore the top o the tide.'

'You never saw the extra passenger?'

'Naw.' The man turned away towards his own boat, leaving Gil staring after him.

'If Mistress Mason was unwilling to go along wi them,' said Syme diffidently at his elbow, 'they might dose her wi Nicol's drops till she couldny stand upright.' He put a sympathetic hand on Gil's arm. 'If they've taken her wi them, she's no harmed, maister.'

That was true, he recognized, standing there in the midnight with Glasgow whirling round him. They would scarcely take so much trouble if they had – if she was –

'I must ha been right,' continued Syme, 'though it's no pleasure to think it. Frankie's death was never natural, if Nicol's up and run like this, and taken Mistress Mason for a hostage.'

'Land or water?' Gil said aloud, hardly hearing him. 'I must catch them.'

'Ye'll be faster by land,' said the man he had spoken to, looking up from whatever he was doing. 'There's no a boatie on the Clyde can out-sail Stockfish Tam's *Cuthbert*, even wi a burthen like yon. You'll be at Dumbarton afore them, on a good horse, and you'll ha what's left of the moon in a few hours and all.'

'I'll ride wi you,' said Syme.

Now, with Syme and the mason's youngest man Luke, he pressed on through the night, plaid wound firmly against the wind, dimly grateful for the absence of rain, his mind churning with hideous visions of Alys bound, injured, terrified. And why had she ventured out to the Renfrew house alone? What had taken her –

She must have thought matters through, and come to some conclusion. And then what? Had she gone to ask for some final scrap of information, and alerted Grace or Nicol to her suspicions? That could surely have waited till the morning, and in any case she had more sense than risk an encounter with someone they thought guilty, after the time out in Lanarkshire.

He pulled his plaid tighter and settled down in the saddle, following Luke's piebald horse through the dark, the lantern held down at the lad's stirrup showing them the next few steps of the road. What had altered since suppertime? What new information had reached them, to prompt Alys to action? The letter from the apothecary in Edinburgh, of course, with the information about the poison. Apple pips. The fragments Adam Forrest showed him must have been apple pips, not almonds, and the workroom had smelled of apples.

But an apple pip was a small thing. What quantity must one need to make up a flask of poison such as came into Bothwell's hand on Hallowe'en? There were five or ten at most in one apple, so how many apples must one slice open to get a cupful? Enough to make one very ill, or to make a very large dish of applemoy, or perhaps some sweetmeat or other. It kept coming back to sweetmeats, he thought, and suddenly recalled Frankie Renfrew complaining about apple-cheese. Robert had said, *We've apple-cheese in plenty*, and later his father had remarked sourly that Grace was a great one for making the stuff. Grace, who had stripped the room where her father-in-law died. Who had expressed what seemed like genuine regret at Robert's death. As well she might, thought Gil, if she had brewed the poison that slew him.

281

Grace, he recalled with a chill down his back, who had saved John's life. We owe her a debt for life, Alys had said. A debt which was more than enough to prompt Alys to warn her that she must be suspected. That must be why she had gone to the Renfrew house. He wondered why he was not angry at the idea, and found he was more angry with Nicol and with Grace, for repaying her in this way. He knew some of his wife's ideas on justice, and felt they were probably nearer to God's justice than to canon law. The question of explaining things to his master the Archbishop or even to the Provost could be dealt with later, after he had Alys safe, after –

'Maister?' Ahead of him, Luke checked. 'There's a fellow on the track, maister.'

'Who's there?' A voice from the darkness in front of them, a moving shadow which made Luke's horse stamp uneasily. 'Who's there at this hour?'

'Who's abroad i the night like this?' said Syme nervously behind Gil. 'Is it thieves?'

'I'd ask you the same. Who are you?' Gil reined in beside Luke. 'We're bound for Dumbarton. Are you afoot? Alone?'

'Aye.' The man came closer, his footsteps squelching. 'Could I beg yez for a lift to Dumbarton? Would any of yir beasts take a second man aboard?'

'You're wet, man,' said Luke, holding the lantern higher to see the stranger's face.

'Aye, I'm wet,' the man agreed, through chattering teeth. 'Piracy on the river, freens, my boatie stole from me and sailed on out my sight, and me left to make my way ashore as best's I can. But I've freens at Dumbarton will sort him for me, him and his extra passenger!'

'Ah,' said Gil. 'Stockfish Tam, is it?'

With the boatman perched behind Luke and wrapped in Syme's great cloak, which he gave up with creditable willingness, they put a fresh candle in Luke's lantern and pressed on through the dark towards Dumbarton, accompanied by a monologue on the subject of piracy and a debt of two groats. Questions about the extra passenger established that she had been alive, conscious and talking to the pirate's wife, though Tam had not heard their conversation, and after that Gil shut his ears to the man's grumbles and thought about Grace Gordon and a poison brewed from apple pips, and about what they would find at Dumbarton. The *Sankt Nikolaas*, if she was big enough to traverse the Irish Sea, the English Channel, the German Sea, was likely to be moored out in the roads off the port, rather than run up on to the shore. Could Nicol sail Tam's boat well enough to find her? Could he sail a boat at all? What if they failed to meet up with the Dutchman and drifted on down the river with the tide?

Most of Dumbarton was still asleep, though as they rounded the town heading for the shore a few lights showed and the smell of rising bread floated on the wind. Stockfish Tam directed them to where the Leven rippled quietly down to join the bigger river, and along the shore where Gil and Pierre had once found a fisherman willing to sail them to Rothesay in a boat of willow and skins. There were a couple of fires showing, with dark shapes squatting round them, waiting for the dawn, waiting for returning fishing-boats.

'Bide here,' said Tam, and slid down from Luke's horse. The animal sighed in relief, and he crunched off along the shore, hailing the nearest fire.

'The custumar,' said Gil, looking about him. Dumbarton Rock loomed over them against the stars, the narrow moon slid in and out of clouds, and one or two windows in the town showed lights. Here on the shore, apart from the two fires, there was little to see. It was still some hours to dawn, he reckoned, and by far too dark for customs work or for loading or unloading goods unless the matter was urgent. As it was now. The custumar would be virtuously asleep in his bed.

'I ken him,' said Syme unexpectedly. 'James Renton. He's a cousin of my oldest brother's wife.'

283

'Where does he stay?'

'One of those, I would think, convenient for the shore.'

Peering where Syme pointed, Gil made out several taller houses. He was debating asking at the fireside which was the custumar's when Stockfish Tam tramped back to them, followed by four or five of the dark shapes from the firesides.

'I've tellt these fellows what's abroad,' he said, 'and there's one of them willing to take you out to the Dutchman, rouse her skipper, and we'll pass the word along the shore and a hantle more o us lie out and wait for *Cuthbert* when she comes down the channel. That's supposing he hasny sunk her off of Bowling,' he added bitterly. 'Right?'

'Right,' said Gil slowly, putting the image that comment generated firmly from his mind. He would by far rather take the first opportunity to get Alys to safety, but he had to admit he would be less use in a brawl in a small boat, if it came to that, than he would be on board the *Sankt Nikolaas* persuading her skipper to help them.

'I could wake the custumar,' said Syme diffidently. 'He'll want to inspect the baggage Nicol has wi him, I've no doubt. If he sends a boat out, it might hold things up.'

'Aye, do that,' said Gil. 'A good notion.'

Crouched in the stern of a small boat, a stout son of Dumbarton hauling on the oars in the darkness, Luke shuddering beside him, he watched the approaching riding-lights swaying high up near the stars.

'How can you tell which is which?' he asked.

'I can mind where yer boatie was by day,' said their oarsman. 'Unless Gerrit moved her after sunset, she'll be in the same place.' It seemed to be a joke; he laughed shortly, leaned on his oars for a moment, then rowed on.

'Maister Gil,' said Luke tremulously. The boy was obviously terrified of being on the water, Gil recognized. He should never have accepted his help. 'Maister Gil, do you speak Dutch? Will you can talk to this skipper?'

'A little,' he said. 'I'm hoping he'll speak Scots.'

'Gerrit?' said the oarsman. 'No a lot. He gets by, the most of them does.'

'Will we get the mistress back, by doing this?'

'We'd better,' said Gil.

Five, six more strokes, and the oarsman backed one oar, swung the little boat round, bumped against the side of a much larger vessel.

'There ye are,' he said. 'Will I hail them for ye, or are ye wanting to take them by surprise?' It was too late for that: a hoarse voice spoke from the darkness above them. 'Aye *Nikolaas*,' said the boatman. 'Here's an archbishop's questioner for you, wanting a word wi Dutch Gerrit.'

Gil found a ladder of rope and wood at his shoulder; he tugged it cautiously, and scrambled up, aware of the familiar scents of tar and salted wood, hemp and damp wool, and climbed over the side on to the deck. Luke tumbled after him, almost sobbing with relief at being on a bigger boat. The deck swung under his feet, a barefoot man beside him held a dagger which gleamed in the light of the lantern slung beside the crucifix on the stern-castle railing, and across the waist someone moved towards him, very large in the shadows.

Deliberately he drew off his hat, saluted the cross, turned to the approaching man. No, men, there were two more, their bearing hostile. Mustering his few words of Low Dutch, he took a breath and said hopefully, 'Skipper Gerrit?'

By the time Syme and the custumar joined them, Gil had contrived to set aside his anxieties, concentrate on his ability with words, and explain matters to the skipper.

He had observed before that the men of the Low Countries seemed to come in two sizes, small and fine-boned or very large. Gerrit van 't Haag was definitely one of the latter, filling the after-cabin, nodding and wrinkling his large nose, his fair head bent to listen to the mixture of Low Dutch, French and Scots they were using.

'Klaas – Nicol t'ief your *vrouw*,' he said disapprovingly. 'Is *niet goed*. I help. Help you,' he clarified, grinning and stabbing a sausage-like finger at Gil.

'And we'll have his baggage sealed afore you sail, captain,' said Maister Renton. The custumar, woken by his kinsman, had apparently reacted strongly to the idea of uncustomed goods leaving his port, and turned out in person, his doublet fastened awry and his clerk rubbing bleary eyes and lugging the canvas bag with the great custom-book in it. 'The idea, slipping past me in the night like this!'

The skipper gave him an innocent look. '*Niet goed*,' he agreed, shaking his head.

'The boatmen are out waiting,' said Syme to Gil. 'They told Maister Renton where they would lie afore we came on board.'

The custumar appeared to be passing the information to the skipper, to judge by his gestures. The big man reached past him, without rising, to open the cabin door.

'*Allons-y*,' he said. But Gil had already slipped out on to the deck, impelled by a sudden surge of fear. Luke followed as if glued to his elbow. Out in the dark there was bustle and movement, several men with cudgels, the mate issuing curt, guttural orders. He stepped to the side, peering into the night past the pre-dawn lights of Dumbarton and the black bulk of the Rock.

Away across the water, a voice suddenly spoke, a woman's voice, high-pitched and frightened. Heart thumping, he stared tensely towards the sound. Alys? He thought not, but – Another voice rose in a loud shout that lifted a flock of flapping seabirds, which whirred over their heads, making Luke cross himself, exclaiming a blessing. Several of the sailors did likewise.

'Ah!' said the skipper behind him. '*Kommt Klaas. Waar sint* other *schouten?*'

Out in the dark there was an exchange with one of the other rocking vessels, and another loud *halloo!* and a shout of *Gerrit!* Then over towards the Rock an outbreak of more shouting, of struggles and splashing, a scream.

'To the boat!' proclaimed the skipper in thick Scots, and seized Gil's elbow. 'Ve save your *vrouw*!'

Six men at the oars shifted the ship's boat across the flat water, across the wind, at a brisk pace. Gerrit in the stern steered towards the noise, Gil beside him. He had persuaded Luke quite readily to stay with Syme and the custumar. Lights showed on another of the merchant vessels, someone shouted a question. Gerrit answered, and shortly another boat followed them. It seemed to take for ever to cross the dark water to where shouting and splashing, a high quivering lantern, the white glimmer of spray identified the battle, and when they reached it and Gerrit's men tumbled over the side into the shallows it was hard to work out who was on which side. Scots voices challenged and answered. The men of Dumbarton seemed to be fighting with one another as much as with Nicol.

'Mind her, Erchie! She's got a knife!'

'And where's my two groats? Where are they? Eh?'

'Alys?' Gil said sharply into the turmoil.

'No to mention you've run her aground!'

'Gerrit!' Nicol's voice. *'Par là! Attrape-elle!'*

Gerrit lurched past him over the side of the boat, splashed into the night, surely not walking on the – it must be a sandbank, Gil surmised, drawing his dagger, and followed, ducked past a whirling cudgel and plunged after the big Dutchman. There was certainly someone out there, hurrying through the shallows towards the lights of the town. Gerrit, more used than he to moving through the tide, was gaining on him and on the running figure, then with a flurry of splashes the big man pounced.

'Waar komms du, ma fille?' he said. *'Votr' mari ist hier.'*

'Alys!' said Gil again.

'Gil!' Her voice was tight with fear. 'Oh, Gil!'

By the time they got back aboard the *Nikolaas* in the greying dawn, one thing was clear to Gil: if and when he got his wife to bed, she was unlikely to turn her back on him as she had done the last few nights. She clung to him as they waded back towards the boats, her teeth chattering with delayed shock; she seemed almost dazed with relief, and when he bent to kiss her she shivered and pressed her body against his as if to assure herself he was really there.

'I thought I might not see you again,' she said.

'So did I.' As they moved her wet skirts dragged through the water, which was surely deeper. 'Is that another gown ruined?'

'And the shoes.'

'*Komm, p'tits pigeons*,' called Gerrit ahead of them. 'Later for that. Mine *schout* drifts, *wir mussen* –' He abandoned the attempt to explain further and shouted abuse at his men in Low Dutch. Two of them splashed after the escaping boat. In the lantern-light Nicol Renfrew and his wife, a number of Dumbarton shoremen, the remainder of the mariners from the *Sankt Nikolaas*, were shouting at one another. Two Dumbarton men held Nicol by the elbows, his nose dripping darkly, Stockfish Tam confronting him from a handspan away with repeated demands for his two groats and the money to make good any damage from the grounding. Grace, also in the clutch of a couple of boatmen, was dishevelled and half-weeping, but when she caught sight of Alys she seemed to relax slightly.

'What here?' demanded Gerrit over the noise. 'What passes?'

Stockfish Tam turned and reiterated his claim. Gerrit heard him, looked at the heap of baggage, kicked *Cuthbert*'s planks where the boat lay on the sand, and nodded.

'Two groat,' he said to Nicol.

'I'd ha given him his money long since,' said Nicol, 'only that these fellows willny let go my arms.'

'And the baggage into mine *schout*,' continued the big Dutchman, 'before water deepens. Hoy there – Martin, Tonius, bring here the *schout*! Klaas, Custumar Renton *t'attend*.'

'The custumar? I suppose I've you to thank for that, maister lawyer,' said Nicol sourly. He handed some coins to Stockfish Tam, who inspected them in the lantern-light, abruptly ceased his complaints and stood aside for the

Sankt Nikolaas men to transfer the boxes and bundles to their own boat. Thus lightened, *Cuthbert* was easily pushed off the sand into the deepening channel. The tide must have turned some time since, Gil understood, as water swirled round his calves.

'You!' Gerrit grasped the arm of one of the shoremen, and indicated Gil and Alys. 'You take these two *Sankt Nikolaas, ja? Is goed.*' He gestured to the men who still held Nicol. 'And you, leave Klaas and *vrouw* in mine *schout*. We see to all now.'

Sitting in the bow of yet another small boat, Alys clamped to his side, Gil contrived not to tell the boatman what was going on, while he thanked him for turning out at low tide.

'Aye, well,' said the man, hauling on the oars in a leisurely way. 'Tam's no a bad sort, even if he is fro Glasgow. We'd no go out all on the mud for just anyone, ye ken.'

'Mud?' said Gil. 'I thought it was sand.'

'Sand where *Cuthbert* ran aground,' agreed the boatman. 'Sand halfway to shore fro that. But it's mud a'most all else. Swallow you to the knees, it will, and hold you till you drown on the next tide.'

Alys drew a horrified breath and tightened her grip of his free hand. Gil registered the risks they had taken, then put the information resolutely aside as the little boat bumped against *Sankt Nikolaas*'s round flank, and concentrated instead on helping his wife on to the rope ladder, holding it taut and steady for her to climb. She reached the top, and he heard her speak gratefully to someone helping her over the side; as he began to ascend he heard feet rush on the deck, a flurry of movement, a cry from Alys and another from Luke.

'Mistress! What –?'

'Nicol!' That was Syme. Gil scrambled up as fast as he might, the ladder swinging across the planks, and reached the top as Nicol Renfrew giggled and said:

289

'Now, ye'll all just stand back, away from me and where I can see you. And if that's you, Gil Cunningham, you'll come no nearer than the rail, or your wee wife finds out how sharp my dagger is.'

The grey light on one side, the lantern-light on the other, showed him a chilling scene. Gerrit, his mate, his mariners stood by the far rail; Syme and the custumars had apparently just emerged from the cabin, and Grace stood in the midst of the waist. All were staring at a point by the mainmast, where Nicol Renfrew held Alys in a close embrace, her black linen hood crooked, the dawn striking pale on the blade of his dagger against her throat.

'Nicol!' said Grace. 'What good does this do? We're on board now, we sail in an hour or two, why are you –'

'He's here to stop us,' Nicol said. 'He's here to take one of us for poisoning Frankie. Is that no right, Maister Cunningham?'

'Poison?' repeated the custumar. 'Is there poison in your baggage, maister? Is that what you're exporting?'

'No, my loon, he canny do that,' said Grace, 'for Frankie took a heart attack, that's certain.'

'Is it?' said Nicol mockingly. 'And who caused that?'

'Not me, Nicol,' she said, a desperate note in her voice, 'and not you, surely?'

'What passes here?' demanded Gerrit. 'Klaas, *was maks u*?'

Alys stared at Gil in the growing light, and swallowed hard.

'Your father had drops for his heart already,' she said carefully to Nicol without turning her head. 'You knew he had them.'

Gil unglued his tongue from the roof of his mouth and said, in a voice he scarcely recognized, 'Nicol, did you poison your father?'

'I never gave him anything he'd not prescribed himself,' Nicol said.

'That's not what I asked you,' Gil said. 'Mistress Grace, did you poison Frankie Renfrew?'

'I did not,' she said. 'I swear by my hope of salvation, I did not.'

There was a pause. Nicol turned to look at his wife. Gil tensed to jump forward, but Alys made a small movement of her hand. *Stay back.*

'Grace? Is that true?'

'I've just sworn it, my loon,' she said.

Nicol's gaze swung back to Gil. 'D'you believe her?'

'Do you?'

'A course I do. No, wee lass, you'll not trick me like that,' he added to Alys, adjusting his grip on her arm. Over by the other rail the mate had begun stealthily moving backwards away from the group. 'Gerrit, tell Hans I can see him. I've still got a blade to this bonnie wee wifie's throat, and I'll use it if he gets too close. A course I believe Grace,' he continued, as if he had not interrupted himself, 'I ken fine when to believe her.'

'And I you, Nicol,' said Grace. 'Give him his answer. You didny poison Frankie either.'

Nicol looked at Gil again, smiling happily. 'Then we needny ha come away like this,' he said.

'This is all nonsense,' said Maister Renton suddenly. 'What's the trouble, anyway? I've still to prove these packages and write you out a docket for whatever port you're headed for, and I've more to do the day than stand here fasting, waiting for you to tell us why you're –'

'Get on and prove them, then,' said Nicol. He drew Alys to one side, and nodded at the heap of boxes. 'There you are, and plenty folk to help you. Grace, you have the keys, haven't you no?'

'But what is it about?' Gil demanded. 'You've never said, man. Why are you threatening my wife? Why did you steal her away down the river in the first place? She's no wish to go wi you, and you've a wife of your own.'

'She's too clever,' said Nicol. The hand holding the dagger shook a little, and a bead of something dark sprang on Alys's neck. 'Too clever by half. She'd worked it all out, afore ever we left Glasgow, and told it all to Grace,

the bits Grace didny tell her, all the way down the Clyde.'
At the words Grace looked over her shoulder from where
she bent to the stack of boxes. She and Alys exchanged a
long look, but Nicol went on, 'Frankie Renfrew brought
about his own death, and I believe that, but I'm none so
sure you do, Gil Cunningham.'

'You believe your wife,' said Gil. 'I'll believe mine,
Nicol, if you'll let her speak. Alys?'

The knife eased away from her white skin, and the dark
bead trickled down towards the band of her shift. She met
Gil's eye and said shakily, 'Grace is guilty only of making
something someone else used. She has told me all. And we
never did think Nicol guilty of – guilty of –'

'You see?' said Syme from the cabin doorway. 'Nicol,
man, this is madness. Let Mistress Mason go and we can
all get home to –'

There was a bloodcurdling yell, and Grace and the
custumar both cried out as something large hurtled out of
the dull sky and swung down on Nicol. He went head-
long, dragging Alys with him, but before they reached the
planks Gil was there, flinging himself on top of him, kneeling on his wrist, snatching at the knife.

They struggled briefly, then Nicol seemed to give up. Gil
dragged the other man to his feet, gave him into the grasp
of two sturdy mariners, and looked about him. Syme was
just helping Alys to rise, and beyond her, the large object
which had appeared so timeously was –

Was Luke, surrounded by coils of rope, also picking
himself up and blowing on his palms.

Two steps took Gil to Alys, to clamp her against his side,
feeling he could never let go of her again. 'Well done,' he
said to the boy. 'Very well done, Luke. What did you do,
anyway?'

'He has climbed the mast, all in the dark,' Gerrit said
admiringly. 'We make you a mariner, *ja*?'

'I sclimmed up all their scaffolding,' said Luke. 'Then
there was a block I saw I could ride down on and get his

attention, so I just did. I couldny call out to you first, maister,' he said earnestly, 'for he'd ha heard me and all.'

'Maister Mason will hear of this,' Gil said, and clapped the boy on the shoulder with his free hand. 'And I thought you were afraid of boats.'

'Oh, aye, boats,' agreed Luke, 'but scaffolding is just scaffolding.'

'Let me understand,' said Maistre Pierre.

It was next day, after dinner, and he had joined them on the settle by the fire, one arm around Alys, his hand gripping Gil's shoulder, as if he could not yet believe they were both safe unless he was touching them. The dog, still slightly offended that they had gone out without him, was sprawled on the hearth. Opposite them, Catherine sat with her beads, bright dark eyes watching them all under her black linen veil.

They had given the household an explanation of sorts when they reached Glasgow the evening before, weary and damp despite the hospitality of Renton and his wife, who had provided food, rest, a fire to dry their clothes. Not that Gil and Alys had rested much, either then or when they fell into their own bed; matters between them were certainly mended, though Gil did not entirely understand why or how.

'This whole case has been all back to front,' he said after a moment.

'How so?' said Maistre Pierre.

'Well – Gibson died, poor fellow, and set us asking questions. We asked so many that by this third death, which I think was the one intended all along, we already had most of the answers. Not that it helped much. And yet what happened to Gibson was an accident.'

'Intended?' repeated Maistre Pierre. 'This woman concocted a deadly poison which killed two people without her intention –'

'So she swore to me,' said Alys. 'I do believe her.'

293

'You think it was intended to kill the third? But you said she also swore she had not killed her good-father. So what was her intention? Simply to see how the poison was made?'

'I can't say,' said Alys, as she had already said to Gil. He was certain the turn of phrase was carefully chosen. 'But she did not use it. Nor did Nicol.'

'I suppose each was protecting the other,' remarked Catherine, 'which is very commendable in a married couple.'

'Why did she change her mind?' demanded Maistre Pierre.

'She said it was a heart attack,' said Alys, and shivered. 'She – she witnessed it. I think she is guilty of that at least.'

'What, of causing a heart attack?' Gil turned his head to look at her, startled by the idea.

'No. Of watching it and doing nothing to help. His drops might have – might have –'

'Might have made things worse,' said Gil.

'You are talking in riddles,' complained Maistre Pierre, but Catherine was nodding, and Alys was staring at him, her eyes wide.

'*Ah, mon Dieu!*' she breathed. 'Of course! And he never – he never –'

'He never swore he did not kill his father,' Gil agreed. 'Though he first told me it was none of his doing, the morning of the quest.'

'And we let him go,' she said.

'Still riddles!'

'I suspect Nicol has been tampering with his father's drops,' said Gil. 'It's only a guess,' he admitted, 'but it would fit. They didn't seem to be helping him much lately. I asked Adam about it this morning. There are things one could add to the mix, obviously, but even putting in too much of something that's already in the compound could be effective, and he hinted as much, you recall, Alys.'

'And we let him go,' she said again.

294

'It would be impossible to prove, even if I could persuade the Provost that it hadn't been a simple heart attack.'

'If his wife suspected it,' Maistre Pierre was considering the idea, 'it would explain why she was so quick to clear Frankie's chamber and wash him.'

Alys shivered again. What was troubling her? Gil wondered. Was she simply tired?

'It was her idea to come to Glasgow, she told me,' she said. 'How she must regret it.'

'You think justice has not been served?' said Maistre Pierre, watching Gil's expression.

'Justice has not been served,' he agreed.

'No, surely,' said Alys, 'it is the law which has not been served. Justice has been done, I think.'

'I think you correct, *ma mie*,' said Catherine. 'The poor lady. She has much to regret.'

'No, that sounds too philosophical for my taste,' said her father. He gripped Gil's shoulder tightly, released it, and got to his feet. 'I must get to work. I have accounts to see to for the quarter day. Not to mention some reward to consider for Luke, since I can hardly offer him my daughter's hand. I leave you to your philosophy.'

Author's note

Ever since it became a kingdom, Scotland has had two native languages, Gaelic (which in the fifteenth century was called Ersche) and Scots, both of which you will find used in the Gil Cunningham books. I have translated the Gaelic where needful, and those who have trouble with the Scots could consult the online *Dictionary of the Scots Language*, to be found at http://www.dsl.ac.uk/dsl/